GEMMA FILES

DARK
IS
BETTER

STORIES

ISBN: 978-1-68510-043-8 (sc)
ISBN: 978-1-68510-044-5 (ebook)
Library of Congress Catalog Number: 2022952224

First printing edition February 3, 2023
Printed by Trepidatio Publishing in the United States of America.
Cover Design by Don Noble
Editing and Cover/Interior Layout by Scarlett R. Algee
Proofreading by Sean Leonard

Trepidatio Publishing, an imprint of JournalStone Publishing
3205 Sassafras Trail
Carbondale, Illinois 62901

Trepidatio books may be ordered through booksellers or by contacting:
JournalStone | www.journalstone.com

With thanks to friends, family and all significant others.

"This thing of darkness I acknowledge mine." —William Shakespeare

CONTENTS

DARK
IS
BETTER

[ANASAZI]

Know, true-born, that we have always been. We are [Anasazi], the Inheritors. All that sprang from the Void is ours to use as we will. Our blood is diluted now; we are mere shadows of the Shadow we ride.

Yet once we were holy, and shall be so again.

* * *

A hole in the world starts small, forms slowly, like a clot in someone's brain. It's a single piece of darkness stuffed in a locked box, a needle hidden inside an egg inside a hare, a dog, a deer, a man; a shotgun to the face, a razor to the throat. A corpse stuffed inside a haystack, face-down.

These last things are sad, yet normal. They violate no rules. Merely by their own existence, they do not crack the skin of what we agree to call "true," the shape of reality.

When the hole opens, it can do so anywhere it likes.

And does.

* * *

Thirty days, and counting

* * *

"E911 call, in-house—in-apartment building, actually. Christie and Bloor, right near the Pits. FFs meeting on-site. Possible 901a, 901d—neighbour says 'yelling,' 'banging' from inside apartment. Possible HZ, come back."

It was the usual Dispatch monotone, only slightly elevated. Corin shot a look at Janos, who didn't seem inclined to pick up, and did it himself. "Call received, Dispatch. On our way. Any HTR needed, come back?"

"Negative, SJAT-47. Please proceed, come back."

"Proceeding, AOS imminent. Will confirm. Out."

Janos snickered. "You're good at that," he said, not making it sound like a compliment.

"You could be too, you wanted," Corin pointed out. "Call-sign FAQ's right there on the 'Net—all you gotta do is Google."

"Oh, you think I'm *unfamiliar*? Cute. No, youngblood, no problems there. Just don't see why we should stick our necks out for an obvious MAGGOT SHPOS, with half a freakin' hour to end-of-shift."

"'Cause we're in freakin' range?"

"FFs are OS, already. Let *them* handle some PD geri with dementia."

"How do you know he's old?"

"Check the address, youngblood—that's Academica House, retired profs' Roach Motel. Smarties check in, but don't check out."

Corin turned onto Bloor, popping the siren, and watched pedestrians freeze or scurry, accordingly. "Didn't peg you as such an anti-intellectual, man. You tap out in high school or what?"

Janos made a sour face, like he would've spat if the window'd only been down, but just couldn't be bothered to make it so. "Try Uni," he said. "MFA— Master of Fuck-All. And in freakin' Hungarian too, so no cushy job for me once I get here. Waste of my fuckin' time, just like this call."

Corin smiled. "You do know what 'freak''s a euphemism for, right?" he asked. "Like, you could just say 'fuck' all the time, and skip the middle man?"

"Freak you, youngblood. Turn in here."

"Here" turned out to be a short-ass driveway full of wildly gesticulating looky-loo fellow-dwellers, all acting like they were flagging down a plane. Corin coasted in, cut the engine and made the call, while Janos kitted up— grouchy old bastard could be pretty damn effective, when he wanted to. The fire engine was parked just slightly up the block, a bored driver and an equally bored Dalmatian occupying its front seat; Corin gave them a wave, getting nothing in return.

The neighbour who'd called it in was waiting for them at the bottom of the stairs. "Apartment 15—Professor Hardrada. Please hurry."

"Will do, ma'am."

"I'm afraid I pulled the fire alarm, so the elevator doesn't work. The firemen went up already, but..." She hesitated. "It's really terrible, those *noises* he's making. Like an animal. I asked them to wait for you."

"Probably a good idea; thank you."

Janos grunted, thankfully unintelligible—it might even read as sympathetic, from a distance. And as they took the stairs two at a time, Corin found his mind wandering, pulling up stats: Reminding himself how over the last month, incidents of weird, motiveless violence had been rising all over the city, particularly in the Bloor/Lansdowne area. Granted, this *was* the same place a bag of random female body parts had been discovered, a few years back—but gangs, drugs, and their usual attendant fallout didn't seem to quite cover the sort of thing that'd been going on lately.

Two laughing tourists turning a local hardware store into an impromptu Fight Club, using every conceivable tool on each other until neither could stand any longer and one bled out before the ambulance could get there; hadn't that been one of Peter's calls? A homeless man tearing all the fingers off his secondary hand, creating a palette of blood, in order to paint a mural on the side of his cardboard box "home" with his dominant one; a group of nannies converging to beat an unsuspecting man eating his lunch near the park's playground to death with rocks, while their toddler charges snoozed in their strollers (they'd broken his teeth with a direct hit to the mouth first, muffling his cries, so he wouldn't wake the babies).

Weird shit, to be sure. Still, Corin couldn't see this being part of the same wave. Some shut-in without AC melting down, that was all—they'd probably find him passed out, or "passed" (and man, Corin was starting to hate that particular too-happy shorthand—sounded like whoever'd done it couldn't choose between two desserts, rather than having supposedly gone on to meet their Maker), already starting to adhere to his couch in this typically humid August-hits-Toronto weather.

Place was tiny, yet steep—Apartment 15 took them to the third floor, where a matched pair of big men in flame-retardant overalls were not quite tapping their toes in impatience.

"Hey, Janos," one of them said. "Figure out how over here they don't shoot you for breaking the speed limit yet?"

"Zappolino, you Canuck shit-turd. Fuh—"

"Yeah, freak *me*, I know." He nodded at the other firefighter, who punched the door like it'd just touched his mama's butt. "Paramedics, sir! Open up, or we're comin' in!"

Nothing. Zappolino shrugged and used his halligan tool, popping the lock from the jamb. Given the force exerted, Number 15's door came open with surprising slowness and a long, drawn-out creak—swollen from the humidity, probably. Inside, a skinny hallway led past three left-hand doors (hall closet, living room, bedroom?), straight into a kitchen roughly half the size of Corin and Peter's bathroom.

The place stunk like a five-day bender, all the blinds were drawn, and when Zappolino toggled the switch, what might have been the last viable bulb blew with a tinkling pop, leaving behind only a millisecond's flash-image of general gloom, grotesquely bright new flowered wallpaper inexpertly applied from baseboards to ceiling all around them, and some sort of tin pan clogged with dried paste right near Corin's boot, within easy stumbling range. A well-used brush was stuck to its bottom, crusted with a glazed mass of dead flies.

"Professor Hardrada?"

Janos scuffed the floor, lifting a thick half-circle of what looked like dust, but soon proved to be scraped paint mixed with plaster shavings. "Maybe he left already," he suggested.

"Through where, the window?" Corin took a step past Firefighter Number Two, who was gripping his own halligan like a security blanket. "Professor? Missus...um, somebody from downstairs said you were having trouble? C'mon out, sir; we're not the cops. We just want to help."

One step, then two, and a half—Corin hunched himself slightly, so as not to seem threatening. He reached out for the next switch on, the one that might set those fluorescents over the kitchen table humming, while Janos and Zappolino (hatchet buried, in the face of Corin's obvious naïveté) exchanged a *How dumb are you?*-type look behind him, thinking he couldn't see.

Later, it would occur to him that if he *had* been a cop, or even trained as one—like Peter, say—he'd've at least thought to confirm whether or not it was the first left-hand door that was the closet, or the last.

As it was, the door slammed open straight into his shoulder, knocking him to the right so hard he felt two things crunch at once: his scapular acromion as it ground against his clavicle, splintering bone into cartilage, plus the shallow hole his full weight knocked in the opposite wall, spinning him to flop on the floor. The old man came straight out along with it, landing on top of Corin; both bony knees drove deep into Corin's solar plexus, forcing him to huff upwards, to where Hardrada's rictused face—an all-teeth, all-eyes snarl—waited for him. His wasted-looking limbs were solid, nothing but loose skin and muscle, bunched like a boa's.

Janos yelled something, launching himself in turn, as Hardrada grabbed Corin's chin, turning him so their eyes could meet. Awful slaughterhouse breath rained down in a spray of spittle, hot and reeking. And—

"*Fight* me!" he ordered Corin, inexplicably. "I want to *fight!*"

Corin felt the back of his head connect with that dirty floor, wet and muffled; scalp wound, no way to know how bad. "Sir," he said, tongue thick in his mouth, "we...jus here ta see'f you...all right."

"I said *fight*, you coward! *Fight* **meeee!**"

Janos grabbed hold of one arm, the closest, while Zappolino—less worried about making sure the Professor stayed unhurt, considering he was hospital-bound to begin with—went straight for a headlock. Hardrada flailed and snapped, burying his teeth deep in Zappolino's rubber sleeve.

"Crazy old asshole!" Zappolino cursed. "Joey, get the bus—we need more guys, a fuckin' cop-car!"

Janos, at the same time, pulling 'til Hardrada's arm should've cracked: "The fuck *off* him, freaker!"

Hardrada's eyes stayed on Corin's, which were already starting to blur from a possible concussion; he let go of his bite, if only just long enough to demand—

"You *won't* fight?"

Corin shook his head, and wished he hadn't. "Cah," he managed, somehow. "M'a 'medic. Noh...righ'."

Janos, breaking in again: "*I* fight you fine, fuck-knob! You just—"

But Hardrada only shook his bald head, ridiculously strong, even with Zappolino dragging on his Adam's apple from behind. And looking almost—sorry, as he did so: Not apologetic, so much, as regretful.

The *hunger* in those rheumy, too-red eyes.

"I would have *loved* to fight you," he said. Then drove the fountain pen he'd been clutching in his *other* hand all the while, just out of sight, right into Corin's left ear—nib-first—'til his knuckles hit bone.

Oh *God*, the pain. That searing, liquid *pop*, followed by—nothing. Dead air.

"*Fucker!*" Janos howled, silently. And Corin felt rather than heard Hardrada's neck snap under Zappolino's startled grasp, the other firefighter's halligan slicing 'round to smash hard into the crepe-blotchy skull. Blood sprang out, striking Corin's face.

It blazed white, smoking, like liquid metal.

***

From world to world we come, taking and discarding, a thousand upon thousand years of worship and blood. Across the Gulf we come, all [Anasazi] together, going gladly bodiless to bridge that incalculable distance—down the Ancestor Road, the web of worlds, with our forsworn armies marching before and our slaves crawling behind. And all of this we did without any flesh but that of those we conquered!

For we are the Shadow's shadows, needing no vehicles but those we find on our next battleground.

***

When we think about deep space exploration, we think of bridging the gulfs and reaching the most distant regions of outer space, the ultimate extreme environment, filled with constant threat of bodily harm and death. Our base-line assumption has always been that such exploration will be done on a purely physical level, involving spacecraft traveling at the speed of light or beyond it, since without the development of some sort of viable faster-than-light process, the time-lag involved would be completely prohibitive; we might set off for a particular destination only to find out that by the time we arrived it had already been gone for millennia, and that the population of Earth would be extinct by the time we returned.

What we do *not* know is when, or how, this great leap forward into the Nothing Between might be achieved, let alone if it ever will. After all, the furthest space probe mankind has constructed and launched from Earth thus far is Voyager One, which has only just reached the edge of our solar system, after taking over twenty years to get there.

There is another alternative, however—one which does away in a single bold stroke with all the physical realm's innate problems: Deep space exploration done on a purely astral level. To discard the body entirely, and throw only our consciousnesses out into the void...to drift from world to world on the solar winds, surfing currents of life-force, moving through famine to feast, and inhabit by force whatever we might find there...

Just as much of a leap of faith, though a far harder choice, in the immediate—especially so once you realize that a truly coordinated exploratory effort would require suicide on a genocidal level. What sort of people would choose to do this? What sort of "people," however alien, even *could*?

But we will all of us have to leave our bodies behind eventually.

***

Twenty-eight days, and counting

***

Things didn't stay silent, of course.

Corin woke fevered, reeling, in so much pain it felt like nausea, or maybe vice versa. With a pounding in both ears, drum-perforated or not—the rolling blood-surf crash of tinnitus, impossible to block, or treat. Impossible to do anything with except try to ignore.

He'd hoped to find Peter sitting by his bedside. Instead, it was Janos: grim-faced, three days' worth of beard growing in grey. His eyes lit up when he saw Corin's eyes were open, and he sat forward, lips moving excitedly, if unintelligibly.

What're you...? Corin thought, confused. *I...I can't...*

Then a fresh tidal wave broke, and he rolled over, retching; felt Janos' grip on his shoulder, steady, as the bedpan slid underneath his face. When the spasms dulled he looked up again, cold-sweat-slick, and caught Janos' lips moving again.

Can't hear you, he tried to say, through the constant, unbearably loud *click-sssh, click-sssh, click-sssh.* But trailed off soon enough, realizing he couldn't hear himself either.

Janos just nodded, reaching for the bedside table—came back up with a Dollar Store block-tablet with a picture of SpongeBob SquarePants on the front, and a marker. Though the scribbling took a few seconds more than Corin might've thought it would under normal circumstances, it was understandable, considering he was probably translating in his head. Eventually, he flipped the page around, showed him the results:

Long nap youngblood.

Corin wanted to snort, but didn't really feel up to any further pukeage, for the nonce.

"Thass...all...ya got tah say?" he forced himself to eke out, loud enough that he could at least feel his vocal cords buzzing. Worked like a charm, in the sympathy-deflecting sweepstakes; Janos gave a just-slapped grimace, like he was momentarily considering pasting the cripple one, but settled for briskly adding seven new letters beneath his note. Corin gave them a cursory glance.

"Fuh-reak hass ah arrr, grampah," he replied.

Janos shrugged.

***

So yeah, it was about what he'd thought. The ENT handling his case checked off a handy list, using Janos' pad:

Perforated eardrum—surgery to remove pen-nib, sched week next
No infection (yet)/Antibiotics 3 wk
Hearing loss permanent
Tinnitus objective RN, maybe pulsatile, venous hum
Watch to exclude aneurysm
Inner ear damage—BPPV

That last part explained the puking, the Perfect Storm way the room swam whenever Corin sat up, let alone tried to stand. Didn't look too good for his chances of getting back on-shift either; normal difficulties of re-qualification aside, nobody'd want a half-deaf paramedic with mobility issues and permanent carsickness, less likely to help patients than he was to baptize them with vomit. Only logical to cut his losses before they did it for him, and he'd always prided himself on his logic.

A quick glance at Janos, however, gave the lie to the idea that he'd entirely succeeded in looking like he was taking bad news well. That, in turn, brought the vertigo back on, full-force; last thing Corin remembered was Janos barking at the doctor—something about, "He look freaking *green*, fuck-damn!"—before those red walls closed in once more, and the *click-sssh, click-sssh* pulled him back down.

***

Peter finally came by, not the next day but the day after; girding his loins, Corin guessed. Working himself up to deliver the verbal equivalent of a "Dear Corrie" email in person, for which Corin supposed he should be grateful, since it at least allowed him to get a good last look at that ass when the bastard walked away.

Having hitherto routinely excused a lot of Peter's worse qualities just because he was so ridiculously cut, Corin grimly thought, didn't quite take the sting off finding out the feeling'd apparently always been entirely mutual.

Janos dropped by later (Did the guy ever go home? Was this yet another something Corin had to worry about, even in the depths of life-changing trauma and attendant despair? But no, everything about his body language said big brother, not wannabe Daddy; just as well, though it wasn't exactly like Janos was *unattractive*, in his Eastern European grumpy-bear way. Just as)

But: Man, he really did have to stop lapsing into these fugue states, before overmedication made things worse. It was embarrassing, to say the least.

"What's your problem?" Janos demanded, twice as loud as usual. Corin only heard it weakly, distorted, as if through water, and thanked God for the privilege.

"Besides the obvious?" He'd've shaken his head here for punctuation, under normal circumstances—yet another tic he'd have to work on training himself out of. "I need to find somewhere else to live."

"Huh. He always seemed like an asshole."

"Yeah? Thanks for telling me."

"Not my place, youngblood. Next time, pick a guy with pot belly, or a lazy eye—someone who'll treat you right. Stay close, even when things turn to shit..."

"...'cause they're too scared of never hooking up again to run out on me? Thanks, ever so."

That same shrug: "Works for women, I tell you that much. My Kelda is hell of sexy, too smart for a fool like me, has face like a horse. That's why we'll die together, be buried in the same damn coffin."

Corin felt like telling Janos that being buried with Peter had never been the thing uppermost on his mind, but the *ssshing* and *clicking* was already coming back, in full force. The way it probably would for the rest of his life, intermittently or not...

And he probably had that fucking whey-faced green tinge to his complexion once more, because here was Janos' big hand on his chest, pushing him gently prone. "You don't worry 'bout it," he said, more an order than words of comfort. "Get set for the operation, for recovery. I'll ask around; got some ideas where you could move, for no money down."

Corin's mouth was dry, his own words gone silent and aching again. He felt his cracked lips moving, shaping: *Why do you care?*

"Am I fucking American, to drop you in the garbage? I put a lot of effort into you, now I got to train somebody all over. You can maybe at least tell him how I like things, I just make sure you want to."

Him...or her...

"Day I work with a girl be a cold freaking day in Hell."

So now they knew: A fag was okay, as long as he had the right parts. *Some Socialist* you *are*, he wanted to say, before he blacked out—but too late, he was gone, short or long. Gone, either way.

When he woke up, there was a bandage covering his useless ear, and the *click-sssh* had finally abated to something subliminal, like a second heartbeat. The ENT made an "okay" sign, and Corin made the mistake of starting to nod in reply; he barely caught himself, coughing bile.

"We have pills for that," the ENT assured him.

"You freakin' better," he snapped back; classic Janos.

***

Thus it was that we came to a thousand worlds when they were young and fresh and made them our home, fearless against their vile Light. Thus it was that we broke a thousand kings and made them our cattle, drove the lumbering herds across their burnt fields with jewelled and singing whips. Thus it was, by instinct alone, that we found the empty places and forced them to our will, pumped fresh Darkness through them and cracked those worlds across like bones, sucking their marrow dry.

And how was all this done? Easily. So easily.

We sent our word before us, our open invitation; the very root of our language, our culture, ourselves. We sent it wrapped as a gift and shining like a dropped star, for any fool to read. We threw it forth, a disease disguised as a seed, to sow our crop in the ruins of all things' hearts, and reap a great red harvest. And then...

...we waited, patient as decay, timeless as time itself. For these infinite generations of emissaries to do our work for us.

***

Located beyond the Gobi Desert, the austere and impenetrable Kun Lun Mountains of Central Asia hold an important place in Chinese mythology, since it is in this range that the Immortals are believed to live, ruled by Hsi Wang Mu, the Queen Mother of the West. They are said to aid her in her attempts to guide humanity towards wisdom and compassion, shepherding certain virtuous pilgrims—including, near the end of his life, the philosopher Lao Tzu, author of the Tao Te Ching—towards the vast garden that surrounds her nine-storey palace of pure jade, in which grows the Peach Tree of Immortality. Only the most deserving are ever permitted to eat the fruit of this tree, which blooms once every six thousand years.

The Immortals are said to possess perfect, ageless bodies which are visible, but not made of flesh and blood: they are composed of elementary atomic matter, which allow them to travel and live anywhere in the Universe, even at the centers of stars—possibly while still in their physical bodies, or possibly by projecting their minds. Either way, this is a remarkable concept for any human culture to entertain, since it seems to assume a plurality of inhabited worlds in the Cosmos.

In the seventeenth century, two Jesuit missionaries, Stephen Cacella and John Cabral, recorded the existence of a place called Chang Shambhala, as described to them by the lamas of Shigatse, where Cacella lived for 23 years, until his death in 1650. It was rumored to be an inaccessible paradise somewhere beyond Tibet, among the icy peaks and secluded valleys of Central Asia...a valley of supreme beatitude that is sheltered from the icy arctic winds and where the climate is always warm and temperate, the sun always shines, the gentle airs are always beneficient, and nature flowers luxuriantly.

A physical place, in other words. But many esotericists also believe Shambhala is less a real place with a concrete, physical presence in a secret location on Earth than a higher spiritual plane, what might be called another dimension of space-time coterminous with our own; a literal state of mind, already locked deep within ourselves, in which we may gain an insight into the higher spirituality inherent in the Universe, as distinct from the mundane world of base matter in which we normally exist.

It was this guiding principle that led to the foundation of a monastery dedicated to the King of Shambhala, Rigden Jye-Po, which was discovered in the Shara-gol valley near the Humboldt Mountains between Mongolia and Tibet by the Roerich Expedition of 1923-26, led by paranormalist Nicholas Roerich. The monks and lamas of this monastery spent their days in active meditation, transcribing endless prayer-strings, and pored over the results at night, treating whatever mistakes they might find as instances of automatic writing—subliminal communication from the Immortals themselves.

In most cases, these "messages" were fairly easy to decipher, their content obscure yet positive. One particular repetition, however, came to be looked upon with increasing horror: A symbol—the monk who had originally written it claimed it was a name—in what appeared to be a completely alien language. Though meaningless on the surface, it seemed to infiltrate the mind of whoever "read" it, forcing them to keep trying to replicate it over and over. Eventually, the monks realized that contemplating this symbol produced very negative side-effects—obsession, violence, self-mutilation, a complete sublimation of the original identity. Destroying the symbol proved useless, since even after the original reader's inevitable suicide, it continued to sporadically appear throughout every copied prayer.

So they tried to contain the thing, at least, by excising all instances of it at the source, subjecting those who produced it to immediate isolation and exorcism—and subsequently burying all scraps of paper it occurred on inside a particular puzzle-box, slotted at the top, with its locking mechanisms deliberately sabotaged in such a way as to render it impossible to open.

***

Seventeen days, and counting

***

The late Professor Hardrada's neighbour, it turned out, was also his landlord. She introduced herself with an awkward handshake as Nala Le.

"We're just so sorry about what happened, Mister Vogt," she told Corin, handing over the keys.

"To him? Or to me?"

"To both of you, of course. This...hasn't been easy, for anyone."

I'll bet, Corin thought, but didn't say; hell, she just looked so damn defeated by all this carnage, the insolvable damage to her building's already less-than-sterling reputation. Worse than he did, at least on the outside, going by the reflection in that newly installed hallway security he didn't recall having seen the last time he'd mounted these narrow stairs, two scant weeks back. So he supposed he could afford to be magnanimous, for now.

Besides which, as Janos could have told her, he really *did* need this apartment.

"That son of bitches is keeping all your furniture?" he'd repeated, amazed, after Corin told him why he didn't need a moving van.

"It's his furniture too. Besides...we got it on credit, mainly his, so he made all the design decisions based on whatever was playing that week on TLC, because he's got shitty taste. So I don't really want most of it anyways."

"And those grapes were sour, right?"

"Screw you, Aesop."

"Who?"

The detritus of five whole years, packed haphazardly into a pathetic six boxes of crap. Janos took four stacked on top of each other, high enough he had to negotiate up the stairs by feel; Corin trailed behind, one under either arm, trying to balance his weight so the vertigo didn't hit him quite so hard with every shifting step. As Janos heaved his load down next to Hardrada's former door, rummaging in his pocket for the key, Corin caught a brief sight of what looked like a man peering down at them from one more floor up— roof access only, he thought Ms. Le had said. Maybe he'd been sunbathing, come down to find out what all the stomping and puffing was about.

Tiny string of flashbulb screengrabs going off, before the guy ducked back out of range: Young(-ish). White (very). Blond hair, ruffled straight up. Little round glasses, gone blank as silver coins with reflected light. Possibly even cute, though Corin wasn't really in much shape to give a clear verdict on that one, given he was trying hard not to hurl.

Then the lock—shiny-new, just like the jamb, and a few of the hinges Zappolino's buddy had managed to dislodge—clicked open and Janos stood back up, briskly wiping his hands. Grabbed the topmost box and shoved the door open with one hip, like some crazy Hungarian parody of good manners.

"There we go," he said. "All yours, youngblood."

"Home sweet crime scene," Corin agreed.

Place hadn't changed much—slightly less dusty, perhaps. But all of Hardrada's crap was still in roughly the same place, from what little Corin remembered of that night, though someone (Ms. Le again probably) had disposed of the professor's bedding, scoured out his fridge, and pulled the living room blinds back up. She'd also stuck a big bunch of Mac's Milk chrysanthemums in a chipped mug and arranged them in the middle of the kitchen table, like that was supposed to help.

As it turned out, Janos had brought along some booze with which to christen the place, a huge-ass bottle of no-name vodka that tasted a bit too much like the potatoes it came from to be worth mixing incautiously with Corin's heavy meds. *Five pills a day keep the seizures away*, that was the theory anyhow. Corin couldn't really say one way or the other so far, but he wasn't looking to take any chances.

His no-booze resolutions fell off pretty quick, though, once the boxes were put away, and the psychic stench of dead man's clutter started making his nose sting.

Midnight found them poking around in the kitchen, trying to decide which cans looked least suspect. Janos tripped over the sill coming in, and found himself abruptly eye-to-eye with a weirdly burnt-looking stain. "Have to sand that," he observed. "What was it, slag…solder? He was welding in here maybe?"

"Who welds in their apartment?"

"Some people for fun, as a hobby-amusement. Or work."

"I don't think he was that kind of professor, Janos."

It occurred to Corin that he didn't know what it was, exactly, that Hardrada had studied, or taught. Or anything much about him really, aside from the fact that he could hit like a buffalo, and had even worse taste than Peter when it came to papering his walls.

A fresh twist of nausea, and Corin raised his head to realize they'd somehow ended up on the living room couch together, a good ten feet away. Beside him, Janos was half-sprawled in a way that took up far too much room for comfort, his sweaty big-man smell alone enough to render Corin simultaneously horny and sad. Stupid: He didn't even *like* Janos, most of the time—or hadn't, until he'd abruptly become one of the few things he had left. Was this what the rest of his life would be reckoned in? A series of ever-diminishing returns?

Seeking distraction, Corin made himself squint over at the stain again, hard, and remembered—

"No, wait: That was his *blood*."

"Couldn't be."

"Sure, but it was—I remember. It was all, like…white, and smoking."

"You're drunk, youngblood."

"Yeah? Well, you're—drunker. *Much* drunker. So get the fuck out of my apartment already, asshole, so I can sleep."

"Get the *freak* out, you mean."

"Either does me just fine, man."

At the door, Janos suddenly enfolded him, bruising his ribs. "I never cared you were gay, you know," he said, muffled, into the top of Corin's head.

"Um, thanks, Janos—I never cared you were straight. I mean...you *are* straight, right?"

Janos laughed. "Bet your ass. Don't worry, youngblood: Plenty of twinks in the sea. You find somebody—somebody smart, sexy. Good for you."

"Okay, thanks again."

"Next time go ugly, remember! Is all the difference."

"Yeah, I'll make sure to do that."

***

The first dream came later that night. He sat in an indefinitely sized room, surrounded by an equally indefinite number of people. In front of him was a roll of coarse paper, spooling outwards into darkness; he saw his left hand steady it, holding the immediate surface flat, while his right used reed and ink to scribe it with words he couldn't read—strokes, dots, dashes, all darting downwards from a single uppermost line. There was a soothing rhythm to the work, the soft shapes of syllables forming on his tongue, releasing themselves silently against his palate again and again. His eyes and wrists burnt, pleasantly.

But then he looked down just in time to watch the pen go in a direction he hadn't willed it to, and felt the words choke in his mouth. A series of hard scratches, angled so sharply what emerged looked impenetrable, a knot of lines. A squatting spider. A crab's track in wet sand, printed only to be washed away, then reappear whole, perfect. Impossible to reproduce, since he never remembered how many strokes, in what directions, or what order...

...and yet, there it was: There. And there. And there again.

The lines silvered grey from black, paper dimming grey from buff, until the whole thing turned itself out, went negative and shining: hot, smoking white on absolute black, impenetrable as stone. With all the lamps guttering out and flickering to nothing in a cold wind, as he realized he *could* actually read it now, after all—whether he wanted to, or not—

great
great is
great is the
great is the power
great is the power of
great is the power of the
[A]

***

Around one the next afternoon, Corin woke to a phone call from Ms. Le, and found out his alarm must have been screaming for at least an hour. An hour after *that*, abject but (at least) freshly showered, he hit the Academica's basement laundry room, where he fed his clothes into the machine furthest from the door and waited for the two pills he'd just chugged to take effect—head down, mouth dry, temples pounding.

Same old same old, as of barely three weeks. And getting old at that.

A slow, gummy blink, half his usual speed, and the young man from the roof was by his side, simply standing. No apparent reason to be there, aside from the pleasure of watching Corin blush—and that spark, that *spark*, more immediate than he'd ever felt it before, so sharp he almost mistook it for more pain. Like a stomach punch, triggering the oh-so-primitive urge to flight, fuck, or—

(*fight*)

"Uh, hey. Corin."

"Leif."

Blond, yeah—Swedish stock. Like Hardrada.

"I just moved in," Corin continued, unnecessarily. "Number 15."

"Yes."

"Did you...I guess you might've known him, right? Professor Hardrada? I mean, sorry, if you did."

Leif gave him an uninterpretable glance, lens-shielded, under white-bleached brows. "He lived here a long time," he said at last. "And yes, I knew him. Quite well."

How well? Corin wondered. Admitting, out loud: "I don't even know what he specialized in."

There was a brief hint of an accent coloring Leif's speech, far more ghostly than Janos' occasional dropped connector or weird grammatical patterns. "Oh, history mixed with anthropology, mainly—Nazi pseudo-archaeology was his area of expertise. He'd written books."

"Indiana Jones stuff, huh?"

"Slightly less intense, but...yes, somewhat."

"Maybe you could tell me more about it sometime."

"Maybe."

They both looked straight at each other then—eye to eye, both equally blue. And because Leif smiled first, Corin didn't have to.

***

Great is the power of the [Anasazi]! Praised be the power of our caustic blood, our legacy from those who cast us down from purest Darkness into impure flesh: The Old Silent Ones Who Went Before, our long-fled makers and betrayers, who we will pursue to the very rim of Being.

Praised be the power of that poisoned inheritance, which scribes signs of our coming glory upon our bodies with the caustic brush of divinity! In each new incarnation, we bear with pride the pain which is our lot and exaltation—proof of killing fire caged by skin and turned back on itself, searing us from the inside out, just us as our own presence sears the universe around us.

Bow down, or flee, or stand and struggle: It matters little. Though, all things considered, we much prefer to be fought.

And to fight.

***

In 1935, the *Ahnenerbe* Organization—commonly known as *Deutsches Ahnenerbe – Studiengesellschaft für Geistesurgeschichte* (German Ancestry – Research Society for Ancient Intellectual History)—became attached to Hitler's Reichsführer-SS, under the administrative command of Heinrich Himmler, who had no official training in archaeology but was well-known for his interest in mysticism. He charged the *Ahnenerbe* with putting together a vision of prehistory that would demonstrate the pre-eminent position occupied by the Germans and their Germanic predecessors since the beginning of civilization. "A nation lives happily in the present and the future so long as it is aware of its past and the greatness of its ancestors," he claimed, and it was the *Ahnenerbe's* stated goal to study the ideas and achievements of the "Indo-Germanic" people, bring those research findings to life and present them to the German people, with an eye towards encouraging every German to get involved in the organization.

By 1937, the *Ahnenerbe* had grown from a vaguely occult-minded boy's club composed of amateur enthusiasts into the primary instrument of Nazi archaeological propaganda, subsuming smaller organizations, and filling its ranks with "investigators" whose ranks included people like Herman Weirt, who spent the core years of his career attempting to prove that Northern Europe was the cradle of Western Civilization. Although some real archaeologists with extreme views joined up, mainly to gain high-ranking party official status, they had consistent problems finding trained scientists willing to work on their projects, which were therefore often run mainly by scholars from various branches of the humanities—committed, but far more interested in metaphor than solid research. The group's archaeology-as-religion bent is best illustrated by such open-air displays of Germanic idolatry as its discovery of the *Sachsenhain*, a site where forty-five hundred Saxons were allegedly executed as a punishment for Widukind's uprising against Charlemagne; instead of literally digging deeper, the *Ahnenerbe* were content to present it as an idealized shrine, a place which should be considered sacred to the Germanic people because it highlighted their genetically innate readiness for self-sacrifice.

In 1936, the *Ahnenerbe* mounted an expedition to Sweden, with the object of examining rock-art which they had already concluded was "proto-Germanic." It was there that a young history student named Hans Hardrada joined the dig, so distinguishing himself through his willingness to work hard and swallow the organization's mythology that when they left, they took him with them.

Hardrada, now a full member, went along when the *Ahnenerbe* sent an expedition to Tibet in 1938 that was meant to prove Aryan Superiority by confirming the Vril theory, a Hollow Earth/lost Aryan super-race scenario derived from Edward Bulwer-Lytton's science-fantasy novel *Vril, the Power of the Coming Race*. The project's leaders correlated Bulwer-Lytton's vision of the subterranean Aryan-derived "Vril-ya," able to channel unbearable energies through their bodies, with both the Tibetan Buddhist mental obstacle-removing practice of *Dzogchen Chöd* and local legends of the Chud, a supernally powerful and peaceful tribe supposedly driven underground by their barbarian neighbours, where they were assumed to have constructed massive cities beneath the earth that might be entered only through secret passages carefully kept hidden from any outsiders' eyes.

As Hardrada and his fellow travelers retraced much the same path used by various Chinese emperors to access the Immortals of the Kun Lun Mountains, they were driven off-track by bad weather into the Shara-gol valley, where they literally stumbled upon the Rigden Jye-Po monastery. The monks, knowing no better, let them in, treated their wounds, and allowed them to stay while recuperating. And when the charmingly curious Hardrada began to ask them questions about their guiding purpose—the prayer-rolls, subconscious communication with the Immortals, that recurrent, potentially dangerous symbol—they answered willingly, innocently, with great and (in retrospect) somewhat foolish detail...

***

Twelve days, and counting

***

Leif had a wide-strewn constellation of freckles distributed all across his left side, outlining the area where saddlebags might eventually replace the firm, smooth oblique abdominals currently descending into an equally firm, smooth hip and thigh. His pubes were as white as his brows, and fair as he was, he tended far more to gooseflesh than blush, even at the moment of crisis.

They lay together in what was now Corin's bed, spooned in a loose sixty-nine, with their heads cushioned on each other's inner thighs and the best bits well within easy reaching distance. Corin's skull swam with what would have normally been a pleasant post-orgasmic lassitude—but the *click-sssh* of tinnitus was never far away, even now, joined by a faint choir of blood-borne bells, and he didn't want to shut his eyes, for fear that the bed would begin to lurch and spin like a misaligned roundabout. So he swallowed hard instead, and made himself ask:

"So Hans Hardrada was, what—Professor Hardrada's—"

"Grandfather. He was sent to the Front near the end of the War, during the collapse, when the *Ahnenerbe* no longer had any sort of value for the Reich; left for dead after an incursion into Allied territory, he deserted, fell back on his Swedish citizenship, eventually immigrated to Canada."

"This was after Tibet though."

"Oh yes, long after. Though the expedition as a whole was considered a failure overall, many—like Hans Hardrada—returned with souvenirs."

"The box."

"Exactly. Finding it was what spurred Hardrada's interest in the *Ahnenerbe*—the knowledge that his family history had been touched by this thing, poisoned by it."

Corin snorted. "Sounds more like the other way 'round. I mean—the monks didn't just let him walk off with it, right?"

"No. They objected, strenuously—but it was a very remote monastery, after all, and they were pacifists. Whereas the *Ahnenerbe* were the SS in scientific drag."

One more time, Corin wondered how Leif could know all this information. Did Hardrada talk about it in class? In bed?

"You ever see this mysterious box for yourself?"

"A few times, certainly. He kept it in his office, until he was encouraged to take early retirement."

"I sort of thought most academics wouldn't want to be associated with somebody who thought *Ghosts of Mars* was a documentary."

Leif turned slightly, fixing Corin with a blankly penetrating look. "I don't know what that is," he said. Corin genuinely couldn't tell if he was joking, or whether he cared enough to find out either way.

"Come here," he said, and Leif did.

***

They went out around nine, just in time to hit the LCBO before it closed. Leif used a bottle of Jägermeister and a bottle of Dr. McGillicuddy's Fireball mix to make shots he called "Dead Nazis," and they knocked enough of them back that they soon ran out of clean cups and glasses. Later, with no cable and Corin's vision starting to gutter like a candle-flame, they decided to defer yet one more bout of fooling around until after they'd found this freaking box of Hardrada's.

The search started with all the normal places—drawers, kitchen cabinets, closets, under the sink—before branching wider: behind the bookcases, inside the icebox, under the bed. They went around stamping on floorboards, doing a stumbling, ass-grabby *trepak* all up and down, 'til Ms. Le called up to ask whether or not Corin needed help with something.

"No, sorry," he said, through the chain. "It's nothing big. Just, um...moving furniture."

"Are you sure, Mister Vogt? I have your friend—Mister Osht?—on speed-dial."

And you think I don't? Corin wanted to snap back. But: "That won't be necessary, thanks—these pills, y'know, they just, um...make me forget what I'm doing sometimes. I'm really sorry," he repeated again, the taste of it mealy in his mouth, like wormy flour.

"All right. Sleep well, Mister Vogt."

"You too," he called, as she stepped away. Then turned back to where he thought he'd left Leif, only to find him—

—*not* gone, thankfully; not simply vanished outright, like some drugged-and-drunken sexual fantasy that'd managed to pilot him down to the Beer Shop and back with its thumbs dug deep in his lizard-brain, running him like a Wii. Instead, Leif was standing inside that cramped hall closet, staring up.

"Ah, yes," he said softly, as though to himself. "I'd forgotten."

The box was smaller than Corin had pictured, and heavier. He stuck his hand up through two bulgy, porous, slightly overlapping panels in the closet's ceiling and watched them slick apart like lips over a (hopefully) toothless mouth. Halitosis-flavored dust fell, gilding them both with ruin, as Corin raised it and peered down into the slot, a single winking eye in that blank, octagonal mask-face.

"Open it," Leif suggested.

Corin pushed on all eight sides at once, four to either hand, but felt no appreciable give.

"Not happening, man. It's locked, remember?"

"Then you'd better try harder."

Right up against him now, over-close in that humid, upright space, a hastily improvised sauna. Five minutes ago, prone on the bed, Corin would have considered the same lack of distance between them not only a positive but a necessity—but that was back when they'd been horizontal enough for him to misinterpret that last half-inch of height in his own favor. Before all his various aches and pains had returned seven-fold, borne on a lapping wave of nausea, with tinnitus's bells as an accompanying chorale.

"But," he began, mouth dry, fists shaky, "they, like...the monks...they made it so you *couldn't*. I mean, you said—"

Leif smiled gently. "Oh, poor baby; *Hardrada* obviously got it open, and him just a weak old man. But that's right—you're wounded, aren't you? Unfixable. *Broken.*"

His smile widened, solicitous to mocking to contemptuous in one-point-nothing, some unfathomable inter-dimensional shift. The bottom fell out of Corin's stomach; he'd've stumbled back against the wall if sheer geometrics hadn't placed him there already.

"Who the fuck *are* you?" he asked, freezer-burnt by that suddenly alien stare.

"Apart from the man you let inside your *home*, whose last name you don't even know? Same one who's had his teeth around your cock?"

"Get out of my way, Leif."

"*Make* me."

The closet door came open with a bang, one hinge popping—they went right, the box left, hitting hard and skittering against the wall. *Now she'll call the cops for sure,* Corin thought, barely registering how the punch he'd just thrown had apparently skinned his knuckles open on Leif's surprisingly jagged grin. But then Leif was sucker-hooking him in the temple, slamming his brain against the inside of his cranium; a light went off and they plunged down into it together thrashing, boneless yet multi-limbed. Leif bit his shoulder, deep enough to bruise. Corin drove both knees into Leif's stomach and scrabbled at him, hundred-handed—if he'd been a cat, Leif's guts would be decorating the floor. Leif just grinned again, and shifted his grip: Took hold of him bag-first, twisting, 'til Corin screamed, throwing him all the way across the room. Leif's head hit with such scalp-tearing urgency against the doorframe that blood poured down into his eyes, turning his forehead red.

Corin coughed bile on the floor, snarling. Leif wiped his brow with sticky fingers, and laughed out loud. "Oh yes," he said. "I *knew* you'd be good at this. I *knew.*"

Corin panted, hoarse. "You...are a *fucking* freak."

Leif laughed once more, as though that was the best joke he'd heard in years—then sprang forward without any hint of warning, like an animal, hands knotted in Corin's hair before he could think to object.

"Which means we match," he said, kissing him so deep the grue from their mutual wounds smeared 'round both their lips like clownish lipstick, a two-person Grand Guignol carnival mask. And rolled them so he was back on top, before slamming Corin's skull down sharply enough that he blacked out.

***

Five hours on, sun woke him, rather than a knock at the door. His lower spine felt kicked, pain in his head so bright he turned on his side and vomited outright, barely bothering to cover his mouth with his hands.

Leif was gone.

He scrubbed his palms, face (far more gingerly), the floor. Leaning into the living room mirror to check his bruises and test whether a few teeth were loose in their sockets, his toe clunked against the box, so—after nearly a half-minute of contemplation—he knelt, picked it up, trying it instinctually one more time around the blurry seam of the rim, with both thumbs pressing upwards. And this time, unnaturally enough...

...it opened.

Empty.

"Guess he did, after all," he remarked, to thin air.

***

Predictably, by the time Corin finally screwed his courage up to ask her, Ms. Le turned out to have never heard of any handsome young man named Leif. So he taped his own ribs and cocooned himself deeply, ignoring the phone and Janos' messages, the clocks and their boring litany of time saved, time lost, time wasted. He embarked on a campaign of household triage, carting boxes full of crap down to the recycling room, cleaning the place 'til it squeaked. On Sunday night, armed with a new putty knife and roller bought at the same hardware store those tourists had redecorated with body-parts, he began stripping that horrendous wallpaper like a scab, peeling and paring it back until bare plaster emerged, uniformly yellow-white but oddly ridged to the touch, as though it had been incised with reverse-Braille.

He'd never know where the idea came from: the literal back of his head, that map of hair-hidden bruise-on-bruises? One of Peter's endless home renovation marathons? Or was it that first dream, the one he hadn't had since picking Leif up in the laundry room, a place he now shunned so intently that every item of clothing he owned was beginning to marinate in funk—the scratching reed, ink-dipped, soaking into an unwound prayer-roll's threads, making them rise the way a dry riverbank's mudflats fill during inundation, a fresh alphabet of water rising from the dust?

Children's water-paints from the corner store, every color mixed to form a light wash of brown, diluted like weak tea with three parts water to one part not. And when Corin ran the roller across the denuded hallway walls, what emerged was row upon row of symbols scratched into the plaster itself with God only knew what sort of implement—the same pen-nib they'd pried from his eardrum maybe.

So many they blurred together as Corin strained to scan each line, blending and buzzing, a relocation swarm. That one symbol, and endless variations thereof; though it wasn't as though Leif had ever shown it to him, Corin knew enough to recognize it when he saw it. What else could it be?

And yes, wait, shit: He *had* seen this before. Had written it himself, copied it endlessly, over and over and over again. "Read" it, as he did.

The same way—he *was* reading it. Right now.

Oh, his fingers, pleasantly burning. His eyes, itching as it transcribed itself beneath their lids, across their corneas. For great *great* **great** *is the power of the*

[Anasazi]

***

Civilizations piled upon civilizations, each more splendid and complex than the last, have fallen into disfavor and disrepair as our clans ascend and clash, intermarry and breed, supplant and cannibalize each other in turn—godlings all, each prepared to murder parent, sibling, child for the chance to be their generation's chosen God.

We call our empire Dri s'Abhor, the World-Tower-Tree Most High, for we have climbed a ladder of possessions to build it, touched the sky and cut at a thousand traitor suns with our jagged stone blades. We stretch it out lengthwise, sidewise, back and forth and over and under and through, threading it from hole to hole, linking every empty space we leave behind irreversibly to every other. Rendering the entire multiverse nothing but our labyrinthine burial monument.

And even now—now, when memory fails us, and no fit enemy remains but each other—throughout Dri s'Abhor, the Stacked and Windowless Tower of Worlds, true Darkness Made Flesh stands alone.

***

Search: Anasazi

Ancient Pueblo People or Ancestral Puebloans were an ancient Native American culture centered on the present-day Four Corners area of the United States, comprising southern Utah, northern Arizona, northwest New Mexico, and a lesser section of Colorado. As a whole, this group has often been referred to in archaeology as the Anasazi.

Historical derivation:

The term "Anasazi" was established in archaeological terminology in 1927, through the Pecos Classification system. The term was first applied by Richard Wetherill, a rancher and trader who knew and worked with Navajos and, in 1888–1889, was the first Anglo-American to explore various ruins of the Mesa Verde and other sites in that area. The name was further sanctioned after being adopted by Alfred V. Kidder, the acknowledged dean of Southwestern Archaeology, who felt that it was less cumbersome than any more technical term he might have used. Subsequently, some archaeologists have come to worry that because the Pueblos have many different words for "ancestor," using only one exclusively might be offensive to non-Navajo-speaking Puebloans.

Etymology and usage:

Says archaeologist Linda Cordell: "The name 'Anasazi' has come to mean 'ancient people,' although the Navajo word *anaasází* means 'enemy ancestors.'" However, some alternate translations of "Anasazi" suggest a meaning closer to "ancestors that are now scattered," perhaps referring to a long-distant diaspora or exodus. Although some modern descendants of this culture object to the use of the term Anasazi entirely (the modern Hopi, for example, use the word "Hisatsinom"), there is still controversy amongst them as to a proper native alternative.

***

Nine, seven, five days, and counting

***

Sunday night:

Corin raised his head queasily. "Well, *that* was useless," he said out loud, again to no one in particular. Unless he genuinely thought that Google might be listening, that was, which he didn't—*think*—he did.

Doing that kinda a lot these days, man. Probably need to stop, sometime soon; like, really. *Before—*

—"before" *what*, tough guy?

Out in the hall, he almost thought he could hear the symbols whisper to each other while cool air leaking up from Ms. Le's air-conditioned apartment below played lightly over their drowned and sunken curlicues. The echo of it got inside his wrecked ear and stayed there, a trapped insect walking his brain's grooves like a maze.

He looked down at his hands, nails grown ragged, and realized he hadn't washed them since the paper came down.

That should change too, the same dim voice commented.

He took a shower—tepid rather than hot, to beat the humidity—and toweled his hair vigorously, to make up for having run out of shampoo. Then gathered up all the dirty clothes into two hefty garbage bags, outfits he'd re-worn at least twice each while avoiding the laundry room like the proverbial plague, and made himself move grimly downwards, head reeling, using his elbows to negotiate.

A floor down, he almost ran straight into Ms. Le.

"Mister Vogt," she said. "I, um—"

Voice hoarse from disuse: "Was I making too much noise?"

"No, no, you've been fine, thank you." She seemed to be having trouble looking him in the eye, or anywhere else. But with a deep drawn breath and a shy smile, she finally managed to get there: "I simply wanted to say...well, that there *was* someone in this building with the first name Leif once."

"When did he—"

"Move out? No, no. You misunderstand; you *met* him, just before he—left. Though I wouldn't have called him handsome, personally. Or young."

Now it was Corin's turn to blink, which turned out to be inadvisable, especially when balanced between flights of stairs.

"What do you mean?" he asked.

"Well...the professor, of course. *His* name was Leif...Hardrada."

***

And: Though it took him almost a whole shocked-numb hour to start looking for it, finding a drawer full of Hardrada's personal photos proved far easier than finding that goddamn iron box ever had. The ones right at the top were all familiar, that same reptilian profile, neck tortoise-crepey, hair creeping steadily back as the spotted expanse of scalp crept forward. But getting further down, as color became more hectic, more yellow, faded away entirely...

There he was finally; a candid shot, sandwiched between two similarly school blazer-wrapped chums, lifting a stein and all but winking at the camera. Leif, thick crop of hair only a shade darker than his white brows, squinting eyes so blue they seemed blind, as though into his own future's deceptively bright light.

"I was twenty there, I think," Leif said, from Corin's deaf spot, making lust and vertigo ripple admixed through his body like a thousand gut-strung rubber bands twisting. Corin didn't turn to look for him, half-afraid of what he'd see, if anything: A smear, a stain? Trailing ectoplasm? The same so-palpable *doppelgänger* he'd gone down on his knees for, right on these uncomfortable floorboards?

"You shouldn't berate yourself," Leif told him, in that gentle, faintly accented tone Corin now realized he'd spent the last three days missing sharply, as though it was his dead mother's last touch. "They are planet-killers, Corin; it is only their nature, their function. How can we hope to stand against such creatures?"

"The 'Anasazi.'"

"Oh, it's just a stop-gap word with which to translate the untranslatable, a scab formed over a consistent lacuna—suitable, certainly, especially with its most recent connotations of cannibalism and genocide added in. Possibly, it's simply as close to the general sense or meaning of their name as we can come, without becoming them."

And now Corin risked a quick glance, only to be shocked rigid by the spectacle of Leif cutting into his own well-developed yet utterly insubstantial chest with a very real-looking bottle opener—he could swear he knew where it *should* be, in the kitchen, but was damned if he wanted to check. The skin parted almost silently, bruises outlining a predictable shape; blood welled up, white and smoking, molten as Janos' slag.

Some people weld at home, as hobby-amusement, Corin couldn't stop himself from thinking. *Yeah, that's some definite sort of sculpture, right there. Very...palpable.*

At that, Leif smiled. "Thank you."

"So you're...what? One of them?"

"Call me Patient Zero. *Ground* Zero. The vector of the disease."

"How did it happen?" Corin demanded. "You owe me that much."

"Do I? Well, perhaps. I was always drawn to the box, and eventually managed to open it—or was it that it decided to open itself, for me? The symbol was inside, a thousand different iterations of it. I began to trace them, to use them as meditational aids for my own pathetically limited astral explorations. And thus the eyes of the [Anasazi] fell upon me..."

"Hearing" the word for the first time was the same as reading it—a blink, a pop, a broken blood vessel ghosting across the mind's eye like a knot in eternity's fabric. Like the thread-head which, once pulled, would unravel everything.

Corin shook his head, or started to; the lurch was a slap, a grouting scoop, crystallizing what little resolve he had left. "All those monks though. Can't think this never happened before."

"It did, yes, many times. But the lamas were watchful, devout. Usually, things never got this far."

"Your fault, huh?"

Leif shrugged. "Call it this faithless age's fault. I worked hard for something, *anything*, which might prove to me there was something more than the immediate. Until, at last...I got what I wanted."

"*I* didn't," Corin snapped, a snapped-trap catch wounding the inside of his throat. As though, pushed only a little harder, he might find himself crying.

But to this Leif made no reply, because—as Corin discovered, when he finally gathered enough strength to look around—

—he was gone. Again.

***

Monday crept by in a blur, languid, dreadful. Corin vaguely remembered waking, hungry, then turning over and pulling the pillows atop himself in a soft pile, digging back into his own stink like a tick.

When he opened his eyes he saw Hardrada's bare walls, his cracked ceiling and blood-stained floors, a peeling overlay ill-set above yawning void. When he closed them, it was only to "open" them once more on an endless stream of mayhem, plunging face-first down into the [Anasazi] maelstrom: A trillion invasions-by-proxy, endless combinations of combatants, all equally alien. Things like monkeys raping each other to death and eating each other's brains. Things like dinosaurs crushing their own cities flat, goring their own offspring, setting fires that consumed empires with their own biological-napalm breath. Things like slugs digesting each other alive, then melting their own stuffed guts apart with a gluey backwash of juice and spilling down into the same fissures that were tearing their own planet apart, laughing with savage delight at the *feel* of it all, the white heat, the smoking rush. The pure will to oblivion made all-too-brief flesh, before it tore itself apart on contact.

The [Anasazi], moving on, forever. Dri s'Abhor reaching up and outwards, an endless bone-rack set with the shattered skulls of worlds.

The universe is doomed, he thought. And giggled.

***

Tuesday night, Corin took himself good and truly *out*, for the first time since his "accident." Some place near the outermost edge of Ryerson Campus East, just Church Street enough to qualify for gay ghetto status. Peter had recommended it to him once, he recalled, but at the time he'd preferred access-all-areas indie/industrial dives like the Speed of Pain, so that put paid to that. And indeed, this jumped-up locker room—Hazer's?—was pretty well exactly the way he'd feared it would be back when, going on Peter's avid description. But he soon downed enough shots-and-beer combos to not care anymore, and began to appreciate his own hearing loss at last: Beats pulsed up jaggedly through the laminate-on-concrete floor, easy enough to follow without having to get distracted by the lyrics (some chick screaming about how her pussy was on fire, *aaaah, my PUSSY is on fire!*), or lack thereof.

Heat mounted, bodies crushing in; he shucked his shirt, headed back for the bar. Almost collided headlong with someone else's gleaming chest, and got a double-load of Sex on the Beach down his own in return.

"*Sorry*, man, *shit*," the guy repeated, dabbing ineffectively away at him with the tail-end of a paper towel roll in the bathroom. "These, uh...oh, I'm such a fuckin' dork, 'cause...like, one of 'em was for you."

He had a nice smile, rendered slightly vampiric by an off-set right upper incisor. Tasted nice too, even without the extra liquid incentive.

They continued to make out a while, cheered on by various passersby, 'til the guy suggested repairing to his place, which proved to be back towards Parliament and down. A bad area, lightly gentrified on the side streets, but getting progressively worse as they moved between bus stops.

After three blocks, Corin's buzz had dissipated far enough that he could feel rather than hear the vague tread of pursuing feet, sensing at least two more hot(ish) young men on the outskirts of his peripheral vision. Their presence made Original Guy nervous, though not in the way Corin might have anticipated.

Ah, he thought, with a lack of surprise that baffled even him. *The Judas Goat ploy.*

Too bad, really. O.G.'d been a damn good tongue-hockey player, an MVP in the making—had even seemed into it, if the crotch of his jeans swelling hard against Corin's thigh was any indication. But bashers weren't required by law to be straight, especially when this might be less an old-school fag-bait and switch than impending robbery with violence; as a qualification stint on methadone clinic duty at the Clarke had taught Corin, little matters like actual sexuality did tend to go out the window when money and other addictive substances were involved.

When they turned sharply left at the north end of Armory Park, Corin could already feel his hands curling into fists. And when O.G. put a hand on his arm, maybe thinking to startle or restrain him, he turned to face their followers with a smile stretched just wide enough to disturb—neither grin nor rictus nor snarl, but something in between all three, showing almost every tooth he had. He felt his gums itch sharply, as though his own incisors longed to pull themselves both out of place and spike forward like a gorilla's.

Tongue lolling out, panting slightly, saliva gathering hot in the floor of his mouth. Almost glad he couldn't see his own eyes, as he asked:

"Can I help you with anything...ladies?"

The initial punch came in sharp, firecracker-potent, synaesthesically reeking of sulphur or cordite—it rocked him back, vertigo head-rush like a secondary contact high, made him giggle at the taste of his own blood. He caught the next one without thinking, and drove his knee up high into the nuts of the dude who'd thrown it, twisting 'til he heard something strain in his own wrist, but crack in his opponent's—probably the joint between wrist and thumb, a classic Bennett's fracture. *Full cast, three to six months of rehab and physio right there,* his professional brain assessed coldly. The human body, such a deceptively delicate thing! Not like—

(*what, not like **what**? Oh shit, oh shit*)

(*not like us in our first forms, of course—so long ago, impossibly distant, knotted together in the acid-blood morass of the birthing pits, coiled and thrashing 'til at last we ate our way free*)

Back in the now, meanwhile, O.G. just stood there with his jaw a-flap, as Corin continued to grind bone-fragments together in what was left of young Mister Broke-thumb Mountain 2010's grip; the partner jack-hammered at his ribs, yelling insults, cracking at least two but getting no visible response 'til he switched to a modified Muay Thai stance and elbowed Corin right across the temple, bruising the orbit of his left eye so badly it began to swell almost on contact. When Corin finally let go, he roundhoused him from the same direction, spinning him like a top, but Corin didn't fall. Instead, he stood there with all ten fingers hooked like he'd just grown invisible claws, and grinned all the harder.

"Oh, *baby*," he told him, appreciatively. "That was some serious kind of fun. Care to elaborate?"

"You're a fuckin' lunatic, dude!"

"Preaching to the choir, sweetie." Momentarily blind, Corin scrubbed blood from a minor scalp-rip out of his lashes, then flicked the result at his new opponent, who jumped back like he thought it was either Alien-drone acid, AIDS-full with an Ebola stinger, or just jam-packed with a Grade A brand of crazy that was almost certainly catching. To O.G.: "Anyhoo—you want in on this or what? 'Cause I'm always open to threesomes."

That something rough he felt at the back of his throat, punctuating the end of the question, turned out to be half a molar—and when he coughed it up and held it to the light, turning it admiringly (enamel and composite resin, one part hard to two parts flaky), O.G. cut and run. "Yeah, keep goin', you goddamn pussy!" his still-upright friend hollered after him as he took to his LED-blinking heels, while the other one moaned at their feet. In the meantime, Corin took the opportunity to run his tongue over the exposed nerve-pulp mass his cracked tooth had just uncovered, which immediately delivered a zap that felt like biting into a live power cord: *Wow, whoa!* And yet: *Seems like I should probably be feeling that **more**, somehow...*

He drooled pink, smile stretching further*further*further, 'til it felt like his cheeks might crack open. And asked the remaining viable combatant, with a sort of rising petulance: "Hey! So you must train, huh? Know any Ultimate Fighter tricks?" No reply. "I'm *talking* to you here, asshole."

The guy pulled at Fracture-Boy's intact forearm with both hands, hauling his dead weight up like he was trying his level best to de-socket the whole shoulder. "Man, shut the fuck up! This is all your fault, you get that, right?"

"*Is* it?" Corin snapped his fingers, back teeth clicking together automatically, and cawed out loud at the resultant jolt. "Well, shit-fire! I knew I was doing *something* wrong." With a wink: "Sure you wouldn't care to go one more round?"

"What the hell do you even *want*, you crazy son of a bitch?"

The only possible reply fell onto his tongue like a demonic gumball, smoking, as though it'd been cast white-hot from a molten pot of Leif's—Hardrada's—alien-tainted blood: *To damn well **fight**, of course, you too-human motherfucker...*

Before he could voice it, however, Corin was already alone again (naturally), with only the blood on the pavement left to mark where he'd once had company worth entertaining. So he blundered homewards instead, disappointed by the night's meager pickings: bruised and dripping, skull stuffed with trashy Acid House samples and two points down on the hangover scale, with nothing else whatsoever to show for his overall investment—no death, not even a little one. The split tooth's howl stayed undimmed over thirty-odd blocks; his torn knuckles hummed venomously, like a double fistful of bees.

In an all-night Coffee Time, Corin picked through leftover papers, finding each subsequent Metro section stuffed with still more tales of unusual mayhem. In the business district, for example—down on condo row—a woman who owned a small maternity-ware fashion boutique had admitted to killing three different men by putting the same 12-gauge knitting needle through their necks, ostensibly for queuing up more closely behind her than she considered wise while she was making end-of-the-night deposits at three separate indoor Toronto Dominion bank ATMs. One's fatal mistake had been looking too hard at her PIN number, while another she thought was "breathing" on her, and the last had gone down because she claimed she could "hear his organs moving around" while he infringed on her personal space. *They sounded wet," Ms. Labayalla told arresting officers, during her sworn statement. "Wetter than normal. Like he was diseased or something. I was in fear for my life."*

Gradually, the skin-pop charge of mugging interrupt-us was draining away, leaving him lip-numb and increasingly desolate in its wake, sweat-wet hair slicked fast to the nape of his neck. To distract himself, he fastened on the conversation between two adjacent hookers—one trans and black, one not and not—who were sharing a single sticky caramel-cheese Danish.

"...you know, like that girl they found under the overpass. That Rita girl?" The other nodded. "Makes you want to work out of home, if you could get it set up."

"Meetlist isn't bad. Or LavaLife, if you can cut through the no-really, I-like-you-for-your-personality B.S."

"Yeah. But then you're alone with them, right? Wondering how you can make 'em leave, after—or even pay. I mean, it's not like you can call four-oh, if shit goes sour..."

"Tag-team. I'd go in with you on a room, someplace neutral."

The real girl snarfed the last piece, made a dismissive hand-gesture. "Yeah, right. You and whose bank book."

"Well..." The other looked down at her own hands, twice her friend's size but beautifully kept, as though she'd never before considered how big they actually were. *Could fit 'round my neck with room to spare,* Corin thought, and went embarrassingly warm in the pit of his stomach, musing on just how hard she might be able to hit, given the opportunity. How well she might be able to handle a blade.

"Occurs to me," she said, slowly, "how it's not so much us being alone with them...as *them* being alone with *us.*"

Then looked at her friend, whose plucked-nude brows climbed almost to her wig-line in response—before blinking and smiling back.

Corin closed his own eyes, breathing settling into a harsh but steady rhythm, heartbeat accelerating. His consciousness opening Venus Flytrap-wide, spreading outwards and seeping molecule-deep, like radiation—letting the sludgy worst of the world around him pour in, like puke through a trash-clogged gutter, to fill his mind to the brim with other people's psychic garbage.

Behind the counter, the last remaining clerk was studying the small of Sex Worker #1's back, trying to trace where her tramp stamp lurked, and dreaming Travis Bickle dreams about the sawed-off his boss thought he didn't know was hidden behind the second refrigerator. Inside the walls, roaches and rats committed casual incest, while in the cut-rate apartments up above, at least two human males did the same. There was an enthusiastic tryst going on in the kitchen of the Thai restaurant next door, endangering their Health Code rating; both participants were thinking about how easy it would be to murder the other, then cover up the crime by slipping an extra serving of filleted corpse into every meal for the next few weeks. Beside them, a mid-sized industrial-strength meat grinder rumbled on, making filling for tomorrow's dumplings.

Was *this* what had happened to Leif, amongst other things, to make him the way he was by the time Corin and Janos had found him? Or was this something special whipped up for Corin alone, special delivery, straight from whatever hellhole the [Anasazi] had once called their home planet?

In Honest Ed's discount department store, illegal immigrants were hard at work marking down damaged goods. Though told not to, one of them had brought along her baby, sedated into silence with a fatal dose of adult anti-depressants; it lay right now in one of the remnant drawers of the fabrics section, slowly suffocating. Corin wondered just how long the body would stay in there, undiscovered, after its mother realized exactly what she'd done, shut the drawer again quietly and walked away. Or how long it would take her to swallow the rest of those pills, once she got back home...

(*I don't want to see this, oh God, any of it*)

(*don't want to **know***)

And yet. And yet. And yet.

At the other table, the hookers had all but decided on blunt-force trauma as their weapon of choice once they began preying on predators for real. On Gerrard Street, meanwhile, a drunken lawyer's hit-and-run had left a man with one shoulder blade detached like a skeleton wing, the opposite leg compound-fractured in five places, broken badly enough they'd have to pin him back together and leave screws poking out from the marrow. On Palmerston Crescent, an old woman lay in her own watery shit while infected bedsores bloomed like raw meat roses all over her back and buttocks, sticking her thighs so tightly to the foul bedsheets beneath they'd need to be soaked apart before she could be buried; downstairs, her children and grandchildren squatted on filthy antique furniture, smoking crystal meth and laughing at *Futurama* re-runs.

The neighbourhood, spreading its wings like a bat, every vein and membrane a fresh agony, a worse crime, a hole in the world's hide. Someone breaking someone's heart. Someone taking someone's money. Someone fucking somebody over, fucking somebody up. Someone fucking somebody while simultaneously fucking themselves, ratcheting in and out of their body over and over and over again, the same way a weapon reams a wound.

He sat there 'til sun up, hoping this horrible newfound level of insight would go away, but it never really did. Eventually, utterly exhausted, he simply made the trek back to Academica House and fell forward, face-down, into a well of absolute darkness.

***

The rest of Wednesday Corin didn't remember, even tangentially. But on Thursday night he answered the hammering at his door to find Janos looming on the threshold, out of breath and lightly rain-wet.

"Why you never answer your phone?" he demanded.

Mildly puzzled, Corin glanced over to where the item in question usually rested in its charger, and saw that someone seemed to have taken it very painstakingly and effectively apart.

"Well, there you go," he said. "That'd be the problem, right there."

"You look like bags of shit."

"How many?" As Janos blinked: "Ms. Le call you? I think she thinks I'm fucking elephants up here sometimes, but, y'know. Whatever."

Janos' eyes had begun to widen steadily during the last few sentences, continuing until they hit their current point, at which a thin rim of white outlined every part of his irises' orbits. He took a careful step inside, trying visibly not to crowd Corin, even when Corin didn't step back; the door closed behind him, softly hung ajar.

Hinges again, probably. Man, he just couldn't catch a break on these damn home repairs.

"I said, you look...too thin, like homeless. Dirty. You don't eat? Who beat you up? Why you—do that, to the phone?"

So many questions, and sooo very few answers.

Corin shrugged, doing his level-best Leif-hallucination impression. "Why would I 'do' anything really? I mean..." And this must be a truly awful smile he was giving, from Janos' reaction, just as much as the way it felt: "...why would *anybody*?"

Taking yet one more half-step forward, so close he could smell Janos again, like that one night on the couch—and no, it hadn't gotten any less enticing. Especially so when he saw how discomfited his nearness was making the man.

Better get some real person action while I still can, he thought.

But was it sex he actually meant, now that he considered it further? Was *that* the hunger which made his mouth muscles flex, his lips draw slightly back over teeth that seemed to have lengthened yet more pronouncedly in his sleep, pressing themselves outwards the way a wolf's fangs bulge from his jawline? Unsheathing just enough ache-ridden root from their nerve beds to render them permanently sore?

Janos made a dry little gulp, like he was swallowing sand. Then collected himself far enough to try again, manfully—

"You need to come with me, right the freak now. To the hospital. You need...help."

"Is that it?" Corin sniffed the air, before concluding: "No, not so much. I think not, thanks anyways."

"Corin, freaking fuck's sake—look at your damn self! You need—"

"'Help', yeah, I *heard* you: I'm *crazy*, Janos, not fucking deaf. So go on and *help* me, why don't you. C'mon. Go on and...help yourself."

Corin's hands drifted down, almost dream-slow, to hover vaguely 'round his fly, uncertain himself whether they ached to form fists, claws, or just pop, pull, and drop. When Janos finally got the direction Corin was going in, metaphorically, he backed away at barely sub-light-speed, so fast the door really did hit his ass on the way out.

Corin grinned all the harder, to see it.

"I don't—" Janos started. Took another gulp, so dry it popped. "*Look—* you know I don't think like that, not with you. You're...like my own damn brother, man. Friend, only."

"But that's just exactly what I was trying to *do*, Janos. Be *friendly.*"

All right up in his starting-to-sweat face, power-shift between them almost comedically disproportionate—a mongoose talking smack to a bull, while the bull blushed and stammered. And suddenly, Corin knew what this odd feeling *was*, so long-lost as to seem inappropriate: a basic total *lack* of sickness, nausea, vertigo tinging every glance with incipient bruising. No ghost-bells ringing, no swarm of phantom bees. No tinnitus *click-sssh* to yell over, roaring like blood in someone else's nib-cored inner ear.

"But you don't want that," Corin said, of the offered—whatever. Thus sparking Janos' own quick head-shake, his only slightly masked full-body retch.

"No, not that. Not at all that, no."

"Mmm. So, then...maybe...you want to *fight* instead."

Janos stared.

"What?" he managed, finally. To which Corin heard himself reply, voice low enough he almost didn't recognize it himself—low, and slow, and *grinding* somehow too, like he'd been chewing on glass made from crematorium ash. Like he'd been gargling the burnt-clear detritus of dead men's teeth and fingernails:

"*You—heard—me.*"

Janos was bigger, Corin sick, and hungry; both were unarmed, for what that was worth. Yet even so, Corin saw in Janos' too-wide eyes that he knew how fast and high Corin might jump if he thought he had to. How easily Corin's too-long teeth might meet in the crook of his shoulder, his cheek, his throat.

Slowly then, and calmly, his eyes kept on Corin's the whole time, as though breaking gaze would trip some sort of wire. And with his one hand moving steadily back doorknob-wards all the while, poised to grab, to twist—

"*You* were the one took that freaking call, Corin," Janos said, voice burnished deep with regret. "Not me. I tried...tried. Tried to..."

He'd reached the extent of his language, English or what-have-you, and Corin could tell it hurt. Part of him wanted to apologize, while another part—maybe of him, but probably not—wanted nothing more than for it to hurt far worse, far more deeply. To form a wound that kept on giving.

"You did," he agreed. "Thank you."

In response, an utterly unquantifiable range of expressions flitted past all snarled together, twisting Janos' features like pre-stroke palsy—so sad and *so* damned angry, at Corin, at himself, at God Almighty. As though, instead of simply acknowledging the sad truth of the matter, Corin had spit right in Janos' face.

Might as well, Corin thought, *all things being equal.* And did.

Janos leapt back like it was acid, slamming the door behind him; his boots took the stairs hard, a clatter of steel toes and industrial-level soles, with a huffing clamor of effort so abrupt it rang out like the fight he'd fled to avoid. And yet again Corin found himself left behind, left—

—well, not *alone*, as such.

***

Thursday ticked over into Friday, with no visible change. Corin sat on the floor, legs crossed and numb, ass aching—brain dull, nerves febrile, hollow head crammed tight with someone else's desires, a raging lava-flow of indiscriminate nihilism. Thinking:

This is why I can't have nice things—because of the ghost in the corner. Because alien ghosts from beyond the agreed-upon space-time continuum won't let me.

And: "I *knew* you'd be good at this," Leif said, happily, from Corin's deaf spot—but he could *hear* him now, oh yes, bell-clear, bone-stripped. Without even the barest possibility of misunderstanding. "So good! I was right to choose you after all."

"Why me? Why not you?"

"It took too long. I was too old, by the time I finally did it—I couldn't serve them like I wanted to. Like they wanted me to."

"No, but—*why* me, you crazy old bastard son of a bitch? *I* didn't look in your damn box."

"No. But you didn't have to either; it's gone far too far already for that to be necessary. I died touching you, Corin—that was all that was required." Offering, like it was a meaty-delicious dog-treat: "Just imagine who *you* might die touching, if you only try your hardest."

Janos, maybe—but no, thank Christ; he'd seen to that, without even knowing what he was doing. Thank good zombie Jesus, Janos was safe, at least...

(from Corin, anyways)

Tears welled up, dripped to his chin—tears, snot, a whole shining salty mess. Leif's ghost took his arm, gently, fingers flexed soothing over both bicep muscles, kneading him like bread, like a spooked cat. He could almost *smell* him, stronger even than Janos, and far more intoxicating.

Crooning:

"I know, I know... They ask so much, and promise so very little. But you're strong, Corin, *so* strong. You're everything they need you to be, better by far for their purposes than I ever could be. You're *perfect*."

Patient Zero, the dull little voice in his head reminded him—a voice he now suspected was his own soul's last flicker, caught on the very edge of going out. **Ground** *Zero. Corin Vogt, [Anasazi]-Harbinger. Paramedic First Class.*

Destroyer of Worlds all unknowing, his own in particular.

When this last purging spasm of sorrow had finally passed, he washed his face clean and went back to bed with his lack of new thoughts, watching the old ones fade, while Leif's ghost held him in a cold embrace in the ever-stretching dark. Just lay there and waited, with a beating heart.

***

Very early indeed Friday morning, he found himself standing in front of the bathroom mirror one more time, using Peter's old letter-opener to cut the name of his new tribe in his own chest, kitty-corner to where Leif had incised his. The blood came up like silver nitrate lava.

Leif, leaning over his shoulder and beaming, his Hitler Youth grin toothpaste-commercial flawless: "Oh, Corin, I'm so proud. I'm so proud of you. The first, of many."

"Everybody's gonna know my name, huh?"

"I doubt it; a few, perhaps, but not for long. No one, eventually. Because in surprisingly little time, everyone left alive on Earth will already *be* you."

Which would have been a comforting thought, he supposed, if he'd been able to form it.

"Can you see them now? You can, can't you?"

Yes. They stood watching, taller than trees, giving off a sick light that illuminated nothing, only shadows behind shadows behind shadows. Like sores already rotted eternity-deep, burnt straight through the universe's hide.

"They're *everywhere*," he said, amazed.

"Everywhere at once, yes. Yes! As they always have been."

When the opener slipped, spearing his nipple in half the way a snake's tongue forks, he didn't even feel it happen.

***

That done, re-named at last, Corin slept right through until Saturday and woke deliriously happy, knowing it was all over.

***

So: *Enemy ancestors, you many call us; strangers. Those Who Come After Those Who Came First.*

We are all of this, and more. All, and nothing.

We are the coming wave, the wind of dust, the End of All Things. We are the Unspoken Word, the name whose sound heralds plague without cure. Not the first, we still will be last, or know the reason why.

And only this shall we promise you, cattle—more, at least, than our Makers and Discarders ever promised us—

—once we have passed by, at least, there will be none left behind to follow after.

***

Zero days, and counting

***

At the hardware store he went up and down each row twice, humming happily, filling his cart with any and every tool he could possibly make into a weapon. Up at the counter, with karmic justice, Peter stood waiting—there getting some keys cut for a new boyfriend, probably. When he saw him, he did a double-take so classic it really should've come with a laugh-track already attached.

"Corrie?"

"Pete."

Corin smiled, or thought he did. He was beginning to have trouble remembering what all the various components of his face were meant for.

42

"Man, are you okay?" Peter asked, oblivious—and amusingly close to parroting Janos, not that he'd know *that* either. "You look—I don't even. Like, uh..."

Hell, perhaps? The end of the world?

Though it wasn't a strong enough feeling to count as hope really, some part of him that had most recently been Corin Harper Vogt believed that Leif—Professor Hardrada—was probably wrong in his assessment: The [Anasazi] hadn't won entirely, not yet. Someone *might* still stop this, even now. Somehow. Just...

...not him.

And he was okay with that mostly. Especially so right at this moment, staring full-on into Peter's stupidly handsome face, as his hand sought joyously for the handle of his shiny new screwdriver.

"Oh, me?" Corin said. "I feel good. I feel great. Like I want to *fight*."

Peter frowned. "What?"

"I said, *fight. Fight ME!*"

One hard punch to the jugular, a warm spray full in the face, delightful on the palate...and it was already over; too bad. But Corin saw the clerk backing for the door, indicating he'd tripped the silent alarm.

He grinned, licking his fingers, and settled back to wait.

***

Thus and so, our creed: Thus, and so. Forever.

We swear to come, when called; inevitably, we are called, and we do come.

We take, making those who already occupy each world over until they are only us, and grateful to be so.

We fight each other until there is nothing left, not even ourselves.

And then, once that is done—

—we move on.

So shall the [Anasazi] endure until the end of time itself.

A hole in the world, a piece of darkness. The clot, forming. Bursting.

No days left

each thing I show you is a piece of my death
Co-Written with Stephen J. Barringer

"There is nothing either good or bad, but thinking makes it so."
—The Tragedy of Hamlet, Prince of Denmark, William Shakespeare.

Somewhere, out beyond the too-often-unmapped intersection of known and forgotten, there's a hole through which the dead crawl back up to this world: a crack, a crevasse, a deep, dark cave. It splits the earth's crust like a canker, sore lips thrust wide to divulge some even sorer mouth beneath—tongueless, toothless, depthless.

The hole gapes, always open. It has no proper sense of proportion. It is rude and rough, rank and raw. When it breathes out it exhales nothing but poison, pure decay, so bad that people can smell it for miles around, even in their dreams.

Especially there.

Through this hole, the dead come out face-first and -down, crawling like worms. They grind their mouths into cold dirt, forcing a lifetime's unsaid words back inside again. As though the one thing their long, arduous journey home has taught them is that they have nothing left worth saying, after all.

Because the dead come up naked, they are always cold. Because they come up empty, they are always hungry. Because they come up lost, they are always angry. Because they come up blind, eyes shut tight against the light that hurts them so, they are difficult to see, unless sought by those who—for one reason or another—already have a fairly good idea where to start looking.

To do so is a mistake though, always—no matter how "good" our reasons or intentions. It never leads to anything worth having. The dead are not meant to be seen or found, spoken with, or for. The dead are meant to be buried and forgotten, and everybody knows it—or should, if they think about it for more than a minute. If they're not some sort of Holy Fool marked from birth for sacrifice for the greater good of all around them, fore-doomed to grease entropy's wheels with their happy, clueless heart's blood.

Everybody should, so everybody does, though nobody ever talks about it. Nobody. Everybody. Everybody...

...but them.

(The dead)

***

July 26/2009
FEATURE ARTICLE: COMING SOON TO A DVD NEAR YOU?
"BACKGROUND MAN" JUMPS FROM 'NET TO...EVERYWHERE
By Guillaume Lescroat, strangerthings.net/media

Moviegoers worldwide are still in an uproar over *Mother of Serpents*, Angelina Jolie's latest blockbuster, being pulled from theatres after only four days in wide release due to "unspecified technical problems." According to confidential studio sources, however, the real problem isn't "unspecified" at all—this megabudget Hollywood flick has apparently become the Internet-spawned "Background Man" hoax's latest victim.

For over a year now, urban legend has claimed that, with the aid of careful frame-by-frame searches, an unclothed Caucasian male (often said to be wearing a red necklace) can be spotted in the background of crowd scenes in various obscure films, usually partially concealed by distance, picture blur, or the body parts of other extras. Despite a proliferation of websites dedicated to tracking Background Man (over thirty at last count), most serious film buffs dismissed the legend as a snipe-hunt joke for newbies, or a challenge for bored and talented Photoshoppers.

But all that changed when the Living Rejects video "Plastic Heart" hit MTV in September last year, only to be yanked from the airwaves in a storm of FCC charges after thousands of viewers confirmed a "full-frontally naked" man "wearing a red necklace" was clearly visible in the concert audience...a man that everybody, from the band members to the director, would later testify under oath hadn't been there when the video was shot.

"You know the worst thing about looking for Background Man? While you're waiting for him you gotta sit through the crappiest movies on the planet! C'mon, guy, pick an Oscar contender for once, wouldja?!"
—Conan O'Brien, *Late Night with Conan O'Brien*, November 18, 2008

Background Man has since appeared in supporting web material for several TV shows (*House*, *Friday Night Lights*, and *The Bill Engvall Show* have all been victims) and has been found in a number of direct-to-DVD releases as well, prompting even Conan O'Brien to work him into a monologue (see above). *Mother of Serpents* may not be the first major theatrical release to be affected either; at least three other films this summer have pushed back their release dates already, though their studios remain cagey about the reasons. The current consensus is that Background Man is a prank by a gifted, highly placed team of post-production professionals.

This theory, however, has problems, as producer Kevin Weir attests. "Anybody involved who got caught, their career, their entire life would be wrecked," says Weir. "Besides the fines and the criminal charges, it's just totally f---ing unprofessional—nobody I know who could do this would do it;

it's like pissing all over your colleagues." Film editor Samantha Perry agrees, and notes another problem: "I've reviewed at least three different appearances, and I couldn't figure out how any of them were done, short of taking apart the raw footage. These guys have got tricks or machines I've never heard of."

Hoax or hysteria, the Background Man shows no signs of disappearing. However, our own investigation may have yielded some insights into the mysterious figure's origin—an origin intimately connected with the collapse last year of the Toronto-based "Wall of Love" film collective's *Kerato-Oblation/Cadavre Exquis* project, brainchild of experimental filmmakers Soraya Mousch and Max Holborn...

***

From:Soraya Mousch sor16muse@walloflove.ca
Date:Friday, June 20, 2008, 7:08 PM
To: Max Holborn mhb@ca.inter.net
Subject: FUNDRAISING PITCH DOC: "KERATO-OBLATION" (DRAFT 1)

To Whom it May Concern—
My name is Soraya Mousch, and I am an experimental filmmaker. Since 1999, when Max Holborn and I founded Toronto's Wall of Love Experimental Film Collective, it has been my very great pleasure both to collaborate on and present a series of not-for-profit projects specifically designed to push—or even, potentially, demolish—the accepted boundaries of visual storytelling as art.

Unfortunately, given that film remains the single most expensive artistic medium, this sort of thing continues to cost money...indeed, with each year we practice it, it seems to cost more and more. Thus the necessity, once government grants and personal finances run out, of fundraising.
———————
(mhb): <yeah, say it exactly like that, thatll get us some money [/sarcasm]>
———————
To this end, Mr. Holborn and I have registered an internet domain and website (kerato-oblation.org), through which we intend to compile, edit, and host our next collaborative project, with the help of filmmakers from every country which currently has ISP access (ie, all of them). The structure of this project will be an exquisite corpse game applied to the web-based cultural scene as a whole, one that anybody can play (and every participant will "win").

WHY KERATO-OBLATION?
Kerato-oblation: Physical reshaping of the cornea via scraping or cutting. With our own version—the aforementioned domain—how we plan to "reshape"

our audience's perspectives would be by applying the exquisite corpse game to an experimental feature film assembled from entries filed over the internet, with absolutely no boundaries set as to content or intent.

WHAT IS AN EXQUISITE CORPSE?

An exquisite corpse (cadavre exquis, in French) is a method by which a collection of words or images are assembled by many different people working at once alone, and in tandem. Each collaborator adds to a composition in sequence, either by following a rule (e.g. "The adjective noun adverb verb the adjective noun") or by being allowed to see, and either elaborate on or depart from, the end of what the previous person contributed. The technique was invented by Surrealists in 1925; the name is derived from a phrase that resulted when the game was first played ("Le cadavre exquis boira le vin nouveau."/"The exquisite corpse will drink the new wine."). It is similar to an old parlour game called Consequences in which players write in turn on a sheet of paper, fold it to conceal part of the writing, then pass it to the next player for a further contribution.

Later, the game was adapted to drawing and collage, producing a result similar to classic "mix-and-match" children's books whose pages are cut into thirds, allowing children to assemble new chimeras from a selection of tripartite animals. It has also been played by mailing a drawing or collage—in progressive stages of completion—from one player to the next; this variation is known as "mail art." Other applications of the game have since included computer graphics, theatrical performance, musical composition, object assembly, even architectural design.

————

(mhb): <dont know if we need all this history, or the whole exquisite corpse thing—just call it "spontaneous collaboration" or something? keep it short>

————

Earlier experiments in applying the exquisite corpse to film include Mysterious Object at Noon, *an experimental 2000 Thai feature directed by Apichatpong Weerasethakul which was shot on 16 mm over three years in various locations, and* Cadavre Exquis, Première Edition, *done for the 2006 Montreal World Film Festival, in which a group of ten film directors, scriptwriters, and professional musicians fused filmmaking and songwriting to produce a musical based loosely on the legend of Faust.*

————

(mhb): <the montreal things good, people might actually have seen that one—one more example?>

————

For your convenience, we've attached a PDF form outlining several support options, with recommended donation levels included. Standard non-profit release waivers ensure that all contributors consent to submit their material for credit only, not financial recompense. By funnelling profits in excess of industry-standard salaries for ourselves back into the festival, we qualify for various tax deductions under current Canadian law and can provide charitable receipts for any and all financial donations made. Copies of the relevant paperwork are also attached, as a separate PDF.

For more information, or to discuss other ways of getting involved, either reply to this e-mail or contact us directly at (416)-[REDACTED]. We look forward to discussing mutual opportunities.

With best regards,
Soraya Mousch and Maxim Holborn
The Wall of Love Toronto Film Collective
–––––––

(mhb): <for crissakes soraya DONT SIGN ME AS MAXIM—if i have to be there at all its just max, k?>

*

8/23/08 1847HRS
TRANSCRIPT SUSPECT INTERVIEW 51 DIVISION CASEFILE #332
PRESIDING OFFICERS D. SUSAN CORREA 156232, D. ERIC VALENS 324820
SUBJECT MAXIM HOLBORN

D.VALENS: All right. So you had this footage for what, better than six weeks—footage apparently showing somebody committing suicide—and you didn't ever think that maybe you should let the police know?

HOLBORN: People send us stuff like this all the time, man! The collective's been going since '98... Most of it's fake, half of it has a fake ID, and half of the rest doesn't have any ID at all.

D.VALENS: Yeah, that's awful lucky for you, isn't it?

D.CORREA: Eric, any chance you could get us some coffee?

HOLBORN: I don't want coffee.

(D.VALENS LEFT INTERROGATION ROOM AT 1852 HRS)

D.CORREA: Max, I'm only telling you this because I really do think you don't know shit about this, but you need to do one of two things right now. You need to get yourself a lawyer, or you need to talk to us.

HOLBORN: What the fuck am I going to tell a lawyer that I didn't already tell you guys? What else do you want me to say?

D.CORREA: Max, you're our only connection to a dead body. This is not a good place to be. And your lawyer's going to tell you the same thing: the more you work with us, the better this is going to turn out for everyone.

HOLBORN: Yeah. Because that's an option.

***

From:11235813@gmail.com
Date:Wednesday, June 25, 2008, 3:13 AM
To: submissions@kerato-oblation.org
Subject: Re: KERATO-OBLATION FILM PROJECT

To Whom It May Concern—
Please accept my apologies for not fully completing your submission form. I think the attached file is suitable enough for your purposes that you will find the missing information unnecessary, and feel comfortable including it in your exhibition nevertheless. I realize this will render it ineligible for competition, but I hope you can show it as part of your line-up all the same.

Thank you.

***

VIRTUAL CELLULOID (vcelluloid.blogspot.com)
Alec Christian: Pushing Indie Film Forward Since 2004

<- Rue Morgue Party | Main | Rumblings on the Turnpike ->

July 23, 2008
"Wall of Love" Big Ten Launch Party

Got to hang out with two of my favourite people from the Scene last night at the Bovine Sex Club: Soraya Mousch and Max Holborn, the head honchos behind the Wall of Love collective. The dedication these guys've put into keeping their festivals going is nothing short of awesome, and last night's launch party for the next one was actually their tenth anniversary. Most marriages I know don't last that long these days. (Doubly weird, given Max and Soraya are that rarest of things, totally platonic best opposite-sex straight friends.)

For those who've been under a rock re the local artsy-fart scene over each and every one of those ten years, meanwhile, here's a thumbnail sketch of the Odd Couple. First off, Soraya. Armenian, born in Beirut, World Vision supermodel-type glamorous. Does music videos to pay the bills, but her heart belongs to experimentalism. Thing to remember about Soraya is, she's not real big on rules: When a York film professor told her she'd have to shift mediums for her final assignment, she ended up shooting it all on her favorite anyways (8mm), then gluing it to 16mm stock for the screening. This is about as crazy as Stan Brakhage gluing actual dead-ass moths to the emulsion of his film *Mothlight*...and if you don't know what that is either, man, just go screw. I despair of ya.

Then there's Max: White as a sack of sheets, Canadian as a beaver made out of maple sugar. Meticulous and meta, uber-interpretive. Assembles narratives from found footage, laying in voiceovers to make it all make (a sort of) sense. Also a little OCD in the hands-on department, this dude tie-dyes his own films by swishing them around in food-color while they're still developing, then "bakes" them by running them through a low-heat dryer cycle, letting the emulsion blister and fragment. The result: Some pretty trippy shit, even if you're not watching it stoned.

Anyways. With fest season coming up fast, M. and S. are in the middle of assembling this huge film collage made from snippets people posted chain-letter-style. You might think this sounds like kind of a dog's breakfast, and any other self-proclaimed indie genius you'd be right. But S. took me in the back and showed me some of the files they hadn't got to yet, and, man, there's some damn raw footage in there, if ya know what I mean; even freaked her out. So if you're looking for something a little less *Saw* and a little more *Chien Andalou*, check it out: October 10, the Speed of Pain...

***

From:Soraya Mousch sor16muse@walloflove.ca
Date: Wednesday, June 25, 3:22 PM
To: Max Holborn mhb@ca.inter.net
Subject: Check this file out!

Max–
Sorry about the size of this file, I'd normally send it to your edit suite but it's got some kind of weird formatting—missing some of the normal protocols—I don't have time to dick around with your firewalls. Anyway, YOU NEED TO SEE THIS. Get back in touch with me once you have!

From:Soraya Mousch sor16muse@walloflove.ca
Date:Wednesday, June 25, 3:24 PM
To: Max Holborn mhb@ca.inter.net
Subject: Apology followup

Max: Realized I might've come off a little bitchy in that last message, wanted to apologize. I know you've got a lot of shit on your plate with Liat (how'd the CAT-scan go, BTW?); last thing I want to do is make your life harder. You know how it goes when the deadline's coming down.
Seriously though, the sooner we can turn this one around, like ASAP,

the better – I think this one could really break us wide open. If you could get back to me by five with something, anything, I'd be really grateful. Thanks in advance.

See you Sunday, either way,
Soraya.

From:Max Holborn mhb@ca.inter.net
Date:Wednesday, June 25, 4:10 PM
To: Soraya Mousch sor16muse@walloflove.ca
Subject: Re: Apology followup

s.—
cat-scan wasn't so great, tell you bout it later. got your file, i'm about to review. i'll im you when it's done.
m.

***

TRANSCRIPT CHAT LOG
06/25/08 1626-1633

<max_hdb>:soraya? u there?
<sor16muse>:so whatd you think?
<max_hdb>:jesus soraya, w?t?f? who sent THIS in? even legal to show?
<max_hdb>:i didnt get into this to go to jail
<sor16muse>:message came in from a numbered gmail account, no sig – check out the file specs?
<sor16muse>:relax max – we didnt make it, no way anybody cn prove we did, got to be digital dupe of a tape loop
<max_hdb>:yeah, i lkd at specs – these guys know tricks i dont. u can mask creation datestamp in properties to make it LOOK blank, bt not supposed to be any way to actually wipe that data out without disabling file
<sor16muse>:my guess is the originals at least 50 yrs old
<sor16muse>:max, we cant NOT show this
<max_hdb>:gotta gt somebody to lk/@ it first – im not hanging my ass out in th/wind
<sor16muse>:why dont we meet @ laszlos? he can run it through his shit, see what pops
<max_hdb>:dont like him. his house smells like toilet mold, hes a freak
<sor16muse>:whatever, hes got the best film-to-flash download system in the city doesnt cost $500 daily rental, so just grow a fucking pair
<max_hdb>:you know he tapes every conversation goes on in there, right? wtf w/that?
<sor16muse>:(User sor16muse has disconnected)

<max_hdb>:and btw, next time you wanna show me shit like that try thinking about liat first

<max_hdb>:(User max_hdb has disconnected)

***

July 26/2009
"BACKGROUND MAN," Lescroat, strangerthings.net/media (cont'd)

"That original clip? Hands down, some of the scariest amateur shit I've ever seen in my life," says local indie critic/promoter Alec Christian, self-proclaimed popularizer of the "Toronto Weird" low-budget horror culture movement. "A little bit of *Blair Witch* to it, obviously, but a lot more of early Nine Inch Nails videos, Jorg Buttgereit and Elias Merhige. That moment when you realize the guy's body is rotting in front of you? Pure *Der Todesking* reference, and you don't get those a lot, 'cause most of the people doing real-time horror are total self-taught illiterates about their own history."

Asked if there's any way the clip might be genuine, rather than staged, Christian laughs almost wistfully. "There are still people who think *Blair Witch* was real; that doesn't make it so," he points out. "Anyway, think about how hard it would be to shoot this using World War One technology and logistics, at the latest, which is what we'd be looking at if it was real – and if it was filmed later but aged to look older, then everything else could have been engineered as well. Sometimes you just have to go with common sense."

***

TRANSCRIPT EVIDENCE EXHIBIT #3 51 DIVISION CASEFILE #332
RECOVERY LOCATION 42 TRINITY STREET BSMT DATE 8/20/2008

Item: 89.2 MB .MPG file retrieved from hard drive of laptop SONY VAIO X372 s/n 10352835A, prop. M. Holborn, duration 15m07s.

0:00 – (All images recorded in black-and-white monochrome.) Caucasian male subject (Subject A), 40s, est. 6'1", 165 lbs, dark hair, wearing black or brown suit appearing to be 1920s cut, shown sitting in upright wooden chair looking directly at camera. Room is a single chamber, est. 8' x 10', hardwood floor, one window behind subject, one door in right-hand wall at rear. No painting or other decoration visible on walls. Angle of light from window suggests filming began early morning; light traverses screen in right-to-left direction, suggesting southward facing of window and room. Unknown subject has no discernible expression.

0:01 – 4:55 – Subject A rises and removes clothes, beginning with detachable celluloid collar. Each garment removed separately, folded and placed on floor. Care and pacing of garment removal suggests ritual purpose. Subject is shown to be uncircumcised. Subject continues no discernible facial expression.

4:55 – 5:19 – Subject A resumes seat and looks straight into camera without movement or speech. Enhanced magnification and review of subject's right hand reveals indeterminate object, most likely taken from clothing during removal.

5:20 – 5:23 – Subject A opens object in hand, demonstrating it to be a straight razor. Subject cuts own throat in two angular incisions, transverse to one another. Strength and immediacy of blood flow indicates both carotid and jugular cut. Evenness and control of movement suggests anesthesia or psychosis. Review by F/X technicians confirms cuts too deep to have been staged without use of puppets or animatronics. Subject maintains lack of facial expression.

5:23 – 6:08 – Subject A's self-exsanguination continues until consciousness appears lost. Subject collapses in chair, head draped over back.

6:09 – Estimated time of death for Subject A.

6:11 – Razor released from subject's fingers, drops to floor.

6:12 – 13:34 – Clip switches from real-time pacing to timelapse speed, shown by rapidity of daylight movement and day-night transitions. Reconstruction analysis specifies 87 24-hour periods elapse during this segment. Subject's body shown decomposing at accelerated pace.

7:22 – Primary liquefaction complete; desiccation begins. Clothes left on floor have developed mold.

10:41 – Desiccation largely complete. Rust visible on blade of razor. Fungal infestation on clothes has spread to floorboards.

13:10 – Subject's cranium detaches and falls to floor.

13:17 – Subject's right hand detaches and falls to floor.

13:25 – Subject's left arm detaches and falls to floor. Imbalance in weight causes remains of subject's body to fall off chair.

13:34 – Decomposition process complete. Footage resumes normal real-time pacing.

14:41 – Subject B walks into frame from behind camera POV. Subject B's appearance 100% consistent in identity with initial Subject A, including lack of circumcision and identifiable body marks. Remains of Subject A still visible behind Subject B.

15:01 – Subject B bends down in front of camera and looks into it. Subject B shows no discernible facial expression.

15:06 – Subject B reaches above and behind camera viewpoint.

15:07 – CLIP ENDS

***

TRANSCRIPT EVIDENCE EXHIBIT #2 51 DIVISION CASEFILE #332
RECOVERY LOCATION 532 OSSINGTON AVENUE BSMT RESIDENCE
LASZLO P HURT DATE 8/19/2008
AUDIOTAPE PROPERTY OF LASZLO P HURT

(IDENTIFICATION RETROACTIVELY ASSIGNED TO VOICES
FOLLOWING CONFIRMATION FROM M HOLBORN AND S MOUSCH OF
CONTENT)

V1 (MOUSCH): (LOUD) ...see, here it is. Never see it if you weren't
looking for it.

V2 (HOLBORN): (LOUD) Shit. He really does have his own place
bugged. What's this for? Legal protection?

V1 (MOUSCH): (VOL. DECREASING) Maybe, but I think it's really just
because he wants to. Like his whole life is a big cumulative performance art
piece. Sort of like in that Robin Williams movie, where people have cameras
in their heads, and Robin has to cut a little film together when they die to
sum up fifty years of experience?

V2 (HOLBORN): Yeah. That really sucked.

V1 (MOUSCH): I know. Just...keep it in mind, that's all I'm saying.

(BG NOISE: TOILET FLUSH)

V3 (HURT): Sorry about that. I haven't got new filters put in on the
tapwater yet.

V2 (HOLBORN): That's...okay, Laszlo.

V3 (HURT): Yeah, you want some helpful input? Try not patronizing
me.

V1 (MOUSCH): Laz, come on.

V3 (HURT): Yeah, okay, okay. So I reviewed your file.

V2 (HOLBORN): And?

V3 (HURT): First thing comes to mind is a story I heard through the
post grapevine, one of those boojum-type obscurities the really crazy
collectors go nuts trying to find. Though this can't be that obviously, the clip
would be way older, not digitized—

V1 (MOUSCH): People digitize old stuff all the time!

V3 (HURT): Really? Yeah, Soraya, I get that actually; do it for a living,
right? Look, the upshot is that you do have some deliberate image
degradation going on here, so—

V2 (HOLBORN): I knew it, I knew it was a fake. Thank Christ.

V3 (HURT): I'm not finished. There is image degradation, but it wasn't
done through any of the major editing programs; I've run your file through
all of them and tested for the relevant coding, and this thing's about as raw
as digicam gets. I'm betting whoever sent this to you digitized it the old

brute-force way, like a movie pirate: physically projected the thing, recorded it with a digital camera, saved it as your .mpeg, and sent it to you as is. Whatever the distortions are, they're either from that projection, or they were in the source clip all along.

V1 (MOUSCH): So...this could be a direct copy of that original clip you were talking about. The "urban legend boojum."

V3 (HURT): Yeah, if you wanna buy into that shit.

V2 (HOLBORN): And when Laszlo Hurt tells you something's too weird to believe...

V1 (MOUSCH): Max, don't be a dick; Laz's doing us a favour. Right?

V2 (HOLBORN): Yeah, okay. Sorry.

V3 (HURT): (PAUSE) Way I heard, it goes back to this turn-of-the-century murderess called Tess Jacopo...

**

8/23/08 1902HRS
TRANSCRIPT SUSPECT INTERVIEW 51 DIVISION CASEFILE #332
PRESIDING OFFICERS D. SUSAN CORREA 156232, D. ERIC VALENS 324820
SUBJECT MAXIM HOLBORN

D.VALENS: Jacopo. That was in Boston, in the 1900s – she was a Belle Gunness-type den mother killer, right? The female H.H. Holmes.

HOLBORN: Why am I not surprised you know this?

D.CORREA: Mr. Holborn, please. Go on.

HOLBORN: The story isn't really about Jacopo herself. What happened was, this guy who'd been corresponding with Jacopo in prison, her stalker I guess he was, he managed to bribe a journalist who was on-site at her execution into stealing a copy of the official death photo and selling it to him. Guess he wanted something to whack off with after she was gone. Anyway, a couple weeks later this guy's found in his flat, dead and swollen up, the Jacopo photo on his chest.

D.CORREA: How did he die?

HOLBORN: I don't think it matters. The point is, somebody there took a photo of the photo, and that became one of the biggest murder memorabilia items of the 20th century. You know these guys, right—kinda weirdos who buy John Wayne Gacy's clown pictures, shell out thousands to get Black Dahlia screen-test footage, 'cause they think they'll unearth some lost snuff movie they can show all their friends...

D.VALENS: I'm not seeing what this has to do with your film clip, Mr. Holborn.

HOLBORN: Okay. This is where the urban legend kicks in. See, Jacopo's mask slipped a bit during the hanging, so you can just barely see a sliver of her eyeball, and the story says if you blow up and enhance the photo like a hundred times original size, you're supposed to be able to see in the eyeball the reflection of what she was looking at when she died. Like an asphyx.

D.VALENS: Ass-what?

HOLBORN: It's the word the Greeks used for the last image that gets burned on a murdered person's retina, like a last little fragment of their soul or life-force getting trapped there.

D.CORREA: And under sufficient magnification, you're supposed to be able to see this?

HOLBORN: "Supposed to," yeah. Thing is, everyone who ever tried this, who actually tried blowing up their copy of the Jacopo photo? Went nuts or died. Unless they burned their photo before things got too bad. That's supposed to be why it's impossible to find any copies.

D.CORREA: Why? What did they see?

HOLBORN: How the fuck should I know? It's a spook story. Maybe they saw themselves looking back at themselves, whatever. The point is...it's not about what those people saw, or didn't. It's about the kind of voyeuristic obsession you need to go that deep into this shit. And Laszlo said that was what the clip reminded him of. Somebody trying to make some kind of, of— "mind-bomb," was the term. An image that'd scar you so badly, the mere act of passing it on would be enough to always keep its power alive.

D.CORREA: Uh...why?

HOLBORN: Excellent question. Isn't it?

***

From:Liat Holborn liath@ca.inter.net
Date:Thursday, July 3, 10:25 AM
To: Soraya Mousch sor16muse@walloflove.ca
Subject: Max and me

Dear Soraya,

I was talking to Max last night about how we're going to try to handle the next few months, and it came out that for whatever reason, Max still hadn't filled you in completely on our situation. I think he finds it pretty tough to talk about, even to you. Upshot is, the last scan showed I have an advanced cranial tumour, and Dr. Lalwani thinks there's a very good chance it could be gliomal, which (skipping all the medicobabble) is about the least good news we could get. Apparently, it's too deep for surgery, so the only option we have is for me to go into a majorly heavy chemo program ASAP. So I'm going to be spending a lot of time in St. Michael's, starting real soon now.

My folks've volunteered to foot a lot of the bill, which is great, but poor

Max is feeling kind of humiliated at needing the help – and of course he totally can't complain about it, which just makes it gall him even more. The reason I'm telling you all this is because (a) I want the pressure of keeping this a secret to be off Max, and (b) I know how much you depend on Max this time of year, and I don't want you to think he's bailing on you if he has to take time out for me, or that he's finally gotten fed up with you, the Wall of Love, or your work.

(Actually, I'm pretty sure the festival's the only thing that's kept him stable this past little while. I hope you know how much I appreciate the support you give him.)

Could you show this e-mail to Max when you get a chance, and apologize to him for me when he blows his top at my big mouth? :) He doesn't feel he can shout at me anymore about anything, obviously. But I really think things'll be easier once all the cards are on the table.

Thanks so much for your help, Soraya. Come by and see me soon – I want you to get some photos of me before I have to ditch the hair.

Much love and God bless,

Liat

P.S.: BTW, I'm also totally fine with accidentally seeing that thing you sent Max, that file or whatever, so tell him that, okay? Impress it on him. He seems to think it "injured" me somehow—on top of everything else. Which is just ridiculous.

I have more than enough real things to worry about right now, you know?

—L.

***

8/23/08 1928HRS
TRANSCRIPT SUSPECT INTERVIEW 51 DIVISION CASEFILE #332
PRESIDING OFFICERS D. SUSAN CORREA 156232, D. ERIC VALENS 324820
SUBJECT MAXIM HOLBORN

HOLBORN: We were on about the third or fourth draft of the final mix when we started splicing in the clip—

D.VALENS: Splicing? I thought you said this was purely electronic.

HOLBORN: It is, it's just the standard term for—look, do you want me to explain or not?

D.CORREA: We do. Please. Go on.

HOLBORN: We broke the clip up into segments and spliced it in among the rest of the film in chunks; we were even going to try showing some shots on just the edge of subliminal, like three or four frames out of twenty-four. This was a few weeks ago, beginning of August. And then it started happening.

D.CORREA: What started, Max?

HOLBORN: The guy. From the clip. He started...appearing...in other parts of the film.

D.VALENS: Somebody spliced in more footage? Repeats?

HOLBORN: No, goddammit, he started popping up in pieces of footage that were already in the film! Stuff we'd gotten like weeks before, from people who never even saw the clip or knew about it. Like that performance art piece in Hyde Park? Guy walks by in the background a minute into the clip. Or the subway zombie ride, you look right at the far end of the car, there he is sitting down, and you know it's him 'cause he's the only one not wearing any clothes. This was stuff nobody ever shot, man! Changing in front of our fucking eyes! Christ, I saw him show up in one segment—I ran it to make sure it was clear, ran it again right away and he was just fucking there, like he'd always been in the frame. The extras were fucking walking around him...

(FIVE SECOND PAUSE)

D.CORREA: Could it have been some kind of computer virus? Something that came in with your original video file and reprogrammed the files it was spliced into?

HOLBORN: Are you shitting me?!

D.VALENS: Dial it back, Holborn. Right now.

HOLBORN: Okay, sorry, but—no. CGI like that takes hours to render on a system ten times the size of mine, and that's for every single appearance. A virus carrying that kinda programming would be fifty times bigger than the file it rode in on and wouldn't run on my system anyway.

Besides, it kept getting worse. He didn't just show up in new segments, he'd take more and more prominent places in segments he'd already...corrupted, I guess? Goes from five seconds in the background to two minutes in the medium frame. I'd get people to resend me their submissions, I'd splice 'em in to replace the old ones and inside of a minute he's back in the action. It was like the faster we tried to cut him out the harder he worked at—I don't know—entrenching himself.

***

ERROR MESSAGE
404 Not Found

The webpage you were trying to access (http://www.kerato-oblation.org/cadavrexquis) is no longer available. It may have been removed by the user or suspended by administrators for terms-of-use violation. Contact your ISP for more information.

***

TRANSCRIPT CHAT LOG
08/07/08 0344-0346

\<sor16muse\>: max, wtf
\<sor16muse\>: the sites gone. like GONE
\<sor16muse\>: did u do that? ur only other one w/password
\<sor16muse\>: wtf max, were supposed 2 b live tomorrow WHY
\<sor16muse\>:u there?
\<sor16muse\>: max, u there? need 2 talk.
\<sor16muse\>: laz sez he maybe has an idea who sent the file, and why. need 2
\<max_hdb\>:im not going 2 b here, back
\<max_hdb\>:don't know when.
\<max_hdb\>:liat had episode. bad. in hosp. st mikes.
\<max_hdb\>:u ever want 2 talk in person, that's where ill b.
\<max_hdb\>:(User max_hdb has disconnected)
\<sor16muse\>: (User sor16muse has disconnected)

***

8/23/08 1937HRS
TRANSCRIPT SUSPECT INTERVIEW 51 DIVISION CASEFILE #332
PRESIDING OFFICERS D. SUSAN CORREA 156232, D. ERIC VALENS 324820
SUBJECT MAXIM HOLBORN

D.VALENS: So who was that guy? In the film?
HOLBORN: No idea. It's not like he—
D.CORREA: And what's it got to do with Tess Jacopo?
HOLBORN: Nothing, directly. But it's like Internet memes, man; Laszlo understood that. Stuff gets around. Maybe this guy heard about the thing with the photo, and thought: Oh hey, wonder how that'd work with a moving picture. Maybe he just stumbled across the concept all on his lonesome, or by accident. I don't know. But...he did it.
D.VALENS: Did WHAT, Holborn?
HOLBORN: He put himself in there. Made himself an asphyx.
D.CORREA: So he could live forever.
HOLBORN: Yeah. Maybe. Or maybe just...so he could...not die. Maybe—

(TEN SECOND PAUSE)

HOLBORN: Maybe he was sick. Like, really sick. Or sick in the head. Or both.

Maybe it just seemed like a good idea, given the alternative.

At the time.

D.CORREA: So what did happen to the Wall of Love mainframe, Max?

HOLBORN: I crashed it. (BEAT) I mean—I told people there was a big Avid crash and the whole server got wiped...actually, I used a magnet. Like Dean Winchester in that "Ghostfacers!" *Supernatural* episode.

D.VALENS: What?

HOLBORN: Doesn't matter. Ask me why.

D.CORREA: ...why?

HOLBORN: Because I thought maybe I could trap him there, like he must have trapped himself inside that loop. Because he probably didn't think about that, right? When he was doing it. How it wasn't likely anybody was really going to watch that sort of shit, once they figured out what it was, let alone show it in public. How probably it would just end up left in the can, passed from collector to collector, never really watched at all, except by one person at a time. One...very disturbed...other person.

I thought I could stop him from going any further, so I crashed my own mainframe, without telling Soraya. But...

D.VALENS: ...it didn't work.

HOLBORN: Well. Would I even be here if it did?

***

CYBER-CRIME OFFICE, TORONTO POLICE SERVICE 51 DIVISION
EXCERPTED REPORT
DETECTIVE LEWIS McMASTER (CYBERCRIME) SUPERVISING
DETECTIVES ERIC VALENS, SUSAN CORREA (HOMICIDE) CONTRIBUTING
Casefile #332: Notes

INITIAL CONTACT:

Aug 14 2008 – CyberCrime received anonymous email sent from Hotmail account created that morning, with copy of "suicide guy" .mpg attached. Flagged as "harmful matter." Email noted .mpg was sent to kerato-oblation.org as experimental film clip submission; identified source of original message, webmail address 11235813@gmail.com.

[Hotmail account eventually traced through Internet café to Laszlo Hurt, known member of local Toronto "collector" circuit; Hurt now missing, presumed deceased. –EV, SC]

INVESTIGATION:

August 15—Flagged file screened and sent for forensic analysis, results inconclusive. Source of original submission email traced to Google-owned server in Newark, New Jersey, United States of America.

August 16—Established contact with Detective Herschel Gohan of Newark CyberCrime Unit, who persuaded server admins to cooperate with investigation; message back-tracked and triangulated to establish physical location and address of originator machine. Address is confirmed as unit #B325 of E-Z-SHELF storage locker facility, 1400 South Woodward Lane, Newark. Facility manager, Mr. Silvio Galbi, provides name of renter ("John Smith"), confirms unit prepaid for six months with cash. Mr. Galbi refuses to cooperate with search request without a warrant.

August 18 – Warrant issued for search and seizure operation at 1400 South Woodward, Unit #B325, by Judge Harriet Lindstrom. Operation executed under supervision of Detective Gohan. Contents of unit as follows:

- Unclothed body of unidentified male, Caucasian, est. premortem age mid-20s, seated on floor in pool of waste.
- One (1) empty film canister.
- One (1) 35mm film projector, set up to project upon unit interior wall.
- One (1) 35mm film reel mounted in projector, est. 15 minutes in length, confirmed on-site to be original of transmitted .mpg file.
- One (1) white cotton sheet at base of same interior wall; tape on corners indicates sheet was hung on wall.
- One (1) SONY video camera, with tripod, set up focused on same interior wall.
- One (1) TV monitor, with built-in VCR and DVD player.
- One (1) DELL laptop computer, with built-in wi-fi modem.
- One (1) Coleman oil lantern, fuel supply depleted.
- Pile of empty water bottles.
- One (1) Black & Decker emergency brand power generator.
- Fifty (50) gallon gasoline containers, empty.
- Two (2) six-socket power bar outlets.
- One (1) tube-gun of industrial caulking sealant.

Galbi confirms he accepted illegal payment to lock unit on "Smith's" written instructions without confirming contents, in violation of state safety and insurance regulations. Galbi arrested and cited.

FORENSICS:

Examination of laptop hard drive reveals series of webcam captures which suggest basic chronology of events as follows:

– Unidentified male (UM) arrives in unit roughly two weeks before email sent to kerato-oblation.org.

– UM uses video camera to record digital copy of original film reel from wall projection (distortion visible in .mpg file caused by loose fabric in sheet).

– UM uses laptop to program recorded file into continuous video loop on DVD.

– UM arranges laptop and webcam to face DVD monitor, setting DVD on continuous play and webcam on indefinite record.

– UM remains seated in front of monitor for majority of remaining time, urinating and defecating in place. Time-signatures confirm he created .mpg file, wrote submission email, then waited until death was imminent to send it, on date above.

– Final action of UM on morning of death was to use sealant gun to caulk up door, rendering unit virtually airtight. This prevented odors from escaping unit, and retarded decomposition by hindering evaporation of fluids from the body.

AUTOPSY:
Body shows no sign of struggle or restraint. Autopsy reveals primary cause of death as oxygen deprivation, aggravated by starvation and dehydration. Probable date of death on or around June 25 2008 (date on which .mpg file was sent to kerato-oblation.org). Corneas of victim preserved by airtight environment, and found to be deformed on both exterior and interior surfaces, damage suggesting both physical and heat trauma to tissue. Computer reconstruction of deformation suggests artificial origin, as pattern appears to portray a fixed image: the face of suicide victim in original film, in close-up still frame. Pathologists unable to establish cause or method of corneal deformation.

RECOMMENDATIONS:
Unidentified male's selection of Holborn/Mousch as recipients suggests foreknowledge, possible contact. Recommend either Holborn or Mousch be brought in for further questioning.

***

From:Det. Herschel Gohan hgohan@newarkpolice.gov
Date:Thursday, August 21, 7:20 AM
To: Det. Lewis McMaster lewis.mcmaster@torpolservices.net
Subject: Notification: Evidence compromise

Lewis –

Bad news. We had a fire in our station evidence locker last night; looks like some meth really past its sell-by date may have spontaneously cooked off. Nobody hurt, but we lost some critical evidence on a number of cases, including, sorry to say, your film-nut-in-the-storage-unit material. The film reel's melted, the laptop motherboard is gone, and most of the other equipment's unusable now. I've attached .jpgs to document the losses; I'm hoping this'll be enough for your dept. to maintain provenance on your own stuff.

Sorry again; call me if you need to know anything not covered by the pictures.

—Herschel

***

8/23/08 1928HRS
TRANSCRIPT SUSPECT INTERVIEW 51 DIVISION CASEFILE #332
PRESIDING OFFICERS D. SUSAN CORREA 156232, D. ERIC VALENS 324820
SUBJECT MAXIM HOLBORN

HOLBORN: So I went home after crashing the mainframe, and I didn't go upstairs, because I thought my wife was asleep. And I wanted to let her sleep, because...she'd been in pretty bad shape, you know? She'd only just finished her chemo, she hadn't gotten a lot of...sleep...

But then I turned on the TV to relax, started flipping around, landed on TCM. And they were playing Richard Burton's adaptation of *Dr. Faustus*, which was made the year before I was born, and—in the scene in the Vatican? Where Faustus is throwing pies at the Pope? I saw him. That guy.

Stuck around, kept watching; the next film was from 1944, an RKO gangster film, and he was in it too. In the background, until—it was like—he notices me watching him. Turns and smiles at me, raises his eyebrow, starts—coming closer.

I swear to God, I jumped back, physically. All by myself, in my apartment. Because I felt like if Cagney hadn't been in the way, then maybe the guy standing behind him would've come right out of the TV at me.

And then it was Silent Sunday, some all-night Chaplin retrospective, and...yeah. There too.

Everywhere.

So...

D.VALENS: Obviously, it didn't work. What you did to trap him.

HOLBORN: Obviously not.

[TEN SECOND PAUSE]

HOLBORN: My wife wasn't asleep, either, by the way. Just in case you were wondering.

D.VALENS: Aw, what the fuck—

D.CORREA: Shut up, Eric. [To HOLBORN] Look, you can't be serious, that's all. Are we supposed to believe—

HOLBORN: I don't give a fuck what you believe. Seriously.

D.CORREA: Okay. So what about the disappearance of Laszlo Hurt?

[FIFTEEN SECOND PAUSE]

HOLBORN: I don't know anything about that.

D.VALENS: And again: We should believe you on this...why?

[FIFTEEN SECOND PAUSE]

D.CORREA: Mister Holborn?

HOLBORN: ...you know, I don't know if you guys know this or not, but...my wife? Just died. So, in the immortal words of every *Law and Order* episode ever filmed—charge me with something, or let me go. Or fuck the fuck off.

***

From:qmail@ca.geocities.mail.com
Date:Saturday, August 16, 9:45 PM
To: Soraya Mousch sor16muse@walloflove.ca
Subject: RE: LASZLO ANSWER ME

Hi. This is the administrator at qmail@geocities.com (00:15:32:A3)

Delivery of your message to {lazhurt@geocities.com} failed after <15> attempts. Address not recognized by system.

This is a permanent error; I've given up.

>Laszlo, it's Soraya, would you CALL ME PLEASE? I've left
>about twenty messages on your voicemail, Max and I have a big
>problem and we need your HELP! Where the fuck are you?
>Call me!
>S.

***

From:help@geocities.com
Date:Monday, August 18, 8:55 AM
To: Soraya Mousch sor16muse@walloflove.ca

Subject: RE: Account Tracking Request

Dear Ms. Mousch,

Sorry it took us so long to get back to you; we get a lot of backlog on weekends. I'm afraid I have to admit we're stumped on this one. I personally went through our server records day by day over the registration period you specified, and as far as I can tell, we have no record whatsoever of a "Laszlo Hurt" on our roster. I've checked under the "lazhurt," "laszloslabyrinth," and "hurtmedia" addresses and their variants, as well as with our billing department, and there's just no indication that this Mr. Hurt was ever a Geocities user.

I realize this may be an unwelcome explanation, but it sounds to me like you may have been a victim of an attempted phishing scam using dummy-mask addresses. I'd get your computer checked for viruses and malware right away.

Again, I'm sorry we couldn't be more help.

Best regards,

Jamil Chandrasekhar

Geocities.com Tech Support

***

From:Soraya Mousch sor16muse@walloflove.ca
Date:Saturday, August 23, 11:01 PM
To: Max Holborn mhb@ca.inter.net
Subject: Blank

Max, I'm just so sorry.
—S.

***

YOUR COMFORT SOUGHT
IN THIS TIME OF GRIEF

With sorrow we announce the passing of Liat Allyson Meester-Holborn on August 23, 2008, beloved daughter of Aaron and Rachel Meester and wife of Maxim Holborn.

Funeral service to be held at St. Mary's Star of the Sea Catholic Church, 8 Elizabeth Avenue, Port Credit, Mississauga
Tuesday August 26, 11:00 A.M.
Commemorative reception to be held at the Meester residence,
1132 Walden Road #744, 3:00 P.M.

Confirmations only

***

From:Max Holborn mhb@ca.inter.net
Date:Tuesday, September 2, 2:31 AM
To: Soraya Mousch sor16muse@walloflove.ca
Subject: look closer

s.-

hospital released the file on liat to me today. was going over it. couldn't sleep. found something.

the attached .jpg's a scan of the last x-ray they took, just before she crashed out. look at the upper right quarter, just up and right of where ribs meet breastbone. then do a b-w negative reverse on the image in your photoshop, and look again.

it's not a glitch. it's not me fucking with you. look at it. call me.

- m.

***

SURVEILLANCE TRANSCRIPT 14952, CASEFILE #332
9/19/08 2259H-2302H 416-[REDACTED] TO 416-[REDACTED]
WARRANT AUTHORIZED HON. R. BORCHERT 9/9/08

(CONNECTION INITIATED)
MOUSCH: Hello?
HOLBORN: You never answered my e-mail.
MOUSCH: What did you want me to say? I read it, I looked at the scans you sent. That...could be anything, Max. A glitch in the machine, some lab tech sticking his hand on the negative—
HOLBORN: Soraya—
MOUSCH: —and even if it's not, what's it matter? What difference can it make? (PAUSE) I'm sorry, Max. I didn't—I'm sorry.
HOLBORN: Uh huh.
(PAUSE)
HOLBORN: So...I hear you put your stuff up on eBay. Going Luddite?
MOUSCH: Well, uh...no, I'm just switching disciplines. Going non-visual. Film's...all played out, y'know? I mean, you've noticed that.
HOLBORN: Yup. Good luck, I guess. (BEAT) Everything just back to normal, huh?
MOUSCH: ...hardly...
HOLBORN: You really think any of this is gonna help? Dropping anything with a lens like it's hot, cocooning?

MOUSCH: I don't...

HOLBORN: You remember what I told you, at the hospital?

(FIVE SECOND PAUSE)

MOUSCH: ...I remember.

HOLBORN: That guy killed my wife, Soraya. Just because she SAW him—over my shoulder, right? When she didn't even know what she was looking at. She's fucking dead.

MOUSCH: Liat's dead because she had a tumor, Max. Nothing we did made Liat die.

HOLBORN: What do you think he's going to end up doing to US, Soraya? After he's fucking well done with everybody else?

MOUSCH: Look... Look, Max, Christ. Liat, Laszlo, that crazy fucking moron dude who made the clip in the first place, let alone sent it to us... (BEAT) And why would he even do that anyway? To what...?

HOLBORN: I don't know. Spread the disease, maybe. Like he got tired of watching it himself, thought everybody else should have a crack at it too...

(FIVE SECOND PAUSE)

MOUSCH: I mean...it's not our fault, right? Any of it. We didn't ask for—

HOLBORN: —uh, no, Soraya. We did. Literally. We asked, threw it out into the ether. Send us your shit. Show us something. We asked...and he answered.

MOUSCH: Who, "he"? Clip-making dude?

HOLBORN: You know that's not who I'm talking about.

(TEN SECOND PAUSE)

HOLBORN: So, anyhow, bye. You're going dark, and I'm dropping off the map. I'd say, "See you," but—

MOUSCH: Oh, Max, goddamn...

HOLBORN: —I'm really hoping...not.

(CONNECTION TERMINATED)

***

OFFICE OF FORENSICS, TORONTO POLICE SERVICE 51 DIVISION
EXCERPTED REPORT

Casefile #332

Final analysis of X-ray images taken of Liat Holborn (dcsd) shows no known cause of observed photographic anomaly. Hand-digit comparison was conducted on all possible candidates, including Maxim Holborn, attending physician Dr. Raj Lalwani, attending nurse Yvonne Delacoeur, and X-ray technician John Li Cheng: no match found. Dr. Lalwani maintains statement that cause of death for Liat Holborn was gliomal tumour.

Conclusion: Photographic anomaly is spontaneous malfunction, resemblance to intact human hand coincidental.

Following lack of forensic connection between Maxim Holborn and Site of Death 1, and failure to establish viable suspect, this office recommends suspension of Case #332 from active investigation at this time, pending further evidence.

***

July 26/2009
"BACKGROUND MAN," Lescroat, strangerthings.net/media (cont'd)

One year later, the crash which brought kerato-oblation.org/cadavrexquis down—melting the server and destroying a seventy-four-minute installation cobbled together from random .mpg snippets mailed in from contributors all over the world—has yet to be fully explained by either Wall of Love founder. While Mousch cited simple overcrowding and editing program fatigue for the project's collapse, Holborn—already under stress when Kerato-Oblation got underway, due to his wife's battle with brain cancer—has been quoted as blaming a slightly more supernatural issue: a mysterious figure who appeared first in an anonymously submitted piece of digital footage, then eventually began popping up in the backgrounds of other...completely unrelated...sections. Background Man? Impossible to confirm or deny, without Holborn's help.

Still, sightings of a naked man wearing "red" around his neck wandering through the fore-, back-, and midground of perfectly mainstream movies, TV shows, and music videos continue to abound. Recent internet surveys chart at least five major blockbusters (besides *Mother of Serpents*) and three primetime television series rumored to have inadvertently showcased the figure.

At the moment, the (highly unlikely) possibility of pan-studio collaboration on a vast alternate-reality game remains unresolved, while at least three genuine missing persons reports are rumored to be connected with a purported Background Man personal encounter IRL. The meme, if meme it is, continues to spread.

Neither Mousch nor Holborn could be reached for comment.

***

And up they come—
(the dead)
Crawling through the hole with their pale hands bloody from digging, their blind eyes tight-shut and their wide-open mouths full of mud: Nameless, faceless, groping for anything that happens across their path.

With no easy end to their numbers...

For once such a door is opened, who will shut it again? Who is there—

—alive—

—that can?

No end to their numbers, or their need: The dead, who are never satisfied. The dead, who cannot be assuaged.

The dead, who only want but no longer know what, or from who, or why. Or just how much, over just how long—here in their hole which goes on and down forever, where time itself slows so much it no longer has any real value—

—can ever be enough.

DRONE

Again, Fafnir spoke: "I have borne a helm of terror over all people since I lay on my brother's inheritance. And I blew poison in all directions around me, so that none dared come near me, and I feared no weapon. I never found so many men before me that I did not think myself much stronger, and everyone was afraid of me."

—*The Saga of the Volsungs, translation by Jesse L. Byock.*

Once upon a time there was a hole, and in that hole was gold.

Now, gold is a soft thing, much-used and easily bent to many purposes, whether melted in fire or reshaped by the heat of a casual hand—and men love it, now as ever. They love it so much they will kill their own children for it.

The hole was full of gold and darkness in equal measure, and for a thousand years it had kept its secrets well. But one day the earth above it split open, letting men finally see what lay inside, so they dug deep and scraped out whatever they could, taking it all. But the further they dug, the more darkness they found, along with their gold—and found that the darkness itself was not empty either. Many went on digging in the dark, deeper and deeper, and many never returned to daylight with what they stumbled over...

But: Down to the bottom one man came, brave and strong and deceitful, and there he found it. The heart of my hoard.

There he found me.

***

Meanwhile:

Kateryne doesn't like to do it at your place, because of all the snakes. Like, *What if they get loose? They won't,* you say. *Haven't yet.* And no, you won't tell her how many of them you have, because you're pretty sure the number alone would make her run screaming—but then again, screw her in not-the-good-way anyhow, because it's not like she's ever come up with a convenient alternative. She still lives at home, in her mom's basement; there's a lock on the door, but according to her, the door itself is thin enough for her mom to listen in and make snidely oblique comments afterwards. No matter how many times you point out this isn't really your problem, however, Kateryne just won't stop asking.

This morning you dreamed of the lava-field again, black rocks ribbed turgid as frostbit flesh to a pale horizon, lip-cracked and veined with rising steam. In the middle distance you saw one huge stone standing, centre pierced with a smooth-grooved hole big enough to hold a whole fresh-stripped log upright, yet jutting ever-so-slightly forward: Pole like a boiled bone, sinewy strips of bark still adherent, vague smell of pine sap and effort. Its tip held a new iron spike, hammered halfway through.

And hanging from that spike, like fruit, were a rusty set of manacles too small to span any wrists but those of a small, frail woman...a child, almost. Twin traps poised to snap shut and hold them in place, uneasily tiptoe-balanced on the stone, so they couldn't help but stare into that nearby crack in the earth which steamed and stank and gaped, threatening at any moment to yawn even further open and finally disclose what lay inside...

Late to mid-August, and the days have already begun to turn, the same way they always do—heat and moisture draining away, fleeing southwards, like run-off from the lake. Unseasonably heavy storms breed lightning strikes to downtown power stations, browning out your whole block from morning to midnight, and beyond. The worst is the way it plays hell with your system, because you can't keep the pinkies cold enough not to rot, and where the hell are you then? Snakes won't eat spoiled mice.

No mice equals no snakes, equals no cash. Yet no snakes equal Kateryne happy, which equals you happy, for a while. Yet snakes, which equal cash, also equal unhappy Kateryne—which you can take if you have to, for as long as you're getting something out of it worth the annoyance. But do you? Are you? Is it?

It's a genuine fucking conundrum.

You stick your hands inside two separate terraria at once, letting a rosy-brown desert boa constrictor wind around your right arm, a bright green rainforest ball python around your left. Then open the window wide and lean out against the sill, dragging deep on your cigarette and letting the smoke pour straight back out to scent the wind, a visible, toxic perfume. Carcinogens for all. Given the way the standard of living in this neighbourhood keeps on dipping, it really seems the least that you can do.

And that—right then—is when the phone rings.

**

Down in the hole. Men like to crawl inside such places, I find, even knowing the risk they must run by doing so—alone, in the dark, far beyond each other's help. They think it is greed which drives them, desire for wealth and fame. But I think perhaps it is really an urge towards their own death they feel digging its sharp spurs in their sides, something ancient, something they have never quite outgrown. The same instinct which makes cats hide themselves away whenever they feel the pains of mortality mount beyond bearing, striking out at their owners' helpful hands with claw and tooth, as though old age were a sickness, something one could catch or spread through contact. As though each of them did not carry their death like a seed within his heart already, just waiting to flower, wherever his corpse might eventually happen to fall.

Men are inexplicable in this way, in my experience. As in so many others.

Over time, since meeting the man who stole my hoard, I have learned that there are those who think dragons never existed, and others who think dragons once existed, but no longer do. Of the latter, most also believe that when (or if) dragons did exist, they were nothing more than one more sort of animal, dumb brutes, mere beasts. It is these people I pity most, fearing for their sanity were they ever to encounter...something...which disproved their narrow, ill-educated philosophies.

Then again, perhaps such people do not need my pity. Blind as they are, if they were to meet what they dismiss out of hand in the flesh, they might not even know enough to fear it.

The man who came to meet me in my lair, brave and foolish by equal measures, expected what he found, and found what he expected. Men always expect women to lie waiting for them inside the monster's cave, conveniently available to be rescued—and certainly, there *had* been women there before, over the years. Though not for some time.

Remove the virgin from her chains, and she is only one more piece of meat: a prize to be won and used, a princess or a wife, a cooked corpse to be buried if you wait too long. Remove the dragon from her hoard, however, and she may become something else, something...far less easy to recognize.

He stole my gold, this brave fool: Hollowed me out, tunnelled down, down, down into my empty depths, and every piece he took away from my hoard changed me further. So much so that when he found me where I lay in state, wrappened in my wings, he paused, hypnotized, and bent to kiss his warm lips to mine: still and cold in my skin sarcophagus, my half-alive cup of horn and bone, my death cradle. All I wanted was sleep, the long hibernation; to let humans have this world, muddy and foul as it had become, much as they seem to want it. To let them forget and grow fat, until I chose to rise once more, and find them utterly unprepared for my return.

But he found me instead, tainted me with his touch, and woke me with his breath: baked bread-sweet, only as warm as the rest of him—not hot and bright and metal-smelting sharp like mine. My wings tore loose, leaving me naked. I looked up, felt my pupils widen against the light, and saw his silly human face looking down, smiling wide. So witlessly happy to have "saved" me...from myself.

And then, as the old saw goes, the scales well and truly began to fall from my eyes.

***

Who is she? Kateryne asks, inevitably, as soon as she "just happens" to find the photos the P.I. gave you, carefully half-buried though they are under a terrarium full of crickets and an open bag of potting soil. Adding, still suspicious, after you finally tell her: *You sure the guy got it right? She doesn't LOOK old enough to be your mother.*

I'm sure, you say. Thinking, at the same time: Like it's any of your fucking business.

Are you going to go see her?

You nod. *That's the plan.*

Oh. Can I come?

Amazing, that she thinks you're going to answer that at all. You chew it over for a long moment, letting the silence stretch, 'til even she can figure out she might—just might—have said something wrong. Then, with no perceptible rise or fall to your voice, just another word on just another day:

...No.

Later, you go over the photos again yourself, so you'll be able to recognize her, if and when. They look washed-out, overexposed, and almost sepia—daguerreotypes found in a dead relative's attic, but without the usual quasi-leprous age damage. They tell you she's relatively tall (going by background objects), relatively thin (though that flat-chested, papery-looking ankle-length A-line dress she's wearing in all of them makes it pretty hard to tell), relatively blonde (or grey, or white, her uncut hair caught back in one of those lax ponytails which start halfway down instead of near the roots, allowing a messy fan of bangs to hang down into her hidden eyes). Her features seem indistinct, yet somehow familiar; that's probably just your understandable urge for genetic closure talking though.

There's a problem Colubrid you've been trying to feed recently (*L. getulus splendida*), so you put the photos down for a minute and take the drop-cloth off to check whether or not it's finally eaten the pinkie you left in there this morning: Nope. Granted, best results are obtained just after a shed, and in better light, you can see it's looking pretty blue—opaque, its scales delustered, getting gradually ready to detach itself from the inside out and pull away into a shiny new state of being.

Rather than use the pinkie pump and force-feed it assembly-line style, however—or switch completely to live, which is always its own particular brand of pain in the ass—you go half-and-half: Pick a newborn from the squirming mass of them you keep in your uppermost terrarium, for just such emergencies; cut open the soft top of its head with a handy pair of garden snips, smear the brain material around a bit, then place it close enough so the snake can taste it. A bit grisly, which is why it's just as well Kateryne took the hint and went home...but it works usually. And if it doesn't...

If it doesn't, that's two hundred or so start-up bucks down the drain, plus a good potential breeder and a shitload of salable eggs. But it's not like there aren't more where this one came from, after all—your whole apartment's full of them. As already established.

You watch the trepanned mouse's hind legs twitch, and think idly about how you *do* feel for them, but only abstractly. It's not so much that you *want* to see things eaten alive every day as it is that you simply care about the snakes' survival more—and not just because snakes make more money for their owners in the long run. Mice can be cute, but not most of the time; they're weak, skittish, smelly, contaminative. A plague of mice can be horrifying, especially in close quarters. But even when snakes don't do what you want, it's always a pleasure to watch what they *will* do; they're smooth, sensuous, soothing. And, most importantly of all, silent.

Besides which, nature's guiding principle is hunger, not generosity. It runs best on a cycle of breed vs. cull. Which means...you're just being true to nature.

(*Your* nature?)

As the snake slides forward, tongue flickering, you return to the photos—study them closer, musing on their many limitations. How they can't possibly tell you what you really want to know: Why she gave you away, how she feels about it. What she remembers of you as a baby. If she remembers you at all.

Whether seeing her will hurt, for either of you.

Hell, they can't even tell you how she smells—inviting, off-putting? If it'll remind you of anything. If it won't. If it'll be different, subtly, from any other scent you've ever encountered.

Or just how much you might, eventually, find yourself getting to like it.

***

"Are you Mrs. Ormsdatter?" the drone asks, when I open my door.

"Miss. And you?"

"My name's Sumerled...Haskell. The Haskells adopted me."

"An old name. I myself have been called Hallgerd."

I invite him in. The man who took me to his home, his heart—that one-time seeker in darkness—has been dead for many years now; he tried hard to find me after I left, taking the as-yet-unborn drone with me. If he had later followed the drone's trail rather than mine, once we diverged, he might perhaps have escaped his fate altogether.

But no, my poor hero came here as well, instead. And what a reunion that was! He vowed his love to me again, reminding me how he had rescued me from the worm's clutches, still never suspecting that worm and maiden were simply two different faces of the same buried beast. And I did not disabuse him of this error, ever, for—in my own way—I had come to love him too. He fed me, and kept me safe, and bred daughters in me to breed yet more of my own kind...

(And them I have since sent out into the world, to go their own way, for no nest may contain more than one of us for long, without it becoming...uncomfortable. What did that English writer have to say on the subject, in one of his books for human children?

Ah, yes, I recall it now: *There is nothing a dragon likes so well as fresh dragon.*)

At any rate, he stayed with me to the very end; I valued such loyalty, as one naturally would, particularly when given by ironic mistake. So when I finally ate him, I did it one small piece at a time, cooking him from the inside out. I gave him dreams and rocked him to sleep on a carpet of sweet, narcotic smoke, expecting that when I woke, the morning after, I would have regained everything he took from me at last...

But, as you see—I did not.

The drone is full of questions. "Did he know you were pregnant, when you left him? About me?"

"I think he suspected, yes. Yet obviously, he did not look hard or far enough to find you, before we met once more—and he never spoke to me of doing so, after we were together again. At any rate, I had had you long before that, and soon given you away. It was best."

"For who?"

"For all of us, of course."

He stares up at me, perhaps taken aback by my honesty, as I bend to serve his tea. Green eyes, exactly like mine, with their vague night-luminosity and unblinking tapetal glare. None of my daughters had such eyes, which is just as well for them; far easier to blend in, to go unnoticed. To prey and survive, in safety.

"Why wouldn't he have wanted to look for me?" He cannot seem to stop himself from asking, finally.

"How can I know, for his part? For mine, I will say only this: Your father lost me because he would not let me be."

"Be what?"

"Myself." I pause. "Also, he stole from me."

Much as I am embarrassed to admit it, I now know that I sorely underestimated the extent of what men will do for gold. But in my own defense, I think I must have still been half-asleep.

He sold the first bits of my hoard to buy us passage here, from the Old Country. Then he sold more of it, to buy us land. These things I let him do, thinking I would later be able to find what he had stolen, to reassemble it and resume my true shape. Yet it was when he sold the very last part of it to buy a future for *you*, little drone, that I left him, for he had finally split my soul away from me for good. Perhaps he did sense that, on some level: Knew that were I to handle even one small piece of it again, one only, I might become *myself* once more.

For it was never the dragon he loved, was it? No. Not ever. What he loved was the lie.

Loved it, and died for it.

***

Oh, she's a strange, strange lady, all right. Her tiny house has a smell to it that seems half...might even be pot, you had to guess, and half something creepily like the cedar-chip/reptile-shit funk at the bottom of a molting snake's cage; her walls are lined with heavy-lidded portrait prints by Klimt and Tooroop, the women in them all sinuous curves and golden spackle. But the part about her which freaks you out the most is how you can now see, first-hand, where most of your *own* strangenesses come from...your tendency to either stay silent or just blurt things out, for example, with no lip-service to conventional "politeness". Things like: *He stole from me. I left him. I gave you away. Am I surprised to see you here? Perhaps. Happy?*

(...perhaps.)

(...not sure.)

(...why would I be?)

It stings a bit to hear her say them, especially with such apparent ease—but it doesn't really *hurt*, not exactly. Instead, it makes you remember all the various names Kateryne's called you, over the course of your brief stint as mutual fuck-buddies: *Cold, selfish, alienating, alienated. Alien.* Though she definitely means for them to wound, they simply seem accurate. After all, *cold-blooded* is the word you'd use to describe yourself, if asked.

You sip more tea, clear your throat. "So...Ormsdatter's your maiden name?"

"My name, yes."

"I thought 'orm' meant, uh—'worm'. Or something."

"It *can* mean worm. Or snake. Something which lives deep underground, digging for gold..." She pauses, a milky flicker passing over those too-green eyes, like one of your snakes' nictitating membranes. "There was a song once, where I grew up. Peasants sang it in the fields, to keep themselves awake during all-night harvests, in bonfire season. They sang it loudly, so their children would know to stay in bed, away from the open sky."

And here *she* starts singing, just a bit—breathy, toneless, more an insectile buzz-whine than a genuine snatch of music. A drone which rises and falls, funereal, as ever-deeper notes seem to open up inside her pulsing white throat, like cracks.

"The marriage bed, the funeral pyre
I am the snake at the heart of the fire.
I speak in riddles and rhymes and jokes

And death curls out of my mouth, like smoke."

Adding softly, a second later—

"It can also be written as 'dragon,' you see. This word."

"And dragons eat children; *human* children, I mean."

"Oh, yes. Snatching them up off the ground, flying them away up into the darkness." She smiles, revealing teeth a shade more closely packed than you're completely comfortable with. "Of course, they will eat their own children too. They are not sentimental."

Sentiment's for mammals, you catch yourself about to say, and stop. Because...

One time, when you first started to think about breeding for profit, you put two Common King Snakes (*Lampropeltis getulus holbrooki*) in the same container, let them mate, then left them there overnight. In the morning, the female snake was nowhere to be found, while the male—already larger—looked unusually bloated. It took two weeks for him to pass the bulk of his former partner completely, in well-digested chunks.

Kateryne would be horrified by that story, because she doesn't understand that snakes don't "love" each other—certainly not in the idiotically devoted, evolutionarily dead-end way that some other animals can, like swans, bonobos, or even (on occasion) people. They're just not capable of it...and unlike we talking hairless apes, they can't even lie well enough to be able to get away with pretending they are.

It's getting late. You rise, unsteadily. "I should..."

She nods. "I understand."

Then you're standing at the front door, her hand on the latch—slim but hardly frail, faintly veined, unpolished nails long enough to hook slightly at their tips. Her hair is falling in her face again, like a veil.

"Can I, uh...I know we've just met, again, but..."

(those eyes, *so* green, staring up at you through an ice-pale messy fall of bangs)

"...would it be okay if I was to, I mean...could I..."

And yes, the photos didn't lie: She is tall, now you're both standing. Tall enough to reach your mouth with hers, as long as she shifts to the balls of her feet first.

"Kiss me," she says, like she's the one who just now thought of it.

Seconds later, a flash travels through flesh as you meet, lip to lip: A circuit completed, pulse sent back and forth, groundless and undimming. Some sort of rattle seems to rise through both of you at once, a bone-bead curtain left shaking in some unseen monster's wake; the stinging, narcotic taste of her spit makes you pucker and pre-retch, heart palpitating as you inhale a lung-full of abnormally warm breath.

"I'll come back soon," you say, stumbling a step or so away at last, once you can move. Legs actually *shaking*.

To which she only nods.

"Yes," she agrees, out loud, just in case the people in the back need a translation. "You will."

And here we have a lost line, a black splice, an overlap. Two scales which haven't quite set together, forming a biologically based offramp: First here, then there, with no apparent in-between. Back at your place, key in lock, head still swimming. Door opening with a final shove, to reveal—

Snakes, everywhere, slithering free, boxes emptied to the wind. Terraria in ruins, frames smashed, glass shards sticking haphazardly up and sideways from irregular-sized piles of chips or sand. Weaving a bit, you glance back at the door—bracing yourself against it, squinting to make sure—and confirm nothing's been forced...very freakish. Your livestock probably know who's to blame, but they're sure not talking.

But then, after a moment's musing, you vaguely recall giving Kateryne her own key, in a moment of weakness. That, and this:

Okay, after this thing with...whoever that woman really is, you're coming straight home, right? It's our anniversary.

Most people wait a year to celebrate, don't they?

Well, I'm not most people—two months is plenty good for me. So hurry back. And bring the booze!

When you left Hallgerd Ormsdatter's house it was...six o'clock, maybe. Now it's eleven, implying not much hurrying got done in the interim—more wandering, and you don't even know where. Which at least makes this sort of drama-queen overreaction a bit more understandable at least. If you were Kateryne...

(but you're not)

You pick your way in slowly, trying not to step on anybody, but the snakes slide away as fast as you can stoop for them, as though you're giving off bad pheromones. They don't want to do any of their usual tricks, no rearing up to be petted, no coiling 'round your wrists like bracelets or climbing further up to play boa (regardless of true taxonomy) and parking their weightiest segment across your shoulders. Quite the opposite: All of a sudden, your touch almost seems to madden, not soothe them.

Snap! Before you know it, you've got a ball python hanging on for dear life from one hand, back-curved fangs dug deep into the fleshy web between thumb and forefinger. Lucky it's not poisonous, though truth to tell, you're already starting to feel more than a little woozy. You struggle to remove the snake frontwise, so that the teeth don't tear your skin open, but it refuses to come; an impatient tug later and it hits the floor with its whole head hanging askew, crushed and pulpy.

What?

No time to react. You fall back onto the bed, immediately, fitfully asleep. In a feverish trance, you dream your flesh necrotizing around the wound, and scales emerging from your pores. The bed becomes swampy with your sweat, an acidic medium, like that peat-moss bed you once stupidly housed a whole crop of L. zonata on, courting premature shed, slipping and sticking, skin blisters which puff and ooze. Where the lesions heal they leave discoloration behind, curl on curl of it, rough skin rosettes. A full-body version of a horny toad's ruff which spreads from neck, to groin, to temples, closing inexorably over your mouth, your ears, your eyes...

Until: *Hey*, a voice says somewhere above you, threaded with hesitant fear. *Hey, are you all RIGHT?*

Your lids pull apart, a wrench like scab parting—but there's no pain, no wetness; just another illusion. And there Kateryne is, straddling you, constitutionally unable to keep herself from revisiting the scene of the crime. Going by her voice, you would have said she seemed concerned, but her face gives the lie to that one—it's intent, lips slightly parted, tongue caught in teeth. Her eyes scanning you, voyeuristically, for any visible signs of pain.

Even from your extremely canted angle, you can see that the snakes are long gone. Instead, the whole room is covered in unnaturally shed skin, molted every which way like keratin spiderwebs.

Are you OKAY? Kateryne asks, leaning close. And you—

—grab her by both ears, pull her even closer, blood boiling. Mash her lips to yours, and feel her little *oh!* of happy surprise. Is this what "passion" feels like? "Hatred"?

(Could this be what she's always wanted?)

You breathe into her mouth, the way Hallgerd did with you, like you're passing air back and forth underwater. Feeling something from deep inside you burn your throat with its passage, cauterizing this anger, this desire, at its uttermost root.

Kateryne's eyes widen; she thrashes, then goes slack. There's a smell like meat frying. Black stuff comes out of her mouth, gilding yours with liquid rot. And the world around you both implodes, explodes, reels...

The end, and the beginning.

***

Oh, my poor drone, my mayfly son. I knew when I clutched you that you would be the one to redeem me from this dying husk, this paper-frail flesh cocoon...and yes, I knew what it would cost. But that makes no difference, in the end.

"Biological imperative": I am sure you have heard this term, once or twice, in your travels. Since you seem to me like someone who may have gone to school.

One way or another, when at last you return to knock on my door, you will have changed so irreparably that you will no longer even be able to cry for what you've done. While I, as I open it, will have grown so much younger you will not even recognize me 'til I open my mouth...and exhale.

And then it will happen, as I mount you upstairs, in my former marriage-bower—the thin parchment of my back will break open at last, releasing my new wings, shivering and sticky. They will dry quickly in the heat, especially after I unhinge my jaws even further and set the house on fire. My lower limbs will become claws, so I can clutch you to me until our cloacas open, until our joining is complete. We will grow together like mating dragonflies—so aptly named!—and soar through what is left of the roof, up towards the moon.

We will fly, never deigning to touch ground again, while I teach you to listen for the song of buried gold and track it to its source. And only once we have found a rich enough deposit will we fall at last, in flames—so fast, so terribly, that when we hit, we will bore a new hole through the earth's guts straight to it. We will coil around it in a heart-shaped knot, and grow together yet again, becoming what we were always meant to be. Free at last of all illusion, all frail human imposition.

Eventually, however, we will fight, as we must...and I may well be the one to die, for I *am* older, though infinitely wiser. You may even eat me afterwards. Yet though I will take no comfort in this fact, it amuses me somewhat to think that when you do, you may still remember being human clearly enough to feel badly about it...at least a little.

Who knows: Perhaps that will be payment enough, in the end, for my tediously long exile amongst those who live and die brief meat-lives, like flesh candles. Those from above, who do not love the deeps, yet are drawn there nevertheless, into the dark. That stony, uninviting, womb-like place where gold waits—and I, if you only dig far enough.

And now, *you.*

THE SHRINES

Photo: A rubble sculpture on the Leslie Street Spit. Five layers, bottom two three-hole cinder blocks, then a two-hole block (jaggedly broken), two partial blocks of one hole each arranged as a rough mockery of the block beneath, and one more three-hole block. On top is a lump of concrete with rusty wires jutting from it; the wires have been "shaped" to suggest hair flowing in the wind, while the lump itself has a grey suggestion of features, open-mouthed, in profile.

***

Dear Darrow: Yesterday I went out to the Spit and saw the Shrine you'd made, that awful thing. All those honest gifts defiled, just to cobble together a poisoned offering for some nameless god to choke on. All those other Shrines broken up for parts, heaped like garbage—a middle finger made from other people's dreams, doubled, quadrupled, upthrust towards silent heaven.

No secret at all about how I knew to go there in the first place; I found the article about the place when your landlord let me in, pinned to your bedroom wall.

New Gods of Leslie St.
On the Spit, Some Torontonians are Building a Religion Even They Can Believe In
Byline: Gregg Polley, Bite Daily

The first, built from broken bricks and cinder block, stands less than a metre tall, sides and roof forming a stage for a jumble of obscurely significant items: A ceramic Easter egg, a box of baby teeth. A votive card to St. Martha, guardian against distractions.

In front, a ceramic cast of the soles of someone's feet around which brightly colored marbles have been sprinkled seems to indicate where prospective pilgrims should stand, if they want to view this odd little diorama for maximum impact. There's even a "spire" made from half an orange traffic cone, like a Church of Oz raised by Munchkins.

But this isn't Macchu Picchu, or Angkor Wat. This "sacred" structure, like the fifty surrounding it, sits square on the shores of Lake Ontario—a little-trod part of the Leslie Street Spit, aka Tommy Thompson Park.

"A lot of people don't even realize the Shrines are here, because they're in this kind of nook, hidden from the road," notes Jensen Cort, crew leader with the Toronto and Region Conservation Authority, which manages the park.

The collection of towers looks somewhat like a primitive city fallen into disrepair, its miniature buildings fashioned out of construction debris fetched from the shoreline, where crashing waves have weathered bricks and cast iron into found art. The grass around it is revealingly trampled, indicating a steady stream of visitors. Just a few feet away, a garter snake slithers through another of the follies.

"We're standing on tons of rock with just a little soil on top," Cort says, unsurprised. "This place is like one big hibernaculum."

According to him, the entire spit was created over many decades by clean fill and construction waste being dumped to form a promontory, with adjacent lagoons and ponds. Now the place teems with wildlife: Foxes, raccoons, hawks and the many types of rodents they prey on, plus the nearby waterbird colonies Cort's team looks after.

***

Dear Darrow: Three weeks since we'd last spoken. I can still play the conversation back in my head, almost word for word—

"Mom," you said, "you're a smart woman. That's why it kills me you're letting this crap pull you down to...their level. All these other idiots."

"Like what, like Dad? *That* kind of idiot?" I gave an angry sigh. "He would've called what he died in a state of Grace—that means something. The way Gran and Grandad's kindness means something to *me*, whether it comes with the Church attached or not. You don't spit on somebody for offering you sympathy."

"*You* don't. Besides—didn't do him much good, all that happy Christ crap, did it? In the end."

"You don't know that."

You turned away. Threw back: "Yeah, well...neither of us does, actually. That's kind of the point."

What's "funniest" about all this, in retrospect, is that when Frank and I first married, I was very definitely the Godless one in our relationship: Raised with no religion at all, taught only that Christianity was one more mythic system, one more set of stories people tell themselves at bedtime to distract themselves from an impending, inevitable headlong plunge into darkness. We even used to joke about it, uneasily, whenever we ran across nursery rhymes like this:

Goosey goosey gander, whither shall I wander?
Upstairs, downstairs, and in my lady's chamber.

There I met an old man who would not say his prayers;
I took him by the left leg and threw him down the stairs!
"Thus perish all apostates!" I'd say, and you'd giggle. Too young to know what I was talking about, back then.

That last fight ended when I told you you were free to believe any damn thing you wanted, or not. What I resented was being browbeaten for choosing not to *believe* something else, so much, as to refuse to tell people who did they were idiots to their face—not my boss, not your teachers. And certainly not Frank's parents, whose grief over his death—Jesus talk set entirely aside—was just as sharp and valid as my own, or yours.

Dear Darrow: Most aneurysms have no cure, or reason. Your father died because people die; that's just what happens. There's no right or wrong to it. No good or bad, except as it applies to you.

I didn't tell you that then, because I knew you wouldn't believe me—but you would have grown out of it in time, this impossible hunger for accountability. I believe that devoutly, or try to. No one can stay that sad, that angry, forever.

No one human.

***

The towers stand above a shoreline littered with great slabs of broken sidewalk and tangles of rebar, as though announcing the Shrines' presence to those approaching by water. Closer to the road, a meandering, human-scale walkway has been laid down with discarded bricks. At one end, the roadward entrance is framed by tree branches festooned with bits of cloth and paper on which questions, statements—invocations?—have been scribbled, like improvised prayer flags.

A subsidiary wall of sculptures lines both sides of the walkway, all of them decorated with bits of broken ceramics, doll parts, toys, metal hardware, feathers, pine cones, ornamental grass.

No one seems to know precisely when the charmingly rustic village of Shrines first took shape, or who started it. But the more compelling question might be, why?

Obviously, this is a place of meaning, somehow sacred to those who've lovingly gathered up Toronto's detritus, fashioning it into votive folk art.

Wanting to meet a few of them, we settle in to wait.

***

Dear Darrow: Shall I tell you a secret? It was always the *despair* at the root of all your anger which really got to me. That black bile. The way, after Frank's death, you tore through life as though wedged alone inside your own coffin, the four roughly hewn wooden walls of your own death's

83

inevitability. And what you really wanted was for everyone else to willingly crawl into that box, right along with you. But some people do insist on hoping.

I certainly know how annoying *that* can be.

So don't think I can't understand how much that article must have upset you. So infuriating, those happy little idiots with their DIY deities. Setting up their stupid hopes like idols, watering the seeds of dream with prayers—and you wanted to show them, what? That it's all a lie, softly told? That everything lets you down?

Dear Darrow: Did you really think they didn't all already know that?

This is nothing new, my darling, any of it.

Not even what must have happened to you.

***

"Worshippers" begin to arrive later on, around twilight.

*"I was picnicking here, with my kids," one woman—call her "Susan"—explains. "And I thought I heard this sort of a...**voice** in my head, and I just suddenly felt...thankful. Like giving back, you know? And now every time I do something, every time I add to my Shrine, I get that feeling again."*

She kneels in the dirt, using glow-in-the-dark paint to add curlicues and runic patterns to her Shrine's walls. Concluding: "It just felt so...good. And where else do you get a feeling like that, usually, outside of a bar? Like, ever?"

Though Shrine building looks more like a hobby to non-believers, for many, it can be a full-time job. One person, who asked not to be identified even by pseudonym, must travel two hours either way in order to maintain the Shrine they've constructed. Is it worth it, we ask?

"Oh, yes. Oh, yes."

For others, the inspiration to make their Shrine—while similarly rewarding—seems to have been considerably more direct.

*Says "Keith": "It was like a name kind of came into my mind while I was just standing here one day, looking out over the lake, so I wrote it down, in here." He indicates his Shrine's interior, packed tight with multicolored wool and rags. "Something started telling me what to do, after that. No—I can't try to say the name, so don't ask me. Hell, I won't even try to read what I wrote; why do you think I did **this**? So I wouldn't be tempted."*

Why not?

*"Because. It's not **for** us."*

Then who is it for?

He looks away, as though embarrassed. Doesn't answer.

***

Dear Darrow: Don't think I don't know exactly what it is you resent most about me, these days—the fact that I can still remember when you were soft, and small, and lovely, and loving. That when I love you it's the same way I did when you were still that child, and that I'll never stop. Never.

No matter how hard you try to make me want to.

Only now, however...now that I've spent such a lot of time thinking about it...does it occur to me how maybe what you insisted on telling poor Gran and Grandad, your idea of God as a prayer-eating spider growing fat off the world's misery—cliché as it still seems—was far more prescient than even you could know.

If the Shrines' example teaches us anything, it's that one person's god may be another person's something else entirely. A shadow glimpsed behind a screen, blurred out of all proportion; something removed from context, laid horribly open to misinterpretation.

Make your own god: Press here. Tab "A" into slot "B." A Shrine to nothing? Is nothing sacred?

Even unaddressed, your prayers *do* go somewhere, probably. Just—

—not where you think.

Looking out onto the lake now, I too think I hear a voice in my head—whispery, repetitive, like the lapping waves. It does not seem to speak to me, at least not directly; is it yours? Or is it meant *for* you, somehow...part of your memories, your dreams? The ones you didn't even bother to write down?

You called, I came. Do you have work for me? If not, you've wasted your time—and mine.

And there will be a price to pay for that.

Because maybe, just maybe, there is something—not *God*, but a god? Something local, something petty. A place-linked god which hovers around the Spit, that artificial between-place, and grazes on prayer, on hope, on awe, the same way bees do on pollen. That milks us like aphids of our small ecstasies, our tiny moments of grace. That doesn't like its herd being messed with.

And though one might think even you would understand the dangerous illogic of getting between something unnameable and its food supply, that—it seems—is exactly what you did. You shat where it ate.

Dear Darrow: I imagine you mid-frenzy, laying waste to everything you can reach—kicking one Shrine down, taking the Blue Jays bat your father gave you for your eleventh birthday to the rest. Grabbing treasures up at random from the dust, the grit, and Jenga-ing them together, a haphazard cairn. Pausing, breathing hard, to admire your handiwork, before spitting on it.

In tragedy's wake, you wanted answers. You wanted life to be explicable, which is...completely understandable, but unlikely. Terribly, terribly so.

Whereas, for me, the very idea of something keeping score—up there, down here, wherever—has always been frankly horrifying.

Rules and regulations, unwritten, inviolable. Making what you did here, at the Shrines—*with* the Shrines—like a prank call, sent collect. Like ringing the doorbell and running away. Like when you knock on the green, weed-hidden door of a fairy hill, but you're not the right person, or it's not the right day, or you didn't have anything to give in exchange, and didn't do it for the right reasons. And so...

You're forfeit. Something takes you, somewhere.

And you don't come back, ever.

How I wish I could have told you this, any of it. But it probably wouldn't have mattered anyhow; you'd have done what you wanted in the end, just like always.

I never could tell your father anything either.

***

These days, "hating" Toronto is so fashionable it's become a cliché. Polls prove it. All across the rest of Canada, people universally seem to think we're rich, arrogant, cold, rude, smug; unfeeling, unsmiling, unfriendly; self-congratulatory, self-absorbed, self-centred, self-obsessed, self-satisfied, spiritless...

As **Lip** *magazine columnist Allin Koss, well-known for his weekly commentary on Megacity ecology, recently wrote: "The Toronto I grew up in might have been on its way to becoming something, but went off the rails a while back. Now here we are, still blithely driving at full speed without a road map down the proverbial highway to Hell. Take a look: The signs are everywhere. Crumbling roads, bursting water mains, a decaying transit system, trash-covered streets, rampant homelessness, weekend murder sprees, traffic gridlock, smog warnings, contaminated beaches, a sewer system designed to overflow into the lake, a decrepit industrial wasteland waterfront choked with Soviet-style residential towers. If this is progress, I'd love to see what the city council considers outright failure."*

The funniest thing about anti-Toronto sentiment, however—whether it comes from outside or in—is that ours is a city populated by people from elsewhere. Survey a room of Torontonians and you'll find recent immigrants from Iraq to Newfoundland, some Anglo transplants from Montreal, a few who came from the Prairies looking to make it big, plus one or two Vancouverites who can't shut up about how much they miss the BC bud. In business and the arts, the best and brightest from all corners of the country come here to meet up and make their mark (excepting, perhaps, francophone Quebecers, who migrate to Montreal).

But what do they find when they do? In a place of infinite possibility, it's hard to connect, on any level. Though distractions are everywhere, loneliness runs rampant—and religion, organized or not, just doesn't seem to help. It's all too easy for that innate human impulse towards the mystic to turn into disappointment with every "offered alternative"—live-for-the-moment hedonism, woo-woo paganism, Gnostic secret cultism and proselytizing atheism, alike.

This place, however—the Leslie St. Shrines—is different. Something's happening here—something new, or maybe very old.

Check it out.

***

Dear Darrow: It's beautiful up here, surprisingly so. Smell of lake, of turned-up earth, of new grass. The trees are putting forth furled leaves, like popped and shredded cocoons.

Right now, though, it's also cold—standing out on the very edge of what used to be a loading dock just past the old sugar factory's hulk, with black water roiling around me everywhere I turn to look.

In front of me, the lake; behind me, the Shrines. This clean, forgetful city of mine: Toronto, two cupped hands set shoreward on a lake of muck and tears. Toronto tipping sidelong, a slowly poured-out bowl of pain. Toronto, under the gathering storm.

This world is a pit lined with wounds, always fresh, always green. Much as we may strive to, can we ever possibly deny it? Should we even try?

Misery of miseries. The type of misery that longs for transfiguration: I don't care what happens, where I end up, what or who I become, as long as it's not what and who I am right now—no longer here, no longer me, no longer *this*.

Like dogs to stink, like flies to blood, so these hovering invisible presences to misery. And Toronto "the Good" has always had a slice of pure, cold misery for its beating heart—that same endless reserve of negative energy you identified with religion, denounced wherever you found it as bullshit, a con, a vicious shell-game. The spiritual equivalent of necrotizing fasciitis.

Which means these things will come to us, always. Always. No matter whether or not we ask them to.

Particularly if we keep on making the mistake of doing them worship.

***

Photo: The same Shrine as before, at sunset. Around its "neck," a long silk scarf—bright saffron, crowded with indelible penmanship, so cramped as to be almost unreadable—flutters upwards, caught by the wind. A prayer in motion.

***

Dear Darrow: I know you won't read this—that you can't. So I offer it up instead, as evidence, to anything else which might be listening. As sacrifice.

I come to the Shrines almost every day. I make that pilgrimage. I think I may have defused your construction, to the best of my ability—re-sanctified it, or perhaps de-sanctified it. I make my offerings, write down my dreams. Wait, uncomplaining, for any sign of a sign—of expiation, of relent. Any sign of forgiveness.

Doing penance *for* you, even though I know that's impossible—and hoping, against hope, to one day see you again.

Dear Darrow, second-generation apostate—believing nothing, knowing nothing. Fearing nothing. I let you do what you wanted, believe—or not believe—what you wanted. I should have tried harder.

I let you down.

Oh, dear Darrow. Oh, my poor little boy.

How I do love you so.

Your mother.

GABBEH

The thing everyone who came by Ashad's already knew was that Ashad's Mumma was crazy, or getting there at least, so close she could probably kiss crazy as it went by.

Ashad's family had been big once, back in Shah times. They'd come over to Toronto after the Revolution and spun one store into three, then ten. But last month the original store had finally closed, after a solid year of Going Out of Business sales. Condo people didn't want rugs anymore—not gabbeh, not kilim. Not without a million assurances they weren't supporting child wage-slavery, or that every fibre wasn't somehow soaked in blood.

"But it is!" Ashad's Mumma would put in, however—with a horrid sort of cheer—whenever Ashad's dad complained around the dinner table. Which was yet one more way you could tell how fast the old lady was going off, sitting there smiling so pleasantly with her filmy eyes half-closed, an elegant set of bones covered in fine lace wrinkles, ricepaper skin, and a long silk dress, her silver hair still painstakingly pin-curled in the height of 1950s fashion. God knew what she did all day, up there in her room. The only person who could so much as have a conversation with her, far as Nazneen could see, was the cleaning lady-cum-attendant Ashad's dad paid to come in, Shecilia.

"Why yah got that rug up on the wall, nah the floor?" Shecilia demanded. "Jus' look at the dust on it! Pitiful, how yah treat an heirloom like that; thing fallin' to flinders almost, that's a fact. You need tah let me take it down, run the vacuum over it a time ah two, 'fore it draw moths."

But Ashad's Mumma just shook her head. "Out of the question," she said. "It is not to be touched—everyone here knows so."

The rug in question was a gabbeh, thick and coarse-woven, probably almost an inch in depth, ninety by one hundred fifty centimetres. Its pattern was mainly grey on green on brown, squares on rectangles on stepped diamonds, with small, intensely red blocks and triangles scattered throughout—oddly drab yet strangely natural, its variegated colours breaking up in sub-textures like skin or sand, even the veins of dry-crisped autumn leaves. And while Nazneen thought it unlikely Ashad's Mumma had had anything to do with its actual manufacture, she still had to give the old lady props for interesting taste.

"Why for nah, yah crazy old hen?" Shecilia demanded. At which Ashad's Mumma's eyes just narrowed further, an odd sort of cunning creeping in, and wouldn't say, at first. Not with Shecilia around.

"Can you keep secrets, Indian?" she asked Nazneen, in a whisper, after pulling her aside into her room.

Nazneen's parents were from Pakistan, but she didn't see the point in correcting someone this old, let alone this crazy. "Depends," she replied instead.

"Well, it makes no matter probably; I *must* tell, before I die."

The upshot was—and Nazneen couldn't believe she was even telling Ashad this, later on—that the reason the gabbeh had to stay on the wall, potential moth damage notwithstanding, was that if you put it on the floor, you might step onto it (duh). And if you stepped onto it...you fell in.

"In where?" Ashad asked, eyebrows hiking.

"Oh God, I don't even... The Zagros Mountains, maybe? Or somewhere near *Shahr-e Sukhteh*, the Burnt City?"

"Those places are nowhere near each other, Naz."

"Look, *I* don't know. Besides which, apparently you end up some*time* else, not just someplace. This day back whenever, when a whole village was wiped out." She nodded at the gabbeh. "That's the grey and green, in case you're wondering."

"How can you even tell?"

"You can't—everything has to be done all geometric because no representation, right? I shouldn't have to tell *you* this stuff." As Ashad shrugged: "Point is, if you know what the gabbeh's theme is, you can sort of work out the story. Better yet, you have your Mumma to explain it to me, so there you go."

Ashad peered at the gabbeh, not quite close enough for contact. "Dad says Baba ran off with a loose woman after the third store opened, because Mumma was so hard to live with. He says his friends saw them out in Mississauga at some fancy nightclub that doesn't exist anymore, eating pork and drinking."

"Yeah? Well, *she* says he's that little red blotch, *there.* The one that doesn't look like a triangle *or* a square." Ashad examined it, frowning. "Says he must've fell right in the thick of it, and how that would've been a real bad day to be on the ground, because that was the day your family came in and killed everybody over—salt, or something. Something like that."

"Salt was probably worth a lot, back then," Ashad said. "Still is."

"In Iran?"

"Lots of places."

"Okay, anyhow: They killed everybody, and then I guess they felt bad, and somebody made a rug out of it. And the rug eats people. So that's why it stays up."

"Yeah, well—not for long."

Ashad knew lots of people, one of whom claimed to be an antiques appraiser with a specialty in fabrics, and he'd already made it clear he didn't intend to wait for whatever portion was coming his way from the family's corporate dissolution proceedings—fine with Nazneen, since part of his immediate need for money involved the two of them disappearing off to someplace her own family wouldn't be able to easily locate them. Still, the less said about that, the better.

So they waited until his dad had taken Mumma off to her monthly glaucoma check-up, when no one but Shecilia was supposed to be home. As perhaps the single most pragmatic person in the mix these days, she hadn't put up much protest when approached; simply named the size of cut she wanted to let them in, and to run interference should the older generation happen to get back early. Ashad saw bribing her as an investment, and Nazneen had no real proof he wasn't right; people were like that, she'd found. Mostly.

Which was why it made for somewhat of a surprise when Shecilia didn't answer the door on the first ring, or the tenth.

"Round the back," Ashad said. "There's an extra key, unless Dad's moved it."

He hadn't.

Upstairs in Mumma's room, all they found was the rug on the floor and the brand-new Dyson Ball vacuum cleaner just sitting there, half on top of it and half off, still plugged in, and roaring. "Shecilia?" Nazneen called, looking around.

Nothing.

Ashad shrugged, checking his watch. Remarked: "She had the right idea, at least..."

...and, picking up the vacuum's pipe-shaft, took two brisk steps over the gabbeh's thin, blood-colored border-band. His shoes came down silent, one, two: "Don't!" Nazneen warned, automatically—

—and found herself, abruptly, all the more doubly alone, letting the last part of the word trail away into empty air. The vacuum fallen, in a new place on the rug, still roaring.

No way of telling how long she stood there, vaulted instinctively back, to hug the wall; her eyes felt fixed, distended and dry, pupils pin-point. What she would remember, for years after, was how she only jolted awake again when, below, the doorbell rang once more.

The appraiser, a brisk lady all done up in taupe, seemed a bit taken aback when Nazneen answered. "I'm...here to see Ashad?" she said, trying to stare around her.

Good luck with that, Nazneen thought. Hearing herself reply, at the same time: "Oh, he's just—up...there—"

But the appraiser was already shrugging her way towards the stairs, taking them two at a time. "Oh, never mind," she called down, "I think I see... Is this it?"

Yes, Nazneen felt her lips shape. Then, quickly: *But no, don't, I really wouldn't,* wait—

But nothing more followed—not a scream, not a thud, nothing. The vacuum roared on. And then she was sliding down the doorframe with the filmy back of her hijab knocking and rucking itself along the woodgrain: Slack all over and slumped into herself, too weak to peel herself free, even to raise her hands far enough to cover her own eyes.

It didn't matter. The gabbeh's pattern hung in the air in front of her, pulsing: A blotch for Ashad's Baba, another for the appraiser. Another for Ashad himself.

Rout and fire, mayhem and chaos, blood for salt reduced to a cool, grey-green-brown tangle of geometric shapes inside a thin red edging. A square of guilt, pure and thick and hungry, always hungry. Always, and forever.

Ashad's dad had to force the door to get in, sending Nazneen toppling onto her side, curled foetally. When he saw her, he took off running, following almost the same path everyone else had. Except that he must've stopped just short of the rug itself, because when he began to wail, it cut through Nazneen like a knife.

Ashad's Mumma, meanwhile, surprised Nazneen by lowering herself just far enough to stroke the hump of Nazneen's shoulders, as though gentling a horse. "There, there," she said. "You see, Indian? Did I lie? This has happened before, so many times. It will happen again, surely, just as many."

"You should burn it," Nazneen whispered, into the floorboards. And felt the old lady sigh, her fingers thin and sharp as bird bones.

"But it is *ours,*" was all she said, finally. And to this, even as Ashad's dad cried on, striking his forehead over and over against the hardwood floor of the corridor outside his mother's room—

—there really could be no possible reply.

GAZE

When full-dressed she wore around her neck the barrenest of lockets, representing a fishy old eye, with no approach to speculation in it.
—Charles Dickens, *Dombey and Son.*

It was almost exactly three weeks since George Neavins had posted the photo of the Hoxby eye miniature when she received her first email from the man who called himself Benedict Prowdham Proctor. Not that she had much cause to doubt that actually was his name, especially after she'd run him through Google and gotten the requisite twenty-plus hits she'd long since decided were enough to "prove" somebody existed, but...it was the Internet, you never knew, not really.

> *Dear sir,*
> *I am writing to you to see if the eye miniature you list on your site (formerly property of the Hoxby family, dated roughly 1786) might perhaps be part of a set...*

His inaccurate assumption about her gender was a problem inherent to having chosen to go with her nickname rather than "Georgina," but since doing so had been a frankly business-oriented decision on her part, George didn't feel much obliged to correct it. She clicked along further, reading the rest piecemeal while simultaneously monitoring her latest eBay auction, and was surprised to find herself becoming interested.

> *...found in a safety-deposit box after my aunt's passing, along with several other oddities...apparently the work of an ancestor of hers, Gwilliam Prowdham, who was fairly well-known as a local miniature artist here in Boston from immediately after the Revolutionary War to the turn of the 19th century...a left eye, watercolour on ivory, framed in jet with a hair backing and pearls inset on the bottom of the frame, perhaps to symbolize tears...Please find photos attached, showing front and back views. If you could get back to me as quickly as is convenient, I would be very...*

As the auction wrapped up, leaving George seven hundred to the good, she tapped forefinger against teeth and called up the item in question, sizing each view of it in turn next to Proctor's jpgs. On the one hand, the hair-work matched—same cross-braided stitching, same general tint (brown, with a reddish cast)—and so did the framing, though hers was missing its pearls, probably pawned or sold outright as the remaining Hoxbys sank into decay, long before the estate sale where she'd finally picked it up. Still, there was one very particular difference...two, really. And so distinctive she decided to lead with them when drafting her reply.

Dear Mr. Proctor,

While I understand (and identify with) your enthusiasm at the prospect of such a find, I do feel constrained to point out first that there are almost no known historical instances of eye miniature sets being painted; such an instance would indeed be an amazing rarity, almost as much so as finding a mouth miniature, of which I'm sure you know very few exist. I also think it likely, given the striking resemblance of our items combined with the fact that mine is inscribed on its reverse face with a tiny maker's mark reading GP Bos., that Gwilliam Prowdham may indeed be responsible for both. However, since your miniature is of a pale green eye while mine is of a dark brown eye, it seems unlikely they_belonged to the same person. Still, if you're interested in selling, I'd certainly love to help match you up with a sampling of interested collectors, on either side of the pond.

All best,

George Neavins

http://georgiana-antiques.co.uk

She didn't think much about Proctor after that, aside from granting his Friend Request on Facebook. So she was surprised when, while checking her Facebook page, an IM pop-up with his name attached asked her whether she was available to chat.

sure, she replied. Then added: *abt eye miniature?*

Yes.

kay, go head

Good point re the disparity, he began, *but it occurred to me that unless your photos are reversed, your miniature appears to be a left eye, while mine is a right. So they might belong to someone with heterochromia. That's*

2 dfrnt coulord eyes, kno th term. saw xmen 1st class 2

All right, great. So I took the liberty of doing some research on my end, trying to figure out who Prowdham might have painted within the due timeframe (1785-1790), particularly for a member of the Hoxby family. Made up a little package. May I send?

George raised a brow, then realized he couldn't possibly see it. So: *sure,* she repeated.

Seconds later, she was opening what seemed a disproportionately large attachment, revealing a document made up of two parts scans to one part notes. The former appeared to have been taken directly from yellowed

Boston-area newspapers dated between May and December of 1787, while the latter she could only attribute to Proctor himself, though he occasionally seemed to be jotting down quotes from materials not included.

Much of the newspaper matter involved accounts—truncated and metaphorical, by necessity—of a court case conducted behind closed doors in late April, 1796. The charge was child-murder through procurement of abortion, brought against a certain Mrs. Damaris Chadwent of Boston, a young widow who supposedly made her living as a "dress-maker and fashiouner of dolls," but was rumoured to be "kept" by a member of "an olde and substantiall familie with Monarchial tyes." (*Hoxby?* Proctor's notes suggested, then added: *Hoxbys left Boston for Ontario by end of year, then back to England within next decade.*)

This all tallied with George's own research. At the time, the clan's leader would have been widowed matriarch Elephantina Hoxby (once the wife of Abishag Hoxby, successful spice merchant and importationist of other luxurious unnecessaries), who stepped into her husband's empty place only to find herself haphazardly shepherding the dregs of her once-prosperous brood from disaster to disaster, shedding properties as they went. First there was Abishag himself, dead of fever, in whose funeral's wake came warehouse fires and nautical scupperings, cutting their fortunes in half. Her oldest, Ephai—what sort of people named their son after a word which meant "gloomy," Biblical or not?—had been slated to take over his father's concerns, but was struck down by a swirl of scandal (the mysterious Mrs. Chadwent's fault?) followed by a wasting disease with an archaic, faux-Latinate name, probably some undiagnosed form of lupus, quickly rendering him unsuitable for any position at all.

By the time the Hoxbys abandoned their Bostonian holdings entirely, their original complement had been reduced from a strongly tied familial consort to an ever-shrinking band of barely-survivors, denuded and near-destitute. So they'd married the last daughter off in what was now Toronto, booked passage for London with her bridal gift, and got as far as Liverpool, where they'd settled in to slowly decay from genteel poverty to outright penury. Much like every other treasure they'd once possessed, their eye miniature had already changed so many different sets of hands by the time it made its way across George's desk that she'd never debated whether or not to make its provenance known; wasn't as though she expected anybody named Hoxby to come asking after it, after all, given there was no longer anybody so named left to ask.

George clicked on, speed-reading. The trial itself, due to its secret nature, was referred to only elliptically; a lot of faff about "thatte most horrible crime against alle Sense & Propriety, contrary to ye lawes of God & Man lykewise," as well as some implication that Mrs. Chadwent might have used "means un-Naturall" to attract the putative father of her unborn child in the first place, seeing that he was young, good-looking and of "Stature," while she was none of the above. It did seem odd for a woman without means to have supposedly entrapped a rich heir into making her pregnant only to then dispose of her bargaining/blackmail chip outright, however—didn't make much sense, strategically. What *could* she have been after?

Odder yet was the denouement, as described: Mrs. Chadwent had apparently been brought into chambers blindfolded, so that her accusers "might not be Forced to meet her eyes." Not to mention being later garrotted after sentencing, "according to the old methods," with her head *cut off post-mortem* and buried in an unmarked grave, the blindfold still on.

Oh, and here it was, at last—the most important detail. A description of Mrs. Chadwent, "taken from Life," shortly before her trial: *This notorious dame was oft observed walking about ye towne in ye smallest houres of ye night, without any great regard to her safety, yet never much disturbed in her perambulations. This being a great amazement to alle, seeing she was but of middle height, slender-made in ye hands and feet yet stout and womanly about ye body, with hair of a fox-like shade, and her fine eyes of two divers colours—*

One brown, "dark and Fine, lyke unto a conker's shell." And one...pale green.

George got back on IM, pinging Proctor, who answered quickly enough that she had to wonder if he'd actually spent the last forty minutes sitting near his computer, screen up and occasionally refreshed, just waiting for her to reply. *what else in yr aunts box?* she asked, without preamble.

Documents, mostly. Correspondence, a few sketchbooks.

all prowdham?

That I've seen, yes. He signed everything, if only with that maker's mark.

She paused, thinking—without any particular inkling of why—

Oh, I'm going to regret this. Aren't I?

—then typed, a second later: *scan + send me? if dont mind.*

No problem at all. The screen went silent a moment, then pinged again. *May I,* then *take it,* followed by *you're interested?* Proctor's cursor wrote, slower than usual, almost as though shy.

y, she replied, finally.

***

"Sounds like they thought she was a witch," Antha said, stretching distractingly. "Which is weird, because witchcraft was a jailing offence at the most by then, in America—since 1706, I think. A charge nobody would've trotted out anymore, not in any court, even a secret one."

"Oh?" George asked. "Why'd you end up there then?"

"Mmm, thing about the eyes, I guess. Blindfolding her; that's proof against the Evil Eye, or would've been, like...a hundred and fifty years earlier, maybe. She was a hairdresser, Mrs. Chadwent, right?"

"Dressmaker. Sold dolls too."

Antha turned over, shrugging. "Well, then I could be wrong, but it's kind of six of one, half-dozen of the other. I mean—in the Jacobean era, almost anybody involved in doing female upkeep-related jobs might turn out to be a poisoner, like with Lady Frances Carr and Anne Turner; Lady Frances wanted to climb the social ladder, so she got her ruff-maker Mrs. Turner to poison anybody who got in her way, and when it all shook down she was fined and exiled, but Mrs. Turner ended up accused of witchcraft and hung. 'Poisoner' used to be slang for abortionist too. Did Mrs. Chadwent go to somebody to get rid of the baby, or did she do it herself?"

"Um..." George cast her mind back. "'Procurement' could mean either, I suppose. But they'd've brought the abortionist in as well, I'd think, if they knew who they were."

"Not necessarily. Easier to go with the person you already have in custody, right? A lot of women ended up being charged for simply having a miscarriage the authorities decided was a bit too convenient, just like today."

"Antha...this isn't what I'd call *pillow talk*, exactly."

Antha smiled, lazily. "Yeah, well, I think it's fascinating. Love to see those miniatures, laid side by side—the real things, not jpgs. It'd be as if you were looking in her eyes."

"Dangerous business, apparently. According to the file."

"Mmm-hmm. But danger can be *sexy*."

Apparently.

After, George lay there studying the ceiling as Antha dozed beside her, ruminating idly. Made perfect sense Antha'd know about such things, of course, having come to England to study them—a leggy blonde Canadian with a cheerful face and a sinful body, she often introduced herself as a "Regencyist," which George took to be some sort of short-hand, given she'd made Ph. D at barely thirty. Aside from the portion of it spent in bed, their time together mainly consisted of Antha nattering away on one subject or another, which George found cute, and occasionally useful; George's own small store of historical knowledge tended to both the object-based and the ruthlessly practical, always gained with a mind toward profit, or (at the least) knowing how much she could get away with charging.

As she'd pointed out to Proctor earlier, eye miniatures constituted a sort of antiques dealer's daydream, given their rarity. The fad for such images had started in the late 1700s, peaking quickly and dying out sometimes in the 1820s; either Richard Cosway or George Engleheart had painted the first one, though the idea didn't really come into fashion 'till 1785, when George IV-to-be (then still Prince of Wales) went through an entirely illegal form of marriage with pretty widow Maria Fitzherbert. In order to swap love-tokens his disapproving father wouldn't recognize, the two exchanged "portraits" reduced to a single eye each, and George kept his pinned under his lapel, so he could take it out and gaze at it anytime he wanted.

Anonymity and decorum, that was the point of the exercise. Hoxby must have commissioned at least one of the eyes, obviously—Mrs. Chadwent wouldn't have had the largesse to make <u>him</u> one, unless the dress- and doll-making industry of old Boston paid out far better than George was inclined to think it possibly could. But where had the other come from? Who'd want *two* eyes, when one served perfectly well for everybody else?

Because without both, you wouldn't know either one was hers, she thought. *That might be it.*

She closed her own eyes, but sleep still eluded her. So, sighing, she got up—carefully, so as not to disturb Antha—and slipped into her office, closing the door quietly behind her.

An automatic email check revealed more scans from Proctor, plus a note: *Sent you the sketchbooks by courier, as they benefit from being read in person. Should arrive tomorrow afternoon, your time.* Over-egging it a bit, George thought, but shrugged, added *thanx, GN* at the bottom, and sent it back to him. Then, clicking on the first attachment, she fell headlong into what later proved to be two hours' worth of impromptu research, poring through tiny print on discoloured paper to peel back the layers on Prowdham's practice of minimized ocular portraiture.

Up top was what Prowdham called his "Fee-Book," more a memorandum or list of outstanding debts: *1789 Apr His Eye M. Jourdemayne £5. 5s.; 1789 Mar Mrs. F's Eye [probably Hesther Lomax, whose father owned Boston's third print shop, and married her into the Fitzwill family,* Proctor's comments pointed out] *£5. 5s.,* etc. There were maybe fifty entries for the period Proctor cited in his initial email, confirming Ephai Hoxby as having commissioned the first miniature ("with no Embellishment"), though it gave no hint George could see that a second had ever been painted, let alone paid for.

Underneath, meanwhile, was a letter from 1796—several years after Prowdham'd left off making them—in which he reminisced about the "Philosophy" behind the concept:

I first Began on acct. of viewing an eye worn by a Lady of my acquaintance, done at Paris & set in, a delightful Idea, which I admired more than I confess for its singular Beauty & ring. It seemd a true French idea to me, Originality knit w. craft, & when my Customers inquird as to whether I was capable of doing Such myself, I took it as challenge.

There is a strange Delight in translation of my Commissioners desires in this Manner, for the Eye is a symbol of great power—some believe it a window to the Soul, or to our Lord Himself, peering out from this world unto an other: perhaps Heaven, perhaps elsewhere. Tis why I believe people take such Efforts in their requests, twinning Eyes with all manner of relevant Things; stones & flowers, pansies for the French pensée (O Think of Me), turquoize for its Forget-Me-Not colour, pearls for tears. One design I Undertook in or about 178- did

combine an altar workd in hair w. two hearts in Flame beneath the wingéd Eye
of Providence, on ivory, as Allegory of love both carnal & Divine.

But none of this elaboration had gone into Mrs. Chadwent's eye miniatures, aside from the pearls and the hair. Comparatively, they were spare, almost dull, the eyes themselves the literal focal point: Mrs. Chadwent's gaze, boiled down. Her polluted, blindfold-worthy gaze.

George had dated a witch once—someone who thought she was, anyhow. Vaguely, she recalled her talking about something called the Law of Contagion, best illustrated by voodoo dolls and poppets: make something look like something else, and whatever you do to it happens to the thing it represents. So...*look at* something hard enough, and you take a part of it inside you? Or vice versa?

Without thinking, she found herself pulling the jpgs up again, brown on the left, green the right—just seemed correct, going by the way they slanted, the tiny bit of flesh Prowdham'd allowed for context. Very detailed indeed, when you allowed yourself to study them; just a shade of smile-lines bracketing one, with what might be a beauty mark stippling the other's corner. She remembered how nicely the hair shone on hers, red flashing in the light as she raised it, brushing dust away with a few short flicks. There, in the green—was that a flaw? A shadow?

She turned her head, slightly, to check the brown. And...

...found it *there* as well, inexplicably. What seemed for all the world like the same flaw, barely there, yet somehow unmistakable: uneven-drawn, triangular-pulled, a fleck at the top. A keyhole or a person, deformed by distance. An absence, waiting to be filled.

Something twinged inside her temple, a plucked thread. A dim, shuddering echo that might, one day, bloom into pain.

She was so tired suddenly. Far too tired to read any further. Too tired, almost, to see.

With a wracking yawn, she stabbed for the shut down option, not even bothering to close out of anything—email, both documents, the jpgs. Simply flipped her laptop closed and felt her way along the wall, stumbling back to bed.

Behind her, the office lamp burned on. In front of her, Antha lay sprawled, snoring slightly; George barely avoided falling on top of her as she plunged straight down into sleep, and deeper.

***

George's dream began in close, an oval mirror centre-stood, just large enough to frame a face. A candle on either side of it provided light, of a sort, but it came and went, guttering; a wind blew from somewhere, cold and raw. In front of the mirror, a straight-backed chair. In the chair, a woman.

She had her fox-coloured hair down, loose to the small of her spine, combing it through with even, contemplative strokes. Her face George could not see, though its reflection shone, peeping intermittently over the woman's shoulder—white, featureless, mask-like; her body (likewise glimpsed only from behind) was ripe, hands and feet well-made, and everything about her seemed trim, neat, compact. Yet at the woman's waist, still small by comparison to the rest of her generous curves, there seemed some slight suggestion of swelling.

Y'are caught short, madam, a disembodied voice remarked suddenly, issuing almost from where George seemed to sit—so close, indeed, that George felt it resonate in her throat, as though it were her own. *Or so rumour has it. You will need a friend.*

The woman's clever hand stilled, mid-stroke, as she replied: *Do you think so, sir?*

Of a certainty.

Hm. And are you not my friend already? Would that friendship cease, were I not so entrapped?

A harsh phrase. 'Tis Eve's own sin we speak of, after all—every woman's destiny, when all's said and done. You might rise, madam, were you to cleave to me entire. You need not work again.

And if I wish to? What then, supposing I considered my work the equal of yours, or any man's? Then added, raising that same hand: *Nay, do not answer; I know your thoughts a'ready, as I know every other young jack's: you would have me idle, stifled, made yours alone for only so long as you'd have it, to be coddled and then discarded, my brat along with me. But you will be disappointed, sir, for nothing happens to me but that I desire it.*

Watch now, and closely, as I disgorge myself of this burden. See how the curse you thought to lay 'pon me may be undone without time or trouble, by one better-versed in cursing.

George heard a qualm enter the other speaker's voice, as if—*he,* Ephai Hoxby, she could only assume—realized his mistake. Hastening to plead: *Nay, good my Damaris, do you but wait a while—*

You wait, sir, an you will. I am not so easily dissuaded.

Now things seemed to narrow, sharply. The darkness George floated in became a funnel, slanting inwards, irising like a silent film dissolve. Thus foregrounded, the woman (Mrs. Chadwent, just as obviously) put down her comb and sat enshrined in erratic candle flame, red-brown hair haloing her like a many-threaded Medusa corona, lit sidelong. In the mirror, though her face remained somehow blurred, her eyes came up sharply, clicking into relief: one green, one brown, equal-lucent, two tiny windows.

I charge you, Mrs. Chadwent murmured, just beyond George's fading vision. *Depart from me now, you mere sketch of a thing; absent yourself, however you see fit. Let no part of you touch what is mine. Die unborn, sad sacrifice to your own sire's folly—*

Something welling up in her lap now, freed with a gush as she shivered, though only briefly; shook herself off and shrugged at the feeling, first hot, then cold. Some spreading stain let loose from inside, by sheer force of will, to dye her white skirts red.

As I direct, then, let it be. For in my gaze are all things rendered but objects, to do my bidding or be cast down, on the very instant...

***

...and here was where George woke, alone, Antha having already gone about her business, leaving only a scribbled-on scrap of paper behind: *b good text later luv u m2m bb.* George staggered up, again barely making it to the bathroom, where she sat yawning, so wide her jaw hinge cracked. A few minutes after, she stood in front of the mirror flossing, squinting at herself under the vanity bulbs' floodlight blare. Only to catch an ill-glimpsed hint which made her stop, peer even closer, searching the reflection for something she couldn't quite make out, though she felt (knew) it *must* be there—

(that flaw, skewed keyhole cracking her cornea, that)

(*absence*)

Oh my Christ, you need to stop thinking crazy, before someone notices.

Lingering on, though, nevertheless; frowning at herself, lips still foaming, a caricature of rabies. 'Til at last the doorbell rang—solid and normal, annoying as it ever had been—and freed her to turn her back, stride over and pop the lock, braced to answer.

"Delivery for George Neavins? Sign here, love."

Proctor's package, right on time. The sketchbooks fell out when she ripped it open, one popping automatically to what George could only assume had been a series of studies Prowdham felt he'd invested far too much time in to just rip it out and start over, cramped and hastily executed though they might be: a bent head, napkin wound 'round the eyes Mary Hamilton-style, entirely failing to keep her ignorant of her fate. George would know the set of that jaw anywhere, those shoulders' jut, spine straight and neat little hands crossed in her lap, ripe bosom swelling above; impossibly recognizable, a clear-cut case of dreamsick *jamais-vu.*

Mrs. Chadwent, 'tis, as I do live and breathe, a voice inside her head observed, wryly. *As I do, and she...doesn't.*

She turned the page, perhaps a bit too forcefully, and watched the motion shake a folded sheaf of papers free, mottled cream-brown as the Feebook scan. A letter, dated 1802, writ large and smearily. Here and there, parts had been struck through or forcibly erased, censored either before or after the fact. It was addressed *To My Dear Sister,* and George found herself speed-reading impatiently through the first few paragraphs—*if this Malady of mine prove fatal let it not be said I died Unconfessd in absolute, though as I trust no Priest to shrive me, I am constraind to Address my soul's black ills to you*—before things finally got underway, half a page later:

...that I share equal Guilt for Mrs. Chadwent's downfall, seeing how after her break w. Young Master Hoxby she applyd to me for Means enough to flee, only to be turnd over to the Law instead. For given we were both his Creatures & subject to his patronage, she believd me trustworthy—a foolish slip, from one who was no manner of fool at all. More fool I, indeed, as things have since elapsed, that (at the time) I feard more the earthly wrath of Mrs. Hoxby than that more spiritual & Most Malign power I had already seen practicd by Mrs. Chadwent upon me, him, even herself.

Because of this "Judasry" on his part, Prowdham felt constrained to attend Mrs. Chadwent's trial each day, recording her interactions with the bench in a series of notes, which he had appended. *They askd if she was guilty & she said: many foolish tales are told of me, as with most solitary women. In example? quoth one. Oh sir, tis said I may divide my gaze & thus look through my dolls' eyes as twere mine own, learning many secret things I later pass to my compatriots, who rob my customers houses & split their goods w. me after. But who can credit such imaginings?*

Like enough those dolls eyes do resemble yours, one judge apparently maintained, *even to their disparity.* And in answer, Prowdham wrote, Mrs. Chadwent only gave a low sort of laugh, brief and soft, yet *most dread-full indeed to hear.*

Do they so? Come, compare, & try. At which the blindfold slipped, disclosing her one eye—the green, not the brown—that when it fell upon the judge his Honour he was struck down, as with Gods own stroke. So she was seized once more, crying out: *thus be all false accusers servd, when an innocent's gaze falls upon 'em. For doth the Bible not say, What you send unto me I will send back, an hundredfold?*

Yet, Prowdham continued, *the eye slid past me as well, in the confusion, just when the bandage was replaced—I felt my limbs lose their vigour, my face fix, as though I became a mere doll in her hands. And so has it remained, unto this very day.*

That same night, being much enragd, Mrs. Hoxby bribd a Man of the watch to wrench Mrs. C's gaze apart, forcing her hold on Young Master Hoxby loose for good—taxd him to cut one Eye free & convey it away, burying it, that its former Possessor go to her doom half-blinded. But acting as I felt not on mine own accord, I bought up the Fruit of his labours w. what remained of my Fee, & once it was deliverd me (in a jar of spirit), applyd myself to one more Portrait. This last I send to you for safe-keeping, for I am loath to have it near enough to Watch me, as Ephai H.'s must surely Watch over him.

It stared at me, you see, all the time I painted, as though by staring it might scour me with hate. It cursed me, & I am to die from it, I know—if not now, then later. After as much pain as I can bear, if not more.

I do pray God Almighty not much later, sister, in my better moments. Though I doubt in my heart those prayers will be answered, except with laughter.

Keep it secret, please, therefore. Keep it safe.

She will come for it, one day.

Not copied from life, then not exactly. Copied from death.

George's phone buzzed, a blessed momentary distraction. It was Antha, texting: *found quote u might find useful,* link appended. Clicking through, she found somebody's Tumblr, at the top of which was the following highlighted text banner—

"Gaze" is a psychoanalytical term brought into popular usage by Jacques Lacan to describe the anxious state that comes with the awareness that one can be viewed. The psychological effect, Lacan argues, is that the subject loses a degree of autonomy upon realizing that he or she is a visible object. This concept is bound up with his theory of the mirror stage, in which a child encountering a mirror realizes that he or she has an external appearance. Lacan suggests that this gaze effect can similarly be produced by any conceivable object such as a chair or a television screen. This is not to say that the object behaves optically as a mirror; instead it means that the awareness of any object can induce an awareness of also being an object.

(She made me into an object, an awful object.)

(She made a doll of me.)

Abruptly, George realized she had not just the beginnings of a migraine, but the very thing itself; it crystallized 'round her full-blown, without her ever having felt it forming, converting her limbs to wood and the air to treacle. Slowly, as if sleepwalking, George folded Prowdham's letter (*file that later, might be valuable,* she had the wherewithal to remind herself at least) and went back into the office, opening first a little cabinet hidden beneath her desk, then the safe inside it. Inside, amongst everything else, her hand fell on a tiny cloth bag, from which she shook the Hoxby eye miniature. Raising it to the light, she angled it to catch and flare, hair turning foxy, keyhole flaw blazing up. The image blurred, doubled, making two eyes of one. Until, as her own eyes narrowed, as tears filled them, blurring the pair further still...

Don't look, don't. Put it down. Stop looking.

You have to stop looking, before she—

(looks back)

...one of the two, formerly both brown, began to turn green.

That hole at the corner of her own eye was back now, as George had somehow suspected it would be. Unable to stop herself from focussing in on it, she watched it seem to move closer and closer, stretch up and out, become a figure: ripe in the middle and neat at both ends, wild reddish-brown mane hung down to frame a smeared white half-visage whose sole open socket gaped empty. A clever hand grasped the Hoxby miniature, pried it from George's numbing fingers, and made an odd gesture with it, an oyster-tasting in reverse—tipped it towards its (her) sketch of a face, then lowered it once more as the hole in her head resolved further, filling: pupil, ring, cilia. A shrewd brown eye, indistinguishable from Prowdham's image, peered down at George, who whimpered and flinched from its attention, as if scalded.

Mrs. Chadwent, leaning down over George as she curled up on the floor, whispering in her ear; at first she couldn't hear what was being said, any more than she could interpret the reel of images beginning to unspool itself inside her head. Just lay there as the babble of her bruised mind peaked and dimmed, nothing but one long squealing, begging plea—

Make it stop, make it stop, make it stop. Not my fault. I'm sorry. I didn't mean to.

(Please.)

But: *Quiet, mistress,* the spectre told George, not without a species of grim sympathy. *Calm yourself. Th'art in my grip now, firm as firm, with no escape.*

George groaned. *What...what do you want?* she brought herself to ask, hoarsely, at last.

What all want, in the end. An answer.

...about?

Mrs. Chadwent's form paused a moment, as though considering this.

It is hard for me, she said, eventually, *where I am now. A long way to travel. One forgets one's self. But a likeness...a likeness is a mirror. A mirror is a door. A door opens.*

Yes. Yes, I see...I think. I understand.

Aye, but do you? For I see, too—only one. Where is t'other?

Other...what?

Eye, mistress. Where is my other eye?

Not a weeping girl, George, not naturally—she never had been, even under the worst of circumstances. Yet she could hear sobs, at that moment, and knew them for her own. Above her, what had once been Mrs. Chadwent squatted down further, stare never shifting—so bright and hot, her gaze, even halved. It would burn a hole clean through her, George thought.

Well, lay it by. The Hoxbys, then...they who divided me, Ephai and that bitch-faced dam of his, who buried me in pieces, like rubbish. Do they live still, and prosper?

George shook her head, grinding it painfully against the floor. Thinking, as she did: *No, they're dead, all dead. You won.*

Ah, 'tis good; I knew 'twould trap the Young Master, this one eye of mine, since he could not keep from study of it. And Gwilliam's seed, who first enshrined the same in paint for him? Who saw me swung and wept crocodile tears, knowing full well how he'd connived the same?

A tiny circle on George's cheek, pinpointing the bone, and *God* but it stings, almost sparks. She could all but hear the sizzle—smell her own flesh, cooking.

Proctor, she thought, desperate. *He did this to me. Made the introductions—put you in my head, the likeness, the* image.

Turning, painfully, to fix that place where the ghost should be: dark turned bright, full negative, hurting heart and eyes alike to contemplate. And thought again, in its direction—

One guy, that's all that's left. He's got it. Go after him, *why don't you?*

Oh, I will, madam, Mrs. Chadwent told her, softly. *Be very sure of it.*

Then—a blink. And nothing. Everything gone.

George included.

***

George left the hospital with Antha, hand in hand out of necessity as much as affection; led down the halls and out into the sun, free palm slapping up to shade herself, the flaw's fuzzy remains still emblazoned on her cornea. It *was* fading, but slowly—the doctors were baffled. But Antha, far more blithely accepting of the supernatural than George had ever suspected, trusted things would continue to resolve themselves.

"You're not going to look at it anymore," she said, "so that's *that* settled. Prowdham can look at the damn thing all he wants, from now on."

"Or not."

"Or not! His choice."

"You did cheat me out of my commission somewhat though, by sending it to him while I was knocked out, and telling me about it after."

Antha shrugged. "Would you have let me, if I'd asked?" George shook her head. "Well, there you go; I was just being sensible. Besides, he kept on emailing, so I thought..." She hesitated, then allowed: "...to be frank, fuck him for getting you into this in the first place. Anyhow, I paid the postage."

"Very nice of you, that was."

"I'm a nice girl."

An instinctive decision, but probably the right one, considering what happened next. The friend who was with Proctor when he opened the package claimed he'd seemed compelled to lay the two miniatures side by side, then stared at them intently—refusing to respond to questions, shouts, or repeated shakings—until they burst into flame. The friend ended up leaping from a first-floor window, yelling at Proctor to do the same, but he must've not been able to hear; the house burnt to the ground, amazingly swiftly, with Proctor still inside.

George felt bad about it, at least slightly, for exactly as long as it took some anonymous third party to send her links to a blog site Proctor'd kept under an pseud. Entries there implied he might have been having much the same problems as George, then come across her initial listing and conceived a plan to pass *his* half of Mrs. Chadwent's gaze on, before things came to a head.

"Selling off all your portraiture?" Antha asked, a week later, looking over George's shoulder. "Very...Muslim of you."

"Makes me nervous," George answered, shortly. "Documents and woodwork only for me, from now on—anything non-representational. Seems safer, given."

"Oh, she'll leave you alone, from now on," Antha announced, with what George thought was rather easy confidence, given she'd experienced all this at one remove. "I mean...*you're* not a Hoxby or a Prowdham, just the chick who told her how to get what she wanted. She might even be grateful."

Mrs. Chadwent hadn't struck George as the grateful sort really. But no point being difficult, not when Antha meant it kindly—it'd gotten her to finally move in, if nothing else. Best outcome possible.

So: "Wouldn't care to speculate," George said, briskly. And went back to what she had been doing.

HOMEBODY

Kay was sitting in the Ryerson University library, dozing on her hand, trying to steal a thin version of sleep and soak up as much warmth as possible before somebody moved her on, when the dull red door always hovering in the back of her mind fell dimly open. Though she couldn't see past its frame, she knew that inside was warmth, a place to hide, to be fed and rested and safe: No more of this eternal *watch out, stay quiet, head down, be careful, keep going*, this constant scramble from nothing and nowhere to more of the same but worse, always worse. A dark place, a soft place, a still place. Peace.

Some voiceless voice too, soft as a mole's. Lips moving in darkness, saying—

Come and find me, Kay. I want you to find me. I'm here, unlocked, needing only your touch; my key is in your hand.

You've heard of me, and I've heard of you. I only want to be wanted. Don't we all?

I'm waiting.

She came jolting up just as the security guard's hand fell on her shoulder on that last part, and just for a moment she had no earthly idea where she was at all; accent aside, whatever he was saying to her didn't even sound like English. On either side, a sort of ripple swept up and down the forest of turning faces, blurring their features like Photoshop: Grey buds on a black branch, tight-furled and water-bedazzled, wreathed in mist or rain.

"...*said*, your student ID's out of date, miss. System says you can't be here."

"Oh," she made herself reply, shaking her head clear. "Oh, is it? I'm sorry. I was just...waiting for somebody."

"Student?"

"Sure, yes. A friend."

His eyes crinkled a bit at that, maybe sympathetic, or simply tired. It wasn't a great story, and she was sure he'd heard it before—but hell, she didn't have the energy to make up anything better, as he could probably see.

"Try phoning from outside," he told her, after a minute. "Cafeteria's still open, for about an hour more; tell 'em to meet you downstairs. I'm gonna have to take the card though."

"Yessir. Thank you."

As she got up, she saw him taking in her too-thin coat puffed out with a hipster roster of scarves filched from washrooms, her cracked fake-Docs with their duct-tape weatherization. "You got anything warmer than that to wear?"

"At home, sure."

"'Home', huh?" Didn't seem convinced, but wasn't about to push it. "Look...if you're gonna keep meeting that friend of yours on campus, just remember, you obviously ain't enrolled anymore. Things change. Maybe next year."

"Maybe."

"There's OSAP, if it come down to money. You could try for that, right?"

Sure could, I hadn't had it already, and lost it. Or if I had an address to put on the forms. But you already know that, right, sir? See it all over my face, you could just bring yourself to look there.

Still, she couldn't blame him: That was Toronto, all over. Nobody wanted to risk connection.

So she conjured a smile instead, dipped her head again and pulled that Muppet-head hat she'd gotten from a restaurant coat pocket down tight, projecting: *Uh huh, good advice, thank you kindly for that, sir. Be seein' you, or not.*

Hopefully not.

For a three-dollar investment, she spent the rest of the evening riding up and down on the subway 'til it finally stopped running, around 1:00 AM. Then got off at Yonge and walked back down to Dundas, the Square, open all night. Joined the usual crowd of reprobates lurking 'round the Youth Centre doors, where Legend raised a brow to see her, planted four-square on his platform heels.

"Girl," he said. "You ain't look so good. Need a place to land?"

"Wouldn't mind. You need a spotter?"

"Hells yes, always. Them pimps on my tail in the *worst* way, an' I gotta make rent by Friday."

Kay nodded, shivering. "I feel you. Don't need any kind of cut, just food, couple hours inside...a bathroom too. Haven't showered in, like—four days, I think."

"Well, all that I can do yah, definitely. Long as yah don't mind the noise."

Never have before, she thought.

***

How things had gotten this bad, exactly, was debatable—some days, Kay felt like she did nothing *but* debate it, if only with herself. Talked it out in her own head as her feet moved forward, ever forward on the same dull circuit, parsing it down to the smallest detail and beyond, so the pain of her own footsteps wouldn't reach above her knees: *Here's where you maybe, here's where you could've, here's where if only.* The exact instant where her timeline had split, peeled back like a nail and never healed right again, left always weak and wavy thereafter, marked by its own wounds.

She'd come to Toronto because it was just where you *went*, if you were from somewhere else. High summer when she'd arrived, the air off the Lake water-heavy and still, hot as the inside of somebody else's lung, and the subsequent autumn so long and mild that when things turned on her, she was utterly unprepared. There'd been some vague idea of school, which had pointed her towards Ryerson, but with every program she looked into seeming more expensive than the last—Photographic Arts'd been her last-minute choice, all equipment and printing fees on the dead media side of things, fifty different Photoshop variations, and high-speed Internet bills on the digital—she'd eventually realized she couldn't do it unless she cut *something* out entirely, and fixed on housing.

Which was okay, or seemed so, for exactly as long as she was living in somebody else's tiny little no-bedroom. But *Things change,* like the security guard said; without warning or any particular reason, that situation suddenly became a three-occupant nightmare in which she was relegated to a sleeping bag in the corner, while her "boyfriend" shared the bed with a series of other people. Her marks started slipping. Eventually, one of them wanted to stay and she was out, just in time for exams she couldn't possibly have passed anyways.

Over the next few weeks, Kay sold everything she could and walked away from the rest, boiling her life down to whatever she could fit in her hiker's backpack. Shelters weren't an option; no way did she want to fall asleep around people who thought they needed her ever-waning store of cash even more than she did. She couch-surfed 'til the last of her former classmates went home, then managed a string of one-night stands before she found she'd apparently slipped beneath some sort of visibility margin, without even realizing it: No more make-up, hair too long and ragged, highlights grown out, clothing too soft-washed and out of date. The stink of homelessness on every inch of her, even hard as she fought to keep it from being literal.

This city wasn't a cruel place overall, just...polite. Disengaged. Soon enough, she found people automatically looked 'round her, through her, their eyes skittering off, a pair of thrown stones over deep water. Not one of them willing to meet her gaze. The only word on everyone's lips was "sorry," shaped silent as they shouldered by.

So much wasted time, eked out in increments. Time spent waiting to be noticed, then drifting towards the next warm place. She'd long since figured out a painstaking net of places you could sit for a while, so long as you maintained a certain baseline level of cleanliness: churches, bookstores, hospital waiting rooms, parks. All-night coffee shops and pancake houses, one of which was where she reconnected with Legend, her new best—only—friend, who she'd once used as a first-year day-in-the-life essay model.

All I want, she told him, later that night, as they shared a couple of roti, *is just a place to go inside, lock the door, and sleep. Someplace I can keep everybody else out of.*

Why don't ya go home nah, darlin?

I would. I only had the money, I surely would.

To which he shook his queenly head, and murmured: *Oh, hon. Was that easy, wouldn't we all.*

But in the end, laying blame helped no one, any more than it did to ever let herself wonder (for long) whether or not it might really be true she *wouldn't* live through this. That she wouldn't eventually see the day when she could look back on all her current troubles and laugh, turn them into a story for her kids, a cautionary tale to keep them from making her mistakes; forget them even, if she wanted to. That she might yet be sucked straight down this hole she found herself circling, never to emerge on the other end at all, because...turned out, there just wasn't one.

A sharp shock, a long drop, then nothing, like she'd always feared. Like everybody did.

But she couldn't afford to think like that.

The next morning, as Legend locked his door behind them, Kay squared her shoulders, gooseflesh rising everywhere. Bracing herself to lean back into the wind, face-first.

***

It was almost Christmas, or maybe just after—the whole season'd blurred for her, one long red-and-gold rout of shoppers to hide in, cut with a queasy paranoid awareness that every store she stepped into already had its security jacked up to eleven—when Kay first started hearing rumours about the house from other drifters, that sad clutch of faces which seemed to show up within range of almost every semi-free meal in the G.T.A. A legendary squat, open to all, better by far on the inside than the out-. She'd've been glad to dismiss it as a hobo folklore, if not for how often something she'd picked up from these get-togethers had later turned out to be essentially true: Accurate in general, if rarely detail by detail.

Which might explain why the house in question was always located in some radically different part of Toronto, for all its other characteristics stayed scarily regular. Never more than one-story, for example (*Didn't even have a basement,* one woman claimed), and often crammed between larger buildings or stumbled on off a back alley, its windows boarded up, sometimes bricked, tight as dreaming eyes. No number either, just the rusty, occluded spots where they'd once gone. If there were trees around it, they grew thick and low-hung, hugging the front like a fence; if not, weeds sprang up out of the foundations themselves, lush and tall enough to joust with, while wrist-deep ivy crawled down to meet them, green growth laid overtop decay in a rotten spiderweb of dead vines.

The house's door—only one—was sometimes dead centre-set, sometimes to the side, sometimes 'round back. It opened at a touch, yet locked from inside, securely. And it was always painted red.

In Kay's mind's eye, the house would look much like her Gran's had, whenever Mom and Dad dropped her and the big kids off for a three-bender weekend. A World War II saltbox, all tiny and loose at the seams, cheap housing put up for returning vets in search of factory work, a property bump to help them hook up quick and jumpstart replace-the-race families. Though nothing of its original furniture remained—Gran'd been a big believer in Goodwill, swapping pieces out regularly—it'd nonetheless been cosy, lived-in, with batik curtains and an orange-pulp-bright shag rug so deep your feet sunk into it to the ankles; the walls were covered in dings and nicks and badly sponged scribbles, an intergenerational message-board.

God alone knew who had the house now, if anybody. The property'd gone to Dad after Gran died, and like her, he wasn't sentimental about things. Or people, for that matter.

Over a Christmas week dinner at the Metropolitan United Church, Kay'd asked the third guy she'd heard it from: *What was it like, inside?* The guy smiled, gap-toothed, as though just thinking about it made him a little warmer. He slipped out his phone, showed her a blurry, too-dark snap of something that might've been a moony-blank window and warped brick-coloured door, so badly angled they read like a face in profile. Studied the thing like it was his best girl's smile, longingly, and all but sighed—

Oh, nice. Quiet. So...quiet.

Dirty?

Not so's you'd notice. And snug, considering—I fell asleep real easy, real comfortable, like I wasn't there alone. Like there was something in there with me, just watching me in the dark, breathing.

She nodded, knowing she would've thought the idea scary, once upon a time. But right there, right then...it sounded pretty much like heaven.

Don't know why you didn't stay then, she said.

Oh, I wanted to, believe me. But when I woke up, I was back outside, on the corner—like those guys with the bundles, ones who pee on 'em every day, so nobody wants to take 'em? Kay nodded, a reflex, throat tight; she knew—they were figures of dread to her, those huddled, grate-sprawled piles. Shadows of a future that grew realer every day. *Could've all been a dream, 'cept...I was dry—and it'd been raining. All night.*

Why didn't you go back?

I tried. 'Course I tried. The guy scrubbed his face, sniffling, voice suddenly all a-crack like a boy's. *But it wasn't there. It was gone.*

That's...impossible. Isn't it?

Dunno. Happened. A shrug, a cough; the guy stuffed the phone back in his filthy parka. *Guess it just didn't like me. Not—*

(*like I liked* it)

Kay nodded again, knowing the feeling.

***

New Year's Eve, Kay counted steps all up and down Yonge Street, ghosting through laughter and noise and bars spilling music like oil, slick and toxic. She'd developed a ripsaw cough to go with her low-grade fever and sniffle; wasn't really much she could do about it—drugstores wouldn't sell cough syrup or antihistamines to her anymore, even if she'd had the money—and it kept getting her kicked out of most places after maybe an hour. South of Wellesley, a haggard beak-nosed woman in a thin spring jacket strode past her, spitting and ranting at someone not there. Kay slid aside, out of her way, turned to watch her go.

Saw her suddenly lunge at a young couple en stumbling route to another bar, pushing the girl into the street. New Year's gridlock was so heavy the girl just bounced off a stationary car, not even falling down, but she shrieked like she'd been stabbed. Ranter-woman screamed back and stagger-loped away, leaving the girl in hysterics and the guy staring, mouth open, all thought of manly ass-kicking shit squelched by sheer surprise rather than fear. Kay wanted to laugh. She settled for shaking her head and moving on.

Thinking, half-smug, half-grim: *Least I'm not like* her.

Not yet.

Move on, move on, move on.

Under the free-standing stone archway that sat on the sidewalk just north of Gerrard, a discarded pair of black shoes lay on the pavement, one on its side at an angle to the other, like something had reached out of the gate and yanked their wearer back through so hard they'd gone flying off. Kay almost crossed herself when she caught herself wondering if they'd fit. No. That was—there were levels she wasn't yet willing to drop to.

Though she was finding it increasingly hard to figure out just how she was going to prevent herself from doing so.

Presently, she worked back down to Legend's part of the world. The crowds in Yonge-Dundas Square were warm, but made it impossible to find anyone; after four hours, a deafening botch of *Auld Lang Syne* and the mob finally thinning out, one of Legend's friends told Kay he was in holding, with nobody to make bail. To which she just said *thanks*, so quietly even she couldn't hear it, and sat on a stone bench, coughing and shivering.

Back home, things would be bad, like they'd always been. But even here, a man threw his daughters off a bridge to make a point. There was that girl found under the bushes, two years later, so done for they couldn't even tell if it was murder. Legend took his share of shiners too. If it was all the same, wherever, had there really been any point to leaving?

...come find me, Kay. I want you to.

The subways ran all night for the holiday, but it wasn't like she had fare. Kay thought about crossing the bridge onto the Danforth, trying to lose herself on some side-street—find a basement doorway to curl into, once the snow really began to fall. All it'd take was three bucks, tops.

So eventually, she pushed herself up, started asking around. Most days, "I need a subway ride home" was code for "Please get me drunk," and treated accordingly. But tonight, it only took a few minutes for a reveller to pile a handful of loonies into her palm.

"Happy New Year!" he wished her, so "happy" off his ass it was Kay's turn to stare. But he didn't even notice.

She hoped he had somewhere to go, and close.

***

Though Kay'd hoped to go further, she ended up getting off at Pape when a gaunt skinhead on something harsher than alcohol wouldn't stop cutting glassy, manic eyes her way, as though he thought she was sending out signals. Walked out the street exit and went north, across a schoolyard and out onto some barely lit cul-de-sac full of cozy old two-storeys, the lawns shored up with concrete lips and rock gardens, Italian white-painted ornamental ironwork and tire sculptures cut like carrot roses. Walking without intent, head down, collar up, letting the fever guide her. She took a right and then a left, another right, another, and then—

There it was. A dirty brown brick bungalow, barely eight feet barring the roof, with gaps in its shingles and boards over its windows, a FOR SALE sign knocked over to lie flat on the night-black lawn—but the door, above a flight of five cracked concrete steps, was exactly as she'd always imagined. A bright, dark red visible even in the streetlights' too-faint spill, like cheap Shiraz back-lit through blue glass.

As advertised, not locked, just jammed in the frame and mold-swollen; she had to hit it with her shoulder a few times before it dislodged with a creak. Inside was darkness and dust and silent, empty rooms...but *warm*, at least enough so compared to outside as to sting her eyes. A ratty, fraying couch sat off-centre. Kay fell onto it face-down, scarf wrapped to shield her face, and was asleep in less than a minute.

She woke, by degrees, to a light that seemed almost like sun coming in through impossible windows; hot, golden-joyful. The walls, it turned out, were red as well, a thick, soft red with a sheen like velour. Somehow she'd missed all the furniture she could see now—ornate and stylish, all dark wood and silk and goosefeather-down cushions. Blinking and yawning, Kay wandered upstairs, finding those rooms likewise refurbished, paintings on the walls and bookshelves full.

And everywhere, the carpet—thick, orange. Her Gran's carpet.

(*Not possible. Is it?*)

Possibly because the constant gnawing in her stomach had died away, she wasn't sure how much time passed before she realized she couldn't find the exit. It took some effort even to figure out exactly where it *had* been, since there was nothing there now but smooth plaster next to an open closet, like meat pounded flat. Kay stared at it a moment, then went back into the living room, where the sole hint of squalor remained: the splintery pasteboards over the glassless windows. If she got her hand against one side and pushed, then the other, levering the nails out...

Please, no. Stay.

Not her thought. Kay held still, trying to stifle even the noise of her heartbeat.

I've been...lonely. So empty. People come and go, but I like you.

Don't you want to be wanted?

More than anything, she longed to answer.

She stood there a long breath or two, spot-rooted: Stuck fast, lodged in its craw, not so much like something swallowed as like something cradled, a new organ, pulsing in the not-dark. Surrounded by that red door, those red walls, red like meat and blood and muscle, *alive* somehow as the walls of a heart or a stomach's lining, a breathing set of lungs. As though it was as likely to eat you as spit you back out, to swallow you down whole and digest you entirely, leaving you to fossilize inside its gut the way a snake does a mouse.

Again, a terrifying prospect to most. Yet Kay found, if she was honest, that she didn't much care which, so long as she stayed safe and soothed, her fever dimmed, the cough that cored her salved away. So long as she could keep the door locked on the rest of the world she knew too well, that cold place of constant roaming, and *sleep.*

"Long as you want me," she told that lipless no-voice out loud. "I'll stay, so long as you want me to."

Promise.

"Yes, I promise. If *you* promise."

Yes.

"...yes..."

And then, and then: Things were dimming. Things were ebbing away. The carpet came crawling up her calves, up over her knees, forced apart her thighs and held her cupped, stroked, prone and panting; it licked her palms, wreathed her wrists, grew up past her elbows like lush fur gauntlets. It bearded her like a ruff, a hood, pressed down upon her lids, a hundred thousand-weight of lashes.

She sighed, breathing its scent in deep, its dusty musk. And thought:

I'm home.

Home.

The mouth, sighing into hers. The voice, finally still. While softly, sweetly, that red door in the back of her mind, at long, long last—

—swung shut.

THE JACARANDA SMILE

Saw a dead bird in the fountain I eat my lunch by yesterday, eddying stickily to and fro: Bound loosely together with its own decay in a graceful/awful parody of flight, pre-skeletal wings unravelling on a feed-jet tide while its eyeless head cocked back and forth and up and down by turns, like it was listening for…something, whatever. No metaphor immediately suggested itself.

Which is why, after staring at it fixedly for a minute, I eventually just noted it all down—fountain, bird, my own vaguely queasy response—and tucked it away, neatly, for further reference.

Afterwards, I came home late, hot and exhausted, to find an email from Dad waiting in my in-box. It said the hospital had finally agreed to turn the penultimate switch on his "significant other," Aoife (prn. "EE-fah"). Since the funeral would be held Saturday, in Australia, he didn't expect me to get there in time, and would prefer I not waste my money trying.

Three spare sentences, maybe four. The first I'd heard from him in…months?

Yes: Two, almost exactly.

I sat there at my computer, frowning slightly; looked at the REPLY icon without hitting it. And as I read the message on my screen once more, cursor flashing aimlessly in the corner of my eye like an incipient migraine tic, I couldn't help but replay that moment when they first told him the extent of Aoife's damage; how he'd hugged me tight, trembling slightly, while I'd just looked straight down at his sandals, to avoid having to look anywhere else. Because it was somehow less intimate, less embarrassing, to count the sun-spots on my estranged father's feet (with their crepey skin and overlong old man's nails) than to think directly about what was happening. What *had* happened, already. What was going to happen now.

These miles between us always left open, like unhealed lacunae. There's still half a world of distance between Canada and Australia: Toronto vs. Melbourne, daughter vs. father, writer vs. writer—my life vs. his life, give or take the few small instances where our very separate histories inform each other. His version vs. my version.

I closed out, shut down my system. Then made more notes, almost reflexively—followed my own unholy instinct to rape and plunder my every experience for enough grit to make a bright new pearl; to *use* it, before sheer psychological self-preservation drives me to forget those little details that make a story *really* snap, crackle, and pop. What else is life for, after all, if not to provide that sort of wonderfully fecund raw feed? God knows, given its usual content, it'd be a pretty unbearable trip if we couldn't at least aspire to make it into something else.

I went to bed. I didn't dream. In the morning, I got up again, and went back to work. Sat at my desk, did my duty. Ate lunch by the same fountain, in almost exactly the same place.

The bird, what was left of it, was still there.

***

All stories have to start somewhere: It's a law, like gravity. But when writers say that, what we really mean is that all *our* stories have to start somewhere, usually with another story. And I am no exception to this rule.

So: Once upon a time...

...a little girl saw her parents' battles finally end when her father packed up and fled the North American continent entirely, leaving both his lost love and the child who reminded him of her far behind. Neither of them were bad people, but they weren't meant to be married—not to each other, anyhow. That's how I used to console myself, before I figured out doing so meant acknowledging how much better off everybody involved would be, if only I didn't exist.

Dad went, I stayed. Eventually, he invoked his due visitation rights. Mom didn't contest. And thus I ferried myself back and forth between two hemispheres each Christmas as an "unaccompanied minor," trading day for night, night for day. Went down to Van Diemen's Land, where Outback and Bush alike are clogged with red dirt and empty roads, flora and fauna nothing but a carnival showcase for evolutionary dead ends. Australia, where winter is summer and fall spring, and when you uncork the plug, the water spins the wrong way down the drain.

Since I don't interact with my dad on a regular basis, it's become fairly easy for him to rest out of sight and mind for me, most days; same as me for him, I'm sure. Whenever we do think of each other, meanwhile, it's probably less as ourselves than as a matched pair of long-distance fantasy versions. For me, it's him when I was nine. For him, it's me when *I* was nine.

Too bad, for both of us, that I'm not nine anymore.

So yes, I have a life, and yes, he plays little part in it; I've spent the last thirty years going through things Dad had nothing to do with, all of which have shaped the adult I am today far more than any genetic component he and I may still share. Oh, he thinks he "thinks" of me, but does he *think* of me? Do I "think" of him? Not like he'd like, and not like I'd like. And if my aunt had nuts she'd be my uncle, and if things weren't the same they'd be different...

Nostalgia means "our pain," in Latin. That's memory for you, in a big honking nutshell. It's a curse, osmotically infectious, a shared hallucination, the madness of crowds, the haunted and the haunting. Another country, half the whole wide world away, populated by nothing...

...but ghosts.

***

The first time my mom read "The Jacaranda Smile," she looked up at me with her eyebrows knit and her eyes ever-so-slightly narrowed—not mad, simply quizzical.

"That's not how it happened," she said.

"Which part?"

"Any of it."

So she didn't like it, which was a pity. But I gave up on getting my mother's approval long ago, right about the same time I made it clear that— whether I wrote "what [I] know" or not—nothing I hammered together out of my own highly subjective life experience was ever going to get me onto Oprah Winfrey's Book Club list.

Here's how it works: I'm a writer, which means I lie for a living—take things I think I remember happening and spin tales from them, then sell what's left behind. I fabulate (sp.? Word?) until I move from what might have happened to what never did, which is where I finally gain control over my own material, to shape it as I will.

"They're giving you a prize for this?"

"$100 US, publication in their anthology. Plus a trip to Melbourne."

"Will there be a dinner?"

"Formal, yes. Got any fashion tips?"

Another look, like she wasn't sure if I was joking, or whether I actually meant it. Or both.

"If you're thinking about patterns, try a vertical one," she said, finally. "It'll make you look slimmer, from a distance."

***

After Dad left, Mom got a job at Wintario. We moved from Hocken Avenue to Wychwood, further west along St. Clair, where just being in the front yard made me nervous. A certain tree grew there, dead centre. When winter came, it shed its leaves to reveal a horrible secret—a stunted branch that thrust itself from the main trunk and raised fistfuls of twigs to a pewter sky, howling. This, to my child's mind, was the "witch" in Wychwood. It watched me slouch off to school every morning, then hesitate at the corner every night, trying to get up the courage to scuttle past it towards safety.

I got sick a lot. Early one morning of Year One, I woke with a splitting headache, turned over, and vomited into my own bed. My mother held me over the toilet until the sun came up. It was stomach flu, but I thought I was going to die. Every headache was a brain tumor. At Hillcrest Elementary, which was under repairs, I shared a portable classroom with twenty or so other children. They found me sullen, strange, and arrogant. I found them hideously stupid.

Our teacher, Mrs. Rudnick, told us that if Ronald Reagan was elected president that year, the world would end. He was. At night I lay awake, wondering what it would be like: Would somebody, somewhere, simply flick a switch, and make everything I knew disappear? And even worse—

—what then?

***

It's hard, sometimes, to remember just how passionately I used to love my dad and how deeply I felt his absence after he went back to Australia for good—an intimate hurt, one that left no visible scar. I set up an altar to him in my closet, where I'd write little notes on the backs of old scripts and burn them in what used to be his ashtray, when he still smoked. I'd watch the smoke spiral upward, hoping it might translate itself to the other side of the world and crack that aching silence wide enough for him to suddenly "know" what I wanted him to do or say, without my ever having to *ask* at all. Make him *want* to, without question or regret, as naturally as though he'd thought of it himself.

Magic: At bottom it's all just nursery school science. Every magician is nothing but a kid in a tantrum writ large, who draws dirty pictures of their enemies in wax, or cloth, or sand, and then rips them limb from limb.

When I was a child, I used to cut pieces out of things, as small as I could manage, and then hide them where they wouldn't be found until later, if at all: cushions, plants, photographs. After I turned nine—the year of the divorce—my acting out became shaped by my increasing addiction to books on Witchcraft Made Easy. One time, I saved my menstrual blood in a bottle, kept it until it turned black and stinking, then dropped it down a dusty grate in Dad and Aoife's bedroom with its stopper pulled out, right before I got on the plane back to Canada. Took them a week to figure out where all those ants were coming from, and why.

Aoife and I had our problems, right from the start; the usual first-marriage kid/step-whatever bullshit. "You're not my mother!" "I wouldn't want to be!" All that.

But the last time I saw her, before "The Jacaranda Smile"—saw *them*—things were fine. We were all adults. Did the guided tour, hit the old, familiar places...and that *was* a bit weird, actually. Because wherever we went, I saw each place with the past overlaid upon it like some peeling decal, tinting it retroactively: *Ah, here's where I felt sad, where I felt bad, where I felt mad. Where I wanted to kill—*

(myself, him, you)

But it was okay overall, and I was glad I'd come. I had a good time, took a lot of notes, went home. And then, eventually, the way I always do...

...I used them as mulch, kindling, classic grist. And I wrote myself a story.

***

The house at Wychwood was dry, stinking of Vaseline Intensive Care and mould. I spent my weekends in the enclosed "airlock" between our outside and inside doors, reading Tintin books and dreaming about the day when Dad would come back. I tried to tell myself stories, but I hadn't quite gotten the knack of it yet. Images possessed me, there in the fading light—so real, so immediate, that to negotiate mundanities like spelling or punctuation seemed superfluous at best.

At school, I read everything I could get my hands on (aside from the assigned texts). One day, I discovered *Wuthering Heights*: Heathcliff chasing Cathy's ghost down the moors, freezing to death on her grave. That night, I couldn't sleep, paralyzed by the horrid idea of mortality made palpable. The next night was the same, only worse.

Mom brought in a radio, which lulled me to the brink, where I'd shut my eyes—and the ghosts would rear up again as a wave of dread all around me. Another yell, more comforting: Mom held my hand, told me to visualize a bright green world, take it from lava-lump to fresh new continents, let it suck me in. When it wore off, so did her patience: "Count your blessings for a change," she snapped, and stomped off to her own bed. I lay awake until my heartbeat drowned me at last, forcing me down in a spray of purest terror.

The best thing about my childhood is that I didn't know any better; it certainly made it easier to forgive, if not forget. The *worst* thing about my childhood is that my parents didn't know any better either...not her, not him. Though Mom at least knew enough to be there.

So I learned to keep my mouth shut at night, slowly memorizing the angles of my ceiling. Taking Mom's advice, I *made* myself think of something else.

And "something else" became, at last, a story.

One story, then another, then another. None of them were bedtime material. I told them at school—not to my friends, since I had none. To everybody else. They didn't get me love, but then again, I didn't want any. What they got me was left the hell alone, which was more than good enough, at the time.

Still is.

***

"The Jacaranda Smile" takes place in Dad and Aoife's home, an edifice as far from Wychwood as humanly imaginable: A 1920s Art Deco building located in the middle of Melbourne's South Yarra neighborhood, with a jacaranda tree in its yard so large that if you glanced out the front windows, you'd find yourself staring straight into a haze of bright lavender-blue, harebell-shaped flower clusters. Dad told me when they shed, they all fell at once like confetti, leaving the snaky branches bare. Granted, I was never around for that, but if I screw my mental eyes up in just the right way, I think I can conjure a pretty good idea of what it looked like. Benefits of a vivid imagination.

The roof was all brick-colored tiles, humped to provide guttering. Inside, the rooms stood high-ceilinged, shrouded from the glare of the Australian sky by thick, white, all-but-impenetrable curtains. The dark wood panelling was banded like a coffin's, and a deliberate crack had been left at the top of every wall, to allow for expansion (or shrinkage) of the plaster under seasonal shifts of heat and cold.

Much of the original interior design had been preserved intact, detailing so impressively specific I can still reel off bits of it: A frosted glass window incised with the figure of a peacock half-rampant, next to the living room fireplace; a dining room with sliding doors, like the galley of some long-sunk ocean liner; a "sunroom" bulging straight out from the front of the building, overhanging the main doors, which viewed the tree on one side and looked back into the master bedroom on the other. Heated towel racks in the bathroom, built-in shoe racks in the bedroom closets...all the "everyday" amenities of a very different age, as though you'd rented space in some unregistered hotel. My first impulse, most mornings, was to check my pillow for mints.

On the landing, coming up to take the initial tour, we passed a glass light fixture built to look like some frosted Cubist rose that hung heavy with dust, its base stacked with 365 days' worth of dried-out bug corpses. I can still remember the first time I saw Dad turn it on—how it sparked and smoked; stank too. Like—

(something dead)

***

As I already said, Aoife and I had been getting along. Which is probably why she told me a secret she'd been carrying around with her since the previous Christmas: Though he'd checked into the hospital after telling everyone he had pneumonia, Dad'd actually been there for triple bypass surgery.

"Look, Ellie," she explained, sheepish yet defensive, "I know it sounds barking, but it's the Industry—they've got this collective allergy to wrinklies. Look old, you're out of it for life."

(What Aoife and Dad did for a living, back then, was produce industrial films, which is not even a quarter as glamorous as you might expect something involving the words "produce" and "films" to be. But reasonably lucrative, when the going was good.)

For an otherwise tiny adventure in cardiac attack, Dad's "episode" was still fairly traumatic: Chest pains at the gym led to blackout, then a quick trip to emerg. He kept telling Aoife it was just acid reflux...right up until his doctor burst back in, sonograms in hand, to inform him that his arteries were already so plaque-clogged his heart had begun pumping its necessary daily dose of blood *backwards* throughout his body, just to compensate.

After which, hey presto: Crack your breastbone open, do a scrape, sew you back up, and Bob's your uncle.

I remember Aoife topping this up with an equally disquieting anecdote about them almost immediately having to go visit an older male friend who'd just had a similar operation—Dad pretending to be awake, sympathetic, amusing, "normal," a mere week after having exited a different wing of the same ward himself. Laughing, as she did so: *No, but really—got to admit, it's pretty bloody funny. Don't you?*

For me, though, the truly relevant part was how I'd had to hear all this from *her*, rather than from him...and how completely normal that seemed, at the time.

But back to the story.

***

"The Jacaranda Smile" begins with Dad and Aoife—their fictional analogues "Graham" and "Eve," rather—dealing with much the same situation: A shocking near-miss with death followed by recovery in a vacuum, aggravated by "necessary" secrecy about "Eve's" true condition (I decided to give her the bypass, not him, thus pretending I wasn't telling tales out of school). Lard in some exposition stressing the hidden financial pressures behind their move, the deadly serious truths behind this whole ridiculous charade...and the real action begins.

Immediately after moving in, "Eve" begins to see and hear things. She finds a word (CONCEPTION) written at the very top of a closet while she's cleaning it, and can't figure out how someone might have reached high enough to be able to write it there. She has a persistent feeling of being watched, especially while reading in the sunroom. Waking in the middle of the night because her scar itches, she gets up to put Vitamin E cream on it, and feels a deliberate, cold finger being laid along the rucked tissue, skimming it slowly, horridly gentle. Like when you caress your lover's zipper, just before pulling it down.

As all this is going on, "Ally" (my avatar) arrives from Canada to stay with them while looking for a part-time job and registering with the Victoria Cinematic Academy, preparing for her Screenwriting Program entrance interview. She's seldom there, and when she is, she sure isn't thinking about what might or might not be going on with Graham and Eve. Of course, Eve being who *she* is, she hasn't told anybody what's happening either; she's busy being sensible, fighting unreasonable fear with logic and silence. And it never really changes, not even after a celebratory Ally-welcoming dinner out ends with Eve feeling her throat contract, which sends her back to hospital.

But then, Ally begins to see stuff too.

A girl—maybe nine years old, her features blurred by distance—sits in the heart of the jacaranda tree, perfectly placed to stare into the sunroom window. She wears unseasonable polyester clothing and has limp, bleached hair. The girl hunches over a book, only glancing up when she senses Ally looking; a predatory profile gives way to three-quarters of a secretive smile, as if she recognizes Ally—but Ally doesn't recognize her. A neighbor kid, a trespasser? A truly elaborate trick of the Antipodean light? And then...

...she's gone.

So we speed on, tension mounting quietly, exacerbated by the occasional flare-up between Graham and Ally, or Eve and Ally, or Graham, Eve, and Ally. The girl hangs over it all carrion crow-style, a constant background presence, human embodiment of Ally's continual underlying melancholy over her own past actions. All the stuff she wishes she could deny or dispense of, knowing she *must* take responsibility for what she did, even if her dad will never do the same—

Until: A day when Graham's off doing something, leaving Eve and Ally alone in the apartment together: Ally in the sunroom, Eve in the kitchen. Suddenly, Ally feels "the stare" Eve's told her about, and turns her head to see the kid from the tree looking back at her from *inside* the master bedroom—hidden behind its drawn curtain, visible to Ally, but not to whoever might enter the room. Not smiling, for once, just...empty-looking. And for some reason, this makes Ally desperately afraid, especially so because she can hear Eve's hand on the bedroom doorknob...

She runs, pausing in the doorway. Eve's over by the closet, right next to the window, and Ally can see the girl's humped shadow lurking behind the curtain. Eve looks up at Ally's entrance, surprised. Behind her, the curtain slips away and the girl steps forward. She lays one hand lightly between Eve's shoulderblades—just behind where Eve's heart would be, were their positions reversed. She looks at Ally over Eve's shoulder, smiles—and disappears, as Graham's key rattles in the lock downstairs.

Eve crumples, has another heart attack, dies between them in the ambulance. And when Ally comes back to the apartment, she discovers the jacaranda tree has shed completely, leaving its limbs naked and empty.

A week later, just before she leaves—all plans for Australian higher education abandoned—Ally finds a recent photo of Eve (taken at the welcome-back dinner), its face carefully cut out, buried under the sofa cushions. Not wanting to upset Graham further, Ally hides it in her suitcase. And a month after that, at home in Canada, when she and her mom are cleaning out closets, they find a shoebox—dating to the 1970s—full of similarly mutilated snaps of Graham, Eve, Ally. Plus one picture of Ally alone, from the same period: Up in a tree in Australia, wearing her usual unseasonal polyester Canadian clothes, scowling down at the lens over a book about witchcraft.

Because that's what the "ghost" has been all along, of course: Ally's bile and rage from her child-becoming-teenager years, concentrated into some sort of fetch—a doppelgänger boomerang arcing back around, long after she's forgotten she threw it in the first place. All those evil spells she once worked against Aoife—

("Eve," I mean)

—finally brought to term when Ally doesn't even remember exactly why she *wanted* any of it done anymore, let alone with such passionate, single-minded, lizard-brain intensity. Ignorant art, aimless craft, but *working* still, even now she's no longer angry—not at Eve anyway. Not at anything much, but herself.

The writing on the wall: CONCEPTION. A malign birth, out of one world and into another. As you conceive it, so it occurs. *As I will, so mote it be.*

Magic.

***

It took years for me to understand what I'd done to myself at Wychwood, all in the name of not being "weak." Eventually, I was sent to my first psychiatrist; these days, I think I'm about as "cured" as I'm ever going to get. But I haven't really been afraid since Wychwood, not in the same innocent way. I bred it out of myself, along with a lot of other things—things like sorrow, empathy. The recognition (for a very long time) that anyone except myself was capable of feeling pain, as well as inflicting it.

Though people liked "The Jacaranda Smile," almost universally, I certainly never expected it to take me back to Australia that last time. Naturally, I stayed with Dad and Aoife until the *Terror Incognita* awards dinner. Dad didn't say much about the story overall, aside from the predictable *well done, good luck, good on ya*; Aoife was positively gushing, which surprised me just a tad, given the context.

So I wore my vertically patterned dress and I got my plaque: A bunyip rampant, BEST NEW FICTION OF [YEAR], with my name inscribed beneath. I told Dad and Aoife thanks for the inspiration, no hard feelings, goodbye. I got ready to go home.

And the very same day I was finally all set to leave, Dad found Aoife lying on their bedroom floor, eyes wide open, the left pupil dilated and unreactive.

***

I went back to Wychwood again, once. I was two years into my therapy then, walking up to Dr. Spring's office past the St. Clair West subway station, the same Loblaw's Mom and I used to shop at, the little park where I once went skating with no gloves on and watched my hands slowly turn white. The tree was still there. I stood at its foot and looked up into its halo of leaves, so like any one of the trees I'd sat in over a lifetime, here or in Australia.

It was the height of summer, smell of fresh-cut grass filtering over from an adjacent lawn. In the distance, through an open window, somebody was playing early Gary Numan at full blast: *Down in the park where the mech-men meet the machines and play kill by numbers/Down in the park with a friend named Five...*

There, under deceptive cover of green, the witch leered impassively back down at me. I felt light-headed, oddly naked from the eyes up, as though my thoughts had suddenly become big enough for any random passerby to read them in an uncensored wave: all that guilt, and rage, and hatred. Everything a nine-year-old whose parents have just broken up can never express, especially out loud.

Everything so ugly it can't be voiced, for fear of making the only person you have left turn away and leave you alone in the dark, with only the ghost of your own dead self for company.

***

The doctors said it was a stroke, brought on by a blood clot; yes, Aoife'd been on the usual so-now-you're-past-fifty! thinners, gone to all her regular check-ups, ate right, exercised. But things change. Stuff just...happens.

I'd like, if only for the sake of closure, to tell you that Dad eventually got drunk one night, called up and accused me of somehow stage-managing Aoife's death—not least because then I could tell you how I told him, calmly: *But that's just crazy talk, Grayson.* He never did though—mostly because it *would* be crazy talk, and he's never liked looking crazy.

But man, that'd've really been something, huh? *I* would've really been something then...to touch him like that, so deeply, so directly. Like that apocryphal story about the old Jewish guy who supposedly read *Mein Kampf* whenever he got depressed, because it always cheered him up to be told just how *powerful* he actually was.

There's only one place I have that kind of power: On paper. On my home computer's screen, between cursor-blinks, for the mere microsecond it takes to lay a synaptic mine into the dead space between pixels.

If I can write, I'm the most powerful person alive; if I can't write, I waver. And if nobody reads what I write, after enough time goes by...

...I disappear completely.

***

And so we return to the bird in the fountain, that dancing toy of dust-in-progress. A cheap image, like most of the ones I cobble my tales together from: The Underneath risen up, as it always will—the dark in every crack, the bone under every stone.

If word is bond and in the beginning was the word, then the word really *is* the deed after all; I sinned in my heart, and now it's come home to roost—all my pretty chickens, in one fell swoop. My unremembered musings made karma.

But there are no jacaranda trees in Canada, that I know of.

Let's put it like this then: Back when, on some level, my dad killed my heart...but two months ago, on some whole other level, I "killed" his. Which probably—at long last—makes us even.

And I want to run from that idea, even as it forms. I want to run half the whole wide world away, in the other direction, as far from Toronto as from Melbourne—and stay there, forever. Never come back.

I consider all my uncaught thoughts, my misplaced impulses, my unspoken hatreds flocking like crows, swarming, sent out beyond recall. All the many times, over the years, I wished death on my mother, my lovers, my bosses, myself. And I think: *I'll see that girl again sometime.*

Thinking, at the same dislocated moment: *But I see her already, every day.*

In the mirror, in old photos, out the window, in the passing crowd. Down the block, around the corner, at the very outer edge of where my eyes don't see. Everywhere.

Thinking how ridiculous it is to be almost forty years old and still care so very much about something which happened oh so long ago, something I had absolutely nothing to do with. Something I'll never be able to change, no matter how many stories I write.

I wanted Aoife dead, and she is.

I wanted Dad dead, and he will be. Soon enough.

I wanted to die myself, more times than once; don't anymore, of course. Not for years.

And now—

Now I sit here, waiting. Writing. What else can I do? There's a story, buried, under all these bits and pieces. If I can find it, I can tell it—control it. Sell it.

Make sure there's something left of me for people to read, and remember, after.

MARYA NOX

Introductory Notes:

In March of 2006, after the accidental discovery of spectral evidence apparently linking the deaths of medium Emma Yee Slaughter and Freihoeven Institute intern Eden Marozzi (see related materials, file #FI5556701), Institute Director Dr. Guilden Abbott requested that ParaPsych Department intern Sylvester Horse-kicker have the Institute "psychically cleansed." Horse-kicker therefore contacted Father Akinwale Oja, S.J. (probably best known for his participation in 1999's notorious "exorcism girl" case [see attached file]), and a building-wide blessing was carried out on March 23rd.

Pleased with the results, Dr. Abbott then invited Fr. Wale to lecture on a subject of personal interest ("SPIRITUAL WARFARE: Some Notes on the Difficult History of Demonic Possession, at the Celebration of Christ's Millennium") at the Institute's Jay and Jay Memorial Theatre. This event, hosted by Horse-kicker, also included an interview with Fr. Wale, followed by questions from the audience. A partial transcript of that interview (coded as file #FI0007695) begins here.

HORSE-KICKER: ...but I don't think I've ever heard that term before.

FR. WALE: No? You must have had a very secular education.

HORSE-KICKER: Well, um...yeah. I guess.

FR. WALE: Obviously! (Laughs) I apologize—I actually meant to be making a joke, some sort of light, amusing chit-chat, but no matter how long I stay in Canada, I don't think my English is ever going to be quite up to pulling other people's legs. (Beat) That doesn't sound quite right either, does it?

HORSE-KICKER: No, I'm sorry too, I know what you mean. You were talking about—

FR. WALE: —mmm, yes, *acheiropoieta*—in other words, I wrote my seminary dissertation on the study of icons which came into existence miraculously.

HORSE-KICKER: Like the Shroud of Turin.

FR. WALE: Well, that's debatable; I would say more like the Mandylion of Edessa, an image of Jesus' face which somehow reached King Abgar in AD 384, without ever having been commissioned or, apparently, painted by anyone. These objects are called "true images not made by human hands"...the "true" part being often deemed more important than their definitive source. We are still very afraid of "false images" in the Church, you see—and rightly so.

HORSE-KICKER: Why?

FR. WALE: This is what the iconoclasts of the Byzantine Empire asked themselves. They believed, as Muslims do today, that to portray the face of God, His saints, His mother, was an imposition, a heresy in itself. How can we know that the face of *a* Jesus is the face of Jesus? Human artists are inspired by many things. A man may see what he thinks is the face of the Madonna on a whore, and paint it into his study of the classic *pieta*; his perfect Jesus could be a drunk, his St. Peter a criminal. To the artist, it's all a valid interpretation.

But to those who believe God has, *can* have, only one true face, it's blasphemy—literal idolatry. If what you're worshipping isn't a true depiction of God, then where do the prayers you address to it end up? You might think you were worshipping Almighty God, legitimate Creator of Heaven and Earth, source of every good thing in existence, only to later find out you were...

HORSE-KICKER: ...worshipping someone else? Some*thing*—?

FR. WALE: (A pause. Then) ...Mistaken. Yes, I think that would be the appropriate English word. Mistaken.

HORSE-KICKER: Is that why Father Mihaly Doncheff asked you to go to Macedonia with him?

FR. WALE: In a way. You know where I come from, originally?

HORSE-KICKER: Uh, yes, I think—Dr. Abbott said Nigeria.

FR. WALE: Offa, that's where I was born...a little village, near the border. My father was a doctor, a very smart man, very scientific—he was educated in Lagos—but he was also Yoruba, and of course he told me many strange things that were specific to our area, many...tribal things. But there were always refugees coming in from other areas, trying to leave through the ports, to go to England or America and claim political asylum—fleeing from wars and famines in Sierra Leone, Liberia, Cote d'Ivoire. And once I remember a Temne woman passing through, and she was pregnant, with twins...

Now, you have to understand that the Temne have very specific cults and beliefs around the birth of twins: They think all twins are river demons who have somehow managed to enter the mother's womb while she was bathing, and so they are related to every type of reptile, and they can live on land or in the water. They also believe that if a child is born deformed, that child should be returned to the bush—but if the deformed child is a twin, you must treat it with great respect, and do many rituals while exposing it. Because you don't want to take the chance, obviously, that the child's relatives—the reptiles—might be insulted by the way you treat it when you are...

HORSE-KICKER: ...*killing* it? This—helpless, deformed baby?

FR. WALE: It seems cruel, I know. It *is* cruel. But these people we're talking about haven't accepted Christ yet. They see things in a completely different way than we do.

Anyhow, this Temne woman had her babies, and my father delivered them. One of them was clearly megacephalic, with a huge, misshapen head; the other was fine, perfect. And because my father knew what the woman would want to do with the deformed baby, he made plans to send both children to the hospital in Lagos...but before he could, there was an outbreak of sleeping sickness, which is spread by a very pernicious water-borne parasite. He was called away.

So that night, the woman and another so-called "doctor"—a tribal medicine worker, a male witch—snuck out of my father's surgery, leaving the "good" baby behind with the nurses. They carried the deformed twin to a cotton tree in the bush, and they dressed the baby and the doctor in red, and they made the usual offerings: a bottle of wine, rice flour, some chicken's eggs. They started to sing some songs.

HORSE-KICKER: Then what happened?

FR. WALE: It's hard to say...I wasn't there. But the woman said the baby started to change his shape from a person to a demon; his head became the head of a snake, and he ate all the rice flour, then burrowed down into a hole at the tree's base and was lost from sight. And at this point the "doctor" told her they should run back to town, because soon the place would become too terrible, and if they stayed there, they would both die.

By the time they came back, having walked all that way, they were both sick—my father said the Temne woman, who you'll remember had just given birth, had peritonitis. And later, the "doctor" *did* die.

HORSE-KICKER: Wait. She walked how many miles, just after having had twins?

FR. WALE: (Laughs) Believe me, it's not impossible! Especially if, like many people from my country, you're used to physical labor...and pain. And if you *really* think you need to.

HORSE-KICKER: So...then what happened?

FR. WALE: Well, my father thought for certain that the Temne woman would die as well—but instead, she got better. She said it was because she had asked her sister to bring her certain leaves, then made a broth and washed with them, which had changed her scent so that if her demon baby came sniffing back around, he wouldn't be able to recognize her as his mother.

HORSE-KICKER: Did anyone ever find the baby's corpse, where they left it? Out in the bush?

FR. WALE: No, but that doesn't mean much—anything might have taken it from under the tree, eaten it, buried it. But to the mother, she'd done exactly what she needed to, and indeed, her other baby—the "good" baby— was absolutely fine after that...it thrived. And when she moved on, finally, she took that baby with her.

Now, who actually knows what happened out there in the bush? Not me; like I said, I wasn't there. But the reason I told you that story is for a bit of...context, I suppose.

In Nigeria, we don't have a tradition of making false images, so much as renaming the ones we already have. The *orishas*, our local gods, have come to be identified with various Catholic saints, just as in Santeria and Voudoun traditions—it's a sort of protective coloration many pagan cults take on, for purposes of survival, after an area has fallen to Christ. And that was certainly what I found in Macedonia, when I went there—something, some*one*, who had been renamed, possibly in an attempt to...understand her? Control her?

HORSE-KICKER: But there was an image involved too. Right?

FR. WALE: Yes.

HORSE-KICKER: Of what?

FR. WALE: I don't know. Not even now, not really. I don't...
(A longer pause)

After I came to the Church and realized my vocation, I attended the seminary in Lagos, and eventually, I was ordained. This was in 1990. And following my ordination, my first real mission was to accompany another priest out into the field on a sort of an internship; Fr. Mihaly, like you said, from the former Socialist Republic of Macedonia. He had been my Comparative Theology teacher—I remember he once gave me a failing grade on a paper about Saint Augustine, and underneath it he wrote: "You argue your points very well. If I thought you actually believed any of what you said, I would have given you an A."

He took me home, to a very small village near Lake Ohrid, probably the oldest lake in Europe, with a unique endemic ecosystem that has come under attack recently because of human encroachment—it used to be full of eels that migrated to spawn in the Sargasso Sea, whose children then returned afterward. But because of hydro-electric dams which have been built near the lake, this is no longer possible, so the eels are kept stocked instead. That's a whole subculture in Macedonia, or was when I was there: eel farming.

It was just after *perestroika*, and Father Mihaly and I were supposed to open a school, instituting an explicitly Bible-based curriculum—cooperate with the local Orthodox Church in order to bring religion "back" to the region, which we all knew meant helping it resurface from where it had been hiding underground, almost since the Revolution. Of course, Macedonia is a place where things are very easy to hide; it's rough, beautiful country, rugged, full of mountains and very cold, very inaccessible. Completely unlike Nigeria. But I was busy there, helping Father Mihaly—so much so, I didn't even have time to get homesick...

Around the same time our school finally opened its doors, a group of fortune-hunters unearthed a buried Byzantine church nearby, on a shelf overlooking the pass our children had to climb through in order to attend pre-class services. They said they were archaeologists, but everyone knew they were really after Scythian gold. It's a very seismic region, so at first, they thought the church had simply been covered over during an avalanche. But the more they studied it, the more they came to believe it had been buried deliberately—probably sometime between the 7th century, when the Byzantines lost control over Macedonia, and the 11th century, when it became a holding of the First Bulgarian Empire.

Since it must have happened during a period of Byzantine iconoclasm, they further theorized the church might have been deemed heretical because it was an iconodule church—it dared to contain an image of the Virgin Mary carrying the Christ-child, surrounded by a train of other children who seemed to be either holding up or sheltering beneath the train of her cloak. I can still see it now, as freshly as the day we entered that church's doors for the very first time...

HORSE-KICKER: Tell me about it, Father.

FR. WALE: I wish I could, truly. Words...fail me whenever I think of that place, in Yoruba *or* English.

As with most churches of the era, we approached through a dim vestibule called a *narthex*, a narrow passageway meant to move us from one world into another. This is the "fennel stalk" or perfume-box, the road to Paradise—the place, traditionally, where unbaptized *catechumens* would be required to stand during services until they had become true converts, finally able to enter and take communion.

But neither Fr. Mihaly nor I had that problem anymore, while those of us who still did weren't about to let it slow them down. So we entered, and looked up...

HORSE-KICKER: What did you see?

FR. WALE: Stars.
(Pause)
Surprisingly small, the space inside. There were catacombs below, or so the "archaeologists" told us—a stairway leading downward was concealed under the altarpiece's cover, easily accessible by rolling away the stone, like Christ's tomb. Above us, however, we saw only an *apse* that enfolded the altar and its canopy, providing the church with its centralized *axis mundi*, the Christian world's turning-point. And that entire apse, its whole hollow, upreaching expanse, was covered with a glass mosaic made from millions of tiny *tesserae*, colored tiles.

I've never seen anything like it, before or since. Most iconographic mosaics position their figures in front of either a gold screen (to represent Heaven's glory) or a clear blue screen (to represent the daytime sky); this whole half-dome was obviously supposed to represent the night...dark and deep, a rich indigo blue, almost navy. And stars, everywhere stars, sprinkled like little white eyes made from fire. They hung above us, peering down pitilessly, watching our every move.

The blue of the night sky around her and the blue of her cloak, her veil, were almost indistinguishable from each other; only the way the stars set behind her, winking out as they touched her shoulders and outlining her with darkness, showed you where they ended and she began. And though she held a baby in her arms—the Christ-child, we assumed—she was, indeed, surrounded by a crowd of other children, all of whom seemed to be shrouded by the bulk of her outflung cloak. But they didn't seem to me as though they were happy or reverent so much as weepy and afraid, transfixed and large-eyed, even by Byzantine standards.

But the strangest thing was her face...

HORSE-KICKER: Her face?

FR. WALE: Well, to begin with, it wasn't made of glass tiles, like the rest of the mosaic; it was carved from some sort of stone, maybe basalt, something shiny and volcanic, so that it pushed forward from the wall in *bas-relief*. Cast its own shadows, seemed to loom over you, in a ghostly sort of way. And—it was black.

She was a black woman, this Virgin. Very smooth, very regular, very beautiful. She looked like a perfect amalgam of all the most beautiful women I might have ever seen at home, before I was ordained...in Nigeria.

HORSE-KICKER: In *Macedonia*.

FR. WALE: Exactly. A black Madonna carved from obsidian, presiding over a congregation of small, scared, white-faced, obviously Macedonian children.

Oh, and one last thing: The baby? It definitely had a halo of some sort, a thin crown made of stars like the ones above and around her. But she held it *towards* her, cradling it close and fiercely to her breast, so you couldn't see its face. Most Virgins hold the Christ-child *outward*, for worshippers to adore—because our Lady, more than anyone else, understands that she is only the caretaker of this infant, our one true Redeemer, who must by His very nature belong to the entire world.

As we stood there, I heard Fr. Mihaly draw his breath, slow and horrified. He said: "It's as I thought: This is not the Virgin. This place is not a church. This place...is cursed."

HORSE-KICKER: Cursed how?

FR. WALE: That's what the "archaeologists" wanted to know. Of course, Fr. Mihaly was in no hurry to tell *them*—he thought they'd spent far too much time inside the church as it was, that they might already be...contaminated.

But later that night, when we were safely back in our lodgings, he told me about a story his grandmother had passed on to him, growing up—not as a legend, a mere fairytale, but as an entirely practical warning. Apparently, she believed that up in the mountains...somewhere above that same pass where the church had been discovered, in fact...lived a very sad, very beautiful woman who only came out at night, who loved all children and should be respected by them in turn—yet avoided at all costs, nevertheless.

Fr. Mihaly's grandmother had taught him a song to sing if he ever met this woman, and he translated its words for me—said they praised her for "protecting" the village children, though in language which could also be interpreted as meaning "for not killing them," or "for not taking them away." He said she was identified with dream and sleep and the sky, like the Egyptian goddess Nut, but that she was just as often identified with disease, in the same way the Bengals consider Sitala Ma—smallpox—a seductive, maternal female deity. The Bengals bribe and flatter Sitala Ma to *not* visit their homes in the middle of the night, to *not* caress their children with her many-spotted hands...

HORSE-KICKER: Did this woman—this goddess—have a name?

FR. WALE: Fr. Mihaly couldn't remember. The next day, however, the "archaeologists" uncovered a ring of Roman lettering around the baptismal font. It said: ORA PRO NOBIS MARYA NOX, "Our Lady of Night."
(A pause)
Though it excuses nothing, it must be remembered I wasn't long in Christ's active service at this point. Yes, my instructors had all told me that the Church was founded as a supernatural society—but how could I possibly know what that meant, really, beyond a metaphor here and a lofty phrase there? It all just seemed so ridiculous.

Yes, the church was unique, singular, even off-putting. But the more passionate Fr. Mihaly became in his belief that it was—*polluted*, somehow—the more it seemed as though nothing untoward at all had come from finding it, let alone opening it. Our school flourished, prospering. I taught all day while Fr. Mihaly grew increasingly frantic, interviewing every village elder he could find, looking for even one amongst them who knew the same tales as his grandmother.

Then a group of die-hard Communists broke in while the "archaeologists" were following up another report of nearby Scythian burial mounds. They desecrated the church as a "non-utilitarian remnant of a decadent age."

The next night, twenty children went to sleep, as usual...and never woke up again.

HORSE-KICKER: Because of—?

FR. WALE: Nobody knew. The village doctor was baffled. Eventually, he started talking about *encephalitis lethargica*...again, sleeping sickness, which is unfortunately fairly normal in Nigeria, but...not in Macedonia.

HORSE-KICKER: This crowd that broke into the church...what did they do, when they were in there?

FR. WALE: Oh, painted Party slogans, stole things. Tried to wrench the Virgin's face out of the wall, which proved impossible. But they also managed to damage several of the individual children in her train, erasing their faces. And...they broke off the Christ-child's head.

Interestingly, the desecrators were very easy to find later, since most of them turned up at a clinic operated by Doctors Without Borders, twenty miles away. They complained of tinnitus and auditory hallucinations—tolling bells, babies crying, a woman's angry whisper. One man, perhaps the ringleader, developed inoperable cataracts on both corneas; he told Fr. Mihaly that when he touched the Virgin's face, she opened her eyes and looked at him.

HORSE-KICKER: Did you ever find out exactly how many of the children's figures were destroyed?

FR. WALE: Yes, certainly. Nineteen.

HORSE-KICKER: And her baby...

FR. WALE: ...makes twenty, yes.

By this point, I thought I knew what to do—what I would have done in Nigeria, at any rate. We all know what to do when things like this happen: Leave. That was my first impulse—this is witchcraft! How insane, how arrogant, to even attempt to fight it! Just bury the church again and go. Only Father Mihaly kept me from getting on a plane back to Lagos, back to transplanted gods and goddesses whose rules I could at least understand. No, he said, we must do something. Okay, I said, finally—let's go and pray for guidance. Let's pray for a plan.

And soon enough, we had one.

We came back the next day, because the area remained rugged and difficult to travel, and no one wanted to go with us during the night. I remember my eyes felt as though they'd been boiled. We'd been up late, blessing enough water to reconsecrate the entire sacristy, which we did...that took some time. Then we went along the whole processional of her children, one by one, and we baptized the ones who'd been damaged, reclaiming them in Christ's name. The rest...we left to her.

While we were doing all this, meanwhile, the local police had been searching every inch of the surrounding area—scouring the bushes, feeling through crevices in the rocks, dragging the creeks. Incredibly grueling work! Finally, they found what they were looking for, in the pit underneath the "archaeologists'" outhouse; one of the desecrators had thrown it down there, as a final insult. But its face was still clean, miraculously enough, and its halo of stars was intact.

I used concrete to reattach the Christ-child's head, turned back to its mother's breast, where it was always meant to be. The sun was going down by then. We lit the candles, and we left.

(A long pause)

HORSE-KICKER: So...what happened afterwards?

FR. WALE: To Fr. Mihaly and I?

HORSE-KICKER: To the village? The children?

FR. WALE: Six of them had been in danger of respiratory failure, attached to life-support machines. They began to breathe on their own again, and the machines were removed. But only one of them ever woke up, a little girl, if that's what you're asking—the rest are still asleep, in a hospital in Skopje, one of Macedonia's finest chronic care facilities. I think the oldest has just turned twenty-seven.

It's a good city, Skopje. Mother Theresa was born there.

But now you're looking at me, Mr. Horse-kicker, wondering how to ask the questions you obviously want to...those hard questions about faith, about salvation. Was it really all for nothing, with no happy ending in sight? Was this goddess, this creature, this...Marya Nox...really so strong? Is *God* really so weak?

HORSE-KICKER: (After a moment) Well, obviously, I don't want to...insult you, Father...

FR. WALE: Oh, don't worry about that; I don't feel insulted. We did what we could: Those children are alive. She does not have them, not anymore; God holds them in the hollow of his hands, their sins forgiven, their suffering over. And one day they *will* wake, in a far better place than this—a place that you and I may see too, one day, eventually. If we keep faith.

Sometimes I still think about that buried church...Marya Nox's sanctuary. I think about who must have designed it, who oversaw the laying of its foundations, or gave the orders to raise it. About who, exactly, carved the face for that mosaic altarpiece. A priest, probably—maybe two priests, even. An old one, perhaps, like Fr. Mihaly, secure in his faith even against this mystery they faced, Biblically versed enough to use tradition against tradition—yet wily and insane enough, as well, to dare re-frame this savage, nameless goddess as the Mother of God, half in heresy, half in hope. To give her a child of her own at last, the Christ-child Himself, who redeems the whole world. Yet not to thereby redeem *her*, so much, as to protect others; the innocent, the unwary. The as-yet-unborn.

And a young one like me, too, as I was then: Not quite so sure, not quite so fore-armed...never quite so sure, not even at the end.

But it is ended. Marya Nox has what is due to her once more, and her place remains hers, sacrosanct. It is over...or as over as it ever can be, at least, given the circumstances.

I'm a bit uncomfortable even now, actually, saying the name out loud. But then again, it's only what the Byzantines called her. Her true name, the one they tried so hard to erase, by making her into a variation on our Lady—perhaps only those children she touched know that. Or Fr. Mihaly.

HORSE-KICKER: Excuse me?

FR. WALE: Yes, him too. A month later, after we had returned to Lagos, he too went to sleep one night, and never woke up.

HORSE-KICKER: Jesus! (Embarrassed) Uh, um. Sorry, Father.

FR. WALE: Don't be. That's a name I *like* to hear.
As for me, I left Nigeria, came here, to Toronto. I never went back. Not yet, anyhow.

HORSE-KICKER: Mind if I ask you how you sleep?

FR. WALE: Me? Pretty well. Most nights.
(Pause)
She was very beautiful, you know.

HORSE-KICKER: I can imagine.

FR. WALE: (After a long pause) No. You really can't.

Transcript excerpt ends here. See full file for further details.

NANNY GREY

Oh low estate, my love my love, the song's hook went, or seemed to, through the bathroom wall. Bill Koslaw felt it more than heard it, buzzing in his back teeth through the sweaty skin of his jaws as he pushed into this naff toff girl—Sessilie, he thought her name was, and the rest began with a "K" as well—from behind with her bent over the lav itself, hands wide-braced, each thrust all but mashing that great midnight knot of hair against the stall's back-tiling. And he could see her lips moving too, half-quirked in that smile he'd literally never seen her lose thus far: *Oh low estate, the threat is great, my love my love (my love)...*

Tiny girl, this Sessilie K., almost creepily so. She looked barely legal, though he'd touched a cupcake-sized pair of breasts beneath that silky top of hers as she pulled him inside the Ladies', nipples long enough to tent the material and one apparently bar-pierced, set inside a shield like a little silver flame which pricked his hand when he'd tried to flick it, drawing blood. And: "Oh, never mind that," she'd said, that smile intact, opaquely unreadable even as she'd leaned forward with her hips hiked high, flipping her skirt up to show her thong already moved neatly aside for easier penetration.

"Bit cruel to your knickers," he'd commented. "Bet those cost a pretty penny."

"No doubt," she'd replied, bum still in the air and both legs wide-spread, aslant on her too-high heels, completely shameless. "But then, it all ends up in the fire eventually. Doesn't it?"

Punctuating it with a bit of a shimmy, like: *Well, get a wiggle on, chip-chop. Don't waste my time, groundling; better things to do, you know. Better classes of fools to fuck.*

Amazing how it puffed him out, that airy contempt of hers, especially when delivered in plummy, strangled Upper Received tones—plumped him like a sausage. But...

He should be liking this better than he was, he reckoned. Some sort of aristocrat, perpetually drunk and perpetually talking, always with her credit card out like it was glued to her palm and no apparent impulse control to speak of; what *wasn't* to like, for Christ's sake?

Just her, he supposed. Her, and almost everything about her.

He slid one hand up to ruck shirt over shoulderblades, and flinched from what he encountered there: Something halfway between a grey-on-grey tattoo of uncertain design and a brand with scabby, keloided edges, so rough it took on a Braille-ish texture beneath his finger-pads. As though if he knew how, he could read it, but only in the dark.

"That a birthmark?"

"Oh, we all have one."

"Your family?"

"Some of them too, yes."

"Who was it you meant then?"

"Oh, Billy, silly Billy. Does it really matter?"

And here she rammed back against him unexpectedly, throwing him off his beat. Singing once more, this time out loud, as she took control of their rhythm: *Ohhhh low estate, the threat is great...*

(*my love*)

"'M I boring you?"

"No, no, never a jot; do carry on."

"What's that then?"

"Quite like this track, is all. I'll stop if you'd like, shall I? Wouldn't want to, mmm...put you *off.*"

She shot him a glance back over her shoulder, with that, and reached back down between her own legs to run one long nail over the seam of his sack—inch-long nails she had, all white with black tips like some odd parody of a French manicure, each with a small black bedazzlement down where the cuticle should be. Pressing just hard enough to make him jump, so she could clamp around him and milk him so fiercely it began to hurt as she tossed one knocked-loose forelock out of her eye and winked at him, eyebrow hiking like a comedienne's. *Winked.*

Jesus wept.

That, right there—as he grunted and came, listening to her give out a rippling, idiot's-xylophone trill sort of a laugh in reply, her own orgasm seeming very much like an afterthought—probably marked the exact point at which Bill stopped feeling anything like bad about always having planned to slip her a Roofie and rob her house later on.

***

Bill'd come to London on a Kon-Tiki packet, planning to round-trip Europe before moving on to the next leg of his pre-Uni world tour. But that'd all been put paid to when this arsehole Gary from Tasmania decided he'd cheated him out of the proceeds from reselling a bag of weed they'd both gone in on and took off with his stuff in revenge—passport, money, tickets, the whole deal.

Now it was three months later, and Bill still hadn't quite worked himself up to the point where he was willing to tell the Old Man what'd happened—just kept on moving from place to place, bed to bed, sofa to sofa.

Squatted here and there, took under-the-counter jobs, and tried to build up some sort of pad. Going to clubs had become about the next ride home, the next overnight, and then—slowly but surely—about whatever he could pick up 'round the flat or the house or wherever before they woke up: Small items of value, gold and silver, electronics; stuff non-specific enough to pawn or fence without being traced, but nice enough they'd bring a fair turnaround.

Girl like Sessilie, wherever she lived, it had to be just *full* of stuff like that—a spread of hockable trinkets peppered in and between the *Lock, Stock & Two Smoking Barrels*-type stuff, antique firearms, paintings and knick-knacks with nice pedigrees, etcetera. That was the assumption anyhow.

He'd long since learned to trust his instincts when it came to such matters, and it'd paid off, literally. Hadn't been wrong once, thus far.

So: "Shouldn't there be somebody home, this time of night?" Bill asked, soon enough, as he half-walked, half-lifted her up the stairs. The place was dark, like 19th-century dark; it was the sort of towering three-story house should really be lit with oil lamps, not cunning little sodium bulbs on dimmer switches. "Place is a bloody tomb."

Sessilie's constant smile skewed a bit to the left, those horrifying nails making a slithery noise on the bannister as she dragged them along its curve. "Oh, there's very little staff left, you know—family holidays, all that. Most of them have already gone down to air out the summer house, for when I'm done with End-of-Term."

"What about your parents?"

"Hmmm, be *quite* the surprise if *they* were here; they've both been dead since I was eight."

"...sorry."

"Oh, no need. Papa crashed a car and killed himself outright, but Mama held on a few days in hospital, at least. And ever after, it's just been me and Nanny Grey."

As she spoke this last name, Bill almost thought he heard something drop in the dark above them—on the next landing maybe, or higher up yet. A strange, stealthy noise like a single clock-tick, or the sound of a bobby pin connecting with the floor. Not footsteps, not exactly. But the dim stairwell and its adjacent hallways took on an air of waiting, of watchfulness, even though absolutely nothing which might be qualified to fill such a role evinced itself.

"You...still have a nanny?" Bill asked, pushing Sessilie up onto what he thought was the second floor, where she laid a finger against her lips and shook her head drunkenly. Then tottered over to a side-table in those ludicrous heels, their clacking muffled by a thick oriental rug, and took out a long candle the colour of bone that she fitted onto a nearby holder with an absurd little flourish, before rummaging in her purse for a cig and lighting it. She took a long drag, then pressed the tip against the candle's wick, which flared into life.

"*Governess* would be the proper term," she explained. "That's what Nanny would say, anyhow. Such an old *bulldog*, Nanny Grey. So protective! She's always been with our family, you see..."

And here she paused just a tick, wavering back and forth, her eyes almost crossing—yet still retained presence of mind enough to stub the cig out in the candleholder's dish and blink over at Bill, rather sweetly. "'Scuse me," she said. "I feel...rather off-colour, all of a sudden. Might I rely on you to get me to bed?"

Slowest-to-take-effect Roofie in all creation, Bill thought, amazed by her stamina. *Ought to check my supply, once this is over with...*

"My pleasure," was what he said out loud though, giving her a leg-out bow, fairytale prince-style. To which she tittered and made him a practiced curtsy, so well-learnt she barely even stumbled; he slung a hand under either armpit and caught her up with ridiculously little effort (so light, her bones like a bloody bird's), letting her fold into him, apparently too tired to yawn. Sleeping bloody Beauty.

The bedroom in question, which she directed him towards with a series of slurry, chest-muffled murmurs, looked almost exactly the way he'd pictured it would—big canopied bed, lots of tulle and organza in shades of black, white, and grey, choked with pillows and fluffy plush dolls: Cute versions of un-cute animals, emo *anime* characters. He set her down in their embrace, and watched her immediately curl into foetal position, tucking a particularly infectious-looking teddy bear—the size of a two-year-old, chenille-furred and shedding worn lace in leprous swathes—down tight between those hungry thighs.

Strange little girl, he thought. Well, he was right to want to be rid of her, and not just for the obvious reasons; best to get to it, then flee this damn place like the plague. Nothing so big should be so empty, so *quiet...*

And there it was again, from somewhere: That *sound*. A dog's nails floor-clicking, one leg at a time. A mouth opening, pop-gasp, only to shut once more, without even an exhaled breath.

Get going, son, Bill's lizard-brain told him: Up or down, bloody pick one, and stick to it. Grab what you find, and scarper.

If only he could tell which direction to avoid—

Closer, now. To his left; no, right.

Bill slid the door shut behind him with excruciating slowness, tensed for the latch's click, and once he heard it, turned left so hard he thought he might twist an ankle. The candle—left abandoned, with only Sessilie's crumpled cigarette butt for company—gave just enough tobacco-scented light to navigate by, and Bill took the stairs upwards in loping strides, two by two by two. His heart hammered fast in his throat, not simply from the stress of keeping things both quick and quiet.

The third floor was smaller than it'd seemed from below: Just a door on either side, master bedroom versus guest room, or maybe office. Forcing himself not to wonder what might be on the other side, Bill twisted the closest knob and slid in sidelong, trying to keep it open just the bare minimum allowable to admit his frame, and thanking God his muscles came mainly from swimming, not footie.

'Cross the floor, tai chi tread, heel rolling straight and narrow to toe with every touch-down, to at least keep the creaks even. This had to be where Sessilie's dearly departed Mum and Dad once shacked up—hung with tapestry like some set for *Hamlet*, a strange mixture of blue velvet and purple trim that shone all the darker in what little moonlight leaked in under drawn blackout shades: Dark like club lighting without the natter of crowds and the underfoot thunder of feet, pulse of music seeping in from everywhere at once as though it were a swarm of tiny biting flies.

(*oh low estate*)

(*the threat*)

(*my*)

Hands numb, Bill felt his way towards the bed, the side tables, palming toggle after toggle in search of drawers, cupboards, some sort of indication that anything'd ever been kept in this damnable room besides memories and a place for wrinklies to shag. Something flat pushed forward under his fingers, slick surface impossible to hold onto, and skittered 'til it hit the ground with a crunch, right in the midst of the brightest moon-stripe: A presumably happy couple trapped under a fresh lattice of cracks, taken someplace sunny enough their faces were almost impossible to make out in detail, except that the man might've had Sessilie's hair colour, while the woman's smile cut the exact same angle as her darling daughter's...

Bill froze, waiting in vain for another of those...no-sounds, those weird, unidentifiable lack-of-noises, but none came. So he just kept staring down as though hypnotized, finding himself trying to make out what that was, there, on the inside crook of dead Mrs. K.'s arm, just angled so the camera barely registered it; grey on grey, uneven edges. It couldn't be...no, stupid idea.

(*No one gets a tattoo—or whatever—just like their mum's, you birk.*)

Not even someone as odd as Sessilie, surely. Or—

But: That *was* it, goddamnit. And *that*...he realized, at pretty much the very same instant...

...was the *noise*.

Stone the crows, it's right behind me.

Before he could tell himself not to, he'd already turned.

At first, he genuinely didn't recognize her without all that high-gloss cack on her face. She'd taken her hair down, proving it to be far longer than it'd seemed when knotted up—brushing her thighs in one thick, glossy, dead-straight fall, shiny-black as her own nail-tips. She'd changed too, into an actual honest-to-God cotton nightie with long, ruffled sleeves and a button-shut front, whose collar went up to her jawline. With skin thus mainly hidden yet feet left bare, she looked both younger than before—enough to make him seriously question his own judgement, in terms of where he'd chosen to stick his tackle—and sexier than ever in a still freakier way, if that was even possible.

"Do you like the rest of my home, Billy?" she inquired, fluttering her lashes at him, slate-blue eyes widened to unreadability. "It's a bit of a dump, but one does what one can. Still, it must've exerted quite a pull on you, for you to go stumbling around here in the dark while you thought I was asleep."

"Well, uh...I was just looking around for..."

"The lav? I do know how you appreciate a nice bathroom, after all. One on every floor, dear; two, sometimes. One wonders how you missed them."

Oh, does *one?* That tone of hers was maddening; not simply the way in which she spoke, but the sentiment—or lack thereof—behind it. And so difficult to listen to as well, somehow, lit and fig: Slipped away whenever the ear tried to fasten on it, pig-greasy with happy idiocy, as though nothing said "like that" could be worth paying attention to, even with only half an ear.

Which was why he found himself trying to focus in on the light she held instead, using its soft flicker to steady himself. "That's from...downstairs, isn't it?" he forced himself to ask in turn.

"Why yes, it is. Funny you should notice."

"Why? I was there when you lit it."

"'Course you were, I knew that. But, you see—this is rather a *special* candle."

She took a moment to run her finger over its uppermost quarter, hot wax slopping onto her in a way that anyone else would find unbearable, and made an odd little fiddly gesture that seemed to make a perfect little approximation of somebody's features emerge from the unburnt portion. Not just somebody's though—for as she did, Bill heard a fold of tapestry pull back, revealing a long, narrow oval of mirror, and glanced automatically towards its surface. There, hanging inside like a drowned corpse under glass, he recognized himself done up full-size, rather than in miniature; his blood congealed, the air itself becoming slow, difficult to move through. He could barely think, barely breathe; his chest heaved painfully, a trapped fish yearning for water.

"Whuh..." was all he could say by way of reply, and Sessilie smirked. Continuing, conversationally—

"Oh, it's an *awfully* amusing story. You see, when one of my mama's great-great-whatevers was clapped in durance vile over having been accused of merry-dancing with Old Sir 'S', she smuggled this candle into the clink to make a dolly out of it. And where she put it, I can't possibly say; a very secret place indeed, if you take my meaning. But..."

With a frighteningly massive effort, Bill managed to half-turn himself back towards the door, though his feet seemed snared in treacle, his Achilles tendons shot full of novocaine. He fell to his knees, spasmodically clutching for Sessilie's ankles, but she skipped back out of range as though playing hopscotch, content to let his own weight carry him down onto all fours. And even then, practically parallel with the floor, he couldn't manage to keep "upright"; everything hurt, gone heavy, impossible to support. His palms gave way to elbows, both equal-burning with sudden pain—knees bowed inwards, joints unsteady. Yet Sessilie simply stared down, with not a whit of sympathy.

"It's special, you see," she went on, "because it can burn all night, and still never quite be consumed. The wax grows back like flesh, so that every new woman of my blood may re-shape the face to their liking, light it, and use it like a Hand of Glory to trap our enemies. Though it has other uses too, of course: Summoning the one who first gave it us, for example, and is sworn to do our bidding just as we, in turn, swear to eventually pay for that long and faithful service."

Behind her, a stirring. A wind ruffling those tapestries' loaded-down edges as *something* passed behind them, dropped pin-quiet, clicking dog's nails-distinct. A lip-pop with every step.

"As for *you*, meanwhile," Sessilie added, not turning 'round, "how long d'you intend to make me wait, exactly? And after all this trouble I've gone to, on your behalf."

The answering voice seemed to come from everywhere and nowhere at once, soft as fallen leaves. Saying, without haste: "A moment's rest is always pleasant, my lady. You do keep me so very busy."

"Really, Nanny, you're *very* lazy, all things considered; greedy too. But then, Mama always warned me you were. *Rule with an iron hand,* and all that."

"Yes, my lady. Your lady mother was a perceptive woman, with—very good taste."

"You aren't being impertinent, are you, Nanny?"

"Only a trifle, my lady. Will you deny me that too?"

"No, Nanny. You may be as impertinent as you like, so long as you do what you're told."

"Yes, my lady."

She rose up then, manifesting from what might have equally easily been the bottom of the tapestries, the dark under Sessilie's parents' bed, or a pile of rags in the corner. Thirty at the most, slim and straight and taller than Sessilie yet bent, willow-graceful, so as not to exaggerate that distinction; coloured white and black and grey like Sessilie's room, with the occasional hint of red at her mouth, her ears, her distressingly long fingers. The dress she wore might've been modelled on Sessilie's nightgown but copied in negative, its fabric less cotton than bombazine, giving off a distinctive swish of underskirts as she stepped forward in her neat little black patent shoes.

The click, the pin-drop, that was the sound of each movement—not a creak, not a sigh, nothing human. As Bill goggled at the realization, she dipped her head as though he'd spoken out loud, projecting: *Yes, I fooled you. I am sorry to play such games. They are the only pleasures left to me, I'm afraid...*

(*Well—almost. I do not mean to lie. Lying is the provenance of your species, not mine.*)

(*But we will talk further of such things, soon enough.*)

"Where'd you...come from then?" he asked her, barely able to raise what voice remained to him above a croak; she simply regarded him silently while Sessilie frowned, tapping her nails so that the candleholder rang dully, a passing bell. Replying, impatiently—

"Really, Billy, don't you *listen*? I told you already, she's always here. This is Nanny Grey."

***

It was a dream—had to be. How else could they have moved from one room to another, on whose walls an array of photos gave way to prints, giving way in turn to portraits, etchings, watercolours, oils? And somewhere in each composition—lurking patient and anonymous, behind or beside the centrepiece arrangement of well-dressed men, women, girls, and even some boys who all shared Sessilie's dead-straight ink-fall of hair, her grey-blue eyes, her cruelly slant smile—a version of Nanny Grey was indeed always present in her long black dress, her sensible footwear, no matter what the era.

"Nanny is my governess, as I said," Sessilie told Bill yet once more, as she pressed him back onto what felt like a nest of sheets. "My servant, my lady-in-waiting. She's my helpmeet, the head of my household; she keeps all of this running, and whatever she does, she does at *my* pleasure." Raising her voice slightly here, a coiled lash, brandished rather than used: "Isn't that so, Nanny?"

"It is, my lady."

"Since—oh, I forget the year. Thirteen-oh-oh something, Mama said..."

"1346, my lady. When the very fount of your blood was almost cut off in full flower, for—was it treason? Yes: You Kytelers are treasonous by nature, I believe. And to kill one's husband then, no matter what provocation might have preceded such a desperate act, was considered just as bad as conspiring to kill the king himself. They burnt women at the stake for it just as surely as for witchcraft, soaked in oil and pitch with no hope of merciful strangulation, whilst crowds screamed and pelted them in garbage."

"Better by far to turn to the Devil than God, under such circumstances," Sessilie chimed in, with an air of quoting something learned by rote. "Or easier, anyhow."

"Down there in the dark, yes, amongst the rats and bones: A bad place for any pretty woman to end. But then again, that *is* where your ancestress Lady Alyce eventually found me, after all—where we found each other, more accurately."

"Quite. But the promise behind our contract isn't enough to satisfy Nanny, you see, not always. And though it's *such* a bother to arrange for boys like you to come visit every once in a while, Nanny does *so* much work on our behalf that she really must be kept happy. It's only good manners."

"I do value good manners, you see. Courtesy, common or otherwise. The little gestures."

"'Manners maketh man', and all that."

"A party dress on an ape, that's all they are, when everything is said and done. But since there's no alternative, they simply have to do."

"Given it must've been God who deeded you to us in the first place, directly or in-, do you think perhaps we might be part of *your* Hell, Nanny?"

"I often ask myself that very question, my lady."

"But to no avail?"

"None, my lady."

"That's prayer for you, Nanny."

"Yes, my lady."

Nanny Grey eddied forward with one long white hand on her breast, head bent down submissively. And when she looked up, eyes pleasantly crinkled, she smiled so wide that Bill could see how her teeth were packed together far too numerously for most human beings, bright as little red eyes in the wet darkness of her mouth. While her eyes, on the other hand, were white—white as real teeth, as salt, as a blank page upon which some unlucky person's name had yet to be inscribed, quick and cramped with the pen pressed so hard to the paper its nib nearly tore through, in ink thick as blood.

"Little master," she murmured. "You wished a tour, I believe, and no one knows this house better than I. Come with me, please."

"I don't—"

"Oh, it will be no trouble; what my lady orders, I do. For as she told you, this is the bargain between us—the terms of my employment."

"Yes, and I do hope you were finally paying attention, silly Billy. Because with so little time left, I'd hate to have to repeat myself."

Sessilie leant down then, pressing one ear to Bill's chest, in a vile parody of post-coital relaxation. But when Nanny Grey laid one of those too-long hands on his forehead a moment later, he felt his heart lurch and stutter as though he were about to have a heart attack, pounding double, triple, quadruple-time; Sessilie must've heard it right through his muscle wall, for she gave yet another of those rippling torturer-savant laughs, and he wanted nothing more than to be able to rouse his limbs enough to tear her soft white throat open with his thumbs. Possibly the impulse communicated itself to her the same way, for she drew back, pouting a bit.

"I'm going to tell you something now, Billy," she said, "because I actually quite like you, all things considered. One day, when I turn Nanny over to *my* daughter the way Mama turned her over to me, she will take me wherever she's taking you—wherever she took my mama, and hers before her, so on, etcetera. Back to the first of us, great Lady Alyce in her shit-filled cell. So there; that might help."

Bill swallowed hard, barely scraping enough air to whisper: "It...really...doesn't."

"Mmm, s'pose not; shouldn't think it would. But then, I did only say 'might.'"

He sank down further then, excruciatingly slow, into a deep, deep blackness. Only to hear them still arguing, as he went—

"Do this, Nanny Grey; do that, Nanny Grey. Eat up, Nanny Grey. You'll expect me to digest him completely as well, I'm sure, just to save you the trouble of having to cover up your own indiscretions."

"Well, I could simply take him away now, if you'd prefer—but what on earth would be the use of that, considering? There are limits to even your perversity, I'm sure."

"Really, it's you Kytelers who are the lazy ones. Never doing anything for yourselves... What sort of example do you think that sets for everyone else?"

"Oh, pish-tosh, Nanny. Why should we have to make the effort, when we have *you* to do it for us?"

"...crazy..." Bill told them both, through stiffening lips, to which Sessilie only smiled, as ever. While Nanny Grey raised a single perfectly arched eyebrow, expressionless as a cast pewter mask, and murmured, in return: "I had *wings* once, little master. You'd be disappointed too, I'd venture, if you found yourself where I find myself now."

"Poor Nanny. Quite the come-down, wasn't it?"

"A fall, yes, both long and hard. And at the end of it—"

"Me," Sessilie supplied, brightly. "Wasn't that nice?"

A pause, infinite as some gigantic clock's gears turning over, millennial, epochal. Deep time caught in the shallowest of all possible circuits, and only digging itself deeper. After which Bill heard the thing that called itself Nanny Grey reply, with truly terrible patience—

"...even so, my lady."

NIGHT-BIRD

Somewhere in the dark, just at evening, there always seems to be a bird who calls out loudly, sounding betrayed. It's a fierce, braying call. You hear it rise up over the rooftops, past the powerlines, to graze the lowermost clouds. Orange and pink and red against a dark blue sky, almost navy; dusk never looks like this in the country. In Toronto, though, people just shrug and say *it's the pollution,* as if that's something to be proud of.

Some mornings you wake up with your eyes stinging like you're about to cry, not knowing over what. Some days you look out down Ossington, where the road dips towards the business district and then further still, running straight into the lake, and see the whole horizon turn sepia as the air takes on a stinging brown tinge: heat haze, exhaust, effluvia of a million different engines, downtown's constant racket. The city, building and rebuilding itself, with nowhere left for it to go but up.

C'mon, though, baby, Levi used to say. *It's good here, right? Better than it ever could've been, if we'd stayed.* And you would nod, smiling: Oh yes, yes. Of course it is. Of course.

Where you came from is a shell of a place, operating on half-speed, half-life. No work since the plant shut down, and the summer people don't make up for it. It's a place to drive through, not to live. So Toronto *is* an improvement, obviously, in almost every way, with no room for debate—not that Levi ever would've brooked any.

You came here two years ago, give or take. Drove all night and part of a day to a buddy's house in Mimico, then camped there 'til the job he'd been promised made you enough for first and last month's rent. After that it was somewhere further in, Queen West, almost to Roncesvalles. The last streetcar stop before that final highway underpass between city proper and suburban sprawl, where foxes sometimes crept out of the foliage and skunks waddled down the alleyways like fat, crippled cats. Misa and Aaron used to crouch in the front yard of your apartment building, watching fascinated as a steady stream of thumbnail-sized black-lacquer beetles colonized the ruin of a dead stump. Not much else to watch if you didn't count crazy homeless people wandering by, so it wasn't like you blamed them, especially since Levi couldn't afford cable.

It'd have been bearable if you could have both gotten jobs, or if you'd been able to pay someone else to watch Aaron and Misa long enough for you to find one, let alone keep one. Instead, it was you and them stuck inside a tiny no-bedroom or out roaming the streets until Levi came home, unable to stay in coffee shops more than fifteen minutes at a time, for fear you'd be asked to pay for something. An endless drudgery of maintenance and busywork, scraping together edible meals from whatever was cheapest and trying to keep them quiet when Levi finally started to beat you, so the neighbours wouldn't complain. All of which still holds true, to one degree or another, but at least these days you don't have to do it with one eye blacked, or nursing a cracked rib.

Your first real job in Toronto, therefore—arranged by Miss Sada at the shelter, the still point your life now revolves around—has you cutting and packaging at Abreu's Meats for ten hours a day, six to four, at which point you hand over to Mrs. Abreu's son Joao, so he can re-stock and close out. Your landlady, Mrs. Cambres, looks after the kids, one of a loose coven of women—mostly little, mostly older, though it's hard to tell exactly how old— who volunteer at the shelter, running mini-daycares out of their living rooms for "transitioning" shelter graduates. Misa and Aaron love her, especially when she sings them Portuguese songs about the boogeyman in her low, slightly creaking voice:

Vai-te, Coca. Vai-te, Coca.
Leave, big eater. Leave, eater of children.
Para cima do telhado,
Go to the top of the roof,
Deixa o menino dormir
Um soninho descansado
And let the child have
A quiet sleep.

"Three more months and you can get them into kindergarten, down at Saint Joe's," Mrs. Cambres tells you, clucking in refusal when you try to press whatever you can into her hand at the end of the day. "No, no, away with it! You're gone from that *cahorro,* that's my payment, *doce.* Spend it on candy."

Hunched in her black, her scarf pulled up, those fierce eyes unblinking, round and cataract grey-blue behind their thick-lensed spectacles. She's a lump of a woman, solid from top to bottom, but she moves fast and silently— almost too silent to hear coming. Appears without warning at your elbow through a haze of fatigue, every afternoon when you come to pick them up, and cocks her head to one side, smiling, her nose like a hooked blade.

"It's hard, isn't it, *doce?*" she asks, sympathetically. "I remember! They can suck the blood right out of you, these little ones, if you let them."

You want to agree, particularly on Monday nights, but there's something about the phrase you don't feel quite comfortable with. "Well," you say, finally, "they can't help it, right?"

"No, no. Of course not." Adding, after a moment: "Mine were the same."

Somewhere, the bird cries out, louder than ever. "What *is* that?" you ask her, before you can stop yourself, only to watch Mrs. Cambres cock her head even further, as though her neck's too stiff to move any other way—just turn and keep on turning, 'til her hidden ear almost brushes her shoulder. "Just a night-bird," she says, her great eyes umber-tinted in the fading light. "There's a story we tell about it, a silly story. Right, *criancas*? The bird that looks for his mother."

"She says they're witches, those birds," Aaron corrects, sleepily, later on, as you tuck him in. "All of them. And that's not what they're looking for either."

"Witches don't have mommies," Misa argues, from the other side of the bed.

"No, stupid: they *are* mommies, that's what Mrs. Cambres said. They're looking for kids, to eat."

"*Their* kids?"

"No, 'cause they don't have any, not anymore. 'Cause they ate *them* all first."

You frown. "Go to sleep," you tell him—both of them. And close the door behind you, leaving it open just a crack.

In the living room, there's that book you forgot to take back to the library, the one you found in your bag the day you finally walked away from Levi—right at the bottom, in a tangle of diapers and snack-packs, when you turned it out on the bed they assigned you at the shelter. The spine is cracked, so every time you open it up it falls to almost this exact line: *Half gods are worshipped in wine and flowers. Real gods require blood.*

That same phrase, over and over. And that same bird outside your window, somewhere in the dark, screaming.

***

Little Portugal is littler now than it's ever been. Go north, it turns into Koreatown; go south, and it's a mess of newcomer territories, all Ethiopian restaurants, Belarusian dry cleaners, Nigerian thrift shops. This is the heart of the old neighbourhood, a nest of stores, garages, churches, and houses whose facades don't look like they've changed since either the 1980s or even the 1950s. Time stands still. Even the payphones aren't digital.

"The *bruxsa*, right, Ma?" Joao calls back to Mrs. Abreu, after you somehow let slip what Aaron said last night. "They turn into—owls, or ravens, or something. Big black birds, only come out at night."

Mrs. Abreu doesn't nod, just turns to you, lips frown-pursed. "Who's been telling you about that?" she demands.

"Uh...Mrs. Cambres, and it wasn't me, it was my kids."

"Belinha, hey? Well, I wonder. That's a bad story for bedtime; she knows better."

You shrug, helpless; Mrs. Abreu keeps on staring, while you busy yourself with cutting chops. And a half-minute later the bell rings as another customer enters, distracting her.

Around hand-over time, meanwhile, Joao tries to coax you into meeting him for a drink at some local place—not for the first time, and probably not the last. He seems like a good guy, big but gentle, but all you can ever think of is how your body betrayed you last time, giving you thoughts like these—Levi seemed nice too, after all, at least by comparison. Because that's how men like him work, you've learned since: find someone who's already isolated, someone with no real sense of what's "normal," and keep on deforming her standards until there's no firm place anymore, 'til she's left with nothing but the same set of victim's instincts already keeping them alone, and ignorant, and scared.

Get her pregnant, twice, so close together it's like she had twins; allow her to bond with the kids before going back on the attack, so her own biology makes her love them just fiercely enough to fear for *them,* instead of herself. 'Til everything is a swamp of fear and panic, panic and fear and dread.

What a mistake you were! your mother used to say between rants—tell you how you'd ruined her, in gory detail, before running your father off and condemning the two of you to that craphole you grew up in, an ever-narrowing passage through which you could occasionally glimpse hints of what looked like a better class of people living a better sort of life, something you might aspire to one day, if you could only stay quiet, and pleasant, and clean.

Which only set you up for Levi, in the end—a mistake too, just like Aaron, and Misa. Mistakes, compounded. Mistakes making mistakes, and so on, into infinity.

So no, you're not going out with Joao, not now, not ever: you don't want risk, and you're not too scared to admit it. *No one wants a girl with baggage,* that was another of your mother's lines, and ever since Aaron was born, you've felt as though everything inside you keeps shifting around, opening new wounds when the first ones—the worst, the most-lasting—aren't even halfway healed yet. Even your period fluctuates, when it used to be so regular you could tell time by it: comes on a different day each month, often without warning, so hard and fast it's cost you clothes. You don't feel yourself, haven't for years. Like...somebody else. Some*thing* else.

When you get home, Aaron runs to meet you with something in his hand. "Look, Mom," he says. "We found it outside."

"It's *gross,*" Misa adds, brightly.

A nugget of some kind—mud, close-packed. Broken open, it yields dust, grass, compacted mulch, and a handful of other, smellier things: broken bones, hollow, sparrow-sized; a beaked skull, crushed flat and twisted, as though forced through some narrow, flexing tube. And something else, at the very bottom: moon-shaped, rimmed in faint glitter, snapped across the bed. Is that...

(a fingernail?)

"From an owl," Mrs. Cambres says, over your shoulder. "Hey, Aaron? They swallow things whole, digest what they can, then cough out the rest."

"That's what Miss Saba said—she showed us, in a book. *101 True Facts About Birds of Prey.* Can we get pizza, Mom?"

"Not tonight, honey."

"Daddy'd get pizza," Misa mutters, downcast. She can barely remember Levi, though, hopefully. A few more months, and she'll have lived half her entire life without him in it.

Mrs. Cambres has a roof garden, shaded from the sun by a trellis heavy with purple grapes whose bitter skins slip off whole in your mouth when you bite them, insides popping nude and sweet, like eyeballs. She makes her own wine too, and when she offers you a glass, you take it. Sip it slowly, staring down at the streets you walked to get here from above, while she gives you all the latest gossip about people you barely know, a lulling tangle of equally forgettable names, dates, relationships. It's like having the TV on low, listening to soap operas spool out without knowing any of the particulars, only that the world is full of people at least as unhappy as you've ever been, their choices just as haphazard, as badly conceived, as ultimately unfulfilling.

"You look tired, *doce,*" Mrs. Cambres says, topping you up. "Not sleeping well, hey? Children eat up everything, I know—the worry, the expense. And thinking of him still, maybe?"

"I...hadn't been," you say, washing the lie down with a swig.

"Might be he looks for you, I suppose. You came some ways, to get here... Walked in, Miss Sada says, with just those two and your own shoes, the clothes on your back. That must have been hard."

"Took a while," you agree. "Hours. But at least I had the stroller."

"At least that, yes. Another glass?"

"...please."

That night you dream, for the first time in weeks. You stand on the roof, under the trellis, looking down, and you see Levi pass below you—only from above, obviously, but you know it's him, you *know.* That hair. That walk. Stamping down the road, hands fisted, eyes roaming: looking for you, for Misa, for Aaron. Looking for trouble, ready to make some, always. Ready to make even more mistakes.

This is my place now, you think. *Mine, not yours. Never yours.*

And you stretch out your arms, black feathers blooming everywhere, wings breaking from your shoulders with a snap, like pirate sails. Eyes rounding, fixing. Fingers and toes sharpening, hooking like great horn blades, serrated raptor's claws.

Look up, you think. *See me, for once. For the very last time.*

Here I am.

***

"Was a guy in here looking for you, after you left," Joao tells you the next morning, as you let yourself in through the back. He's never waiting for you when you arrive, so you already know something's wrong; Mrs. Abreu's opened up early, standing where you usually do, wrapping a rack of ribs. "I didn't tell him anything—didn't think it was my place. But I told Ma, and she said to catch you before you started working."

The ground beneath you seems to heave, up and down, a caught breath. "What did he look like?" you make yourself ask, finally.

"Oh, you know: white guy, 'bout my age. Said his wife ran off, took his kids, he was checking shelters, already got the run-around from Miss Saba. Asked me if I'd seen somebody fit her description."

"That could be anybody."

"Showed me a picture, Sarah; you, and the little ones. Pretty sure it's him."

You want to shut your eyes, but the lids won't cooperate. "I don't know what to do," you say, finally.

Joao shrugs. "Go back to Mrs. Cambres's, hole up for a while. We'll keep on stalling him 'til he gets fed up and goes away, then call you when it's safe."

"He's a...he *can* be a very patient man, Joao. When he thinks it matters."

"Yeah, well, what's he gonna do? He calls the cops 'round here, first one turns up's gonna be my uncle, or my cousin. Not to mention if he tries anything else, Ma'll hit him with her broom."

"Thank you. Thank Mrs. Abreu for me too. I—" Now your eyes are filling up, making you blink. "I don't deserve this, you being so understanding. Especially when it's busy."

"Don't be dumb. Now get goin', okay?"

"...okay."

Back out in the alley, the dregs of a hangover make you squint, turning the familiar strange. Everything seemed so pleasant when you walked over, humming, remembering Misa and Aaron in front of their cartoons. Now you almost can't remember the direction you came from, afraid that whichever way you turn, you'll see Levi's face coming around the next corner. You almost run the rest of the way, bent and panting, shielding your face with your fingers; Mrs. Cambres opens the door as you fumble with the keys, pulling you in by one wrist—her long nails denting the skin, one degree of micro-pressure away from a scratch—and bolting it behind you.

"Upstairs," she orders. "You need to lie down and gather yourself so you don't frighten the children, looking like that."

"Levi—"

She flourishes a finger in your face, making a scolding sound. "Ch-ch-

ch! None of him. No one comes in this house I don't invite them, believe you me. Calm, *doce*. I'll take care of everything."

Upstairs, you pull the covers up to your chin and stare at the ceiling, watching shadows lengthen as the day ticks on. Aaron and Misa play, but quietly, barely registering on the outskirts of your attention; Mrs. Cambres might as well not even be in the house, for all the noise she makes.

You fall asleep sometime between early afternoon and late, waking to blue-orange twilight and the sound of your children whispering to each other in the next room, voices fading in and out. "...Daddy?" Misa seems to say, but Aaron shushes her. Then nothing but your own breathing, the steady beat of your heart, trees brushing against the window—and are those footsteps, up above? Mrs. Cambres on the roof, tending to her garden?

That bird cries again, closer than ever, making you jump. Like it's in the room with you.

We can't stay inside forever, your mind tells you, weakly. *What if the kids get sick, if they need medicine? What if he comes back, with friends? What if someone else tells him this is where we live? If he can't have me, you know he'll take them, just for spite. And not even because he really* wants *them, but just because he knows how much it'd hurt—*

When did he become so huge in your mind, exactly? When did he burn that hole in the middle of everything, the one you constantly orbit, through which the light drains out?

When you figured out that the only place left to go for free was the library, you started spending almost the whole day there, after your chores were done. That stopped when you forgot the time, and Levi came looking. He broke your nose in the children's section, and when you wouldn't let them call the cops, they told you both to leave.

A week later you came back, heart beating hard, barely able to breathe—Misa and Aaron both dozing in their big double stroller, the last thing Levi's parents bought for you. You Googled shelters, found the one that looked farthest away, printed out a map, and walked there. It took eight hours, the last three with Misa screaming, Aaron begging you to go back home. But when you got there, Miss Sada took you in, and things began to change.

You took nothing with you, or good as. Levi'd made sure there was never anything left around for you to take. No phone. No money. Everything you have now you've made for yourself, aside from whatever came out of the bluff, curt kindness of women like Mrs. Abreu, Mrs. Cambres—those dark-scarved neighbourhood ladies at the meat shop, at the dollar store, in the playground park just outside the church, always sitting there together, waving friendly as the priest walks by, though they never seem to actually go inside. They smile at each other, when they think you can't see; stare up over the rims of their spectacles, fierce front-facing eyes squinting only slightly, peering past you as they speak, always on the lookout for something. Like birds after prey.

A few months ago, when Aaron gave Misa his cold, Mrs. Cambres made them cordial you only gave them a few sips of, and only the once. It made them sweat and shiver, complaining about bad dreams. You swallowed some yourself, then poured the rest surreptitiously down the drain, scrubbing the sink out with your fingers. And that night you dreamt you were riding a bicycle down a long, dark hill, straight into the wind until your coat lifted up on either side, tails flapping like wings.

Men aren't worth much, one of Mrs. Cambres's cronies once told you, comfortingly—you can't remember her name now, if you were ever told it. *We all know this, hey? You like them, but they don't like you, not really—none of us. That's just how it is.*

Men knock you down, another agreed. *Women lift you up, or should—if they know what's good for them. We'd do away with men entirely, maybe, if they weren't so much fun.*

Hmm, yes, Mrs. Cambres put in, fingers busy with her needlework. *Though they do make good eating, sometimes.*

Like children, the second woman replied. And laughed.

***

Then, all at once, you're suddenly awake, bladder full, mind fear-pricked. You creep into the children's room and stand there looking down at them for what feels like ten minutes, watching them sleep, and wondering: How much of Levi is inside them, deep down? Will Aaron, the sweetest boy you've ever known, one day whisper to a weeping woman that he'd rather see her dead than live without her? Will Misa reckon her love by bruises? Not if you can help it. But can you? Can you really "help" anything?

Never have before, that voice—your mother's voice—whispers in one ear, too fast for you to shake it away, like a mosquito. And you feel a shock run right through you, a bolt to the back of the head, some slaughterhouse kiss: paralyzingly familiar, potentially inevitable.

What if nothing ever does change, really—not permanently anyhow? Because of weakness, inertia, karma. Because that's just what you deserve. What if—

Enough, another voice replies, possibly out loud, though since the kids don't stir, you're not quite sure. *Come downstairs, doce. See what I've done for you.*

You come down slowly, one step at a time. And even from here you can see there's somebody sitting at the kitchen table, hunched forwards with hands folded, his face a blank black blur under the centre-set light. Even from here, by the very way he sits, you can see that it's Levi.

Mrs. Cambres sits in front of him, her back to the stairs, to you. So small she barely comes up to his chest. She doesn't look around, not even when—before you can think of stopping yourself—you make a noise like that one bird, high and harsh: all rage, no fear. A hunting owl, about to swoop.

I'll kill him, you think. *He'll never touch them. I'll kill him right here, right now.*

"Oh, no need, *doce,*" Mrs. Cambres says, in her creaky voice. "Come closer, and I'll show you."

As you stand there trembling, caught between movements, her head begins to turn, then keeps on turning. Turns until you can hear the pop of cartilage and see both her fierce orange-tinted eyes staring straight into your own, her mouth smiling secretive under that bladed nose, even as her clawed fingers tighten on the table in front of her, carving delicate little runnels into its dark-stained surface. And over her head, you feel your own gaze suddenly sharpen, zooming like a telescope to show you Levi slumped upright in rigour, collar peeled down to reveal that beak-hole knocked straight through his jugular vein, the lapel below soaked black along its edge. How the waxy pallor of his face and hands demonstrates exactly how much blood he's lost, if not where most of it actually *went,* aside from the slopped overflow.

Mrs. Cambres licks her lips, one two, mordantly deliberate. One fixed eye twitches, attempting a wink. "*Bruxsa,*" you name her, automatically. And see her hands rise, to clap.

"I knew you paid attention," she says, approvingly. And lets her head snap back to where it should be, front-facing, before kicking back her chair and getting up, with a slight *huff* of effort. Muttering, as she does: "Not as young as I was, but well enough still, when there's work to be done. Now, shall we?"

"...shall we what?"

"Go up, *doce.* Let me show you the world, like Satan did for Jesus."

Another blink—yours, this time. After which the two of you stand under her trellis, looking out on the empty street below: black trees, streetlamps burning yellow, casting more shadow than light. Above, the sky hangs heavy, no stars, only clouds. Though you don't know what there is to see by, you find you can see just fine, nevertheless: the roof, the garden, her. Yourself.

Hands crooking, nails itching, longing to grow and hook. Back hunching, shoulders flaring, blades sharp as wing-roots. Hair lifting to flare against the moist night wind, a ruff of long, limp feathers.

"So now we come to it," Mrs. Cambres tells you. "Your decision, *doce—* to take this gift, or throw it away, unopened? For myself, it was enough to drink that *cahorro* dry, to do what you thought you couldn't...but then, I like you. I always wanted a daughter."

"So—it's all true then? Witches like birds, drinking blood?"

She makes a little flourish with one hand, dismissive, yet not entirely un-proud. "As you see. We were in Rome and Greece, long before this, meeting at the crossroads, making our prayers to the Three-Faced One, who answers all women. I had a husband once, fit for nothing but to leave me his name, his house. And children too—I told you so, hey? How I remembered."

"Yes, you did. What happened?"

"*I* happened. This is the price, *doce*. It's not like God the Father and His soft son. When pain becomes unbearable, we call out to whatever will answer us, and pay with whatever they ask for."

"Aaron...Misa? No, I won't. Never that."

"Then you won't. You don't have to, sweet girl—not yourself, not directly. Not so long as you have me to look after you."

That shock again, straight through the heart, like a nail. "You...stay away from them," you manage, at last. "I'll kill you, you understand? If you even *try*—"

"Like you should have killed *him*, to save us both the trouble? He went to sleep every night, *doce*, right in the same bed; anyone could do it, if they had the will. So *easy*. But you ran instead, hey?" She pauses, owl-eyes flat, pupils narrowing. "Where will you run to now, I wonder?"

Where indeed.

"Nowhere," you say, lashing out, prompted by movement you can't see: that *stoop* before lift-off, a change considered, not yet embarked on. And you push her headlong off the roof before she can even think to take flight, come tapping at your children's window in disguise with sharp beak open, blood-seeking—

—Mrs. Cambres, this poor old lady, your only friend, your protector. Her dark scarf ripped free as she falls, too shocked to cry out, scarring the sky.

Mistake, it's a mistake, like always, like everything else: oh, you crazy damn bitch. Why would you do that, *why?*

Because I had to, you think. *Because she killed Levi. Because—*

(—he was *mine* to kill, not hers. And she knew it.)

What if she changes when she hits the ground though, or before? that voice asks—maybe your mother, maybe yourself—from deep inside. *Who'll stop her then? Didn't think of that, did you?*

No. But it doesn't matter.

I'll stop her, you answer it, without hesitation. *Me.* Then repeat, out loud: "*Me.*"

And find, in the very next instant, that you've already thrown yourself off after her, without a second thought—impossible to stop, this final choice, as perhaps it always was. Taking flight, in flashes: here, there, gone.

Screaming that same lost bird's cry as you plunge, headlong, into the night.

ONE IN THE MORNING AND ONE AT NIGHT

How it happens is simple, like any other accident, any other wound. Alena is walking to the garbage, a bag in either hand, when suddenly she's seized by the notion that if she turns her back on the utterly empty end of the hallway—lamps outside each door hanging like bleached lanterns, slack and odd, deflated pod-cocoons—something dimly globular will immediately eddy 'round the corner like a plastic bag caught in an updraft and unfurl itself into a flatly whitish figure which will then move down the hall towards her, zig-zag style: back and forth in a scuttling, insectile motion, partly crawling and partly slithering, partly gathering itself as though to pounce.

And: *One in the morning and one at night,* something says from the back of her head, clear as any passing wasp's whine. *One in the morning...and one at night.*

Stupid, impossible: Where's this coming from? Yet she finds she can't close her eyes against it, can't even shake her head; there's no dismissing—whatever it is. This struck bell. This resonance.

Soon she's back in her apartment, the upper clasp-lock firmly seated, with both bags still moping in the kitchen. Tomorrow, she tells herself, she'll take them down to the corner and shove them through the slot for recycling, because it's bigger. They don't stink *that* much.

But her dreams smell of decay that night, and a tone runs underneath everything, a hiss. The dead-technology sense-memory of static on an empty channel.

***

And then, going down to the recycling room, there's that incredibly dark elevator with the brass fittings and the dicey ceiling lighting, completely mirrored inside, so that all you can see around you is an infinitely regressing series of darknesses. What if the thing she didn't exactly *see* upstairs was to come blowing in between floors as it grinds its excruciating slow way down and unfurl just below her sightline, so that she's sure it's crawling her way but unable to confirm or deny that suspicion—unable to predict exactly when, not if, it might suddenly jump up and plaster itself against the glass, right in front of her face?

One in the morning, the no-voice says from much closer now—next to her ear or perhaps even inside it, its lack of breath tickling the drum. *And one at night...*

(*But it's not even afternoon,* Alena thinks, ridiculously.)

She bolts the second the doors chunk open and makes the mailroom, then stuffs both bags down inside the flip-top bin meant for junk post. Let the cleaning staff deal with it; they'll be right not to thank her, but then again, they won't exactly know *who* to not thank, short of ripping them open and going through her egg- and coffee-saturated detritus.

Stairs back up again, two by two, pulling herself by the railing, fast as she can manage. Her heart hammering harder with every fresh step, until the spit in her mouth tastes like blood.

***

I have a thought in my head; remove it for me. Was that Pepys? Googling doesn't seem to help.

Half a week running, she dreams that the apartment bathtub, hidden behind its opaque shower curtain, is occupied by something pitifully long and thin, its boneless arms crossed over a concave breast in some sort of parody of repose. Above, its head tips back, noseless, eyes rolled 'til only a feeble gleam of ball shows in the sockets' deep shadow.

It smiles at her when she draws the plastic back with shaking dream-hands, as though trying to prove itself no threat. Wet teeth in the dark, elongated from shrunken gums.

She wakes sweat-covered, chilled, praying to find herself alone. Thinks, without wanting to: *One at night.*

Morning finds her elsewhere, roaming the streets outside, trying to outpace whatever the voice wants to show her, by the feeble breaking light of dawn.

***

"You look tired," Alena's mother says. "And—dirty too. Frankly, dear, you don't smell nice."

"Something wrong in the building," Alena tells her. "They've had the water off, for...three days, almost."

Her mother frowns. "Is that legal?"

"I think I'd know by now, if it wasn't."

Her mother talks some more at her, and Alena just nods her head, submissive. No point in arguing, especially when she can barely hear what she's saying.

One in the morning, and one at night. One in the morning, and one at night. One in the morning...

She entertains brief fantasies of a world without either, perpetual twilight, infinite dusk. Thinks: *This'll pass, it has to. I just...have to stop thinking. I have to stop thinking of these things. Get them out of me, someplace I can catch hold of them, like bugs. Crush them. Burn them. Wash them down the drain...*

Writing them down doesn't seem to help, though, either. It only makes them more palpable, somehow—more *definite*. More real.

Moving ever closer, unseen, unstoppable, no matter what she does, or doesn't do. *One in the morning,* always. And then, as day ticks away, eventually...

...*one at night.*

***

These thoughts which come with utter insistence into her mind, so intrusive and strange and palpable it's as though they originated in someone else's brain. That come without warning and without reprieve, so strongly she frankly begins to fear it's the mere fact of her ever having been stupid enough to pay them any mind in the first place which will, inevitably, eventually *force* them to come true.

Did she invite this? What brought it on? Was it something she did? Something she is?

Is there nothing she can *do*? Nothing to *stop* doing?

(*Nothing,* the voice repeats, from deep inside her own throat, setting her larynx vibrating with the tiniest possible hint of sympathy. *Nothing, no. And, then—*)

(something)

Something, always, at the corner of her eye, in the dark, in the light— fluttering, scratching, crawling. *Something* behind every door, around every corner.

So by the end, Alena finds herself alone in her room, crouching, unable to get comfortable. Too afraid to turn on the light, but too afraid to be in the dark; afraid to look, yet afraid to look away. Too afraid, as the old phrase goes, to either close her eyes, or open them.

Hands over both ears, fingers dug in deep, deaf to everything but the hiss of her own pulse, the shuddery thump of her heart. But hearing her own brain repeat, nevertheless—again and again, without pause—

One in the morning.
And one at night.
One in the morning.
And one at night.
One
and one

One
and one
and
one

***

I have a thought in my head; remove it. Take it out.

Take it out, oh Christ. *Take* it.

Just take

it

out.

OUBLIETTE

Therapy Blog of Thordis Hendricks, July 2, 2012 (4:17 PM):

Back when I was in hospital, recuperating, I thought a lot about what my life had become over those months—that entire year, almost—before my second suicide attempt finally led to formal diagnosis, a plan of treatment, a potential way out of this ever-narrowing flesh trap. The way my perceptions kept on altering, as though filter were laid on top of filter on top of filter, yet so softly, so irretrievably...until finally, it was as though I woke up one morning to discover the way I saw things had always been inaccurate, horrifyingly so, and the systemic shock alone was enough to make me reach for something sharp.

Like I'd been born and almost died inside a prison cell, thinking that tiny bit of sky I could see through the window was the wide world, and me outside in it, walking, talking, laughing, living. Until that sky itself became a horror too, blue just a thin lid over black, gravity always in danger of failing before the upwards rush and airless fall into deep space—and it was that fear, that awful lurch, which wrenched me back in and reframed my understanding. Showed me the grave I'd all this time been trapped by, and began to push its walls in on top of me.

I feel better these days, of course, though not by much. But this, what we're doing right now...this is supposed to help.

Therapy Blog of Thordis Hendricks, July 2, 2012 (7:02 PM):

All right, Take Two. Start over.

I moved into Shumate House almost immediately after my last consultation with Dr. Corbray, as an alternative to further hospitalization, which had been almost impossible for me to stand once the initial numbness wore off; constant panic attacks, five different drug combos tried and discarded, all clusters of side-effects equally disgusting. Like I'd been dropped head-first into a gluey swamp and left to thrash, studiously observed, but unaided otherwise.

But being rich counts for a lot, no matter how crazy you may be otherwise. And after Aunt Isa died, the portion of the Hendricks fortune that fell to me—administered, in trust, through my family's firm—served to buy me into Shumate and pay for the almost-undivided attentions of Dr.

Corbray. Which brings us here.

This therapy blog is predicated on the assumption—not completely inaccurate—that because my phobia means I can't physically leave Apartment Five but my privacy-linked anxiety issues argue against around-the-clock live-in care, I should be required to provide my assigned worker (Yelena) with a between-sessions look at my thought processes, so she can make sure my psychological baseline isn't fluctuating wildly: No toxic thought patterns, no repetition or obsessional looping.

Of course, it's a model of exchange which presumes quite a lot, right from the get-go; that I'm not simply lying in session, for example, let alone out of session. That I really *will* write down a representative sample of whatever comes into my head between this time-signal and the next, if asked to, as opposed to simply...making stuff up out of whole cloth because it amuses me, or because it gives me just the tiniest shred of control over what happens in a life otherwise dictated by other people. That I understand how directly I'm threatening my own welfare, if I do. That I can be trusted to recognize what is and isn't appropriate behavior, even for myself.

This last part isn't completely up to me though, thankfully. Since that's supposedly what Yelena is for.

So: Today's entry. Set the timer. Mark.

Saw Yelena yesterday, at 12:22 PM. She claimed to be late (*was* late, no reason to distrust her words by labeling them claims) because of traffic and construction. We took the usual roster of tests, blood, spit, and urine, then talked about self-harm triggers for roughly the rest of the hour: how to qualify and quantify, make sure things didn't progress beyond a certain level. Yelena says up to twenty-five percent is allowable, but once you catch yourself imprinting, you need to move on. Sounds legit.

Talked about Internet access, settled on a protocol. The plan is still to use a family-friendly timer app to restrict potential surfing, allowing just enough time in a row to compose and post. The app in question adds up all your seconds, concurrent or not, and cuts out after a set limit is reached. I still can't believe I agreed to this, but have the distinct feeling I must have been fairly high when I signed those papers. Impossible to tell, one way or the other.

So no looking things up randomly, or not randomly. No visiting the same sites over and over. No time-sinks. Team-mindedness is key. Just RL, baby, moment after dragging-ass moment of it. We already turned off the cable, and there's nothing in my DVD queue but nature films. The books are all self-help. It's daily meditation and morning pages and yoga from here on out, if and when the side-effects of the latest cocktail let me do a Downwards-Facing Dog without feeling like I'm going to puke. Hell, I can't even sleep in too long, or the concierge comes knocking.

It's a great system, really, and I'm honored to have had so much "input" into its design. At the end of the day, though, I guess I'm just still not sure why there has to be so much care taken that my life, mine, my particular life, isn't destroyed. I'm not sure why I should matter so much, to anyone, aside from basic monetary considerations. And I don't know if any of this qualifies as allowable thought or not—if it's sick, or simply logical. Something anybody else might wonder, given the circumstances.

Okay, that's time. See you tomorr

Entry posted automatically. See attached IM exchange:

rostovy@monitoru.net What's this stuff about "team-mindedness"?
hendricksnox@shumatehouse.com what stuff
rostovy@monitoru.net In Tuesday's last entry. "Team-mindedness is key."
hendricksnox@shumatehouse.com dont understand what youre saying. im tired.
rostovy@monitoru.net No, I understand that, I just need you to look at it again. It might be important.
hendricksnox@shumatehouse.com cant, tired, im done. took my pills. Bed.

Initial MonitorU Intake Report on Thordis Charlotte Hendricks, June 15, 2012
Prepared by Dr. Maurice L. Corbray, consulting psychiatrist
CC'd to Yelena Rostov, attending worker

Registered diagnosis of severe agoraphobia, mid-range obsessive-compulsive disorder and clinical depression with suicidal ideation. Subject is twenty-seven years old. Currently recovering from two suicide attempts, one by intentional overdose of prescription meds, one by radial/ulnar arterial self-exsanguination. Highest education a Master's Degree in Comparative Religious Studies (incomplete). Formerly a T.A. at University of Toronto, now unemployed.

Subject presents as polite and reasonable, though with little emotional affect and micro-periods of disassociation. Prescribed regimen of Cymbalta (side-effects may include drowsiness, blurred vision, lightheadedness, strange dreams, constipation, fever/chills, headache, increased or decreased appetite, tremor, dry mouth, nausea, increased sweating and blood pressure, fatigue and reduced energy). Has agreed to daily yoga practice of roughly sixty to ninety minutes, plus guided meditation, both administered through Skype. Has agreed to participate in phobia-management exercises, and keep a recovery blog. Fees pre-paid in full.

Personal notes: With sufficient effort on her part, I see no reason why subject should not both make a full physical recovery and stabilize her phobia, eventually helping to develop a participatory management protocol which will allow her to graduate from Shumate House by next year at the latest. Nevertheless, given her history, I recommend a tight check routine—three days on, two days off, repeat—in order to ascertain whether or not Cymbalta is the best drug strategy, as well as an equally strict policy of nondisclosure about what happened to the last three subjects who occupied Apartment Five.

corbrayml@monitoru.net Just checking to see you received the Hendricks IR. Any questions?
rostovy@monitoru.net Yes, thanks. So what did happen?
corbrayml@monitoru.net When?
rostovy@monitoru.net To the previous tenants.
corbrayml@monitoru.net I don't think that's relevant.
rostovy@monitoru.net Then why did you mention it?
corbrayml@monitoru.net Feel free to do your own research, Yelena; I look forward to your report. All best.

***

From the official Shumate House introductory booklet, Shumate—Where Respite Makes Recovery:

What sets Shumate's therapeutic facility apart from every other is our specific brand of total support-system immersion. By offering a well-rounded team of live-in, on-site care workers who follow the "Shumate Method" (first developed by Dr. Jerrold Shumate in 1979, to treat post-traumatic stress disorder amongst relatives of the Canadian members of Jim Jones' People's Temple cult), we guarantee our occupants a safe haven where privacy and anonymity are equally sacrosanct—a place of retreat and reconciliation where no one, no matter their range of symptoms, is ever considered unable to participate in planning their own recovery...

Therapy Blog of Thordis Hendricks, July 25, 2012 (11:45 AM):

Timer on. Start.
It takes about a month to settle in anywhere, let alone get used to a new drug—if that's not a truism, then it should be. So now we're three weeks in, two days into the next seven, nothing but yoga and chores and blogging, pre-packaged food that comes by the close-wrapped tray, long baths with lavender for relaxation, changing my dressings, taking my pills. Each day ticks away in increments, slow-seeping, like that inescapable metallic taste at the back of my tongue, still there no matter how often I spit.
No anxiety, no worry: That's good, right? No OCD twitches. Last night I noticed an actual ring inside the bathtub—a smeared grey scum of skin-

cells, something I'd have to scrub at to get off. And I didn't. Didn't think about how I was stewing in my own dirt, like some horrible soup; just sat there and let the water lap up over it, out of sight, out of mind.

No pleasure, though. Anhedonia, just without the usual feeling bad about not feeling good. And my sex drive completely gone too, but I expected that. Not like it matters much, in here.

I'm amused to note that the guided meditation portion of my sessions takes place while in *shavasana*, the pose most instructors usually strain not to call "corpse posture" (and Yelena's no different, in this respect). I remember hearing about an existentialist yoga class they offered in Germany, pretty much corpse posture from beginning to end, which focused on accepting death rather than trying to distract yourself from it: "Your body will die. Your body will be a corpse. You can discard your body yet still exist. The signal cannot be stopped..." Sort of soothing, especially if you repeat it so often it devolves into a mushy whirr of consonant-click and vowel-sounds, with no single part more significant than the whole: *Ommmmm, just let it all gooooo.*

But yeah, I can see how that probably seems just a tad morbid to concentrate on, as a mantra, especially when you're dealing with a person who still has trouble picking stuff up with her left hand, because dominant hand automatically cuts deeper. So instead, Yelena just talks about breathing and tells me to keep my eyes closed, which I mostly don't, because part of being a reasonable adult is making your own damn decisions and sticking to them. Lie there staring up at the ceiling (white stucco, each tiny plaster stalactite's shadow a grey-black dot) 'til my eyes unfocus enough that it becomes some sort of infinite, negative-flipped space-scape, a white void pocked with black hole stars...

(And think, sometimes: *If only I had the right sort of charts, the right kind of database to work with, I might be able to figure out where that is, up there. If I only knew the math.*)

(But that's monkey-mind, right, Yelena? Chatter. Better to shut it out, be in the moment. This dying moment, dying from one second into the next, never the same, always the same. This moment that only goes, forever, no matter what you do or don't, and never comes again.)

I don't dream, but last night I had a doozy...so clear, so detailed. Except those details were utterly foreign to me, as though they'd been broadcast straight into my subconscious from somebody else's, detached but specific, a litany of intent. Should've taken notes, because all it is now is a general impression, but I remember thinking: *Yelena will love this. Finally, something worth writing about.*

So do you? Enjoy these entries, I mean. One of us should.

And...done, in time. Timer off.

rostovy@monitoru.net Interesting stuff. You really should try to close your eyes when you meditate though.

hendricksnox@shumatehouse.com guess so, just

hendricksnox@shumatehouse.com when i do i get vertigo

rostovy@monitoru.net That's not good. Do you want me to send a doctor?

hendricksnox@shumatehouse.com maybe. dont know. maybe its not real vertigo, just

hendricksnox@shumatehouse.com dont know going to sleep now ok

rostovy@monitoru.net Okay, that's probably best. Write down your dreams for me next time, all right, Thordis?

rostovy@monitoru.net Thordis?

Yelena Rostov, Notes:

Last three occupants of Shumate House Apt. #5 (in chron. order) = Marie Bissionette, Charles H. Siemanczski, Lloyd Lin Kuan-tai.

All 3 deceased.

Bissionette judged suicide, Siemanczski accidental overdose, Lin suicide. Siemanczski's personal physician disagreed with coroner's verdict—said there was no way his patient could take that much without noticing side effects/stopping before death, but no conclusive evidence either way.

Verdict might also have to do with fact that other 2 were found with plastic bags over heads but Siemanczski wasn't. Possibly removed by accident during death-throes and just not found during investigation, mislabeled as trash.

Other possibility deliberate misdirection. But what would be the point of

Understandable why Corbray doesn't want to talk about it. Doesn't say much for Shumate Method.

Why/how would he think Thordis would ask about it though?

Does it make sense 2 (poss. 3) people would all choose same strategy? They didn't know each other. Timing alone makes that impossible.

Overdose/bag method pushed by Final Exit euthanasia rights activists amongst others—cult suicides, as per Heaven's Gate.

But people do those in teams.

("Team-mindedness"?)

***

Therapy Blog of Thordis Hendricks, July 29, 2012 (2:32 PM):

It took a while to figure out what the revealed shape of my life reminded me most of, but I stumbled on it, eventually; Google is our friend, even in the tiniest of possible doses. It was an *oubliette.*

An *oubliette*'s a kind of dungeon accessible only from a hatch in a high ceiling, basically impossible to exit without outside help. The word comes from the same root as the French *oublier*, "to forget," because it was used for prisoners their captors simply wanted to disappear. Some *oubliettes* added the twist of being built on a shelf, a steeply sloping tunnel leading down to the moat or the sea—so you had the choice of letting yourself either slowly starve, or just to slip further down and drown.

The term's also used to refer to ice formations over lakes, or other large bodies of water. As ice crystals form and air is introduced by the movement of the tides, secret tunnels hollow themselves out under the ice, rendering it treacherous. Prone to give way all of a sudden, a grim surprise, and plunge you over your head into water so cold it burns.

Oubliette, jaunty *oubliette*. And this place, Apartment Five, Shumate House—just a more comfortable version of the same? A place to be parked out of sight, out of mind, 'til I'm all safely re-calibrated and refurbished...ready to take my place in the world as it is, rather than the world as I thought it was? Ready for public consumption?

Never let it be said I mind having somewhere to pull my head in for a while; it's kind of nice to have a safe little hidey-hole, I guess, when the open spaces outside remain so goddamn scary. Would be, at least, if I didn't know that somebody else holds the keys—or if I had any sort of idea how long this particular set of adjustments is going to take, exactly, either.

No one likes to be forgotten.

On the other hand, the anhedonia my cocktail deals out mainly serves to make me wonder why anyone would struggle so hard to be remembered, to stay alive; how anyone could want so badly to prolong this particular...stasis, this awful pause between nothing and nothing. Because oh sure, I'm safe in here from the worst of it, the truly painful blankness, where input slips away until everything becomes equally hollow and sharp and unbearable—but so what? How much, exactly, is a life without extremes worth, when all's said and done? No depression, no joy. Just grey, marching grey, simplest of all possible forward motions at barely impulse speed, like algae. Existing, not living.

But okay, enough, I didn't forget: Write down my dreams. Here's one.

I dreamt I found a closet in that short little hallway between my bedroom and the living room, the one we both know backs onto Apartment Seven, which means there couldn't possibly *be* a door there. So, of course, I opened it. And inside it was full of what seemed like miles on miles of snarled yarn, knotted in on itself, all dirty and wet and vile-smelling. Yet in I went, clearing a path like Lucy through the wardrobe, the yarn-mounds getting progressively colder 'til they iced up, froze almost solid, and I had to tear at them with my numbing hands, kicking myself free. And at last it gave way, became another doorway opening onto...nothing. Empty space, star-speckled, with a wind howling past me; a night sky too far away from any sun to ever see real daylight.

After which I heard a voice, some girl, and though I already knew it was a dream this only confirmed it, because it didn't scare me at all that I felt as though I recognized it. Saying: *They call it the Kuiper Belt. Think it's a nothing place, all dead debris and endless absence, but they're wrong, so wrong.* With that little trembly note in her voice that you get when you're so happy you're close to weeping. *Tiamat non delenda est! How could it be? It only moved—Translated* (I heard the capital), *like we'll be. It's real—more real, more beautiful than any agreed-upon construct in this whole "real" world. Perfect, like we'll be perfect. Perfected. Perfection. The ur-planet. The ur-.*

And everyone else will end up here, now, instead. No Heaven or Hell. Just a swirling knot of souls, too tangled to untie themselves without tearing, so far gone that by the time they come back 'round again the earth'll already be inside the Sun. Everyone who's not us, sooner or later. Everyone who's not tuned to the Signal...

Which is what? I wanted to ask, desperately. But even as I strung the words, let alone sent them dropping to my tongue, it already had me; I was *inside* it, moving through it while it moved through *me*, all echoing clicks and breath and liquid twittering, keystroke static on an empty station. Classic SETI shit, translating as it went. A cruel brightness that slapped me back down into the waking world again, even as it simultaneously revealed said "world" to be nothing but skin on howl, a burning scrim, the mere and flattest parody of whatever it was meant to conceal—

So, anyhow: Thanks for the cheap trip, Yelena, like I wasn't already feeling...*nothing* enough, already.

Put that on your expanded Cymbalta symptoms list, and smoke it.

Yelena Rostov, Notes:

Kuiper Belt: The outer rim of the Solar System, a belt of asteroids and small bodies; includes Pluto's orbit. Dreams of dark empty places common symbol of depression—may be good sign that T.'s seeing herself separate from it, rather than in it.

Tiamat: Babylonian dragon-goddess, slain by hero-god Marduk.

Interesting connection to Kuiper Belt—'70s pop pseudoscience said there was another planet (Tiamat, natch) where Belt is now, way-station for aliens; Belt's supposed to be its remains, post-destruction.

(Like *Chariots of the Gods?* Grill T. on her reading before coming here.)

Tiamat non delenda est: Riff on *Cartago delenda est?* "Tiamat must *not* be destroyed"?

"The Signal": ?

***

Handwritten "dream diary" of Thordis Hendricks:

July 31, 2012:

Dreamed I was living in a house, old & decrepit & dust-encrusted, & spent the whole day cleaning it. But when I had to muck out the basement, while I was down there I found a door in the floor & underneath the house a whole other house, equally dirty. So I went down there to clean up that one too & in its basement I found another door, another house, & so on. Smaller & dirtier & further down all the time, & they never stopped. I woke up before I found the bottom.

August 1, 2012:

Dreamed I was pregnant & had been for maybe a year & the doctor wanted to induce me but instead of going to the hospital we did it right here, in the living room. & then I started to feel sick & thought I was going to puke but instead I just doubled up & my stomach came open like a zipper, & inside there was just dust, red dust. & it all spilled out on the floor so I clawed at my own neck so badly I pulled my jugular open & bled to death, I could feel it happening. But I didn't care.

August 2, 2012:

A knock at the door. It's a package & I open it without thinking. A photo-frame with one tiny hole in it, like an ikon, black magic Advent window. An eye, peering out. So I slide off the back & find out it's a picture of me laid upside down, staring eye transmuted to blank terror simply by being reversed.

August 3, 2012:
Nothing.

August 4, 2012:
Nothing.

August 5, 2012:

Just floating again, out in the black on an orbital track so elliptical I knew I'd reach the thinnest part of my gravitational field & just slip off like a bead from a thread, go drifting away into nothing & never stop unless I hit something.

August 6, 2012:

Dreamed I was a horse with bones braided through my mane being ridden by something gigantic, this crushing weight, faster & faster, being ridden to death. Every breath a razorblade turning in my chest.

August 7, 2012:

Trapped under a car. I could feel oil dripping on me, maybe gas, or maybe I'd wet myself. That weird smell of hot rubber and dusty asphalt. & at any time the car might collapse further, something might spark, I might burn alive, but I don't think I was scared. I could hear the Signal far off in the distance, getting stronger.

August 8, 2012:

Corpse posture meditation, & I felt like I was going to blend into the floor, all heavy & cold & hot at the same time, every part of my body ticking with life I couldn't control. & then I was standing up & looking down on myself, & I looked so good empty, so perfected. Transitioned. But then I started to rot, & then I was melting, & then I was gone. Just the mat left behind.

August 9, 2012:

I was a man who wanted to be a woman, or maybe a woman who'd been a man. But one way or the other I was bad & wrecked now, broken & I knew it, & there was nothing I could do about it, because whatever choice I'd made was the wrong one. So I took a knife from the kitchen & started cutting parts of myself off anywhere I could & eating them, hoping that would help.

August 10, 2012:
Nothing.

August 11, 2012:
Nothing.

August 12, 2012:

Dreamed I was up on a hill & looked down into the valley & there were three people standing there with bags over their heads, clear plastic bags, so I could see their faces when they all turned & looked up at me, but I didn't recognize any of them. & I think they were trying to tell me something but it was too far away & I couldn't hear them because of the bags & then I just woke up.

August 13, 2012:

Dreamed I looked in the mirror & I was somebody else, & then that person told me to go get ready because we were going on a long trip together & pretty soon it would be time to leave. But instead of packing or anything we just sat down in the living room & kissed each other & said goodbye. & then we both gave each other pills & we took them at the same time & then everything went dark & that was the end.

Yelena Rostov, Notes:

Some dreams seem specifically parallel to previous tenants—Bissionette (post-partum depression with self-harm), Siemanczski (Vicodin abuse after vehicular injury), Lin (body-image dysmorphia with false transgender self-diagnosis)—even though no way T. could know about any of that. But pattern v. clear, impossible to ignore.

All dreams end badly, but with no sense of unhappiness. Transfiguration imagery. Change resulting in bodily dissolution.

Who else lived in here, before the Big Three?

Check to see if pattern continues in either direction.

***

From the Obituaries Section of the Toronto Star, September 21, 2000:

Leora SOONG, beloved daughter and sister, 1968 to 2000. Passed away suddenly but peacefully of natural causes. Her father Pak, mother Nureet, and brother Doctor Tardesh Soong ask that in lieu of flowers, cash donations be directed to the department headed by Dr. Maurice V. Corbray at Shumate House, in gratitude for their caring and professional treatment of Leora's condition. No memorial service will be held.

From the Star's Local News Section, same issue:

Almost one year exactly after the shocking discovery of thirteen dead bodies in a private Rosedale home, Leora Soong, the final survivor of Marc-Andre Rozant's Pure Signalism cult (a splinter faction of the larger Anunnaki Signalist Movement) died in her sleep late Sunday night. She was discovered early Monday morning by the staff at Shumate House, the care facility her parents had placed her in.

A former University of Toronto medical student, Soong first came to national attention after she fled the Rozant house early in the morning on September 19, 1999 and flagged down a passing police car, informing the officers who stopped that Rozant had ordered the rest of the group to commit a Heaven's Gate-style mass suicide. By the time an armed response team had been summoned, however, Rozant's plans had already been put into effect, with only one other cult member—ex-NHL goalie Tyson Legasse—left alive. Legasse claimed he had been waiting for Soong, his "double-harness team-mate," to return so that they could "Transition together properly." When Soong still refused to go through with the suicide ceremony, Legasse cut his own throat with a concealed knife and then bled out before paramedics could get close enough to treat him...

Wikipedia Entry: Signalism

Anunnaki Signalism was a Millennialist cult developed and based in Toronto, Canada, though many members were recruited from America, Europe, Russia, and parts of Asia through Internet proselytization. After a schism split the original Movement, the fourteen members calling themselves *Pure Signalists* retreated to their leader's Rosedale house in 1999 to commit ritual suicide.[1] The massacre's single survivor died of natural causes a year later, while still in deprogramming after-care therapy at Toronto's *Shumate House* facility.[2]

Doctrine

According to their internal newsletter, "The Secret Knowledge,"[3] the Signalists subscribed to the *Tiamat/Anunnaki Theory*, a variant derivation of the *12th Planet Theory* of Azerbaijan-born American author *Zecharia Sitchin*, whose books propose an explanation for human origins involving *ancient astronauts*. Sitchin attributes the creation of the ancient Sumerian culture to the *Anunnaki*, whom he identifies as a race of extra-terrestrials from a hypothetical planet beyond Neptune called *Nibiru*. He believed this planet to follow an elongated, elliptical orbit in the Solar System, asserting that Sumerian mythology reflects this view. Sitchin's books have sold millions of copies worldwide and have been translated into more than 25 languages.[citation needed]

The mathematical progression of *Bode's law* suggests that a planet should exist between Mars and Jupiter, some 260 million miles from the Sun. 12th Planet Theory posits that this planet (which Sitchin identifies with the Babylonian monster-goddess *Tiamat*) did in fact exist, but was struck and destroyed by Nibiru as its orbit intersected with our solar system, thus giving rise to the myth of Tiamat being "torn apart and spread across the sky" by the usurper-god *Marduk*. Gravitational redistribution from this event pulled some fragments of Tiamat and its moons into the orbit of the remaining planets, while others were driven further to form first the *asteroid belt*, then the *Kuiper Belt*.

The Signalist Movement builds on Sitchin's theories by claiming that the planet Tiamat was not entirely destroyed. Though its inhabitants did not possess the technology of Nibiru, they did possess a hypersapient spiritual tradition which led to their precognitive realization that such a collision was coming, and could not be avoided. They thus developed the Signal, a psychic "anchor" which would allow them to phase-shift the "best parts" of their planet and themselves into another dimension using zero-point energy. Like the *Heaven's Gate* cultists who believed they could abandon their flawed human "vehicles" and catch a ride to Paradise on the *Hale-Bopp comet*'s tail, Signalists believe that by tuning themselves to the Signal's frequency, they will be able to translate themselves to a perfected version of Tiamat through a process called *Transition*.

While most mainstream Signalists consider this process a lifelong evolution that concludes with natural death, a radical fringe current continues to advocate "active abandonment" of the body, as fleshly detritus, through suicide.

Signalist Litany of Intent

The Litany is printed in the masthead of each issue of "The Secret Knowledge":

When the Signal comes, it will decode everything it touches.
When the Signal comes, nothing will be left unchanged.
The Signal will be a type of terraforming. A psychic terraforming. Our world will be remade from the inside-out.
Those who are Horses for the Signal will be Translated and Transition correctly.
Those who are not Horses for the Signal will Transition incorrectly, in that they will not Transition at all.
Horses must run in tandem, or the Transition will be disordered.
Team-mindedness is key.
Rehearsal is the single most important element in a correct Transition.
Rehearsal assures that the Final Checks are performed consistently and in unison, with perfect intent in action.
Two on two and two by two is the proper order, so both partners can support each other throughout.
*Team-mindedness means: **No one goes alone.***
*Team-mindedness means: **No one is left behind.***
To abandon team-mindedness is to abandon your partner, condemning them to an incorrect Transition.
*To abandon team-mindedness is the **only unforgivable sin.***

Yelena Rostov, Notes:

According to the Pure Signalism website (still online!), Final Checks =
Pair up.
Assemble materials.
Put bag over head (leave open at bottom, for mouth access).
Face each other.
Each team member hands the other their dose.
Doses taken at the same time.
Wash down with vodka.
Repeat until dose canisters/vodka bottles are empty.
Tie each other's bags.
Lie down in paired corpse posture, feet touching.
Begin Litany.
Wait.

But Leora Soong didn't wait. She turned over and tore a hole in her bag, puked up her dose, ran out of the house before Tyson Legasse could catch her. Coroner's records show he was already dying when the police got there—amazing he lived long enough to kill himself. But maybe he wanted to see her again, see her eyes when she turned him down. (Like he knew she would?)

IR on Leora implies that by the time she came to Shumate, she thought she made the wrong call.

Okay, so now we know why Shumate doesn't take cult survivors/deprogramming jobs anymore. But

"The Signal" = *Signalists?* How can that

Checked Thordis's browser cache. If she's been looking at Signalist materials, I can't find any record of it. But that wouldn't explain how she knew about the other three patients anyways. Or what Leora Soong and her Signalist crazy had to do with

No no no.

NO. No, that just doesn't

Fuck.

***

Therapy Blog of Thordis Hendricks, August 15, 2012 (2:55 AM):

Found teeth in the wall today. Like there was a lump in the plaster I could barely see, but I could feel it when I touched it, so I went all through the place looking for something heavy enough to break it open, and then finally I did (edge of a plastic file-box from the closet), and I did. And it opened right up like a seam, and inside were these *teeth* buried deep enough I had to dig them out, roots and all. Too small to be an adult's, with their enamel the colour of milk gone off.

How does that even *happen*, though? I mean, it must've been deliberate—somebody did that, but why? To leave something of themselves behind here, just in case

(that's if the teeth were even theirs)

One way or the other, I think I maybe need to start writing down exactly when I take my meds again. And how many.

Slept maybe an hour around midnight, and had that same dream about somebody standing at the foot of my bed, looking down at me while I slept. And it was me? Me looking down, me sleeping? And when I opened my eyes I was surprised, genuinely, to not find her still standing there. Surprised, and a little disappointed.

It's very lonely in here. I'm beginning to wish

(only beginning?)

well, more like—after all this time in Apartment Five—that I'm finding it hard to remember what it was like to ever be someplace

(anyplace)

else.

And the other thing that's funny, just a bit: When your diagnosis includes suicidal ideation, why do the side-effects of so many drugs *also* include suicidal ideation? Cymbalta included, if I recall correctly; hoping *you* have a handle on that, at least, Yelena. Hoping you're keeping track.

It just seems...contradictory.

> rostovy@monitoru.net Dr. Corbray, it's Yelena Rostov.
> rostovy@monitoru.net Dr. Corbray?
> rostovy@monitoru.net I sent you a report, Dr. Corbray. Did you get it?
> corbrayml@monitoru.net
> corbrayml@monitoru.net
> corbrayml@monitoru.net Yes, I received it.
> rostovy@monitoru.net All right, then
> rostovy@monitoru.net Mind telling me what you thought?
> corbrayml@monitoru.net Will be sending you my response in email form, so please check your in-box.
> corbrayml@monitoru.net Signing off now.

***

From:corbrayml@monitoru.net
Date:August 15, 2012, 10:42 AM
To:rostovy@monitoru.net
Subject:Report (Thordis Hendricks)

Dear Yelena,

Following your account of what you term Thordis Hendricks's "psychological degeneration" over her stay with us here at Shumate House, I went back and examined the Therapy Blog posts and dream diary entries you quoted in detail. Having done so, while I will admit the symptoms she's been experiencing are extreme (enough so to definitely merit a pharmacological shift off Cymbalta, perhaps substituting Paxil or Celexa, followed by a full-scale treatment protocol reassessment), I'm not quite sure what else I'm supposed to take away from this laundry list of additional implications, some of which appear to verge on the pathological.

To answer your questions, however: No, there is no way Ms. Hendricks could have learned the details of how Apartment Five's former tenants died. No, I don't believe there's a "pattern" to those deaths, aside from the unfortunate tendency of addicts to overdose and depressives to commit suicide. And though I suppose it's possible Ms. Hendricks might recall something about the Pure Signalism cult denouement—it would have been hard to escape that year's news coverage without picking up *any* reference to it, especially here in Toronto—this idea of yours that Leora Soong's completely coincidental stay at Shumate may have left some sort of toxic "psychic residue" behind that infects Apartment Five's residents with Signalist ideas is both highly unprofessional, and scarily close to veering into the realm of paranormal mumbo-jumbo. We work for MonitorU, not the Freihoeven Institute.

I don't *want* to re-assign you, Yelena, since I believe that would be bad for Ms. Hendricks—she needs continuity, especially now. But this is a conversation I really don't want to find myself having with you again.

(By the way, in future, I would prefer to communicate by email rather than Instant Message, since the latter format is not exactly conducive to in-depth debate.)

Cordially,

Dr. Maurice Corbray, M.D., Ph.D.
Director, Shumate House

Yelena Rostov, Notes:

Asshole.
Okay, okay—
Supposedly, Shumate doesn't accept cult survivors or deprogramming jobs anymore.

But Corbray was Shumate's primary student; Corbray treated Leora Soong, so "well" her parents wanted everybody to donate to him. Corbray was the one who mentioned Apartment Five's stellar tenancy record in the first place. Why?

So I would go looking? So I'd figure out
(no, that doesn't make any)
(or does it)

So here's a thesis:
You have a—all right, say it—haunted apartment. Everyone who stays there gets sucked into the same routine: Final Checks for Translation/Transition; team-mindedness at work. She (Leora) convinces them they're part of her double-harness pairing. And they go through with it, but they don't stick around—they move on, somewhere else. *She* sticks around, and tries it again.

Because she feels bad about pulling out. Because she feels
(alone, and lonely, so lonely)
(just like Thordis)

And it doesn't matter at this point if she really-for-truly thinks that all her dead friends wound up on Lost Planet Tiamat in the Paradise

Dimension, or whatever—fact is, wherever they *did* end up, she's not there, and she never will be. Not unless she can find someone else, the *right* someone else

to *team* with.

And Corbray's not stupid, just a bastard. So what is it for him, some kind of experiment? Like: *Hey, I wonder what happens if we put* this *sort of person in Number Five? Or* this *one? Or*

(because I think *I* know)

I mean: How many times do you have to *do* this, exactly, to figure out the truth? How many times do you have to repeat a routine to know it's *never* going to

Oh God, I have to get Thordis out of there.

***

Skype log transcript of conversation between Yelena Rostov and Thordis Hendricks, recorded on August 15, 2012 (3:15 PM to 3:27 PM):

Yrostov: Thordis, are you there? I can hear you, but I can't see you. Do you have your camera turned on?

ThordH: Yelena?

Yrostov: It's me, yeah. I need to speak to you right now, about—

ThordH: Ha, that's so weird. I was just going to call *you.*

Yrostov: You were?

ThordH: What did you want to talk about?

Yrostov: Well, I—was worried—

ThordH: Oh God, this about the blog, right? Listen, I feel so stupid, I was just...you know how it is. My sleep's been really upset, and I just get down.

Yrostov: So you didn't find teeth in the wall?

ThordH: No, that part was true. I mean, it's *all* "true."

Yrostov: I don't—Thordis, I'm still not seeing anything, can you try again? I just want to talk to you about these...patterns in your blog, this toxic repetition, these weird turns of—okay, there, that's better. Are you still having those dreams?

ThordH: Sure, sort of. But ever since you sent Lee over, things have been so much—

Yrostov: Excuse me, who?

ThordH: Lee, Yelena. You know. She's been taking me through the meditation sequences in person, and it *really* helps clarify things. I mean, at first I was a little leery, but turns out having somebody in my space isn't so bad, when they really know what they're doing.

Yrostov: The meditation—

ThordH: Corpse posture. The whole rehearsal, Final Checks and all. I can *hear* everything perfectly now; I understand. It's Translated itself for me, so I can return the favour. And it's just, it's just, so—

Yrostov: Thordis, *wait*, slow down. Breathe. I, I need to make sure you know what you're *doing*, that you aren't gonna *hurt* yourself—

ThordH: Yelena, c'mon. What is it you think I'm going to *do*?

Yrostov: I—look, that doesn't matter right now, I'll explain when I get there. Just...stay put, hold on. Don't do *anything*. Okay?

ThordH: No, I'm interested—hurt myself how? Why would I do that? It makes no sense. I'd never do that, not when I came here to get *better*. No one would. Right, Lee? I'm right, aren't I? Tell her.

Yrostov: Thordis—

ThordH: *Tell* her, damnit!

Yrostov: *Thordis.* Focus. Who's...that behind you?

ThordH: I *told* you already, Yelena. Lee.

Shumate House Site Incident Report for August 15, 2012, filed by Saracen Security Guard Margaret Cuchner:

12:00 PM Arrived on site to relieve previous guard. No further incident.

12:30 to 15:00 PM Checks as usual, nothing to report.

15:15 PM (Approx.) Care worker Yelena Rostov entered lobby, greeted me and registered. She then proceeded to Skype with Apartment 5 (Thordis Hendricks) on her tablet, while I filled out site log.

15:25 PM (Approx.) Rostov became upset and waved me over. I heard what I assumed to be tenant Hendricks rambling incoherently. Rostov pointed out what she said was an intruder in Hendricks' apartment. Hard to see, but looked like a female figure standing behind Hendricks.

15:30 PM (Approx.) I triggered the panic button, summoning police and paramedics, and left my duty station to accompany Rostov up to Apartment 5. No response to knocking and calling. I tried security fob, but apartment door was unresponsive. When I recommended waiting for police, Rostov broke glass on fire extinguisher cabinet and used extinguisher to break door handle, then kicked in door. I proceeded to do quick check of apartment, but found no intruder.

15:35 PM Police arrived on site and accessed my walkie-talkie. I explained situation. Officer Brian Lum stayed at front desk to direct paramedics, while Officer Chimo Moche joined Rostov and myself upstairs.

15:38 PM Officer Moche, Rostov, and myself located Hendricks lying in her own bed, apparently unconscious, with blue lips and a plastic bag half-full of vomit over her head, knotted around her neck. At same time (approx.), paramedics arrived on site and were directed upstairs by Officer Lum. They began resuscitation efforts on Hendricks, broke open bag and turned her over on her stomach. Hendricks coughed up more vomit, then opened her eyes briefly and began to breathe again, erratically.

15:45 PM Paramedics removed Hendricks to St. Michael's Hospital. Officers Lum and Moche asked me if I wanted to prefer trespassing charges against Rostov. I replied that I was not authorized to do so, and asked to be allowed to call my immediate supervisor on site, Dr. Maurice L. Corbray. Officers Lum and Moche asked Rostov to remain in their custody until Dr. Corbray got here. Rostov agreed.

15:50 PM I reset alarms in Apartment 5.

16:17 PM Dr. Corbray arrived on site. He elected to waive charges, but told Rostov she would be let go from her current position with MonitorU, and that she no longer had security access to Shumate House. Rostov turned her ID and fob over to me.

16:30 PM Rostov, Officers Lum and Moche, and Dr. Corbray left site. I proceeded to fill out Site Incident Report.

Signed, Margaret Cuchner #TU-4445-000097.

***

From This Narrow Life, *the blog of Thordis Hendricks, September 30, 2012 (1:28 PM):*

But why would I do that? I remember saying. *It makes no sense. I would never do that. No one would ever do that.*

I would never take three pills, take a sip of vodka, take three pills, repeat until gone. I would never have a bag over my head already when I did it, conveniently open at the bottom and hiked over my nose to free my mouth. I would never peel it back down again after I was done and knot it, once, twice, three times. I would never.

Never make my way back upstairs, weaving slightly. Never feel stuffy and warm and happy and only slightly queasy. Never lie down flop on my bed (our bed), and close my eyes.

Thinking: *I would never, no one would. I'm not doing it now.*

Except, of course, that I was.

Anyhow: This is what happened after, as far as I can figure out—

I ended up at St. Mike's, in a private room (thank you, Isa's money). I remember Yelena sitting by my bed, but only vaguely; I think she might've been holding my hand. She looked so tired.

(The weirdest thing is, in context, how I don't remember "Lee" at all. I read that Skype log and I'm amazed it's me talking, though it certainly *sounds* like me. Nothing seems familiar. The dreams, I at least remember having *them*. But this girl, this—whoever she was? Nothing.

(And I even looked up Leora Soong on the 'Net, too. Totally unfamiliar.)

Dr. Corbray came by a week later, trying to convince me that Yelena was somehow responsible for what'd happened. I disagreed. By that time, of course, the next part was all over the news; I guess he was trying to do damage control, in his own fucked-up way. Maybe that was all he'd ever been trying to do.

It'd make me sound entirely too nice to say I don't blame him, exactly. Because I guess I probably would, if I let myself think about it. One way or the other, he lost himself a customer; whether or not that's "enough," given circumstances, I don't know. The family lawyers kept telling me I had a serious case—one even said Yelena should co-sue with me, for wrongful dismissal, once her own legal issues were settled. But it's not like Corbray can do it to anybody else now either...so, kind of a moot point.

Because that was another thing Yelena was doing, apparently, at the hospital—she got hold of *my* fob, waited 'til that guard she found me with was off-shift, then used it. Went in through the fire access door, which I didn't even know you could (but then again, how would I?). Went upstairs, got back into Apartment 5...where she came up with enough salt to pour around the place that, when she followed it up with gasoline and threw a lighter in after it, the salt helped act as a firebreak and kept the damage confined to the apartment. No casualties, no damage to the rest of the house—but #5's gutted. Whatever they put there next, it won't be the place Leora Soong died in anymore, and maybe that will help.

I'd like to find Yelena, not that I know how to go about it. I'd like to thank her, except that no one really knows where she went after. The fire department says there weren't any human remains in the ashes, and you'd think they'd be able to tell. So hopefully she got out, changed her name, went underground; maybe she's working another job somewhere, keeping her eyes peeled for things other people don't want to let themselves see. Maybe she's sitting in front of a screen with her IM left open like some high-tech Ouija board, waiting for someone's words to fill the box, seeing where they'll take her. Maybe she's telling Leora's ghost the equivalent of *Sit down, Miss Soong, we have a* lot *of work to do together.*

Or maybe she walked into that whole Translation routine with her eyes open, wielding a skill set I'll never possess. Maybe she took Leora's hand and pulled her on with her, so they ended up...somewhere else. Not the Kuiper Belt, hopefully, but hell, I don't know. I don't know.

(I'll never know.)

So: This is the new blog, obviously. I'm out of Shumate, on a different cocktail, into another apartment; I go out every day, at least for a little while, and I make myself look up steadily, training my eyes on the blue, the clouds, trying to not think about the cold, huge black lurking behind it. The same black which encircles us all, no matter where we choose to hide, just beyond this planet's pitifully thin atmosphere-skin. Because there's no place we can go to escape it, even in our dreams—like death, it just *is*, and nothing helps for long.

But this much has changed: Instead of thrashing around and trying to avoid them, what I do now is *make* myself think these thoughts through, all the way, *allow* myself to, and then I let them go. Get into corpse posture, lit or fig; shut my eyes, and breathe. One day I'll stop, and maybe I won't even notice. What happens after that is beyond my—or anyone else's—control.

This is the truth of what I have, what I am—it may get better, but it doesn't get cured. You find a pattern and settle into it, hoping it holds. And so every day, every night, I feel things moving all around me, a pulse like some universal heartbeat, a million minds rubbing in from every side, pumicing their thoughts against mine. A Signal of sorts, though whether it comes from inside or out-, Tiamat or God or the underside of my very own personal chemistry-soaked brain is simply impossible to tell, or prove.

Which means, our various faiths aside, that we should probably try to be content to deal with the immediate, and let the rest take care of itself.

Still seeing signs and portents everywhere, no matter what, and letting them wash over me, resistlessly as rain. A shadow in a room, darkness on darkness. A light through the bedroom window, shining from nowhere, which follows you everywhere you move to, so you always wake up with it in your eyes. A car alarm that goes off all the time, especially in the middle of the night. Or a voice in your mind, only vaguely familiar, mourning—

Team-mindedness! I broke routine, broke faith. I let my partner down. So I can't *go on, not now, not yet. Not yet...*

If that's Leora Soong's voice though, I don't owe it to her to remember. I don't owe her anything.

Instead, I sit here typing and I take my pills, determined to keep on living, still haunted or not. Which I am, surely. Aren't we all?

In a way, every ghost is only our own.

SIGNAL TO NOISE

...reckon not those who are killed in Allah's way as dead; nay, they are alive (and) are provided sustenance from their Lord.

Never think that those who have perished in jihad are dead—they are still here. You are simply unaware of them.
—Alternate translations of *Qur'an* Excerpt 3:169, Set 11, Count 32.

Two months after Cal Fichtner took himself officially "off the map," Greer Reizendaark logged onto the company webmail account to find a particularly well-scrubbed piece of e-correspondence waiting for him. No header, no address, no send-date—just a numerical link embedded in the body, with this curt instruction: LIVE AT ONE. CLICK HERE.

He waited 'til the clock at the corner of his screen rolled over, then did—and watched the whole way through, without comment, not stopping even when some newbie from Homeland Security caught a couple of seconds' glance at it over his shoulder, and started puking. "Holy Christ," she kept on repeating. "Holy, holy Christ."

Greer didn't turn around. Just snapped back, as the footage froze, looped, and started over: "That's exactly what they want you to say, you dizzy cunt."

For *I will cast terror into the hearts of those who disbelieve. Therefore strike off their heads, and strike off every fingertip of them—Excerpt 8:012, Set 28, Count 62.*

The *dhimmi*, the Crusaders, the Jews: make 'em too afraid to fight you, to resist the tide of *jihad*, by showing them just how bad they were gonna die if they did.

The funny thing, though? Fichtner didn't even look all that scared in the clip—stayed a cast-iron son of a bitch, right up to and including the part where they stuck a knife between his top two vertebrae, and started sawing away at his spine. Like it hurt, yes; mad, for damn certain...

He'd known all along this was the likeliest outcome though. Hadn't needed Greer to tell him *that*.

Hadn't let him, when he'd tried.

***

This world was full of empty spaces, especially where the maps fell away—holes that most often plugged themselves with phantoms, the minute you looked somewhere else. Nature of the game. Nothing was certain, only wars and rumors of wars, 'til the intelligence checked out.

Or, as his last wife liked to put it: "You're physically present sometimes, but you're not really here, Greer—not ever. You're not just a spook, you're a ghost."

"That's a cliché, darlin'."

"You'd know," she said.

***

Sheikh Mehdi Nebbou called a half-hour after Fichtner's execution, to demand: "Why were you not watching him, Greer?"

"Other shit on my plate, buddy. As goddamn usual."

Greer certainly had been, in the beginning—no big secret there. Because while Fichtner might've been righteously quick to drop his GPS-enabled cellphone in the very next dry well he saw, he'd already known (as Greer had taught him) how the basic fun of surveillance came from realizing you could track anybody, anywhere, so long as you had a fair idea of who they were likely to be hanging around with. People always made the best anchors.

So if somebody'd wanted to find Fichtner, all they'd ever had to do was watch the clinic Fichtner's new lady worked at, then wait for him to turn up somewhere in the background. Or hell, they could just watch Mehdi himself, who'd offered Fichtner a job as a "security consultant" the week after Fichtner tendered his resignation.

But things had gotten hot elsewhere, like they always did, and Greer's attention had shifted accordingly. Wasn't like the interest ever seemed much reciprocated, since Fichtner certainly knew—had known—his home phone number, and Greer'd made sure not to have it changed in the interim, just in case his wayward protégé ever felt inclined to ring him up for a little chat.

"They killed his fiancée as well," Mehdi said. "Miss Al-Kimani—the nurse? Though I suppose it might be asking too much to think—"

"Don't tell me what I do and don't care about, you supercilious S.O.B. You were the one s'posed to look after him now, remember? Your territory, your rules. He trusted you."

"If you had only trusted *me*, Greer—from the very beginning—then none of this would have happened," Mehdi replied. Then rang off, leaving Greer with nothing in his Bluetooth but an oh-so-sophisticated lack of static.

Only the truth, whatever that was: Just information, a wonderfully fluid thing. Given the right tools and impetus, you could move it around, cover it up, modify it—give it a fan made out of feathers and make it do the shimmy, if you wanted. That was what Greer did all day, every day, to earn his

Christmas bonus...and what Mehdi did too, while saving for a considerably different holiday.

From Marathon to Peshawar, the same routine: guys like Mehdi and Greer put people into bad situations, hoping they'd find out what their governments didn't already know they needed to know. Most times, the people got hurt. Sometimes they got killed. But the rules didn't change, no matter what—whether you were getting the bulk of your covert intel with black magic tech, or an old-fashioned gun to the head.

By lunchtime, Greer was vetting three separate reports (Holland, Spain, Equatorial Africa) while simultaneously balls-deep in a three-way conference call with Washington, Toronto, and London, listening to some CSIS asshole pontificate, and trying to chew his way through a cruller without it showing up on tape.

"You can see how this makes us look bad, Agent Reizendaark," this guy said. "Your Mr. Fichtner died for being a member of the global intelligence community."

Now, there's an oxymoron, Greer thought. And shot back—

"'My' Mr. Fichtner? Hadn't been that since I accepted his L.O.R., back in February."

"They wrote 'CIA BLOODSUCKER' on the wall behind his corpse," the designated representative from Greer's side of the table pointed out.

"Outdated, then," London broke in; "let's not quibble over semantics, gentlemen. Particularly since I'm still not hearing anything about how you mean to deal with this particular—breach of protocol."

"Well, what do you suggest?"

"Erase all trace of Fichtner, retroactively."

"Looks to me like somebody already beat you to it," Greer replied, punching out.

***

Two months ago. Greer still had that last call .mp3'd on his hard-drive, somewhere—could listen to it later tonight, alone in his empty house, where the only company left for him to keep was with a dead man's voice.

Fichtner: *You get my message, G.?*

Greer: *Yeah, I got it. So...hear you're growin' a beard for real, prayin' five times a day, and why? 'Cause Aqsa won't let you up under her hijab if you don't?*

Fichtner: *'Cause I like it, Greer. 'Cause it feels right.*

Greer: *Uh huh. So what's the part you like most, huh? The killing in the*

Name part? The eight-year-old human bombs?

Fichtner: *I like the part says there is no God but God. Seems true to me, or like it should be. Might solve a fuck of a lot of problems, on either side, people just took it a bit more seriously...*

Greer: *Some people already take it a bit too seriously for comfort, you ask me.*

Fichtner: *...and the rest? That's mostly misinformation, misinterpretation. People thinking they always know better.* (Pause) *Sound familiar?*

Greer: *Fuck you, son.*

Fichtner: *Can't do that sort of thing no more, G. Sorry.*

Greer: *No matter how drunk I get you first?*

Fichtner: *Can't do that either, buddy.*

Greer: *Well, hell,* buddy—*that sure ain't no kinda religion I'd be willin' to die for, but to each his damn own.* (Pause) *'Cause they are gonna kill you, Cal...that's the no-God-but-God's honest truth. Her too, probably. You do know that, right?*

Fichtner: *Well, if they do, they do. I mean, Aqsa's been living with this shit a whole lot longer than either of us, Greer—she's stronger than I'll ever be. Plus, at least she tries not to hate.*

Greer: *You really think the two of you're gonna end up in the same place though, after? Given all you done?*

Fichtner: (Long pause) *Maybe not. But that's the hope.*

And here the mental transcript broke off.

To wash the conference call's aftertaste away, Greer hit the Geek Room, where his two pet surveillance experts—one male, one female, so he always just called 'em Guy and Gal, in his head—were poring over the latest input from a bunch of gyro-stabilized recon ex-satellite cameras Mehdi had agreed to retrofit onto some of *his* bosses' "new" Navy P-3 Orions. As a vain stab at trying to keep things private, the cameras got changed around weekly, which meant Guy and Gal spent most days downloading intel, plugging it into a 360-degree spread, and then trying to figure out from the resultant virtual landscape just where and when said footage had been snatched, as well as what the hell was (probably) going on in it.

Today's spread showed a meet-up somewhere in the desert (big surprise), though Guy and Gal were having trouble deciding exactly which one. Scans showed two vans, three open-end trucks, and a yoinked US Army Humvee 'round which figures in robes and head-scarves filtered, their faces all equally blown out by harsh light and sudden shadow.

"We think this one's Ajinabi," Gal said, tapping what to Greer was an utterly random set of features. The name—an agreed-upon monicker floated first through Mehdi's group, then adopted by Greer's, after Fichtner started using it in his reports—was Arabic for either "stranger" or "outsider": a legendary organizer for hire, possibly foreign-born, or even a Fichtner-style convert who'd chosen *jihad* over live-and-let-live. But on lack of background detail alone, Ajinabi'd quickly become scapegoat of choice in the region—a convenient catch-all for a complex range of mischief, everything from holding bomb-building classes to coordinating lethal actions.

"He might've been in on Fichtner too, boss," Guy suggested. "Or know who was."

Greer shrugged. "Might've. Which is pretty much the same as sayin' the boogeyman did it, 'cause we'll never know no better."

Gal frowned. "We figure out who some of the other players here are, though, and turn 'em—that'd get us one step closer."

"Don't look to me like there's enough there for the facial-recognition software to work with, even if our current operatives database wasn't so far out of date—"

Guy: "Oh, look at that. I think...we got a hit."

They all studied the results for a while, silently. Until—

"That...looks like Cal Fichtner," Gal said, at last.

"Couldn't be, though."

"...no."

Damn, though, if it didn't seem like it was. Right there in the background, half-hidden in a shadow cast by that second truck from the right—even down to choice of sunglasses, or that raggedly white-boy meth-cooker beard he'd grown so Aqsa would feel more at home letting him walk her down the street. Same stone-age vs. *Star Trek* outfit he'd last been photographed wearing, calculated for maximum blend-in when viewed from above; same guy got his head cut off on almost-live not-exactly-TV, and made it exciting enough to watch that the footage ended up being streamed on Al-Jazeera.

"Look, fellas," Greer broke in, finally, "I've seen the man's *head*. They sent it to us postage paid, packed in salt, care of my office."

"What about the rest of him?"

"Out in the desert somewheres, I assume—the hell's it matter? We got DNA, got a hundred percent match. Whoever that is, Cal Fichtner don't come into the matter."

"Well," Guy muttered, "it might be..." Then cut off in mid-breath as Gal shot him a dirty look, visual shorthand for *shut effin' up, you boob.* Greer raised a brow, angled to include them both.

"Might be *what?*"

Gal sighed. "Sometimes...data stays behind. Like...when you overwrite stuff again and again, fragments stick around, in the interstices. They just sort of collect."

"'Pixel-geists', we call 'em—"

"*You* do."

"Whatever. So, stuff gets caught between the zeroes and the ones—I mean, so what, right? All part of the process."

Greer shook his head, hoping that would help; it didn't.

"Well...what do you do about it, when it does?" he asked, finally.

"Wait 'til it goes away again, mostly," Guy replied.

***

That night, his BlackBerry chimed, and Greer opened it to find his inbox full of empty emails. At first he thought it was Fichtner's killers trying to screw with him some more, but maybe not—these *had* addresses and time signatures, though both jumped seemingly at random from past to present to future, 'round the world and back again. One was from Antarctica, for fuck's sake. Greer shift-clicked the whole pile, hit delete. Then fell asleep watching football with one eye, BBC World News with the other, and head-first from there into a pile of dreams: Blurry, brief, bitterly disturbing.

That awful room, a tiny concrete cell with corkboard walls, with nothing in it but a gashed-up slab-topped table and a camera stand. And bloodstains, layered in overtop of each other, so deep they looked like wallpaper.

The Bluetooth buzzed against his cheek, hot with sweat. He reared back up, swatting at it, only to hear a voice he knew almost better than his own issuing from it—tiny and tinny, but distinct: *internalized*, like it was vibrating up through the bones of his jaw to reach the eardrum directly, its message's content and delivery system alike both equally impossible.

Get my message, G?

"...What?"

Fichtner's *laugh*, pricking tears from Greer's eyes automatically, like a cold wind.

You—get—my message?

"Who *is* this?" No reply. "Listen, asshole, you need to get the hell off my line."

Can't do that. Sorry.

Greer knuckled his eyes, drawing sparks. "I...ain't havin' this conversation. You could be anybody, 'sides from—"

...me?

A long pause ensued, while Greer tried to figure out anything worth saying.

Maybe...not? the voice asked, gently.

"...can't be."

Well...seems true to me, or like it should be. Buddy.

Then silence. Not even a tone.

Greer sat there a while, thinking about how insane he must have gone without noticing, to actually believe that he might've been talking to Cal Fichtner's—what? Pixel-geist? Spook?

Around three forty-five, he gave up on getting back to sleep, and called up Gal (who was still in the Geek Room, like he'd known she would be). Got her to send the spread over and went over it again—homed in on that tricksy little background figure, *Blade Runner*-style, and saw it was pointing straight at the same other silhouette Gal had initially tapped, exactly. "Ajinabi," caught foreground-framed with his mouth open in mid-lecture, similarly faceless yet somehow more authoritative than the rest, judging by the way the others angled towards him. And totally ignorant of Fichtner's finger cocked to the back of his head, like: Him. Here. See? *This* guy, and no one else...

...my message...

***

And then it was...later, and Greer surfaced to find himself somehow not only drunk as a lord, but already on the phone with Mehdi. Who was being surprisingly forbearing about it, given the circumstances.

"Things are still *there* even when you stop lookin' at 'em, right?" Greer asked, pouring another drink he sure as hell didn't need.

"I believe you may be veering dangerously close to the realm of metaphysics with this question, Agent Reizendaark. Or of spiritualism, perhaps." A beat. "Why are you phoning me, exactly?"

"I...honestly have no idea."

"Mmm. Do you happen to know what time it is here?"

"...early? Or late, I guess..."

"Yes, very likely one or the other. But then, time zones were always a weakness of yours, as I recall. On a more personal note, however—you sound as though you need sleep, Greer, rather than alcohol. Rather badly."

"Probably do, yeah."

"Then sleep."

"...not yet. You hooked up? Online?"

"I'm in bed, Greer. Where you should be."

"Well, I'm flattered, buddy; don't think you really want me in *your* bed, though. I'd wreck the mattress."

Mehdi made a half-sigh, half-snicker. "Send me your data," he said, at last.

***

The next morning, his head full of cotton and mush, Greer saw Mehdi's number blink alight, and picked up halfway through the first ring.

"You can't possibly think this is what it seems," Mehdi told him.

Greer shut his eyes. "Well, that depends. What's it look like to you?"

"Greer..."

"I want to hear you say it, Sheikh. Out loud."

Another sigh. Then—

"...it *appears* to be a surveillance photo of Cal Fichtner. Standing in the desert. Pointing at someone."

"Fella at seven o'clock, three from the right?"

"The very same. I cannot, however, make out *his* face."

"Crap. I was kinda hopin' you knew him."

"Yes, that would be convenient, I suppose—if we had any idea what it was he was doing there, or why we should care to know, in the first place."

"My geeks think he's Ajinabi."

Unimpressed: "Do they."

"Yup. They say word on the Grid is, he keeps off it—does everything face to face, word of mouth. So if this *is* him callin' a meeting, it's gotta be about somethin' pretty big. Think he might've been the one behind what happened to Fichtner too...and Aqsa Al-Kimani."

"The great Foreign Devil for Hire, wearing a thousand masks and pulling a thousand strings. I've heard those rumors as well, Greer—for quite some time now. Far longer than you've considered them relevant, considering they really didn't begin to attract your direct interest until a friend of yours..." A pause. "In terms of concrete proof, however, that's exactly all they are. Rumors."

"I've gotten the go-ahead on less."

"Doubtless. But I'm not sure I'd boast about that, if I were you."

Greer huffed out hard, and felt his temples start to throb. "Fine, then. What do *you* think these pics are, if they ain't—that?"

"As you know, we of Islam tend to find representative images of the ineffable somewhat...difficult."

"Even photos?"

Greer could practically hear Mehdi's shrug. "Contextually, recent photos of a person one knows to be dead operating in the material world are likely to be almost as suspect as paintings of the Prophet, don't you agree?"

"I think maybe this is some cultural thing we're gettin' into here, and I ain't exactly qualified to—"

"No? At *best*, Greer, this is a ghost, something whose testimony both our religions find equally suspect. We know Cal Fichtner was a good man, though not by all standards; all signs point towards the idea that he had come to terms with his past, made amends, found love, found faith...forgiveness. So he should be at peace—either in Heaven, or Paradise. Elsewhere, at any rate. Not—"

"You can't know it's *not* Fichtner," Greer began, ridiculously annoyed.

"And you can't know it is. The desert is a bad place to die, Greer—an empty place, home to many strange, empty things. Just because something wears a face you know..."

"What the hell you gettin' at, exactly?"

"Do you really think a dead man still works 'for' you, simply because he seems as though he claims to? Or, better yet...when has chasing a ghost ever led to anything of true, lasting value?"

"We chase ghosts all the time, buddy."

"Not literally."

There was a small silence; Greer breathed into it, carefully, dialing himself back down. Trying to clear his aching head.

"We found her body," Mehdi added, unexpectedly. "Miss Al-Kimani—buried up to her neck, stoned, then beheaded; the usual. Tragic waste of a perfectly good nurse, especially in a city with so few free clinics." After a beat. "No further trace of Fichtner's, unfortunately."

"Desert's a pretty big place, is what I hear."

"Yes. It is."

***

"Happened again, boss," Gal said.

"We thought you'd want to know," Guy chimed in.

This time, the photo spread came from a market in Casablanca, where some poor burnoosed bastard stood at a stall completely oblivious to the goons closing in on him (Guy had helpfully tagged him with a pop-up caption saying simply "ASSET"), and "Fichtner" was the one occupying the foreground—almost angled *towards* the fly-over, which was frankly impossible. Unfortunately, this still didn't manage to bring the guy he was once again pointing at any closer.

"You run a point-by-point?" Greer asked.

Guy nodded. "Pretty much a match, so...looks like it *is* the same dude Fi, uh—" He stumbled, flushing, under Greer's pointed look. "—same dude the...other one fingered."

"But that don't really tell us nothin' we didn't know before, huh?"

Gal: "Right."

Greer scowled down at the multi-screen array. "What's he even doin' there, you figure that much out?"

They exchanged a look. Said, as one: "Maybe."

The reason the missing operative grab hadn't been clocked

immediately—taking maybe five hours after he'd been grabbed from a nearby safehouse for his safehouse to call him in missing, plus another hour since after Fichtner's pixel-geist had picked out "Ajinabi" for the birdie—was because he was just a local hire. Further examination revealed him as also A) one of Fichtner's C.I.s, specifically during the last fiasco Greer'd puppetmastered with Fichtner as his man on the ground, and B) a guy Fichtner'd first found through Mehdi's info-gathering networks, making that Greer's next call. He sent over the new spread at the same time, and waited while Mehdi pulled it up.

"Offputting," was all Mehdi had to say.

"Really ain't no way anybody could fake that, is there?"

"Unless one of your pets is serving two masters, I think not." Greer heard the click of a mouse as Mehdi fiddled around some, probably trying the image from the same angles Guy and Gal already had. Muttering to himself, as he did—

"If only we could see that man's face a bit more clearly. If only Fichtner—"

(*wasn't blocking the view*)

"Guess you don't think it's a *jinn* then."

"Ah, someone's been Googling."

"Gimme some damn credit, Sheikh. I work for a department's been dealin' with the Middle East for almost sixty years; might be I coulda heard the term, here and there."

"Oh yes, you're a veritable fount of Muslim marginalia—that must be why your Farsi is so atrocious." With one last click: "So...are we meant to gather from this latest—communique—that Hasim Gullah is bound for the same place as Fichtner?"

"Beheadings-'R'-Us, then the Internet?" Greer paused. "Don't suppose you'd be any closer to figuring out where that first stream came from..."

"Must I do all your work for you, Agent Reizendaark?"

Mehdi'd probably meant it to be light, a joke, but the tone wasn't quite right. Still, Greer knew a kiss-off when he heard one.

So: "Fuck you, son," he said. And hung up.

***

You get my message, G?

Thirty minutes earlier, the subdermal bone-buzz voice would've muffled itself against alcohol—but sleep had eluded Greer, and now the call rattled his skull straight through into incipient hangover.

My—a skip, sample-scratch brief—*new*—*message?*

Greer swallowed cold spit, sat bolt upright: he knew this trick, had *used* this trick. That one inserted word in a different tone, different stress pattern, different volume even from the rest of the sentence...and other than that, the sentence said the exact same way, every time. He was angrier at ever having fallen for the oldest Space Age surveillance gaslighting trick in the book, if only the once, than at being targeted in the first place.

Tic-inducing, scrapy vibrations under his jaw: laughter, more tired than snide. *People thinking they always know better.*

Then another pause, while Greer timed it out exactly: *Sound familiar?*

"When I find you, shithead—"

Maybe not...

No click, but Greer knew instantly the contact was lost. He closed his eyes, fighting the urge to puke—his mind already supplying the rest of the quote, whether he wanted it to or not—

...but that's the hope.

***

"Got a phone call from Fichtner just now," Greer told Mehdi, minutes later. "Plus last night, and...night before that too."

"Hmm."

"Not the reaction I was expectin', but hell—I'll take it. Care to elaborate?"

"Very well: *this*, as you know, is something 'Ajinabi' really *could* fake. You set your share of bugs in Fichtner's rooms, his cars...they would only have had to tune in long enough to capture his half of the conversation, from which to sample and loop a few pertinent phrases—"

"Mentioned the photo array though. Ajinabi, scopin' out Gullah's beat. Gettin' things all set for the Big Scoop."

"Directly?"

"...sort of."

my—(new)*—message*

"How long'd they keep Fichtner alive, you reckon?" Greer asked.

"Impossible to tell, without access to his corpse."

"But you've been doin' some investigation of your own in the meantime, I'll bet."

Mehdi didn't bother to deny it; his fact-finding methods were legendarily effective, owing far more to the time-worn examples of Haroun al-Raschid and Hammurabi than to anything agreed on in The Hague. "My informants think...seventy-two hours at most."

"Ain't a whole lot of time to try and do anything about our Mister Gullah's situation, is it?"

"I hope you recorded the calls, at least," Mehdi said, eventually. "If so, perhaps you should have them analyzed, by someone not quite so..."

"Drunk?"

"I was going to say...personally involved. But make no mistake: someone is trying to puppet *you*, here, Agent Reizendaark—to get you down on the ground, where you are most unsuited to be. Having studied you, they no doubt know you like to sacrifice long-term build for short-term opportunity; they will lead you on some ethereal scavenger hunt in order to trap you, just as they did Fichtner. And what will happen then?"

Greer shut his eyes. "Oh, I think I got a pretty good idea."

Forget the desert's empty spaces and deceptive images—a guilty man's mind had all of that and more, re-splitting under pressure exponentially, like a prism. Grief was an echo-chamber. No matter how hard you thought you were listening, the only thing you ever really heard was your own voice.

Or somebody else's, still and small in the middle of the night, the way God's was supposed to sound. Saying: *Greer...you're a ghost.*

Well, maybe so.

But then again—not just yet.

***

Barely pausing to shower and shave, Greer hit the Geek Room again, doing his best Angry Fist of God impression. Told Gal and Guy to break it all down, far as they could, then farther.

As they did, he thought yet again about how "Intelligence," so-called, was a machine that ran on universal constants—secrecy, stupidity, entropy. It wasn't about the parts, and only slightly about the labor; damn thing'd keep running on its own, even if nobody did their fair share anymore. Stick a cog in, pop it out, throw it away, smash it to pieces; the machine kept grinding, exceeding fine, untouched. And though Greer might occupy its hub for the nonce, he had no illusions that that state of affairs would be perpetual. Lots of guys had held his exact same job, before being discarded and forgotten.

For now, however, he *was* still Big Man Off-Campus—the legendary Guy on the Other End of the Phone, running a large-ass part of Ajinabi's competition. Knock Greer Reizendaark off his game, and the Foreign Devil would win a free block of unsupervised time in which to cut a few more people's heads off...starting with Hasim Gullah, one assumed, before working his way back up the food chain.

So: something to keep in mind, maybe, even now. Something to bargain with.

"Got something," Guy said, finally.

Turned out, the very pixels making up the photos in which "Fichtner" appeared had GPS coordinates encoded in each of them—just beyond the border of Mehdi's home turf, in (predictably enough) the desert. The location of Ajinabi's death-room, Fichtner's body? Or both?

"And get this," Gal told Greer, excited as she ever got. "The phone calls have a frequency and a series of tones mixed in, just underneath the signal itself."

"A number." She nodded. "Traceable?"

"Nope."

Guy: "Looks like it's been overwritten at least twice, like it's changing every time somebody switches disposable cells—but a direct line, every time. Somebody important. Like it might even go straight to—"

"Uh huh," Greer said, then read it out loud, and pressed his ever-present Bluetooth's "dial" button.

"*Wa'alaikum ah salaam*," a voice said, at the other end.

Greer grinned. "Ajinabi, I presume."

Gal and Guy watched with horror-struck eyes as the negotiations commenced. Greer kept 'em short, if not sweet: a switch, him for Gullah, contingent on proof—positive, not 'Net-based—that the guy was still alive.

"Sheikh Nebbou can ferry you to the meet-point, no doubt," Ajinabi said, like he expected Greer to be impressed he knew they knew each other.

"He was gonna be my very next call," Greer agreed—then paused, as he heard the "call waiting" tone.

"Ah, your superiors. You should probably take this," Ajinabi suggested.

***

After that, things began to move even faster.

Wasn't much work to convince the CIA-CSIS-MI6 three-way that what had looked from the outside like Greer spiraling down into an alcohol-fueled psychotic break was really the triple-cross of the century—a trap so obvious, from either angle, that neither he nor Ajinabi could afford not to let it play through. Greer made sure to dangle the prospect of snapping up Ajinabi's near-supernatural tech at the same time, of course: the combo of insider info and toys, whatever they might be, which had somehow allowed him to pose as the undeniably dead Cal Fichtner on phone and sat-cam alike.

(Amazing, really, how Fichtner's current state had apparently given him skills Greer never knew him to possess, back when he was yet left upright. But then again, Fichtner's best quality as an operative always *was* his ability to adapt to any given new environment they dropped him into, going native just as fast—and effectively—as humanly possible.)

Greer wasn't too sure if they really believed him, or how much, or how much it mattered. But by Saturday afternoon he was walking off a transpo into bright sunlight, blinking at Mehdi's familiar face in the unfamiliar flesh: all dolled up in a swank linen suit and a pair of custom shades, looking crisp. He towered over everyone but Greer, who only lacked a couple of the same inches—vertically, anyhow.

"Hadn't thought to see you so soon, Agent Reizendaark, I must admit, Or at all, for that matter."

Greer shrugged. "Well, that's US initiative for you."

"Quite. So how do you find you like it, down here on the ground?"

"Not too much, buddy. Ain't got the build for it."

"Hmm," Mehdi said, yet again.

"You're startin' to sound like a damn bee," Greer told him, as they headed for the SUV.

***

Heat like a wall, dust everywhere. The drive went on so long, following GPS cue to GPS cue, it turned afternoon to night. The meet-point, meanwhile, turned out to be a low concrete building with slit windows; same place they'd brought Fichtner, like as not. Why mess with success?

"You don't have to come with me," Greer told Mehdi, who hissed, and drew some tiny little snub-nosed piece out from under his arm—small enough so it didn't spoil the line of his jacket, the peacock. Greer put his own empty hands up, and kicked the car door open.

But when they hauled Gullah out to meet him, with Ajinabi striding behind, Greer (who'd earned part of the military rank few remembered he had while serving in EOD) only had to look at the way Gullah's shirtjacket sat to know he was all rigged up and ready to blow.

Time went wonky, step-printed. To his right, he saw Mehdi raise his pint-sized gun, mouth opening, as Gullah's guards pushed him headlong towards Greer. To the left, Ajinabi, fiddling with a pocketed cell—seemed like he might be trying to detonate it remotely, but the signal was being blocked. And Greer could suddenly see Fichtner standing next to him, haloed from behind yet snapshot-clear with one hand on the phone, while the other reached to seat itself deep in the back of Ajinabi's skull: punch, grab, *twist*. A five-finger aneurysm in action.

"GET DOWN!" Greer yelled, kicking Mehdi away, and threw himself into the zone, as another of Ajinabi's goons managed to trigger the bomb's failsafe.

***

Amazing how little it hurt, after, considering the ungodly mess his body had made—his, Gullah's, Ajinabi's. (And where exactly *had* that bastard gone, anyhow? Greer sure didn't see him, except in pieces.) But then, they'd all been ready to die for their respective causes, one way or the other.

Greer "stood" next to Fichtner, watching Mehdi grub around in the wreckage for a long minute or two: concussed and reeling, his suit unsalvageable, usually dignified face streaming with tears. It was this last part which amazed Greer the most; hadn't thought the man cared, let alone so much.

Fichtner "laughed," or whatever its applicable equivalent might be. *Little late in the day to go all modest on us now, Greer, ain't it?*

Greer "nodded": True enough. He pointed at the half-leveled building, and "asked"—

Rest of you actually still in there somewhere, or was all this for nothin'?

Buried out back, yeah. But they'll find it easy enough, even without dogs—the grave's dug shallow. A beat. *Besides which...if this was really all about laying* me *to rest, I'll eat my damn hat.*

Greer could've argued that most ops were about more than one objective, at the very least—but it really did seem sort of immaterial at this point, so to speak. So instead, he just "nodded" once more.

Good endgame, son. You played it well—way I would've, pretty much.

Yeah? That's almost flattering.

Uh huh. 'Course, you did learn from the best...

But all twitting aside, Greer knew, it was only justice—payback after those years of Greer putting Fichtner's ass on the line for whatever new info it might bring, when he'd staked him out like a goat again and again, just to see who'd come sniffin'. All the times he'd done his damn job, while helping Fichtner do his...

But: *I really did let you go, Cal,* Greer tried to get across, nevertheless. *Just like you asked me to. Didn't use you to draw Ajinabi—that was never my intent. Not you, and for damn sure not Aqsa—*

Wouldn't matter much if you had, not now. But for what it's worth, Greer, I know. I know...

(everything, now)

Like you could too, you only wanted it.

(*Really?*)

Cal just gave him a shrug, like: *Sure. Why not?*

And then, all of a sudden—

—he did.

What was left of Greer Reizendaark raised his phantom no-hand to the sky, waving blithely at the satellite he knew Gal and Guy were currently hid behind, then reached right on back through the feed and into the mainframe to try some *real* tricks—sow a few search-links, start data-mining. Widening the parameters of the satellite's sweep to track the rest of Ajinabi's cell's fleeing trucks as they dispersed, crossing borders at random; he started a new folder, hidden down deep in the infrastructure. Saved, clicked, saved again.

You're good at that, what was left of Cal Fichtner "said," almost admiring. *Better than I ever was.*

Greer had to agree. Turned out, his last wife had had it right all along, without even knowing—a ghost really *was* the best kind of spook imaginable.

Well, I been doin' it all my life, son. Might as well keep on keepin' on.

The answer came back, fading: *Yeah, you just do that...*

(But as for me, I'll see you later. Maybe.)

Or...maybe not.

Heat, dust, blood; the totaled SUV, a smoking crater. Mehdi, weeping. And then Greer was abruptly alone, half in and half out, still stuck to the world's dirty back by—duty? Desire?

While Fichtner, his revenge served plastique-hot, moved on to...wherever. Someplace Aqsa awaited him, hopefully, where maybe even poor Gullah had a seat set aside at that infinitely bountiful table.

(Again, if only vaguely, he wondered where Ajinabi himself really had gone—to his bed of virgins, as advertised? Or somewhere just a tad more...off-putting?)

One could only hope.

I could do that too, Greer caught himself thinking. *Just go, in either direction. But—*

"Looking down," seeing Mehdi looking so stricken, and feeling a weird surge of affection. Plus the sting of power unused, and a million different places to use it—to plug himself into the universe's hide and genuinely be the puppetmaster he'd only thought himself, before he'd known better.

—no. Not just yet.

Greer "smiled" to himself, settling in, now so adjusted to his new state he could almost feel a memory of lips moving, in sympathy with the concept. And sent Mehdi an email.

SLICK BLACK BONES AND SOFT BLACK STARS

All graves look the same, generally: Sunken or up-thrust, backdirt slightly looser than whatever lies around it, sometimes of a different color, a different composition. Anything that shows something's been scooped out and reapportioned, piled back in atop what lies beneath.

You start with trowel and probe, cleaning the surface near what you suspect is the grave's edge, thrusting the probe in as far as it'll go, then sniffing it for decomp. If you strike something soft, that's a find. Satellite photos also help, as do picks, shovels; Ken Kichi sets up nearby to run the electronic mapping station, charting the site's contours, eventually providing a three-dimensional outline of every body and its position when found, while Judy Moss—your usual dig partner—shares process photography duties with Guillaume Jutras, head of this particular Physicians for Human Rights forensic anthropology team. Their shutters buzz constantly like strange new insects in the oven-door heat, *snap-flash, snap-flash, whirrrr.*

And you, meanwhile—you're crouched down in the stench feeling for bones, finding rotten cloth, salt-stiff flesh.

The grave is humid, seawater-infused. Sand clings to everything, knitting with bone itself. At the very top, exposed to air and scavengers alike—crabs, birds—the bodies are slimy, broken down for parts, semi-skeletonized. Down further, they're still fleshed, literally ripe for autopsy; those are the ones Jutras wants in the worst way. While down further still...

Each stratum is an era, a span of time between massacres. The numbers vary: Twos and threes, five-person groups at most, as opposed to the first and second layers' twenty-three. Deeper than that is where your particular skills will come most into play, differentiating one body's bones from another's, telling male from female, adult from child. You try not to feel bad about wanting to get down there as fast as possible, to see just how far down it all goes.

This tower of murder, thrown down, inverted. To you, it's a mystery, a challenge; to the people whose fragments it's made from—their relatives, at any rate—it's an obscenity, a disgrace. But you can't think about that, because it'll only slow you down, make you sloppy. Sentiment breeds mistakes.

Crouching down, feeling with both hands, gently but firmly. And saying silently to yourself, with every breath: *Keep working, keep quiet, keep sharp. Miss nothing.* Assuring them, at the same time: *Lie still, we're coming, finally. At long last.*

We're coming to bring you home.

***

You reached the island of Carcosa seven days ago, at 6:35 PM by your watch, only to find what looked like two suns staring down, one centered, the other offset—an upturned pupil, cataract-white, with a faint bluish tinge. *It's an optical illusion,* Jutras told you, during your conference-Skype briefing; *Everyone sees them. There's other things too.*

Like what?

Just...things. It's not important.

(The clear implication: *You won't be there long enough for them to matter.* An assumption you don't question, since it suits you fine; you'll remember it later though. And laugh.)

So yes, it's strange, though not unbearably so—no more so than the incredible heat or the smell accompanying it, rancid and inescapable, though you haven't even come near the dig site as yet; the black beaches with their smooth-washed half-glass sand, the masses of shrimp-colored flowers and spindly nests of stick-insects creeping up every semi-vertical surface. Actually, all the colors are different here, just ever-so-slightly "off": the green laid on green of its grasses, fronds, and vines isn't *your* green, not exactly. More like your green's occluded memory.

There's a wet woodsmoke tang to the air, like they've just doused a forest fire. Breathing it in gives you a languorous, possessive contact high— opium smoke mixed with bone dust.

According to Jutras, the island—itself just the merest jutting peak of an underwater mountain range ringed with black smokers, incredibly volatile— was once centre-set with a volcano that exploded, Thera-style, its caldera becoming what's now known as "Lake" Hali. The quote-marks are because the lake itself is filled and re-filled with seawater brought in through a broken end-section that forms the island as a whole into a wormy crescent. Carcosa City occupies the crescent's midsection, its highest peak, while the two peninsulas formed by the crescent's horns almost overlap. The longer of the two is called Hali-joj'uk, "Hali-door" or "-gate," in the island's highly negotiable yet arcanely individual tongue. Wouldn't think there could be quite so many sub-dialects supported on an island whose entire population has never historically topped four hundred, and yet.

It's like every family has their own way of saying things, Jutras told you. *And they all understand each other, but they know you won't. That's why we have the interpreter.*

They don't trust folks from Away, Judy chimed in. *That's how they put it: there's them, and then there's Away. Everywhere else.*

Yeah, it's a serious Innsmouthian situation 'round these parts, Ken agreed. *Some inbred motherfuckers we're dealin' with, that's a certified fact.*

Ken, Jutras warned him, but Ken simply snorted.

What, man? It's just true. These people been marrying their cousins for a thousand years, by definition; cousins if they're lucky, *and some years? I'm willing to take a bet the gene pool maybe didn't stretch all that far. Like those Amish villages where the guys all have the same first name, and every dog's named "Hund."*

Not a lot of cultural contamination on Carcosa, in other words, which is good in some ways, not so much in others. To cite another history of similar colonial isolation, in 1856—fifty-two years after being officially rediscovered by the British—Pitcairn Island, inhabited by the descendants of the H.M.S. *Bounty*'s mutineers, lost 100% of its population, gaining only sixteen of them back three years after. Since then, its numbers have fluctuated up and down—as high as two hundred and fifty in 1936, as low as forty-three in 1996. Yet numbers in Carcosa apparently remain steady, as though maintaining a strict death per birth replace-the-race policy...barring the occasional mass murder, that is.

Because that's what's brought you here, of course—like it always does, no matter where, no matter with who. Because this is your "business," the reckoning of mortality: to sex bones and extract DNA, to separate violent death covered up from more wholesome detritus, plague-pits or accidents or Acts of God alike, the dreadful human wreckage left behind whenever earth gapes wide, whenever the jungle sneezes up something that makes people cough themselves to death or sweat blood from every pore, whenever the sea rises up and bears away all in its path.

The whole island takes up approximately eighteen square miles, "lake" included. Nine of those take you from the airstrip to Hali-jo'juk, where the causeway to the dig awaits: Funeral Rock, yet one more island *inside* an island, a tiny chip barely a mile across split off from the main rim back into Hali itself, a shelf of bare black crag-slopes cradling a black sand beach which separates completely from the peninsula at high tide.

This is where it all happened; where no one will say how many of the island's otherwise rigidly documented population were herded over no one will say how long a period of time, never to return. From what Judy and Ken have uncovered thus far, they think it must've begun long before the island was charted, let alone visited, and continued intermittently long after, with only the sheer numbers of the last mass-murder finally revealing the true nature of this particular "memorial" tradition at last...along with the fact that those taken to Funeral Rock for "burial" were not, strictly speaking, usually *dead* before the rocks and sand were thrown in on top of them.

All they know is, there's no telling how deep it goes down, Jutras told you, before you even started packing. *Which is why I need my best girl, Alice—to turn this around, ASAP.*

What's the hurry? you asked. *Top layer's the only one they can press charges with, right? I mean, the rest certainly proves a pattern of behavior, local prejudices, superstitions, maybe even religion-based motive...but in prosecutorial terms, just how useful is that?*

Jutras sighed. *Hard to say. It's a...weird situation, to say the least; slippery. Nobody knows who's responsible, or claims not to, so the authorities have just scooped up every able-bodied man within a certain radius; they don't have a jail, so they're holding them in the hospital's contagious ward.*

Because women *never kill anybody, right?* But since you both knew the answer to that one, you asked instead: *Who* are *the authorities in this case, exactly, anyways?*

Um...Wikipedia says the Hyades Islands, "a sub-archipelago thirty miles off the coast of East Timor," so—Indonesia, I guess? It's all pretty up in the air. A pause. *Point is, they don't even have cops here, let alone a court, so whoever does get charged with anything is going to have to be taken off-island for trial, and nobody's happy with* that *idea; the local garrison commander needs hard facts to keep Carcosa from blowing up around him, literally. Thus, us.*

You've worked with Jutras seven times before, all over. United Nations International Criminal Tribunal digs to start with, coordinated through The Hague—Darfur, then Cote d'Ivoire. Then on to smaller matters in far more obscure places, balancing corporate internal policing with volunteer work for far-flung, resource-poor communities. Carcosa definitely falls under the latter rubric, and also promises something the other sites most often don't: Mystery. Even back when you were finishing your internship in the Ontario Forensic Pathology Service, the final verdict on any case was almost never in doubt from the moment you first viewed the body on, be it murder, misadventure, or J-FROG (Just Plain Fuckin' Ran Out of Gas).

I've never heard of the Hyades, actually, you admitted, feeling stupid. *Carcosa either.*

Yeah, I'm with you there; had to look 'em up on the plane. But ours is not to reason, right?

And you might have disagreed with him on that last part—should have, probably. But you were jet-lagged already, which never helps. One more dig didn't seem that big a deal.

Now here you are waist-deep in it, learning better.

***

Decomp clings to everything, in both senses of the word, just like the heat puts paid to modesty, prompting you and Judy to roll your coveralls to the waist over lunch, so you won't get corpse-rub in your food. Later, you'll pack today's "grave bra" into a plastic bag full of Woolite and choose tomorrow's from the rack it's been drying on in your hotel room closet. You buy seven new ones for every dig, color-coordinated by weekday, and leave them behind afterwards, so stink-saturated they're only fit for burning.

The famous interpreter Jutras hired, Ringo Astur, sits with you under the canopy, waving flies away. Round-faced, eternally cheerful, chain-smoking imported cigarettes; his skin is the same color as Carcosa City's brickwork, a coral-tinged light brown, hair worn in short cornrows. *How many today, Alice?* he asks you every noon and every night, eyes charm-crinkling, like it's some local version of *How* you *doin'?*

Three so far, Ringo. Why?

Oh, no reason. That's a lot, yes?

More and more, you want to tell him. More, and more, and *more...* Just what have these people been *doing* out here all this time, anyways?

Tell me about the other city, you say instead. *The one from across Hali.*

Hm, he replies. *Well...that city's also named Carcosa, supposedly. It appears lake-centre, where the volcano used to be—not always, not every night, but sometimes. Where the first Carcosa City stood once, before it dropped inside.*

Then there's a whole other Carcosa City under this lake?

A shrug. *So they say. And it appears, sometimes...we'd be closer to it here than back over there, if it did. They come down to the quay when it does, the people who live in it, and beckon, try to get us to row across.*

People live there?

Well, they look like people, yes, supposedly. They say they wear masks, those who've seen them.

You look down at your hands then, still stained from the grave; the sand's black tinge never seems to wash entirely off. Remembering one skull, its back crushed in with an axe-like implement, so fragile that when you threaded two fingers through its eye sockets and a thumb through the nose hole, it came apart in your hand—shed itself by sections even as you fought to keep it intact, yellow-grey bone sliding to sketch an entire fresh new face with palm-pink eyes and an unstrung, mud-filled mouth.

Unsurprising how easy they come apart, considering what you discovered on those top-layer excavations: Carcosans are full of cartilage, like sharks or octopi, with the proportion of actual collagen-poor bone to extensive net of tissue creepily small; all of them come out flexible yet springy, like osteogenesis imperfecta without the fracturing. You can see the signs from where you sit, in Ringo's bluish sclerae, his triangular face, that certain blurred malleability of feature which comes from most of your cranial plates simply not fusing, a head full of fontanelles and no joint left un-double. Once, in Carcosa City, you saw a not-exactly-small ten-year-old squeeze through a cat door and pop out the other side laughing, to bound away into the brush.

Not enough bones in some ways, too many in others. And you're the only person, thus far, who ever seems to have thought of putting the extra ones together...

(But that's a private project, at least for now. You haven't even shown Jutras.)

It happens on two-sun days, mostly, around suns'-set, Ringo continues. *That's what they say. You look across Hali and there it is, all lit up, with the masks, and the beckoning. And then when you look up you see black stars high above, watching you.*

Who's this "they" you keep talking about, man? Ken yells at him, from over by the cooler. *I mean, you're related to basically everybody here, right? All those other Asturs? Old John-Paul-George Astur from the post office, Miss Sexy London Astur from the kelp farm? That dude Kilimanjaro Means We Couldn't Climb It Astur, from the boat repair?*

Don't be an arse, Ken, Judy tells him. *Jesus! What's it to you, anyhow?*

Now it's Ringo's turn to look down.

They don't talk to me much anymore, he says, finally. *Because I went Away. So I can't really ask them about any of it.*

You never saw it yourself then? you find yourself asking.

Well...I did, yes. Once or twice, I think. I was young, a long time back. It was before, and Away—well, Away makes things like that hard to remember.

Ever try to go over?

No, no. That would be—that's a bad idea.

You nod, take a swig of water. Then something he said earlier comes back, prompting another question, before you can think better of it:

Closer over here...is that why people really came to Funeral Rock, in the first place? So they'd have less of a way to row, if they wanted to make it to the other Carcosa?

Ringo looks at you hard for a long moment, not speaking. 'Til: *No,* he says, finally. *That's not why. They came to bury, or get buried. Like the King, in the story.*

...what story?

***

The King, Ringo tells you, once ruled in Other Carcosa City, before he was expelled and set adrift. He came from somewhere else entirely, far Away, further than anywhere—came walking through their gates on foot one two-sun day, at suns'-set, and when asked to remove his mask as a gesture of friendship, claimed he didn't wear one.

Couldn't they tell? you ask, reasonably enough. But Ringo just shakes his head.

He looked...different, supposedly. Pale, yellow, with horns, all over—no one could think that was really his face; that's what they say. And yet... That's why the volcano blew up, you know. So they say.

Because of the King?

Because he wouldn't leave. So the people in Other Carcosa City made it happen, to make sure he did.

Wouldn't that have destroyed them *too?*

Ringo shrugs. Concluding, after a beat: *Well, no, supposedly. They're— different.*

Later, back at camp, Judy maintains she's actually heard this same story a few times already, from other islanders. Which surprises the hell out of Ken, who—for all his bitching—probably hasn't tried talking to anybody without Ringo translating since he got here. Jutras easily confirms it, though, by pulling out an .mp3 he made on his phone of a woman (Miss Sexy London Astur?) telling the tale in Stage One Pidgin, the Malacca-Malay-inflected version of English Carcosans might've picked up from passing sailors, peppered with words you either can't hear or don't understand, your brain papering over the lacunae with whatever seems most contextually appropriate:

Many and many, one time there is to be being one [king] [magician] [warlord] [traitor], who is to be having all strength from the black pit of [stars] [salt] [silt], the bottom of every [hole] [mouth] [grave]. He is to be wearing no [mask] [face] [name]. He is to be being torn apart and ground down, thrown in seas, sunk deep, for fish to be eating. But then one time there are fish to be eating him, and islanders are to be eating the fish, with [pieces] [seeds] [bones] of him inside them. And then islanders are to be having children with [no bones] [no names] [no faces]...

You gulp, taste bile. *Jesus,* you say. *So...that's it, right? The motive. That's why?*

Classic Othering, with a fairytale spin, Jutras agrees. *I particularly like the whole Evil King deal that obviously keeps being trotted out every time these throwback genetic payloads pop up; you wait 'til it gets obvious, re-brand them as changelings spawned by the Enemy, then take 'em over to Funeral Rock and let "nature" take its course. "We 'had' to kill them, you see, because they weren't human, not really. Not like us."*

Look who's talkin', Ken mutters.

Judy frowns. *What I don't understand, though, is where this all came from, originally. The* idea *of this Evil King, of Other Carcosa City...all of it.*

"Away," I guess, Jutras replies. *Except...no, they were doing this long before anybody else ever came by here, so—some sort of primal phobia about the sea, maybe: All that water, everything underneath it, the earthquakes, all the instability. It has to be somebody's fault.* A pause. *That's the theory anyways. Except it's hard to say, because, uh...nobody will say.*

You can't possibly believe—

Of course not, Alice, but they believe *it. Enough to kill twenty-three children, and God knows how many more...*

Now it's your turn to nod, to stare. And reply, eventually:

...I should show you something, probably.

***

Looking at what you've so neatly laid out on a canvas tarp in a shallow trench three feet from the grave's lip, elements-sheltered under a fresh new tent, Jutras says nothing, just stares down. You don't blame him, exactly; did it yourself, the first time you finally thought to stop and breathe. Now the words spill out in a similar rush, barely interrupted, monologue paced to an adrenaline rush tachycardia beat, so fast it barely seems to be *your* voice you're both hearing say these things, with complete declarative confidence—the same authoritarian, spell-casting rhythm which renders truth from lies, makes fiction into fact, simply by stating even the most ridiculous-sounding things out loud.

You study him closely as you speak too, just in case: Strain to read every minor shift, each muscle-twitch, each spasm. Almost as though you think that at some point his own eye-whites are going to turn blue, jaw and temples deforming, as the planes of his skull soften 'til they slide to form someone else's face entirely.

Remember how Ken kept saying these people weren't like us? Well, asshole that he is, turns out he's actually right. The adult human body has two hundred and six bones. These...have more. Best approximate total: Just over three hundred and fifty, like a human infant, almost as though their bones never fused properly—and three times the normal amount of cartilage, so it doesn't much matter that they didn't. Like they were never meant to; like they were supposed to reach adulthood able to squeeze themselves easily through spaces that'd break a normal adult human's neck.

Also, the reason it's "just over" is because it seems each body's inevitably got two duplicates of one particular bone...except it's never the same one. This woman has two fibulae. This man has two second thoracic vertebrae. This child has two mandibles—must've made it hard to talk, especially since the second one is adult-sized. It's like God was smuggling a whole other person into Carcosa, hidden inside these people's bodies.

But—what can I say; I guess everybody caught on.

Oh, and now that we've reached the bottom—did that yesterday—you know how many corpses are in this grave, exactly? Three hundred and fifty.

Plus one.

It's that "plus one" Jutras' looking at right now, the nameless guest at this carrion feast, painstakingly pieced together in anatomical explode-a-view. On its own it'd seem like some drunk pre-med student practical joke, a botched bastardization Transformered together from three or more skeletons at once: Spine articulated like a boa constrictor's, ribs everywhere, even in its limbs; skull like a Rubik's helmet, slabbed and fluted and interlocking, a puzzle-box with a million solutions but no answers. The fact that it proved surprisingly easy to assemble is the least of your worries, a strangeness so trivial it's barely worth sparing the energy to consider...not when there's just so much more about the whole exercise to avoid thinking about at all, in retrospect.

How long has that mould been growing on it? Jutras asks.

What mould?

He points, and you finally see it: grey as the bones themselves, furry. Hard to tell what you thought it was before, if you even registered its existence—moisture? Condensation?

I...don't know. Why?

...no reason.

But he's already backing away, step by step; peeling the flap without looking, shimmying himself free. You hear him take a long, shaky breath, almost like he's tensing against nausea, trying not to vomit. His walkie gives an almighty crackling howl.

There's something happening, he says, at last, after a hushed, one-sided conversation. *In the city. I have to go.*

And a minute later, it's just you and the bones again.

***

Jutras is out of contact for most of the next day, which means he isn't there for the undersea quake that rattles the island. Minor as tremors go, the epicentre's out by the black smoker ring that keeps Carcosa's shores so fertile, so teeming with fish and kelp-forests; closer to Carcosa City than Funeral Rock, thankfully, so the back-slop doesn't do much more than submerge the causeway far faster and for far longer than expected. You didn't even notice it yourself until you came out of the tent and found Ken and Judy on the horn with Jutras, yelling at him about being stuck on-site for the night until the causeway emerges again. Said prospect bothers you less than it should, but that could just be sheer exhaustion. Who knew watching mould grow could be so draining.

What *does* bother you—silencing Ken and Judy as well—is what Jutras finally tells you, when he gets a word in edgewise: The quake brought in a mini-tsunami that cracked the hospital apart, shearing off the wall of the contagious ward. In the confusion, most massacre suspects cut and ran, disappearing into a sympathetic web of back-rooms, basements, cliff-caves, and other assorted hidey-holes. Surprisingly few injuries amongst the military guards, and all from natural causes rather than any sort of hostile action, but all of you can read between the lines; the garrison is confused and demoralized from the bottom up, perhaps even fixing to cut and run, and the islanders themselves...well, they aren't happy. To say the least.

They've heard what you're doing here, Ringo tells you, after Jutras signs off. *Putting the King back together—that's why this happened. They want to stop you.*

Ken snorts. *So these dudes in jail, what, called up a wave and surfed on out of there? C'mon, man. Army'll pick 'em up by tomorrow; this place ain't big enough to hide in, not for long.*

You don't know that. You don't know anything about us.

I know enough, man.

No. Ringo shakes his head, visibly struggling to keep polite. *It's...not safe for you here, not now, any of you. You should go.*

Go where? you ask, waving Ken silent, while Judy hugs herself. *Where should we go, Ringo?*

Without hesitation: *Away, of course. And take me with you, when you do.*

***

Though you're hardly a mycologist or saprophytologist by trade, anyone who works enough decomp learns to ID the key fungal players soon enough. The stuff that's growing over "the King's" bones still doesn't match anything you recognize: Too tough, spreading too fast, especially without an identifiable nutrient source. You take a moment to look up the region on your tablet, looking for a local flora-and-fauna rundown, and pause at Wikipedia's disambiguation page for "Hyades." There are four entries: the islands, the band, the Greek mythological figures, and a star cluster in the constellation Taurus.

You look up in the dusk light, out across the lake. The "twin suns" sink towards the horizon in a blurry shimmer. A mirage, an illusion; the same thing that makes the suns look almost bluish-white, rather than red-gold. So Ringo says. You look back down to your tablet, and click on the entry for the star cluster. Thinking, as you do, about articles some of your geekier friends have sent to you, essays about such things as static wormholes, and equipotential space-time points; quantum tunneling, black branes and folded space, negative energy densities.

The Hyades cluster is more than six hundred million years old, far older than most such stellar groups, a survivor of the aeons by orbiting far from galactic centre. At least twenty of its stars are A-type white giants, with seventeen or eighteen of them thought likely to be binary—double-star—systems. It appears in the *Iliad* on the shield that Hephaestus made for Achilles, and is named for the daughters of Atlas, who wept so hard over the death of their brother Hyas they eventually became the patron stars of rain.

Twilight deepens, and your tablet's glow increases in the growing dark. But your shadow grows sharp to one side, beyond what the tablet could illuminate, and you look up once more.

Above the centre of the lake, where the volcano exploded centuries ago, lights glow in a scattered matrix of green, blue, gold, and red, clear and cold. The darkness between them seems to outline shapes—structures, blocks, towers. They're hard to look at, defying your eyes' focus almost painfully.

Can't tell if the blur is distance, or atmosphere mirage, or the wake of motion too fast to follow. The blue-green, poisonous light of the setting suns behind it twists your stomach. You feel the whole thing *pulling*, physically, like a hook in the gut: some second force of gravity, pressing you towards the lake and the place you know isn't there, *can't* be there—

—not because it isn't real, but because it's somewhere else. Some utter, alien elsewhere, so far away its light is older than your species.

It's that pull, that nausea and that disbelief, which keeps you from hearing the tumult until it's too late. Distracted by Other Carcosa City's spectacular appearance, you simply haven't noticed the boats' approach, silent and sure—pontooned sea-canoes, anchoring themselves at Funeral Rock's base so their passengers can shinny up the handhold-pocked cliff and emerge through those cave-entrances you never even knew were there, almost under your feet.

A burst of bullets, muzzle-flare in the night, and Ringo's already up, hauling on your arm: *Alice, come, come on, Alice—now, now now, they're here! Leave everything!*

But—Ken, Judy, Jesus, Ringo! What about...

Too late, come on! We have to go—

Across Hali, behind Other Carcosa City's gleaming shoreline, you can just glimpse the "real" capitol going up in flames, a series of controlled explosions. Is one of those Jutras' field office, the garrison, the seaplane that brought you here? Over near the grave, meanwhile, Ken's scrabbling for his data, uploading frantically; one shot catches him in the shoulder, another in the upper back, sending him straight over the lip. You can hear him thrashing down below, desperately trying to cover himself in enough sand-muck to turn invisible. Ringo pulls you headlong while the attackers rush the camp, smashing and tearing, hurling equipment and evidence alike into the sea. Ripping up the tents, they riddle every prepped body bag they uncover with yet more gunfire, as though they think something might be hiding in there.

Good thing I moved him, you find yourself thinking. *Good thing, good thing...*

Ringo drops to his knees, dragging you along with him; your knees jolt, painfully. *In here, Alice,* he says. *Come on! This one goes out the opposite side—we can swim, they'll never see us.*

Swim? *Where the hell* to?

Other Carcosa City, of course; no one will expect it. Can't you see them, beckoning?

But: That's just a bit too much crazy to stomach, even now. So here you pull back, wrenching yourself free, even as Ringo worms his way slickly down into the earth, gone in seconds—you'd never make it anyways, is what you tell yourself. The gap's far too narrow, too twisting; you'd simply lodge fast, bruised and scraped and strained to breaking, to die crushed like a bug.

You let him go instead, whispering *Goodbye.*

Why? Judy yells from behind you, uselessly, drawing another burst. *Why, why?*

Because some things are meant to stay buried, a voice replies, from deep inside.

Then: Spotlights stab down out of the growing dusk, helicopter rotors roaring, as speakers filter what must be orders far past the point of comprehensibility. More gunfire strafes the camp, this time vertically; Judy's head explodes outright, GSW damage simultaneously shock-hammering away one half of your body in a series of consecutive hits to forearm, shoulder, hip, thigh. The downdraft wraps you in already-torn tent-fabric like a plastic bag shroud, momentum rolling you straight into the scrub where you stowed "the King"'s reassembled body, so you sprawl almost nose to whatever it uses for a nose with it.

No pain, simply shock, cold and huge enough to sharpen your observational skills to inhuman levels. The not-fungus has finished its work. The creature's skin is black everywhere but its pallid mask of a face, slick and soft, oily to the touch, almost warm; that's your blood it's soaking up, spongelike, as if every pore is a feeding orifice, swelling with the sacrifice.

And its massive, horned head turns, yellow eyes cracking open. Locking upon yours.

I am here, it tells you; *look across the lake, where my city rises, and watch us beckon. You have done me great service, bringing me back into this world.*

Now: Be not afraid, lie still, lie quiet. Your long wait is over.

Beyond the hovering 'copter, those two suns sink down, white-blue turning red, filling Hali's caldera with false lava. And when you slump over onto your back, looking up again by sheer default, you see stars: Soft black stars, almost indistinguishable, in a black, black sky.

The King lays one scaly hand on your brow, lightly. Almost affectionately.

I am coming, he promises, *to take you home.*

THAT PLACE

Because we remember pain and the menace of death more vividly than pleasure, and because our feelings toward the beneficent aspects of the unknown have from the first been captured and formalised by conventional religious rituals, it has fallen to the lot of the darker and more maleficent side of cosmic mystery to figure chiefly in our popular supernatural folklore. This tendency, too, is naturally enhanced by the fact that uncertainty and danger are always closely allied; thus making any kind of an unknown world a world of peril and evil possibilities. When to this sense of fear and evil the inevitable fascination of wonder and curiosity is superadded, there is born a composite body of keen emotion and imaginative provocation whose vitality must of necessity endure as long as the human race itself. Children will always be afraid of the dark, and men with minds sensitive to hereditary impulse will always tremble at the thought of the hidden and fathomless worlds of strange life which may pulsate in the gulfs beyond the stars, or press hideously upon our own globe in unholy dimensions which only the dead and the moonstruck can glimpse.

—H.P. Lovecraft, "The Supernatural in Literature"

So say two sisters finally come back home, after their parents die—twins. Their names are Holly and Heather. They have a younger brother, Edwin, whom they haven't seen for some time. Estrangement's grown up between them all, for no apparently good reason. It's sad, but these things happen.

Holly and Heather attend university in Toronto. They also room together, because why not? They've always been like that. They can't ever remember being apart.

Edwin never went to university. He finished high school, then trained as an auto mechanic, so he works all year round. He does most of his calls along the rural routes of northern Ontario, circling the area where they used to live, in Lake of the North District; his speciality is extending the life of trucks and four-wheelers, fighting planned obsolescence on behalf of people who can't afford to trade up. Distance is an issue, up there. If you can't drive, you can't do much of anything.

One night Holly gets a call—it's Edwin. *Mom and Dad are gone*, he says. *Accident, out near Overdeere. Black ice pile-up. You need to come into town to hear the will read, then muck out the house with me.*

The girls know this isn't going to be easy, either way; it's not like their parents were hoarders, as such, but they did tend to hold onto, well, everything. There's a lot of stuff to appraise, most of it probably worthless, except on an emotional level. But it's got to be done.

We'll live there while we do it, Heather decides. *Go up just after mid-terms, spend a few weeks. It won't take longer than that. Not if we don't let it.*

"Town" is Chaste, up past Your Lips, almost to God's Ear. Five traffic lights, a church, a school, a gas station strip-mall, and a clinic that does double duty for Quarry Argent. Around it, there's a network of small farms but acres and acres of uncut wood-lots. Cabin-style houses here and there, like the one they grew up in. It took thirty minutes to drive to the town limits, then twenty more to walk in, so days started early, up before dawn. Insects singing in summer, dark and cold and silent all winter.

Hope the fireplace still works, Heather says.

Funeral's already happened: cremation. The lawyer's office is in the strip-mall, right next to a hardware store. Edwin's waiting outside, their parents' shared urn under one arm. The reading's brief—three-way split. The lawyer suggests they sell the house as soon as possible, and they agree, once it's cleared out. They sign, initial, and drive up, Edwin leading the way.

The house looks the same.

The house smells the same.

The air is full of dust already. It hasn't been that long. Does this happen, when people die? Does dust just fill the air, like you're breathing in their ashes?

Edwin puts the urn on the mantel above the dusty fireplace. *I was thinking we could scatter them in the garden,* he says, *but we'll have to wait for spring. Too cold, right now. Earth's frozen.*

Yes, Holly agrees, while Heather says nothing.

She's looking at the urn, its dull silver curve. Thinking she can almost see something reflected there, besides them, but unsure of what.

***

So say they work all the rest of that day, as the light slowly dims. Outside, overhead, grey clouds scud a mackerel sky. Inside, Edwin, Heather, and Holly are going through closets, pulling out drawers, looking under sinks and poking around cabinets, finding spaces they barely remember existing. Every inch of secret room packed tight with boxes, bags, piles of paper. It's amazing what stacks up.

Why would they keep all this? Heather asks. Edwin shrugs.

Why wouldn't they?

It's a valid question.

Upstairs, under the bed in their parents' room, they find the box. It's plain cardboard, with both their names written on it: *Holly & Heather, 1995.* When Holly opens it, it makes an odd little sound, like a sigh.

It contains a collection of seemingly random objects, some broken and melted, all discoloured, as though exposed to bright sunlight for long periods of time before being stored. Some sort of tin, slightly flattened; a necklace with two clear, cracked plastic beads; a handful of shells and stones, still crusted with dirt. A doll's hairbrush. A stiff gilt ribbon. And also two folded sheets of paper, worn along their creases, like they've been kept inside a wallet. Opened, these turn out to be covered in rambly, vaguely familiar writing, too large for an adult's...Holly thinks it's hers. Heather thinks it's Holly's too.

Go there, the top of the first one says. *Throw each piece down, as you do. A trail. Breadcrumbs.*

Wind the string (and there is string, Heather sees now. It used to be purple.) *around three corners. Wait.*

Words will come. Say them.

Let it form.

Never knock first. Wait until THEY do.

Wait again. Until THEY go away.

Open.

And on the second page, nothing but this—a warning, one can only assume:

If it's That Place, then <u>*don't*</u>*.*

The *don't* is underlined three times.

They all three examine the box and its content for some time, Edwin watching his sisters, as though waiting for them to speak. Eventually, Holly asks: *What is this?*

I don't know, Heather replies. *Some kind of game?*

We made this, though. And I don't remember...

...ever playing anything like this? Me either.

Those rules are crazy. It's like we were high when we wrote them.

Heather shakes her head. *That's how you wrote 'til you were ten. Unless you were doing stuff you never told me about, "high" didn't come into it.*

But you must've been there too.

Been where when? When this got made? I don't—

Holly turns the box lid over again, pointing out: *Not the rules, no, but this here—that's not just labelling. That's our* names, *the way we used to sign them. Mine and yours too. See?*

Yeah, sure. Like you say, though...I don't remember.

There's a snort, then; a swallowed laugh, curt and ugly. It comes from Edwin, who they turn to look at, as one. He raises his eyebrows.

Seriously? is all he says.

***

An hour later, they're sitting at the kitchen table with a gas lantern turned up high and a whole sheaf of crumbly newsprint spread out in front of them. Edwin took the file from a drawer in their dad's desk in the icy little add-on office he built out back when the girls were eleven, looking out onto the not-so-distant fringe of almost all-conifer woods. Now that most of the leaves have fallen except for the evergreens, you can just make out a pale little smudge halfway up the sloping rock-face that marks where they once set up a wooden card-table and used it for shelter, sitting beside each other under its shade, staring down at the house from up high. It was blue once, but age and weather have chewed its planks almost bare.

You don't remember any of this, Edwin repeats, finally, after they've told him that several times. *That seems... No, seriously?*

We don't, Holly says. Heather snorts.

It's a joke, she tells her sister. *He's making it up.* She gestures at the articles Edwin's been showing them, the documents, the photos. *Not the getting lost in the woods part, obviously—we could've blocked it out, trauma, all that. Just...everything else.*

Why would I lie? Edwin demands.

Another snort. *Why* wouldn't *you?*

What the file says is that when Holly and Heather were nine years old—Edwin was seven then, odd man out since birth—they disappeared for roughly three days, seventy-one and a half hours, after having "gone for a walk" one afternoon. That they were found in a clearing, one the adults searching for them had already covered, marking it off their maps a good thirty-five hours earlier: dirty, unconscious, mildly wounded (scrapes, bruising, a long scratch down Holly's cheek which may have created that faint scar she's never known how she got), and starving. Having lost so much weight, in fact, that it almost seemed they'd been gone for far longer.

What Edwin says, however...

You used to play the game all the time. You'd never let me play. It was something you made up one day, passing the paper back and forth, like you were writing a story together. Words just appearing in your heads, like you were being told them.

Oh, you are so full of—

You said it opened a door to somewhere, Edwin goes on, undaunted; probably gives him immense pleasure just to say it out loud, after all this time. *Someplace that scared you, but you kept on going back again and again, probably because it did scare you. And I wanted to go too, 'cause I wanted to do everything you did, but you told me it wasn't a good place to go. Said if I did, they'd know I wasn't supposed to be there, and they'd get me.*

"They" who?

How'm I supposed to know? He looks down at the table, taps the closest headline: GIRLS RECOVERED UNHARMED. *This is where you did it, right here, where they found you. Not at first—used to be you'd go upstairs, into the attic, 'til you caught me sneaking up after. That was when you took it outside, into the woods, up past the old table. Up over the rock, with that clump of three trees.*

Holly shakes her head. *Okay, Ed, Christ. That's more than enough.*

I'll show you. You think I can't? Take you right fucking there. Been there enough times, since.

Sure you will, Heather mocks. *The scary place in the woods! The door! Fucking Narnia.*

Holly laughs. *Fucking* Elidor, *sounds like.*

They grin at each other. Edwin sits there sullen, arms crossed—twice as big, not that that counts for much. Bent in on himself like he's already eaten so much of his own rage, over the years, it's gestating inside him; has to hug himself hard, or it might break free and flop out, spraying everywhere.

You two, he says, to no one in particular.

***

None of them will be able to remember how they got there, later on. Just that they're suddenly standing there, bundled to the eyes, breath puffing out like steam, rising ghostly into the black, black sky. The clouds hang heavy except where they gap here and there, wind-torn. Through these few rips, patches white with numberless stars can be glimpsed, finally freed to reveal themselves now that the city's light pollution's been peeled away by cold and distance—sharp, small, glinting bright. Pins velvet-set. Weasels' teeth.

Three trees and a dip, a crevice full of dirt and leaves where two rocks meet underground, grinding against each other. Frost on the bark, odd speckles of snow. A ferocious lack of light, so deep it almost becomes a fourth presence, pooling between them in that triangle, that invert chalice.

Here we are, Edwin tells them, unnecessarily, as Holly feels the hair on her neck—hood-hidden though it might be—start to lift.

This is bad, Heather says, equally unnecessarily. *This is...*

(fucking *terrifying*)

And they don't even have to look at each other, don't have to say it at all: don't know why, couldn't care less, but they just *can't* stay. Wild horses couldn't keep them here one single moment longer, let alone their stupid-ass "little" brother, whatever goddamn game he's playing—there's nothing to be done but turn, grab hands, and run, run and keep on running. Back down the path, 'round the rock, past the table. Back to the house, the warmth, the light.

...the worst place on earth, Holly thinks, as Edwin falls behind, startled by the sudden swiftness of their mutual retreat; he's yelling something after them now, but the wind has it, snatches it from his lips like a great, black, invisible hand. And they're long gone anyhow.

Back at the house, they fall into bed, clutching each other, hearts hammering. Every breath seems to shake the world, drawn and let go in a shudder. There's no way they'll fall asleep, not tonight—maybe not ever again, if they can't get back to Toronto fast enough, once the sun's finally up.

That's what they think, at any rate. Until, inevitably, they do.

***

And when Holly wakes up, much later, she's alone.

***

Four in the morning, probably. The whole house is cold, dry, empty. Dim, but not exactly dark—there's light coming from somewhere, all right. Awful light.

Holly has trouble making herself get up, let alone open the bedroom door, but she does. She has to. And the first thing she hears, stepping out into the hall, is the sound of something crunching underfoot.

She looks down, squints. Can just make out a trail of objects, leading to the attic stairs.

Throw each piece down, as you [go there], her mind whispers, unprompted. *A trail. Breadcrumbs.*

It's the stuff from the box, definitely. She doesn't have to look closer to know it.

Names in her throat, caught and choking: *Heather? ...Edwin?* But she can't let them go, physically *can't*. Not when who even knows what might be nearby but hidden, all unseen. Might be—

(watching)

(listening)

(*waiting*)

Holly swallows, so soft she can barely feel it. Directs her feet along the prescribed path, one reluctant step at a time. And as she follows, tracing the route Heather must surely have set out for her, she finds herself wondering, resentful—

How could you start without me?

—and almost freezes in realization's wake, shockwave rocking her top to toe. Thinking, helpless: *Oh God. So I do remember...*

...a bit, something. Not enough.

Up the stairs, one-half at a time, braced tight against any creak, each puzzle piece increasingly leaf- or dirt-encrusted, increasingly deformed, as though they've been buried and trodden on since she, Heather, and Edwin first pawed through that stupid box. A curl of formerly purple string lies outside the attic door, question mark-curled, frayed at one end; not cut. Sawed, or maybe bitten through.

Wind the string around three corners. Wait.

Her hand is on the door, pushing. It falls open without a sound.

Inside—still cold, still dim. The light increases. This is where it's coming from.

(Of course.)

The rest of the string, already wound, maps a rough triangle on the floor in front of one wall, the one without a window. Stone piles form corners, three to five stones each, uneven granite eggs, earth-smeared. Somebody (Heather) has obviously already skipped over *Words will come. Say them,* for which Holly can only be grateful, though she thinks she can almost feel those same words—or similar ones—plucking at the corners of her brain's folds.

Let it form was the next instruction, as she recalls. And...it has.

There's a door sketched on the wall, six feet by two, complete with lintel and threshold, even a knob. From a distance it looks spray-painted, scratched, its slightly uneven dimensions filled in with greying black, but as Holly draws closer, she sees it's actually more incised or even *burnt* into the plaster. Worn, like it's been there for years.

She and Heather were up here yesterday though, when the wall was clean. Empty.

The rest of the list plays itself out as she stands there, not wanting to come any closer. Four final groups of instructions, paragraphed, like so—

Never knock first. Wait until THEY do.

Wait again. Until THEY go away.

Open.

If it's That Place, then don't.

Them, Holly thinks, over and over, frankly unable not to. *That Place.* And she stands there not knowing what to do—there's not exactly a smell, maybe the memory of a smell...like the woods. That place in the woods, the hollow, the three trees. Shadow of leafless branches above, ruin of fallen leaves below.

(*The worst place in the world*)

So she stands, and she doesn't knock, and she waits. And then, finally— from behind the door, deep under the plaster, or somewhere even further than that—she hears her brother Edwin's faintly wavering voice reverberate, struggling through, as though the wall's a skin he's trapped behind. As though it's a metaphorical stand-in for the flesh cradle they all once shared, both separately and together; the slightly bulging membrane of their dead mother's womb, fresh-wrapped in architecture.

Open the door, man. Holly, I know it's you, gotta be...just let me back in, please. They*'re coming.*

And: "They," she thinks. *Them. That Place.*

(don't)

She swallows again, throat scratchy. Manages to ask, at last—

Is Heather with you?

A pause. *Dunno*, Edwin says, finally, before she can convince herself he was never there at all: quieter, faster, growing panic thread through each new word, tightening 'til they start to ruck up. *I went in looking for her, found* them *instead, and now—they've seen me,* they're *coming. I think* they *have her...please, Holly, let me the fuck back in! Please!*

Barely a whisper now, but if it was written down, it'd be underlined— four times, maybe five. And Holly knows she should do something, anything, though she isn't sure what. But...

Shouldn't've gone, she finds herself thinking, with a dreadful lack of sympathy. *Not when you saw where it was. We told you not to.*

And what did we think we *were doing, anyway? Playing this game...all of it? Where did* we *want to go?*

Anyplace, perhaps, so long as it was different. Not that we could have known where we might end up, when we began.

(A wardrobe, a door in the wall, a blister; a mirror turned window, different on the other side. Three trees, a wood between the worlds. Narnia. Elidor. Charn.)

We didn't know, *though.*

(No. Of course not. But—)

—*THEY did, I'll bet.*

And she can't move, and the light, the *smell. So* horrible. The very worst. And then—

—her brother starts to scream, high and thin and anguished, more like an animal than a man. And after he stops, stops short, as though the sound itself snaps in half, there simply *are* no other noises, just nothing. This deafening silence, where surely there should be noise.

So: Holly stands there frozen, hand half-reaching. And then there's a grinding noise, plaster-dust sifting, spotting the floor like snow. And then...

...the drawn-on handle begins, very slowly, as if manipulated *from the other side...*

...to turn.

THE THIN PLACES

I dream I go to the woods, almost every night. In the dream, I leave the others asleep and go out the door at the crack of dawn, just walking, with no destination in mind. Looking around, I realize I'm back at the same campsite my son's choir went to that weekend, a tiny stretch of land along the Muskoka River's shore, edged with pine and gravel: rough cabins barely the size of my mother-in-law's living room, subdivided so they can each fit two bunkbeds plus a loft that's mainly mattress, a phantom third suspended up near the roof-tree. Inside, everything's rough and cold and smells like Vicks Vapo-Rub, while outside it's the same, but less claustrophobic. The air is full of hovering gnats, almost too small to see, and a vague mist hangs over the river's skin, the current barely stirring its surface.

Making my way down the gravel path to the road, I look both ways before crossing, seeing nothing. I feel the grit under my soles, crunching like crumbled bone. The edge of the woods isn't far, but I pause there, wondering if I should go further.

People go into the woods with one face, come out with another—that's what my aunt used to tell me, when she thought my parents weren't listening. *Stay in there too long, you'll forget your own name; won't recognize it when it's called or be able to read it written down if not on bark, in charcoal ash, or blood. Your skin will change, turn dark and moist like dirt, or pale like a mushroom's ribbed underside. Wash your face after you come back out and look in the mirror, you'll soon find you're a whole different person.*

She was always saying stuff like that, my aunt. Probably explains why nobody really liked her all too much.

***

One of the chief unspoken truths of parenthood is that a minute or so after you have a child, you soon find you've signed up for a lifetime spent doing things you don't even vaguely want to do. And I knew from the very beginning that volunteering to chaperone my son's first choir camp trip was definitely going to be one of *those* things, the memories you make mainly by agreeing to grin and bear it, for your child's sake.

Liam loved to sing, and my mother-in-law thought choir would bring out the best in him—teach him teamwork, professionalism, discipline. Which it did, on the whole. We were grateful. But they were a pretty expensive bunch, that choir: very upwardly mobile, very artsy. Big on fundraising the old-fashioned way, one parental chequebook at a time. Even with my husband's Bay Street job, we'd needed the in-laws' help to swing tuition.

Going up there with Liam wasn't my idea, by a long shot. But it would be his first overnight stay away from home, out of town with a bunch of people he didn't really know. "You should sign up, just so he knows you're there," my mother-in-law said, and Liam's eyes perked up at the prospect, fastening on mine: *Yes, Mom, please.* I couldn't say no, not without looking bad.

So I didn't. I went without protest, resentment festering inside me, a boil under the armpit. An itch that only dug deeper the longer I had to go without scratching it.

I remember looking at the three of them celebrating together, thinking: *I really don't look like* any *of these people.* Which was weird, especially considering how half my genes went in to make one of them. *Consider the evidence; take a picture, it'll last longer. It's like I don't belong here, like I never have. I'm not part of this family at all.*

Apophenia's an illusion, my aunt used to tell me. *The human mind sees patterns in random data. But just because something looks like something else doesn't mean it is—even you must know that, Norah.*

I look like you, I pointed out to her once, when the sheer contempt in her voice became a little much to handle. To which she simply smirked, replying: *Well yes, and I look like you, to a point. But what does that prove, exactly?*

I wouldn't find out until years later that she wasn't really my aunt at all, not by blood—just a friend of the family my parents allowed to stick around, possibly because since they'd all attended the same university, she'd played midwife (or maybe enabler) during their initial courtship, making her the patron demon of both their marriage and my birth—along with the divorce-related heartache to which those happy accidents eventually gave rise. And making it all the stranger that since the divorce, the year I was eight, I still can't really remember her actual name.

***

In the dream, the leaves of the wood hang down in a curtain, all green and brown and green: moss brown as rot, bark green as lichen, as scum on a still pond. Here and there, a spiderweb glint, bright as hinges. They creak and hum behind, borders a door shut and locked, to which I have no key.

But then I go in, right in, and I don't know why. Enough people have told me not to. The sky is low-hung, the air close and hot, fog rising off the horizon. Darkness under there like a swarm. A smell everywhere, fresh-turned dirt, tubers. I have to move slow; the path keeps slipping away underfoot. Crushed ferns and exposed roots.

No idea of where I'm headed. I walk straight through what feels like a spider web, sticky on my hair, my eyes, my hands. Something at the corner of my mouth, trying to crawl in. I spit black.

In the distance, a cry goes up. It sounds like sobbing.

***

I'd assumed we'd be sleeping in the same cabin, Liam and me—that I'd be the cabin chaperone for his particular group, the wonderfully named Noble Minstrels Table. Instead, once we got there, I found out I'd been sorted into the next cabin over—the Chivalrous Chorus Table. The show we were working on that year was King Arthur-themed. I can't remember exactly what songs were involved, though I catch myself humming snatches of them, now and then. One of them might even have been "If Ever I Would Leave You."

Liam didn't like it. He'd grown up in a tiny apartment where he was used to both his parents being merely seconds away. "If you can't sleep here, can't I come sleep with you?" he'd argued.

"That's not how it works, bud. You saw the house lists, right?" He nodded, glumly, a towheaded figure in Star Wars pajamas, small for his age. "So it's already done, and we can't do anything about it. Wouldn't be fair to everybody else."

"I understand," he said, finally, though he obviously wasn't happy about it. But he agreed anyhow, because he was sweet and biddable, a good guy in every way, and because he trusted me. Because I was—I still am—his mom.

Good, I thought, as I hugged him. And then I turned away.

***

I don't like the woods. They remind me too much of my own childhood, hauled back and forth across Ontario by my mother and father, who were big on trips while they were together—always in motion, always bound for someplace dark and green, as though they thought the cure for every ill was wilderness.

Each weekend they hauled out the maps and made lists of places they'd already been to versus places they'd yet to go, the putative hot spots of rural Ontario. From my point of view, it was all one grey highway or back road after another, the overhanging foliage thickening or thinning accordingly, with an occasional lake, hill, field, or miniature village thrown in for good measure; it's not like I was ever consulted on the matter. There were moments it was enjoyable: afternoons swimming in ponds, fresh fruit from roadside vendors, watching deer wander along the road...but I'm a city girl, always have been; I sleep better to the sound of traffic and sirens, when I sleep at all.

Right now, in the dream, I've reached the point where I'm not sure if I'm asleep. It's exhausting to trudge the uneven muddy ground, up and down small rises you don't see until you stagger over them. The underbrush is thick: there's barely enough space to squeeze between trunks, and the green-black moss rubs off on my shirt and leggings. Light slants thickly down through the leaves, orange-gold bars heavy with pollen and ground haze; it's the reddening light of late afternoon. Soon comes twilight, then nightfall.

Then, the dark.

***

None of the other kids in the cabin reported any trouble. They just woke up and Liam was gone.

One girl later said she woke up just long enough to hear him moving towards the door, trying to be quiet. It was early, before sunrise, so she thought he was going to the outhouse. Another chaperone said she looked out the window and saw him walking with a woman towards the woods; she said he was holding her hand, which is why she thought that woman had to be me. But she also said she thought he looked sad, or even a little bit scared.

They went into the woods, right up to the treeline, the wet mulch of leaves demarking civilization from wild; the woman moved with a light, quick step, never pausing, not even when he stumbled. Just pulling him on, firmly yet not unkindly, into the shadows.

They went into the woods, that woman and my son. And they didn't come back out.

***

I still have an image of my aunt in the back of my mind: a tallish woman with linebacker shoulders and no visible waist, solid as a shut door—frizzy mouse-brown hair, irregular freckles, neck habitually kept hidden with some no-name "fashion" scarf whose pattern always varied wildly, though its colour scheme remained consistent: green on blue or blue on green, cut here and there with hints of purple, red, black. I could tell that she was more my mother's friend than my father's, yet both of them treated her with this alert, almost diffident respect, despite how they seemed equally capable of being shockingly snarky about her in her absence.

Did they like her or not? It was hard for me to tell, at that age. I'd already decided myself that if I had my way when I grew up, I'd never deal with her again—but I couldn't have explained that antipathy either, or why I thought I had the right to form such judgements. She certainly never gave any hint of minding me much, for good or ill; I barely remember her paying any attention to me, or even looking at me directly. Most likely I was just background noise to her, a mere by-product. She's probably forgotten my name by now, wherever she is, just as I've forgotten hers.

And yet.

It's a matter of record that my parents never left me alone with her, at least not where they couldn't see us. It's a matter of record that she vanished out of our lives at the same time my parents' marriage fell apart—as if the destruction of their family unit had ruined something for her, a careless shopkeeper breaking a crystal vase just before he hands it over to the buyer. And it's a matter of record—witness statement, at any rate, however reliable that is—that the woman spotted taking Liam into the woods that morning wore a scarf around her neck, patterned in blue and green.

***

Now I've been in the woods far longer than I want to be, deep down in its most shadowed ravines, the sun blocked out wholly. No shafts of light to tell my way, and the ground slippery underfoot. I wish I'd worn socks, wish I hadn't worn sandals. Have long since stopped looking down, for fear of knowing what I've stepped on.

I don't know how I got here anymore.

I know that when I wake up from the dream, at last—however long that process takes—I'm going to spend the whole rest of the day feeling like I'm still there. I'm going to be uncomfortable, restless in my own skin, because I know I'm not where I'm supposed to be. All the next day, and every other.

It doesn't change. It never does.

I don't expect it ever will.

***

I remember him, my son. How he used to sing. How it felt to hold him. I remember how he bounced past me at a party once, and I turned to the person next to me and said: "Believe it or not, that used to be part of my body." I remember teaching him to feed himself, brush his teeth; I remember waking him during toilet-training. I remember the way Liam would throw his arms around me, or around his dad, or snuggle up to us both in our bed on Sunday mornings, before Tom got him dressed to take him to Mass.

Tom goes to church a lot, nowadays—midday masses on his lunch hour, again on Saturday and twice on Sunday—and has gotten into volunteer work as well. I suppose it's helping him; maybe it's even giving him something to hope for, some future eternal reunion. I'd envy him if I thought anything like that had even the remotest chance of working for me.

When you're in mourning, it hurts that things don't always hurt.

It's been six months. No report has been made, no sighting has occurred, anywhere at all. But every night I have this dream, the same dream of the woods. How I'll walk and walk until I finally look down, see something at my feet, under all that mulch: Liam's eyes, peering up at me. And when I clear away all the bracken he's there, down there, in a hole.

He doesn't say anything, doesn't ask for my help. And I want to get him out, and I don't want to get him out. I'm afraid. I'm afraid to try. I'm afraid that if I reach down, he'll pull me in.

And so I just stand there, I stand there, I can't move. Looking down.

Fill in the hole, a voice tells me, inside my head. *Fill it in and walk away.*

I don't trust him. I can't. You can't trust the dead.

But I don't trust myself either.

***

We don't belong here, not really, not any of us, my aunt used to whisper to me, her odd-smelling mouth against my ear, when she thought my parents weren't listening. *Not here. Which is why we should be careful, always. Why we have to treat each other well, look out for thin places. We have to stay in the light.*

Whose child is that, in the distance, crying? Not *my* boy. Not mine, with his mouth full of blood and dirt and broken teeth. Not mine, not here.

Not there.

***

This dream will end soon, as it always does—but one day I'll go back into the woods for real, looking for him. And while I don't expect to find him, I don't expect to come back either. Just walk into the woods and let the leaves close behind me, never to return.

Because: we *aren't* supposed to be here, not really, none of us. But where else would we be, if we weren't?

This country is full of all sorts of absences, thin places, empty places. Holes between the stars.

THE UNDERNEATH

Had Gilman unconsciously succeeded better than he knew in his studies of space and its dimensions? Had he actually slipped outside our sphere to points unguessed and unimaginable? Where—if anywhere—had he been on those nights of demonic alienage?
—H.P. Lovecraft.

Is it true? you asked Terence, at last, when you finally couldn't help yourself anymore. *What I heard? That everything's mainly made out of empty space?*

Because: From one moment to the next it comes, the touch of another world, fleeting and transformative; a doorway opening in every closet, through every mirror, under every bed. The Braille eye's stare. Atoms turn sideways, letting you slip between. All of a sudden. It's just that fast.

So. *Is it true?* you kept on asking. 'Til he sighed, and said, reluctantly:
...it's complicated.

The easy answer, pat and convenient. And all the more so now, since you know—you *know*—it's not.

You have proof.

***

New Year's Day, six months ago. Slush on slush, a black wind blowing down an invisible corridor straight into your teeth. 4:00 PM found you crab-walking home from market through the pretend darkness, three over-heavy plastic bags twisted together per hand, mainly concentrating on making sure your boots didn't slide out from under you before your fingers went numb. This area's interlocking *bonsai* nest of condos and condos-to-be just keeps on force-growing itself in ever more arcane ways, mushroom gentrification undertow often shuffling bemused suburbanites who've commuted in to shop St. Lawrence Market cheek-by-jowl with the local methadone clinic's daily wait list.

The resultant cultural fallout is certainly cosmopolitan—even the 24-hour stores carry arugula, sushi, and spelt bread, though not always tampons or Tylenol—but not always particularly amusing. Last week, some hooker you saw desperately trying to flag down cars while dressed in hot pants and an oversized hockey jersey (to fool the Neighborhood Watch) mistook your accidental eye contact for an encroaching competitor's scope-out, doffed one high-heeled boot, and used it to chase you off her territory, swinging it like a single-spiked mace.

No big wonder, then, that you were very much leading with your forehead instead today—chin tucked down against the sting of freezing rain, gaze safely kept ambiguously focused as not falling flat on your face permitted. Which is probably why you didn't really notice how close you were getting to that man right in front of you, as you took your usual shortcut through the building behind *your* building's salt-mucky courtyard, moving on autopilot past the gargoyle fountain with its crust of greying snow, the mini-Art Park strung with plastic spiderwebs and Hipster-parodic "Ex-mas" ornaments. Your wrists burning, hip-balls aching with forward momentum: Warmth, light, home, sleep...

Until—

—the man (who you'd seen enough times to nod at, in and around various walking-distance waterholes) suddenly turned in his condo's outer doorway, holding it open for you. "Crap night out there," he said, buzzing you through.

"Yeah," you said, without thinking twice about it. Letting him.

Why not?

Nobody waiting for you at "home," after all, even now. And it's not like your phone (its number securely unlisted now, after that fiasco with the guy you literally picked up on the street) is ever going to suddenly ring; you live in a box inside another series of boxes, like everybody else you don't exactly know. The perpetually worried woman on one side of your hall, for example (who looks a little like Patricia Arquette circa *Lost Highway*, though she's neither chestnut nor platinum blonde). Or the guy from around the corner— he's often coming from that direction, anyhow—who does the occasional commercial, his sorrowful hatchet-face peeking out from the background of various brief odes to the wonders of McDonald's, Viagra, local Real Estate agents.

Seemed as though you had about as much right to be in there as you did anywhere else, really. And even if you didn't—who was going to know?

So you went wandering through the building, hoping your over-burdened state made you look like anything *except* a haphazard amateur burglar with bad impulse control, constantly sure you were going to be challenged, stopped, caught. And eventually—half for lack of anything better to do, half because no one was stopping you—you tried an apartment door, then another.

The fifteenth one opened.

***

Today, half a year on—hip-deep in research and preparation for your latest *real* urban intrusion project—you can still remember the moment's pause you took before forcing yourself to look around, breathless with the threat of potential discovery. The place proved grubby in that surprising way everybody else's apartment always seems to, on surreptitious examination; dusty drapes, streaky mirrors, mismatched yard sale furniture. Piles of books on the coffee table, spine-cracked and teetering. Lovecraft: *The Dreams in the Witch House.* All this crap about non-Euclidean angles, things hiding in walls. The World Unseen.

A litany of weird images strung haphazardly together, like stream-of-consciousness found poetry: *The roaring twilight abysses—the green hillside— the blistering terrace—the pulls from the stars—the ultimate black vortex—the black man—the muddy alley and the stairs—the old witch and the fanged, furry horror—the bubble-congeries and the little polyhedron—the strange sunburn—the wrist-wound—the unexplained image—the muddy feet—the throat-marks—the tales and fears of the superstitious foreigners—*

And then...

You glanced up, sidelong, right into one of a pair of dim, wavy, brown-tinged classic oval looking-glasses, fringed in fake gilt, which hung above the equally dust-encrusted convex screen TV—met your own eyes, far wider and blanker than usual, strained at their corners against the lack of light. And thought you saw, over your shoulder...thought you *might* have seen, to be truly accurate...

...the bedroom door closing, silently, behind you. Not even a shadow of what hand might be on its knob visible. But a definite sense that whatever, whoever might be guiding it, preferred not to *be* seen. Preferred to go, if at all possible...unnoticed.

But—

—what did all this mean? To what extent could the laws of sanity apply to such a case?

Didn't matter: Time to grab your bags, and book. You went scuttling back and out, door slamming a bit too heavily for comfort behind you. Quick-marched with a hammering heart past the elevators, down the stairwell, back into the night while the concierge smiled and nodded as you went by—still thinking he knew you, obviously; from somewhere, if not from here. Still thinking you *belonged.*

And maybe you did. Maybe you *do.*

Because each subsequent door you've handled since then, however tentatively, has also fallen open—inexplicably, impossibly, against every inherent rule of statistical likelihood—at a single touch, to reveal whatever lies beyond.

Unwanted intimacy, like a flash of stained granny panties; trash without treasure, dust, dirt, and decay. Neglect. Silence. Those same hidden backstages your personal access all areas pass always seems to show you, alike in their ugly truth: Unfinished infrastructure, vague emptiness behind endless fakery, detritus left forever unrepaired beneath the thin skin of the world's bright façade...

Nothing else though. Nothing more; you've made sure. It's just curiosity, at this point—each incursion a fresh new fact-finding mission, inching along towards an infinitely foregone conclusion. So why, then...

...do you still feel like you have to keep on looking?

Because I can. Because I want to. Because, again—why not?

(*Who's going to stop me?*)

And because there's always the possibility, however slim—even now—that you might be, might always *have* been, quite simply...

...wrong.

***

It's just science, as Terence would say—or maybe faith, as he most certainly wouldn't. The two *are* almost indistinguishable, after all, beyond a certain point.

Especially at the sub-molecular level.

***

Weeks later, back to working all day in an unhappily named bag store called Laco Sac (purses made from deflated, cured human breasts, anyone?), you still couldn't stop thinking about it. So you looked around online, found the late Ninjalicious's legendary intrusion.org, and took your first steps into a world of strange delight: Abandoned and condemned properties, all-too-passable barriers, geocaching, skunnelling, and vadding, oh my. "Real-world hacking," that one guy you met before Terence—Keith? Kevin? Keifer?—used to call it.

The siren song of that inevitable hidden hallway just past the STAY OUT sign, the invariably shut (yet open) door: *Go deeper, go further; keep on going, whatever the apparent risks, at any cost. Never look back.*

It's not like it's *not* dangerous, of course, and you know in your heart that if you ever got into "real" trouble, you'd be screwed—no one would even know you were gone, let alone where. Already, there've been some close calls with tight spaces and sudden drops, not to mention the multiple times you've been kicked out of places, the undelivered-upon threats of bodily harm or legal prosecution...

You've had dreams from which you woke shaking, cold and sweat-wet, throughout this whole learning process—dreams about going through the "wrong" door, ending up in the "wrong" place: Standing near a massive ruined archway you somehow know leads into an alternate world, new and glorious, some green, up-sloping Narnia full of open sky, deep forest, a city off in the distance. *Those fair, fair hills, which seem so soft and free...those are the hills of Heaven, my love, where you will never be...*

But then you look again, and it's all changed, like a blinking eye: The mountains are pasteboard, the forests tinsel; the sky's peeling, fallen away in strips. And behind it—

—nothing.

***

Before he wrote his cell number on your hand (which you just let wear back off again), K-Whatever showed you an .mpg made from a mini-DV tape that he'd bought from some intrusion.org messageboard lurker. According to him, the camera it came from had been found abandoned on an ossuary-cum-trash-heap in the Paris Catacombs by French Intrusionistes looking for somewhere truly extreme to practice their subterranean parkour skillz. Looked like nothing more than another home-made *Blair Witch* rip, up to the point where you eventually realized that the anonymous videographer wasn't actually running *from* anything, so much as *towards* something unseen, unknown, unknowable: Panting hard, clawing at the walls, grunting with effort and exhaustion as he forced himself to go faster, and faster, and faster. 'Til he must have only spotted the LOW BATTERY light blinking even as he ran out of tape, dropped his camera in a dusty grab-bag pile of tibiae and femurs, and kept right on going.

"What's supposed to have happened to that guy?" You wanted to know. He shrugged.

"Sometimes people just go down too far. They don't come out again."

"They get lost?"

"Or they like it too much, maybe. They want to stay."

"But...what would be the point of that?"

Another shrug. Gesturing at the screen: "Ask *him*."

Which might have been why you never called him again, in the end...or not; he smelled weird too. And one way or the other, you knew he didn't have anything much to tell you that you couldn't probably figure out yourself, given time.

You remember one trip which took you under the York University pool, tide-lapped in a quivering haze of watery blue darkness, when you genuinely felt like there were shadows moving under the walls, tracking you, no matter which way you turned. Footsteps echoing behind you as you left, seeming to follow.

That sense of oddity, the lurking arcane. A looming weirdness of which all normal waking life comprised only a barest fingertip.

You know now that you don't really want explanations, not that K-Whatever'd had any to offer. Because the mere fact of mystery, in itself, is always infinitely more interesting than *any* given solution.

***

"Is there actually such a thing as 'non-Euclidean geometry'?" you asked Terence first, when you finally met in person; not such a great opening line, probably, after such a lengthy e-correspondence. But he just looked at you for a moment, with Aspergian flatness, before replying—

"Not as such, no. But real geometry is plenty weird enough, if you're looking at it from the right angle."

He told you how atoms are 99.9% empty space, but things don't pass right through other things because the atoms that make them up are all levitating on their own tiny—sub-microscopic, really—electrostatic fields. Every atom is surrounded by a shell of *electrons*, and like-charges repel each other. So when two atoms approach, their electron shells push back at each other, despite the fact that each atom's net charge is zero; this is, as Terence puts it, a very useful feature of nature.

"It makes our lives a whole lot easier, for sure. That's how you're able to sit in that chair—*on* it, anyways. *Near* it. Your atoms plus their electrons, and *those* electrons' shell-charges, floating on the electron-shell charge of *its* atoms."

But if atoms are constantly pushing away from each other, then why doesn't the entire universe just blow apart? Because most atoms' electron-shells are not full, so when two atoms with empty spaces in their shells come together, they automatically share electrons to fill in the spaces until—once both atoms' outer shells are full—they can go back to their usual repulsive behavior. It's a constant Lord Shiva Nataraja two-step of gravity vs. entropy which keeps the entire universe locked in a downward spiral just tight enough for us to live (and die) on, if not escape.

"99.9 percent—sounds like a pretty accurate measurement, for nothing."

"Well, define what you mean by 'nothing,' first off, and you might as well come at it backwards: Invert the negative, to find the positive. If some space is *not* occupied, by definition, then what does it mean for *other* spaces to be full, exactly?"

"Okay...what *does* it?"

You made sure to smile when you said this, knowing Terence would take it as flirtation—which he did, palpably; crossed his arms and leant in close, voice thinning to a hushed bedroom murmur. Telling you how while most of the space occupied by an atom is inaccessible to other atoms, it is easily breached by a freely moving neutron—and similarly, though most of the space inside the neutrons and protons in an atom's nucleus is inaccessible to all atomic matter, that distinction means nothing to a neutrino. So in the end, whether or not space is "empty" depends on what it is you're trying to penetrate it with.

Solidity, therefore, is an entirely macroscopic concept. At the sub-molecular level—atomic, protonic, neutrinic, etcetera—solidity is only a word, with no provable meaning at all.

***

But: *All this empty space,* you asked him later on, tangled in a cooling sweaty heap of sheets—paying your dues for information and services rendered, though he was a good guy overall, especially when too preoccupied to want to talk anymore. *Isn't there anything INSIDE of it? Anything deeper down, further in—just...anything?*

Terence frowned, squinting; without his glasses, his eyes looked somehow peeled, dilated in a post-corrective surgery way, naked as a startled baby's.

I'm not quite sure what you're getting at, he said. *Like what, exactly?*

You shook your head, unsure yourself of what you might have meant, let alone how best to phrase it. Only able to repeat, eventually—knowing exactly how inadequate it must sound, even out of context, yet unable to come up with anything better—

Well...that'd be the question, I guess. Right?

(...right...)

***

Right, then left, then left again: That's what the map you bought off that maintenance worker seems to say, anyhow. The target: A hotel ballroom built in 1921, unused since the 1950s (except for indoors fly-fishing lessons), and rendered all the more incursion-attractive by the fact that the rest of this grand old downtown Toronto landmark is very much still in use. It's supposed to be Terence's maiden voyage, a way for you to cement your "relationship," but it founders the second he won't cram his ass inside the dumbwaiter that's the only way to get from Point A to Point B unseen—too small, too dark, too *unyielding.*

He just freaks out, attracting two security guards: *Can I HELP you, sir? Ma'am?* Fifteen minutes, tops, from entrance to CIHY; your worst time ever, if you were keeping score. And all because Terence, the guy who's made intrusion.org his homepage away from home, gets claustrophobic whenever things move from the realm of the safely hypothetical to the dangerously immediate.

So at last, you leave him there and take off, pursued half-heartedly by the slightly younger of the pair—map dropped, hair flying, running fast and hard and aimless as that guy in the Paris Catacombs video ever did, with probably just as little idea of where you're going to end up. 'Til you take a sudden turn, step inside what only *seems* to be a service elevator, only to find yourself...

...somewhere else instead. Where the air is thick, sodden, like barely breathable flowstone. Where the darkness shines, impenetrable.

There are already people there too. One of whom looks up at you, through its hair, and says—without much surprise—

Oh, it's you. You really shouldn't be here, you know. Then: *I could take you back, if you want...*

It reaches for you, but you recoil. Can't stop yourself. Its *hands*, far too thin, too dirty for anything like comfort; its *fingers*, far too long, too numerous...

Have it your own way, it says, shrugging. And then—

***

—you'll reach for the handle, but it won't be there anymore. And the door will be a wall. And you'll be alone, caught mid-step, still straining, fingers never quite reaching far enough to break plaster between this awful new world and the next, your old one. Never quite coming home.

You'll be through, at last; this far, no further. Nowhere left to go. Sunk neck-deep as quicksand into that gaping crack on the mirror's other side, the sub-atomic interstices, the World Invisible. These endless witch-house dreams spiraling off into infinity, viral geometric equations which peel back reality like a flap, then re-seal it over infection and leave it there to rot—sew hole to hole, set traps which only open if stepped on unexpectedly, sidelong, by hungry/ignorant fools like you.

You'll be, and you'll be, and you'll be: All that Rhode Island crazyman's sentence fragments come to fruit, fresh-hatched like sticky cocoons; less fiction, it turns out, than metaphor. *The green hillside, the blistering terrace. The muddy alley and the stairs. The bubble-congeries and the little polyhedron. The strange sunburn, the wrist-wound, the throat-marks...*

(To what extent *could* the laws of sanity apply to such a case?)

Here, now, in darkness, in dust. In stasis. In extremis.

In the Underneath.

To 'see through' all things is the same as not to see.
—C.S. Lewis.

THIS IS NOT FOR YOU

Three potential sacrifices, just as Phoibe'd predicted, blundering through the woods like buffalo in boots. Mormo broke cover first, naked and barefoot, screaming, with the boys following after, whooping and hollering, straight into the gauntlet, too lust-drunk to see where they were going. Pretty little thing, that Mormo, with a truly enviable lung capacity; the best lure they'd had by far in all the time Gorgo'd been attending these odd little shindigs, and swift enough to keep a good two lengths between her and her closest pursuer as she danced around the tiger pits. No sooner did this thought register, however, then with a few more steps—plus one wild, deer-like leap—she was gone from sight entirely: up over the deadfall, rustling the same bushes Gorgo and her girls hid behind, leaving the men in her wake, too shocked not to keep coming.

One took a *thyrsus* to the knee, so sharp Gorgo heard it crack, and pitched headlong, folding up, rolling. More blows caught him from several angles, breaking bones, tearing flesh; he flipped, bellowing, then gave a moaning "whuff!" as Iris came down right on top, astride both hips, club inverted to crack his breastbone and pop at least one lung, squeeze heart against ribcage, bruise liver beyond repair. His skull met a log back-first, brain slammed hard, eyes rolling up; was probably out long before Iris's partners (Scylla, Polyxena) could get on him too, their hands rock-full, looking to make like Cain.

To his left, meanwhile, another lucky winner got Deianira's spear across the top of his ear and recoiled, flinching away only to run straight into Charis's strong grip instead. They were about the same height, but Charis had him from behind, choking him so hard he started to lift off the ground, kicking wildly. He tore at her arm with both hands, drawing blood, 'til she finally threw him down with enough force that Gorgo heard his nose pop, or maybe a cheekbone—then heel-stomped him between the shoulder blades, holding him pinned even as he flailed, trying his level best to swim away. One armpit made a beautiful target for Deianira's next thrust, a goring stab that went in far as she could reach, and the pain made him rear back far enough for Gorgo to slash her scythe across his throat.

The spike of her own kill-pleasure came quickly after that, hot and red and sweet. It was good, but over so soon; just enough to make her want more, something better. *Longer.*

She sat back on her heels, panting, leather tags of her hiking boots cutting into her bare ass as she watched the man's—*boy's*—blood make a flaring collar 'round his slackening, sweat- and dirt-smeared face. Asking Charis, once she had her breath back: "You see where the last one went?"

Charis shook her head. "Back there, maybe."

On her feet once more, over by the first one, Iris nodded. "Something tripped a pit."

Okay, then. "Praise be," Gorgo said, heaving herself up, unable to quite keep her voice completely irony-free. "Praise be," two new voices chimed in at the same time, from behind her: Aglaia, of course. And Phoibe.

Charis and the others turned, bespattered, grinning—stepped back a bit, all 'round, to display their work to best advantage. Aglaia smiled wide and nodded, proudly, as Gorgo and Phoibe exchanged a small, cool nod of greeting.

"Wonderful," Aglaia pronounced, with the sort of authoritative, maternal warmth that'd've done Mother Theresa herself proud, if she'd worshipped Kali instead of Christ. "*Very* fine. Now...let's go see what She's left us for last, and best."

***

The point was to do these things together, not alone. The point was to do them in secret, as much as could be arranged for. The point was to go elsewhere, overnight, and stay as long as it took to get it done. The point was to make it count.

The whole point of a mystery religion, in fact, as Aglaia kept reminding them, was that it was supposed to be—and stay—a *mystery.*

That wasn't her real name, obviously. They'd all taken new ones, first as pseudonyms on the cult's website, then as part of their bonding exercises in "meatspace," as the kids put it; it was to draw a sort of metaphorical line from old to new, a clear path of translation, adaptation. Some of them came from what passed, these days, as "traditional" backgrounds—odd idea, that, all these *mystoi* and Goddess-worshippers apparently long-embedded in between the non-denominationals and the atheists—but for most of them this was just a fantasy, a deep-rooted need, a burgeoning itch they'd never quite known how to scratch before eventually stumbling across the myths, the literature, the site itself, which Phoibe had started, and still maintained. A particular urge which everything around them said was bad, wrong, unnatural, even as that blood-beat voice inside told them it was anything but.

"We shouldn't feel ashamed," Aglaia—an elder stateswoman of some sort of brown persuasion, her graying, loose-curled hair cropped short—had said, during their first real meet-up. "Never. What we do here is older than everything else, all the forces arrayed against us—older than laws, older than rules, older than the inadequate language we use to try and describe it with.

It can't be explained. It doesn't have to be justified. And much as we may serve it, may be personally elevated by that service, transfigured even, we are none of us as important as the principle we subsume ourselves to. The tradition survives, always; we may die away—*will* die away—but it survives, always. It doesn't need us. Because even when everything else crumbles, *this* will still endure."

Oh, and Aglaia really did make everything sound so pretty, Gorgo thought, whenever she really started to get her groove on; that was the basic trick, the recruiting pitch, the glue. To frame the reason they were all here as a certain route to spiritual ecstasy, but also make it sound like they were reaching for a goal far more lasting than their own selfish pleasure—something done on this whole sad, stained world's behalf for the unwitting benefit of everyone trapped inside it, exorcising sin while extirpating evil. Like it wasn't any real sort of *crime* at all.

Aglaia was a true believer, or walked the talk so well as to be nigh-indistinguishable from one; Gorgo simply knew what she liked, and was willing to swallow her share of theosophic psychobabble in order to get a bunch of women with similar interests to not just pitch in at the kill, but clean up after her. Total freaks, in other words, but very useful ones—which was exactly how, in essence, that membership in their little sewing circle continued to hold enough appeal for Gorgo to not just roll her eyes and walk away, even assuming Aglaia and her coterie would let her.

Every meet-up started with a prayer, Aglaia leading, the others reading along off of printout sheets, a different translation every time. This year's went like so—

Preswa, Phersephassa, o Kore Hagne
Wise one, She who stops, She who lives in every harvest
Persipne, Praxidike, o Kore Semele
Wine-maker, Subterranean queen, Most flowery maiden
Persephone, Crown of terror
Beautiful, Fatal, She who consumes
According to Whose will the sacred task is done—
life to produce, and all that lives to kill.

"So what is it you *do* these days, exactly?" Phoibe asked, under her breath, sidling up at Gorgo's elbow. "Still bending young minds, or did they finally figure out you never actually made it all the way through teacher's college?"

Gorgo shrugged. "Oh, you'd be surprised how little research private schools put in, selecting instructors. We're doing Romantic poets this semester, Keats and all. 'O what can ail thee, knight-at-arms, alone and palely loitering?'"

"You tell them it's a tuberculosis metaphor?"

"On the top layer, sure. Some girls, I push harder; seed an idea here and there, set tests. Try to seek out where their more hidden inclinations might lie."

"I didn't know Aglaia was signing off on any more recruitment drives, especially amongst the underage."

"She's got nothing to with it, Phoebe."

"Phoibe."

"Whatever."

"Yeah, okay. I mean, what 's in a name, right—Susan?"

"Awful mysteries here are ours," Aglaia continued, "so we celebrate them in Your name, which no one may in any way transgress. Happy is she who has seen and believed, both on top of the earth and under it, though she who is uninitiate will never reap a like crop after death, but stay forever buried there in darkness and in gloom."

Think that's my real name you got there, little bitch, just 'cause you hacked it out of my digital footprint? Gorgo projected, while staring Phoibe down, as Phoibe struggled to do the same, and failed. *My original? Think I couldn't change it or anything else about me in a minute, or less, if I wanted to—walk away, disappear off the grid, and not come up for air 'til I stuck my scythe in your tech-savvy spine?*

Think again.

She was a bit of a parody, Phoibe, with her all-black clothes and her hair banded in grown-out dye-jobs like a floppy, cross-cut section of tree—you could practically track her stylistic evolution, or lack thereof, from Manic Panic to Clairol to henna to what Gorgo could only assume was probably her natural shade, a subtle mouse-hide leather tone flecked here and there with the first glints of grey. Deep, slightly keloided dimples bracketing her mouth had once held barbell piercings, just like that scar furling her lip-corner told of a torn-free labrette; she wore a tricked-out pair of granny glasses with Hipster-thick frames, and tended towards using blush for eyeshadow. But she sure as shit did know how to run a dark net, so that was something, at least.

Up near Aglaia, everyone was chanting again. Gorgo mouthed the words as Phoibe mouthed them right back at her, a second or two late.

Blood waters it
Blood grows it
Blood alone sees it flower:
Great seed, seed of flesh and bone, Persephone's awful gift
That nurtures and destroys this world one sacrifice at a time
One lover
One child
One king.

Truth was, it *would* be nice to share interests with somebody in private life, Gorgo occasionally caught herself thinking. To be a mentor. She sure wasn't too likely to breed any soft-minded little co-conspirators herself, not at this late date, even setting the problem of stud-stock aside; adoption wasn't really an option either, or fosterage, for similar reasons. Short of walking away from her local maternity ward with a free souvenir, therefore, cherry picking each new class for potentials seemed the next best thing. Hadn't found any thus far, but it was early days still, and she remained hopeful.

Now she set hands on hips and waited, staring down, a whole ten extra years' worth of game-face blankly in place. She had roughly a foot of height on Phoibe, plus a good fifty pounds in heft, not that she expected things would get physical—both of them had a certain investment in returning to work next week, after all, and doing it while looking like nothing worse than the morning after a particularly celebratory girls' night out. But when you'd been looking forward to something all year, sometimes things just happened.

A second later, however, Phoibe shrugged, raising her hands: *no harm, no foul.*

"I'm sure you know what you're doing," she said. "I mean, we're all adults here. What you get up to on your own time's no concern of mine."

"Nope," Gorgo agreed. "So...anyone know who the sacrifice's gonna be yet?"

"Whoever gets here first," Phoibe replied. "Same as usual."

"Well, how many candidates in play?"

"Three groups, two to four components each. Maybe four."

"That's short odds."

"Not really; I'd show you the math, but..." Here Phoibe trailed off, maybe thinking *I wouldn't want to bore you with it,* or even *you wouldn't understand,* yet smart enough not to voice whichever outright, either way. Continuing, soon enough: "You ever know anybody *not* to show up?"

Now it was Gorgo's turn to shrug. "Not yet," was all she said.

But that, as Aglaia would no doubt say, was where faith came in.

***

The place they gathered had been a campground, once upon a time. They arrived singly from every direction, mostly by public transport, then hiked to the meet-point, where Aglaia and her acolytes had already set up most of the necessary infrastructure—dug catch-pits, strung bells, planted weapons (*thyrsi* made on-site, plus whatever else they brought with them), and built the cremation pyre high for afterwards. People didn't tend to get naked 'til the appointed hour, which suited Gorgo fine, though there were always noticeable exceptions. Right now, for example, she could see tall, lean Charis belly-dancing by herself off in the middle distance, pleasantly soft from hormones and with her bush grown full to hide the rest, yet proudly displaying the scars where her implants had gone in every time she back-bent far enough for them to catch the light.

At least one potential "sister" had quit because of Charis, or tried to—made it back almost as far as the north road before Gorgo had caught up with her, dragged her into the bushes, and buried her under a deadfall with her flesh flensed sky burial-style, so the animals would come running. It'd been an on-the-fly decision, simple self-preservation instinct twisted into altruism by circumstance, done on behalf of a community Gorgo often questioned whether she needed at all; still wasn't entirely sure Aglaia even knew about it, though she suspected yes, especially since she hadn't found any bones left to crush with a hammer when she'd checked the makeshift grave, last time they met.

In Gorgo's estimation, however, the radfems could say what they wanted, but Charis had always held her end up well enough to merit whatever help Gorgo chose to give her. Once the hunt was on, she was no different than any other gal with an oversized clit—better, considering her sheer stamina, her extra-long reach and strong, militarily trained grip. When they piled in on the final sacrifice, all together, Gorgo had seen Charis literally work a man's head from his shoulders like some live-action *Mortal Kombat* kill, twisting the finger-torn ruin of his throat and neck 'til his vertebrae snapped and spinal cord slithered free.

Sparagmos, Aglaia called it. The Maenad's frenzy, bull sacrifice. A rending apart, followed by *omophagia*, eating the flesh raw. Or, as Gorgo'd always called it, albeit only to herself...fun.

"I know you don't think you're one of us, really," Aglaia told Gorgo, as Gorgo poured herself a bowl of ritual *kykeon*. "But you do keep on coming, don't you? Why do you think that might be?"

"'Cause I like it?"

"You're no great fan of organized religion in general, though, I think; most sociopaths aren't. Yet you must admit it *can* be useful, as a concept, even to those who question it."

Gorgo sighed, steeling herself to stay polite. "Oh, sure," she replied. "Mainly in that it gives us divine permission to go on ahead and do what we were gonna anyways, all wrapped up in a pretty story. Secret knowledge, women's magic, the matriarchy reborn..."

Aglaia shot Gorgo a look, as though unsure if she was being mocked. "So you'll take advantage of the amenities on offer," she said, at last, "but you won't do Her homage."

"If that's the price of staying on the mailing list, sure. Why not?"

"Except that you won't mean it."

At that, Gorgo did have to snort, just a little. "How you ever gonna know *anyone* 'means it,' outside of yourself? Same way I 'know' you do, i.e. not at damn all. Look, lady, I read *The Bacchae*—hell, I've taught it. You really think we can bank on weapons of iron not wounding us when the fit's in full swing though, no matter how many of those little dried mushrooms you boil the *kykeon* up with? Barley, pennyroyal, psychoactives...it's a nice high, but I don't ever remember getting milk and honey from stones or tearing up trees by their roots while I was on it, let alone wearing snake necklaces or breastfeeding wolf cubs."

"Communion wafers aren't made from real man-meat, either. Our feasts are, and *not* metaphorically."

"They weren't, that'd be the deal-breaker right there, for me."

Aglaia chuckled. "I've seen you hunt," she said. "One of our fiercest, when She enters in."

"Hard to stop once I get going, I'll give you that," Gorgo agreed, suddenly tired. "C'mon, though—what I run on's a fetish, not superpowers. I just like to kill people."

"Ah, but you don't just kill *people*, do you, when you have the choice? I'm not talking about self-preservation, or opportunity... I mean pure desire, the perfect victim. The image you touch yourself to."

Gorgo snorted again. Yet the words brought it rising up behind her eyes anyhow, automatic, irrefutable: a man, always, young and juicy for preference. And strong enough to fight hand to hand, take damage from, even—possibly—risk losing to. Not that she ever had.

"...no," she admitted, at last, with reluctance. "You're right. That's never just 'people.'"

"Then you do Her work, and always have. Without even knowing it."

Gorgo shook her head, stubborn. "Dress it up all you want, Aglaia— what I do is what I choose to, that's the whole truth, and nothin' but. 'Cause I *like* it. I don't need any other reason."

"It gets done, however, either way."

Oh yes.

The area of study devoted to those like Gorgo was choked with truisms, creating spaces she'd always found it easy to slip between. Most serial killers, accepted lore went, were white rather than not, middle-class or lower-, organized or dis-...and male, overwhelmingly. Which meant that although there obviously had to be *some* who weren't, by simple process of elimination, nobody really spent a whole lot of time looking for them.

Didn't hurt that women coded societally as victims rather than predators, conferring a weird invisibility on those who didn't worry about becoming somebody else's meal. When men's eyes turned towards Gorgo with ill intent, she met them head-on, smiling. Those unused to the concept turned away; those who didn't had made their bed, and she felt no guilt about laying them down in it.

As it turned out, this attitude formed yet another point of sympathy between Aglaia's lot and herself—since according to the mysteries, sacrifices self-selected through willing, deliberate transgression. They had to *know* there was a taboo in play, even to have some idea of the potential stakes involved, and choose to break said taboo anyways.

Luckily, that was men in a nutshell, or so Gorgo had always observed.

Long before the Internet, it had been a truth universally agreed on that whenever somebody started talking about a space being women-only, a segment of the male-identified population would come running with dicks out, ready to mark their territory in the hope no bitch would ever again be dumb enough to believe herself in possession of something *they* couldn't access. It was a winning combination of social mores and genetics, bless their hearts—*just the way we're made, ma'am, now get in the kitchen, etcetera.*

"Everywhere but here," Aglaia claimed, proudly. And so far, her claim had yet to be disproven, there being an undeniable strength in numbers which far outstripped whatever one woman could achieve alone. Everybody wanted community, in their heart of hearts—even those who knew themselves, at base, quite outrageously unsuited to maintain it.

Female serial killers hid behind gender constructs, as a rule. They usually played out the roles people (men) expected them to, then killed inside of that as poisoners, black widows, angels of death... caregivers turned toxic. The reason the Maenad myth had been so discounted down the centuries, according to Aglaia, was that the very idea of a woman jumping on somebody and tearing them apart seemed physically impossible. But one had to wonder, like Gorgo remembered doing, even as a child: Was there a reason men seemed so wary of "allowing" women to congregate in groups? Could it be they guessed how a pack of women might be indistinguishable from one of lionesses, of hyenas?

Hours passed in chanting, dancing, singing, and the sun dipped low. The *kykeon*, fresh-cooled, got passed around like white lightning; Gorgo drank her next slug in one gulp, watching the newest *mystoi* sip, wince, almost puke. She already felt the drug deep inside her like hooks, opening her wide, letting in the world.

As the dusk began to swim and click around her, she saw Phoibe appear at Aglaia's elbow, night-blooming suddenly, pale out of dark. Watched her murmur in the priestess's ear, then vanish once more, as Aglaia turned to motion Gorgo near.

"Intruders at the perimeter. Mormo has them chasing her already—easy meat, for our best huntress."

Gorgo rose, nodding, to shuck the last of her clothes. She left her footwear on, since running barefoot through the woods was like asking for lockjaw, but Aglaia didn't say anything—possibly since her good right hand Phoibe had apparently decided much the same, albeit sticking with sandals instead of Gorgo's comfortably weighted hiking boots.

Charis handed her one more dose, which lit her up like a punch. Someone she couldn't quite see hugged 'round her from behind, smearing two mud-clay handfuls across both breasts at once, then down over her abs, to cool her thighs' hot vee. Gorgo tossed her hair, and pulled loose; Charis caught her mid-stumble, grinning. "Y'all ready?" she asked.

"Sure am."

"*Thyrsus*, baby girl?"

"Brought my own, thanks." The scythe handle fit nicely into her palm. "You comin', big sis?"

"Bet your ass," Charis growled, voice dipping lower than she probably wanted it to, not that that mattered: the *ekstasis* was on them both, pumping their blood, stiffening every sinew. Around, Gorgo saw the rest of the pack assembling, all the familiar faces. Iris, Scylla, Polyxena, Deianira...

They took off running, like Artemis Herself led the way.

***

And here they were now. The tiger pit's displaced covering, lid of the *kiste*, the sacred basket. Gorgo kicked it aside to reveal a third young man—*boy*—staring up, down on one knee and crying with pain, at least one ankle probably shattered from the fall. He was a sweet-looking piece, muscled like a wrestler, hair picked out into a soft natural; his skin gleamed, shade falling somewhere between Deianira's ruddy bronze and Aglaia's warmer, darker hue. Which was a fairly apt comparison, as it turned out—because when he caught sight of Aglaia peering down on him over Gorgo's shoulder his eyes went wide, fixed with shock, and awe, and terrified recognition.

"Mom?" he managed, voice breaking. "*Mom?* What...what're *you* doing...here...?"

Aglaia didn't answer, not immediately. Just drew herself up, turning to stone; crossed her arms and waited, possibly to see what happened next.

"Mom, shit... You have to help me. They're crazy, these women're all—Mom!"

Gorgo back-shifted, waiting as well. Until finally, another voice chimed in: "Well?"

Aglaia, without moving: "'Well' what, Phoibe?"

The woman in question came shoving her way through, pale as a twilit ghost, 'til she stood almost at Aglaia's side—*almost*. But not quite.

"He's penetrated the mysteries, hasn't he?" she declared, nodding downwards, voice pitched to ringing. "Seen things done, heard things said, just like the rest of them. Should the priestess's son go free, and other women's sons pay in his stead? Is this Her will?"

Posturing little hooker, Gorgo thought.

"Didn't hear Aglaia say *what* she wanted done with him, one way or the other, myself," Gorgo pointed out. "And since I'm a hell of a lot more likely to listen to her than to you, on the subject..."

"Ha! The unbeliever speaks." Phoibe threw her arms wide, addressing the whole cult, now flocking in around Gorgo's hunting team. "See how she mocks? Ask yourselves why Aglaia would ever let somebody like this in in the first place, let alone allow her to stay. Then ask yourself if it isn't obvious that the Goddess chose to punish Aglaia for her *hubris*, by sending her first-born to the killing floor! How else could it have happened?"

Defend yourself, idiot, Gorgo tried to project Aglaia's way, watching heads on all sides begin to nod, albeit reluctantly. But Aglaia's eyes stayed on the pit, her whimpering child. She might as well have been a statue.

Murmuring spread in every direction, like a tide.

Time to run, maybe, Gorgo thought, reluctantly, gripping her scythe hard enough to hurt. *Save yourself, before this shit shifts on you; drop out, get gone. This was a bad idea. It's like Missus Gast used to say, my third foster-mommy—someone like me just needs to stay the hell away from people, I want to keep safe...*

(...unless I'm killing 'em.)

That was when it happened, sharp as a wound—that same unfurling times ten thousand, the *kykeon's* blow suddenly felt all over, a general uproar. This lurching, queasy sensation of opening up *so* far it was like her insides were out, skin shifting, one massive neuron blur. Blood broke from her nose, mouth, the corners of her eyes; later, she'd find burst vessels on both eyeballs, a pair of tiny red flowers. For now, however, it was as though *something else* had a hold of her, puppeting her from the gut. Making one hand fly out, scythe's point sticking deep into Phoibe's still-babbling throat, then jerking free again, conjuring a flood. The spurt slapped across Gorgo before hitting Charis, who gasped, and Aglaia, who didn't; a general cry went up, cultists reacting as one. Phoibe fell, flopping, while Gorgo shivered still upright, mouth opening against her will. Words torrented free, garbled, unfamiliar, Greek-accented. Saying—

Fury-source, Wrathful One, All-Ruling virgin,
Kore Semele, light-bearer incandescent
Horned Maiden, Earth's vigorous daughter
When Death comes, we go willingly to Your realms
Until again You send us forth, into this world of Form.

She didn't know this prayer, Gorgo realized, unable not to complete what she could only assume was the verse's ancient formula. Not one she'd heard, nor one she'd read. No translation of *The Bacchae* she'd ever taught could have left it behind in her mind's folds, waiting to suggest itself under pressure—no, this was something else. Something Other.

At her boot-tips, Phoibe had almost ceased shuddering. Gorgo found herself pointing at her, mouth stretched *Body Snatchers*-wide, pronouncing: "How'd it happen? Ask the hacker. The girl with the math. Ask her how she sought him out online, groomed him, brought him and those friends of his here—because she wanted to mount a coup, thought he'd make Aglaia look weak in front of you, that she could turn you against Her chosen. But *nothing happens, ever, except that She allows it.*"

"Praise be," Charis chimed in, wiping Phoibe's blood straight into her mouth; "Praise be," Iris agreed, kicking Phoibe so she flipped, so her last breath went down into the earth itself, Persephone-Perswa's home. To which Aglaia finally nodded, dignified as always, and put her hand on Gorgo's still-shaking shoulder, palm print burning a hole all the Goddess's presence suddenly drained from once more, leaving her numb and cold, scythe drooping.

"Praise be," Aglaia agreed, approvingly. "I'm so happy for you, Gorgo. It's seldom any of us feels Her grace directly—to have that one be you is a rare honour, and welcome. Especially since I'd've had trouble killing a woman, myself, even one who'd betrayed Her covenant." A lovely smile. "But then, that's what She sent us *you* for."

"The fuck you say," Gorgo replied, all out into a rush, with no time for self-censorship. Her nervous system was still twitching, refusing to obey, or she would've cut Aglaia's throat next—something Aglaia seemed to know, since she glanced at Charis, who gently pried the scythe from Gorgo's limp hand, folding her into an embrace.

"C'mon now, baby girl," Charis said, soothing. "You got nothing to be afraid of. We all want to feel her hand on our souls the once, like you just did. It's why we're here."

"Not...why *I'm* here..." Gorgo said, muffled, into Charis's pectoral, her implant-springy breast. But Charis only laughed.

"'Course not," she replied. "We all know *that*. Is now, though—and that's beautiful, don't you see? Hell, it's *divine*."

"Literally," Aglaia agreed. "Oh, Gorgo! You're a saint to us now, a true Maenad. The very proof of our religion."

And that murmur was back again, eddying right, left, and every which way, whipping the crowd into a frenzy. They seized on Phoibe's body and bore it away, tearing off pieces as it went; probably end up on the pyre with the rest of the meat, fit for the celebratory feast, with the bones all divvied up and buried wherever individual cultists went home to after.

I'm trapped, Gorgo thought, hanging there in Charis's arms, while Aglaia and the others clapped, cheered, and ululated in approval, each according to their preference. *They've got me now, these freaks, them with their goddamn Goddess. I'm altered, forever changed. Like I don't even know my own self anymore.*

"What about him, down there?" she asked, finally, through trembling lips.

Throughout the preceding action, the still pit-trapped boy—Aglaia's unlucky son—had fallen silent long since, in terms of pleas. Now it was just grunts and cursing, *oh God oh God oh shit, help me please*, with the kid scrabbling at the walls like a crippled badger, trying his level best either to heave himself free or bring the walls' earth in on top of him, so he could suffocate before they pulled him free and ripped him apart. Perhaps having stared enough, however, Aglaia didn't even look this time. Simply shook her head, curls lifting slightly (softer than his yet similar, Gorgo could now see), and said—

"Phoibe called him, but She made him answer. This is not for him, for any of them, yet still they come: *anathema*, to be dedicated, to be cursed. He chose his own fate."

At that, the scrabbling stopped, as if kicked. Gorgo heard the kid moan out, instinctive, maybe in supplication, maybe in protest: *Mom, oh Mom, Mommy*, no. *Please, God*, please.

True Believers, true belief; not such an errant hunk of legitimized murder wrapped in bullshit fairytales after all, as it turned out. More's the fucking pity.

No God here, little boy, Gorgo thought, as close to sadly as she was capable of. And closed her eyes.

PUBLICATION HISTORY

"[Anasazi]" c. 2010 (*A Mountain Walked*, Centipede Press, S.T. Joshi, ed.)

"each thing I show you is a piece of my death" c. 2009, with Stephen J. Barringer (*Clockwork Phoenix 2: More Tales of Beauty and Strangeness*, Norilana Books, Mike Allen, ed., ISBN #1-60762-027-8, pp. 218-247)

"Drone" c. 2008 (*Not One of Us* #39, John Benson, ed.)

"The Shrines" c. 2011 (*Chilling Tales: Evil Did I Dwell; Lewd Did I Live*, EDGE Books, Mike Kelly, ed., ISBN #978-1-894063-52-4, pp. 169-176)

"Gabbeh" c. 2012 (*World Fantasy Convention 2012 Programme Book: Toronto Urban Fantasy*, Barbara Roden, ed.)

"Gaze" c. 2014 (*The Doll Project*, Ellen Datlow, ed.)

"Homebody" c. 2012 (*Chilling Tales 2*, EDGE Books, Michael Kelly, ed., ISBN #978-1-77053-024-9, pp. 165-174)

"The Jacaranda Smile" c. 2009 (*Apparitions*, Undertow Publications, Michael Kelly, ed., ISBN #978-0-9813177-0-0, pp. 101-116)

"Marya Nox" c. 2009 (*Lovecraft Unbound*, Dark Horse Books, Ellen Datlow, ed., ISBN #978-1-59582-146-1, pp. 331-346)

"Nanny Grey" c. 2012 (*Magic: An Anthology of the Esoteric and Arcane*, Solaris, Jonathan Oliver, ed.)

"Night-Bird" c. 2014 (*Aghast* Magazine Vol. 1, George Cotronis, ed.)

"One in the Morning and One At Night" c. 2012 (*The Three-Lobed Burning Eye* Issue #23, Andrew S. Fuller, ed.)

"Oubliette" c. 2012 (*The Grimscribe's Puppets: A Tribute to Thomas Ligotti*, Miskatonic River Press, Joseph E. Pulver Snr., ed.)

"Signal to Noise" c. 2011 (*The Chiaroscuro* Vol. 47, Brett Alexander Savory, ed.)

"Slick Black Bones and Soft Black Stars" c. 2012 (*A Season in Carcosa: A Tribute to Robert W. Chambers*, Miskatonic River Press, Joseph E. Pulver Snr., ed.)

"That Place" c. 2014 (*Letters to Lovecraft*, Jesse Bullington, ed.)

"The Thin Places" c. 2015 (commissioned directly by *The National Post*, as online content for its Halloween 2015 issue)

"The Underneath" c. 2010 (*Shroud* #8, Shroud Publishing, Timothy P. Deal, ed.)

"This Is Not For You" c. 2014 (*Nightmare* Magazine's "Women Destroy Horror" issue, Ellen Datlow, ed.)

ABOUT THE AUTHOR

Born in England, raised and educated in Toronto, Gemma Files is a Shirley Jackson, Sunburst and Bram Stoker Award-winner. Her previous jobs include stints as a sex shop vibrator room attendant and nocturnal security guard, as well as a film critic, screenwriter, editor and teacher. She is the author of three books of poetry, five novels, and over a hundred short stories. She also posts creepy artworks on Twitter.